MARIE RUTKOSKI is a professor of English literature at Brooklyn College, where she teaches Shakespeare, children's literature and creative writing. She lives in New York City with her husband and two sons. Marie can tie a good double figure-eight knot and is very fond of perfume, tea and excellent bread and butter.

ALSO BY MARIE RUTKOSKI

The Winner's Curse

THE WINNER'S

CRIME

THE WINNER'S TRILOGY: BOOK TWO

A NOVEL BY

MARIE RUTKOSKI

BLOOMSBURY

LONDON • NEW DELHI • NEW YORK • SYDNEY

Bloomsbury Publishing, London, New Delhi, New York and Sydney

First published in Great Britain in March 2015 by Bloomsbury Publishing Plc
50 Bedford Square, London WC1B 3DP

www.bloomsbury.com

Bloomsbury is a registered trademark of Bloomsbury Publishing Plc

First published in the United States of America by
Farrar Straus Giroux Books for Young Readers
175 Fifth Avenue, New York 10010

A CIP catalogue record for this book is available from the British Library

ISBN 978 1 4088 5869 1

Printed and bound in Great Britain by CPI Group (UK) Ltd, Croydon CR0 4YY

3 5 7 9 10 8 6 4

For Kristin Cashore

THE FROZEN WASTES

TUNDRA
(TATH)

SULFUR MINES

WORK CAMP

VALORIA

CAPITAL
(VAL)

CITY
(LAHIRRIN)

HERRAN

THE EMPTY
ISLANDS

ITHRYA
ISLAND

SOUTHERN ISLES
(CAYN SARATU)

SHE CUT HERSELF OPENING THE ENVELOPE.

Kestrel had been eager, she'd been a fool, tearing into the letter simply because it had been addressed in Herrani script. The letter opener slipped. Seeds of blood hit the paper and bloomed bright.

It wasn't, of course, from him. The letter was from Herran's new minister of agriculture. He wrote to introduce himself, and to say he looked forward to when they would meet. *I believe you and I have much in common and much to discuss,* he wrote.

Kestrel wasn't sure what he meant by that. She didn't know him, or even of him. Although she supposed she would have to meet with the minister at some point—she was, after all, the imperial ambassador to the now independent territory of Herran—Kestrel didn't anticipate spending time with the minister of *agriculture.* She had nothing to say on crop rotation or fertilizer.

Kestrel caught the haughty tone of her thoughts. She

felt the way it thinned her mouth. She realized that she was furious at this letter.

At herself. At the way her heart had leaped to see her name scrawled in the Herrani alphabet on the envelope. She had hoped so hard that it was from Arin.

But she'd had no contact with him for nearly a month, not since she'd offered him his country's freedom. And the envelope hadn't even been addressed in his hand. She knew his writing. She knew the fingers that would hold the pen. Blunt-cut nails, silver scars from old burns, the calloused scrape of his palm, all very at odds with his elegant cursive. Kestrel should have known right away that the letter wasn't from him.

But still: the quick slice of paper. Still: the disappointment.

Kestrel set aside the letter. She pulled the silk sash from her waist, threading it out from under the dagger that she, like all Valorians, wore strapped to her hip. She wound the sash around her bleeding hand. She was ruining the sash's ivory silk. Her blood spotted it. But a ruined sash didn't matter, not to her. Kestrel was engaged to Prince Verex, heir to the Valorian empire. The proof of it was marked daily on her brow in an oiled, glittering line. She had sashes upon sashes, dresses upon dresses, a river of jewels. She was the future empress.

Yet when she stood from her carved ebony chair, she was unsteady. She looked around her study, one of many rooms in her suite, and was unsettled by the stone walls, the corners set insistently into perfect right angles, the way two narrow hallways cut into the room. It should have made sense to Kestrel, who knew that the imperial palace was also a fortress. Tight hallways were a way to bottleneck an invading force. Yet it looked unfriendly and alien. It was so different from her home.

Kestrel reminded herself that her home in Herran had never really been hers. She may have been raised in that colony, but she was Valorian. She was where she was supposed to be. Where she had chosen to be.

The cut had stopped bleeding.

Kestrel left the letter and went to change her day dress for dinner. This was her life: rich fabric and watered silk trim. A dinner with the emperor . . . and the prince.

Yes, this was her life.

She must get used to it.

The emperor was alone. He smiled when she entered his stone-walled dining room. His gray hair was cropped in the same military style as her father's, his eyes dark and keen. He didn't stand from the long table to greet her.

"Your Imperial Majesty." She bowed her head.

"Daughter." His voice echoed in the vaulted chamber. It rang against the empty plates and glasses. "Sit."

She moved to do so.

"No," he said. "Here, at my right hand."

"That's the prince's place."

"The prince, it seems, is not here."

She sat. Slaves served the first course. They poured white

wine. She could have asked why he had summoned her to dinner, and where the prince might be, but Kestrel had seen how the emperor loved to shape silence into a tool that pried open the anxieties of others. She let the silence grow until it was of her making as well as his, and only when the third course arrived did she speak. "I hear the campaign against the east goes well."

"So your father writes from the front. I must reward him for an excellently waged war. Or perhaps, Lady Kestrel, it's you I should reward."

She drank from her cup. "His success is none of my doing."

"No? *You* urged me to put an end to the Herrani rebellion by giving that territory self-governance under my law. *You* argued that this would free up troops and money to fuel my eastern war, and lo"—he flourished a hand—"it did. What clever advice from one so young."

His words made her nervous. If he knew the real reason she had argued for Herrani independence, she would pay for it. Kestrel tried the painstakingly prepared food. There were boats made from a meat terrine, their sails clear gelatin. She ate slowly.

"Don't you like it?" said the emperor.

"I'm not very hungry."

He rang a golden bell. "Dessert," he told the serving boy who instantly appeared. "We'll skip ahead to dessert. I know how young ladies enjoy sweet things." But when the boy returned bearing two small plates made from porcelain so fine Kestrel could see light sheer through the rims, the emperor said, "None for me," and one plate was set before Kestrel along with a strangely light and translucent fork.

She calmed herself. The emperor didn't know the truth about the day she had pushed for an end to the Herrani rebellion. No one did. Not even Arin knew that she had bought his freedom with a few strategic words . . . and the promise to wed the crown prince.

If Arin knew, he would fight it. He'd ruin himself.

If the emperor knew *why* she had done it, he would ruin her.

Kestrel looked at the pile of pink whipped cream on her plate, and at the clear fork, as if they composed the whole of her world. She must speak cautiously. "What need have I of a reward, when you have given me your only son?"

"And such a prize he is. Yet we've no date set for the wedding. When shall it be? You've been quiet on the subject."

"I thought Prince Verex should decide." If the choice were left to the prince, the wedding date would be never.

"Why don't *we* decide?"

"Without him?"

"My dear girl, if the prince's slippery mind cannot remember something so simple as the day and time of a dinner with his father and lady, how can we expect him to plan any part of the most important state event in decades?"

Kestrel said nothing.

"You're not eating," he said.

She sank the clear fork into the cream and lifted it to her mouth. The fork's tines dissolved against her tongue. "Sugar," she said with surprise. "The fork is made of hardened sugar."

"Do you like the dessert?"

"Yes."

"Then you must eat it all."

But how to finish the cream if the fork continued to dissolve each time she took a mouthful? Most of the fork remained in her hand, but it wouldn't last.

A game. The dessert was a game, the conversation a game. The emperor wanted to see how she would play.

He said, "I think the end of this month would be ideal for a wedding."

Kestrel ate more of the cream. The tines completely vanished, leaving something that resembled an aborted spoon. "A winter wedding? There will be no flowers."

"You don't need flowers."

"If you know that young ladies like dessert, you must also know that they like flowers."

"I suppose you'd prefer a spring wedding, then."

Kestrel lifted one shoulder in a shrug. "Summer would be best."

"Luckily my palace has hothouses. Even in winter, we could carpet the great hall with petals."

Kestrel silently ate more of the dessert. Her fork turned into a flat stick.

"Unless you want to postpone the wedding," said the emperor.

"I'm thinking of our guests. The empire is vast. People will come from every province. Winter is a terrible time to travel and spring little better. It rains. The roads become muddy."

The emperor leaned back in his chair, studying her with an amused expression.

"Also," she said, "I'd hate to waste an opportunity. You know that the nobles and governors will give you what they can—favors, information, gold—for the best seats at the wedding. The mystery of what I'll wear and what music will be played will distract the empire. No one would notice if you made a political decision that would otherwise outrage thousands. If I were you, I would enjoy my long engagement. Use it for all it's worth."

He laughed. "Oh, Kestrel. What an empress you will be." He raised his glass. "To your happy union, on the day of Firstsummer."

She would have had to drink to that, had not Prince Verex entered the dining room and stopped short, his large eyes showing every shift of emotion: surprise, hurt, anger.

"You're late," his father said.

"I am not." Verex's hands clenched.

"Kestrel managed to be here on time. Why couldn't you?"

"Because you told me the wrong hour."

The emperor tsked. "You misremember."

"You're making me look the fool!"

"*I* am making you look nothing of the kind."

Verex's mouth snapped shut. His head bobbed on his thin neck like something caught in a current.

"Come," Kestrel said gently. "Have dessert with us."

The look he shot her told Kestrel that he might hate his father's games, but he hated her pity more. He fled the room.

Kestrel toyed with her stub of a sugar fork. Even after the prince's noisy course down the hall had dwindled into silence, she knew better than to speak.

"Look at me," the emperor said.

She raised her eyes.

"You don't want a summer wedding for the sake of flowers, or guests, or political purchase," he said. "You want to postpone it for as long as possible."

Kestrel held the fork tightly.

"I'll give you what you want, within reason," he said, "and I will tell you why. Because I don't blame you, given your bridegroom. Because you don't whine for what you want, but seek to win it. Like I would. When you look at me, you see who you will become. A ruler. I have chosen you, Kestrel, and will make you into everything my son cannot be. Someone fit to take my place."

Kestrel looked, and her look became a stare that searched for her future in an old man capable of cruelty to his own child.

He smiled. "Tomorrow I'd like for you to meet with the captain of the imperial guard."

She had never met the captain before, but was familiar enough with his role. Officially, he was responsible for the emperor's personal safety. Unofficially, this duty spread to others that no one discussed. Surveillance. Assassinations. The captain was good at making people vanish.

"He has something to show you," the emperor said.

"What is it?"

"A surprise. Now look happy, Kestrel. I'm giving you everything that you could want."

Sometimes the emperor *was* generous. She'd seen audiences with him where he'd given senators private land in new colonies, or powerful seats in the Quorum. But she'd also seen how his generosity tempted others to ask for just a little more. Then his eyes went heavy-lidded, like a cat's, and she would see how his gifts made people reveal what they really wanted.

Nonetheless, she couldn't help hoping that the wedding could be put off for longer than a few months. Firstsummer was better than next week, of course, but still too soon. Much too soon. Would the emperor agree to a year? More? She said, "Firstsummer—"

"Is the perfect date."

Kestrel's gaze fell to her closed hand. It opened with a sweet scent and rested empty on the table.

The sugar fork had vanished against the heat of her palm.

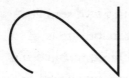

ARIN WAS IN HIS FATHER'S STUDY, WHICH HE probably would never be able to think of as his own, no matter how old the ghosts of his dead family grew.

It was a clear day. The view from the study window showed the city in detail, with its ruined patches left by the rebellion. The pale wafer of a winter sun gave Herran's harbor a blurry glow.

Arin wasn't thinking of her. He wasn't. He was thinking of how slowly the city walls were being rebuilt. Of the hearthnut harvest soon to come in the southern countryside, and how it would bring much-needed food and trade to Herran. He wasn't thinking of Kestrel, or of the past month and a week of not thinking of her. But not thinking was like lifting slabs of rock, and he was so distracted by the strain of it that he didn't hear Sarsine enter the room, or notice his cousin at all until she had shoved an opened letter at him.

The broken seal showed the sigil of crossed swords. A

letter from the Valorian emperor. Sarsine's face told Arin that he wouldn't like what he was about to read.

"What is it?" he asked. "Another tax?" He rubbed his eyes. "The emperor must know we can't pay, not again, not so soon after the last levy. This is ruinous."

"Well, now we see why the emperor so kindly returned Herran to the Herrani."

They had discussed this before. It seemed the only explanation to such an unexpected decision. Revenues from Herran used to go into the pockets of the Valorian aristocrats who had colonized it. Then came the Firstwinter Rebellion and the emperor's decree, and those aristocrats had returned to the capital, the loss of their land named as a cost of war. Now the emperor was able to bleed Herran dry through taxes its people were unable to protest. The territory's wealth flowed directly into imperial coffers.

A devious move. But what worried Arin most was the nagging sense that he was missing something. It had been hard to think that day when Kestrel had handed him the emperor's offer and demands. It had been hard to see anything but the gold line that had marked her brow.

"Just tell me how much it'll cost this time," he said to Sarsine.

Her mouth screwed into a knot. "Not a tax. An invitation." She left the room.

Arin unfolded the paper. His hands went still.

As governor of Herran, Arin was requested to attend a ball in the Valorian capital. *In honor of the engagement of Lady Kestrel to Crown Prince Verex*, read the letter.

Sarsine had called it an invitation, but Arin recognized it for what it was: an order, one that he had no power to disobey, even though he was supposedly no longer a slave.

Arin's eyes lifted from the page and gazed upon the harbor. When Arin had worked on the docks, one of the other slaves was known as the Favor-Keeper.

Slaves had no possessions, or at least nothing that their Valorian conquerors would recognize as such. Even if Arin *had* had something of his own, he had no pockets to hold it. Clothes with pockets went to house slaves only. This was the measure of life under the Valorians: that the Herrani people knew their place according to whether they had pockets and the illusion of being able to keep something private within them.

Yet slaves still had a currency. They traded favors. Extra food. A thicker pallet. The luxury of a few minutes of rest while someone else worked. If a slave on the docks wanted something, he asked the Favor-Keeper, the oldest Herrani among them.

The Favor-Keeper kept a ball of thread with a different-colored string for each man. If Arin had had a request, his string would have been spooled and looped and spindled around another one, perhaps yellow, and that yellow string might have wound its way about a green one, depending on who owed what. The Favor-Keeper's knot recorded it all.

But Arin had had no string. He had asked for nothing. He gave nothing. Already a young man then, he had despised the thought of being in debt to anyone.

Now he studied the Valorian emperor's letter. It was

beautifully inked. Artfully phrased. It fit well with Arin's surroundings, with the liquid-like varnish of his father's desk and the leaded glass windows that shot winter light into the study.

The light made the emperor's words all too easy to read.

Arin crushed the paper into his fist and squeezed hard. He wished for a Favor-Keeper. He would forsake his pride to become a simple string, if only he could have what he wanted.

Arin would trade his heart for a snarled knot of thread if it meant he would never have to see Kestrel again.

He consulted with Tensen. The elderly man studied the uncrumpled and flattened invitation, his pale green eyes gleaming. He set the thick, wrinkled page on Arin's desk and tapped the first line of writing with one dry finger. "This," he said, "is an excellent opportunity."

"Then you'll go," said Arin.

"Of course."

"Without me."

Tensen pursed his lips. He gave Arin that schoolmaster's look that had served him well as a tutor to Valorian children. "Arin. Let's not be proud."

"It's not pride. I'm too busy. You'll represent Herran at the ball."

"I don't think that the emperor will be satisfied with a mere minister of agriculture."

"I don't care for the emperor's satisfaction."

"Sending me, *alone*, will either insult the emperor or reveal to him that I'm more important than I seem." Tensen rubbed his grizzled jaw, considering Arin. "You need to go. It's a part you must play. You're a good actor."

Arin shook his head.

Tensen's eyes darkened. "I was there that day."

The day last summer when Kestrel had bought him.

Arin could feel again the sweat crawling down his back as he waited in the holding pen below in the auction pit. The structure was roofed, which meant that Arin couldn't see the crowd of Valorians ranged above at ground level, only Cheat in the center of the pit.

Arin smelled the stink of his skin, felt the grit beneath his bare feet. He was sore. As he listened to Cheat's voice rise and fall in the bantering singsong of an expert auctioneer, he pressed tentative fingers to his bruised cheek. His face was like a rotten fruit.

Cheat had been furious with him that morning. "Two days," he'd growled. "I rent you out for only *two days* and you come back looking like this. What's so hard about laying a road and keeping your mouth shut?"

Waiting in the holding pen, not really listening to the drone of the auction, Arin didn't want to think about the beating and everything that had led up to it.

In truth, the bruises changed nothing. Arin couldn't fool himself that Cheat would ever be able to sell him into a Valorian household. Valorians cared about their house slaves' appearance, and Arin didn't fit the part even when his face wasn't half-masked in various shades of purple. He looked like a laborer. He *was* one. Laborers were not brought into the house, and houses were where Cheat needed to plant slaves devoted to the rebellion.

Arin tipped his head back against the rough wood of the pen's wall. He fought his frustration.

There came a long silence in the pit. The lull meant that Cheat had closed the sale while Arin wasn't paying attention and had stepped into the auction house for a break.

Then: a locust-like whir from the crowd. Cheat was returning to the pit, stepping close to the block on which another slave was about to stand.

To his audience, Cheat said, "I have something very special for you."

Each slave in the holding pen straightened. The afternoon torpor was gone. Even the old man, whose name Arin would later learn was Tensen, became sharply alert.

Cheat had spoken in code. "Something very special" conveyed a secret meaning to the slaves: the chance to be sold in a way to contribute to the rebellion. To spy. Steal. Maybe murder. Cheat had many plans.

It was the *very* in what Cheat had said that made Arin sick with himself, because that word signaled the most important sale of all, the one they'd been waiting for: the opportunity for a rebel to be placed in General Trajan's household.

Who was there, above in the crowd of Valorians?

The general himself?

And Arin, stupid Arin, had squandered his chance at revenge. Cheat would never choose him for the sale.

Yet when the auctioneer turned to face the holding pen,

his eyes looked straight into Arin's. Cheat's fingers twitched twice. The signal.

Arin had been chosen.

"That day," Arin told Tensen as they sat in the winter light of his father's study, "was different. Everything was different."

"Was it? You were ready to do anything for your people then. Aren't you now?"

"It's a *ball*, Tensen."

"It's an opportunity. At the very least, we could use it to find out how much the emperor plans to take of the hearth-nut harvest."

The harvest would be soon. Their people needed it badly for food and trade. Arin pressed his fingertips against his brow. A headache was building behind his eyes. "What is there to know? Whatever he will take will be too much."

For a moment, Tensen said nothing. Then, grimly: "I've heard nothing from Thrynne for weeks."

"Maybe he hasn't been able to get out of the palace and into the city to reach our contact."

"Maybe. But we have precious few sources in the imperial palace as it is. This is a dicey time. The empire's elite are pouring out gold to prepare themselves for the most lavish winter season in Valorian history, what with the engagement. And the colonists who once lived in Herran grow increasingly resentful. They didn't like returning their stolen homes to us. They're a minority, and the military is solidly with the emperor, so he can ignore them. But all signs point to the court being a volatile place, and we can never forget that we are at the emperor's mercy. Who knows what

he'll choose to do next? Or how it will affect us? *This*"—
Tensen nodded at the invitation—"would be a good means
to look into Thrynne's silence. Arin, are you listening? We
can't afford to lose such a well-placed spy."

Just as Arin had been well-placed. Expertly placed. He
hadn't been sure, that day in the market, how Cheat had
known that Arin was the perfect slave to pitch. Cheat had
a knack for spotting weakness. An eye for desire. Somehow
he had peered into the heart of the bidder and had known
how to work her.

Arin hadn't seen her at first. The sun had blinded him
when he stepped into the pit. There was a roar of laughter.
He couldn't see the mass of Valorians above. Yet he heard
them. He didn't mind the prickling shame spidering up his
skin. He told himself that he didn't. He didn't mind what
they said or what he heard.

Then his vision cleared. He blinked the sun away. He
saw the girl. She raised one hand to bid.

The sight of her was an assault. He couldn't quite see
her face—he did not *want* to see her face, not when everything else about her made him want to shut his eyes. She
looked very Valorian. Golden tones. Burnished, almost, like
a weapon raised into the light. He had trouble believing
she was a living thing.

And she was clean. A purity of skin and form. It made
him feel filthy. It distracted him for a moment from noticing that the girl was small. Slight.

Absurd. It was absurd to think that someone like that
could have any power over him. Yet she would, if she won
the auction.

MARIE RUTKOSKI

He wanted her to. The thought swept Arin with a merciless, ugly joy. He'd never seen her before, but he guessed who she was: Lady Kestrel, General Trajan's daughter.

The crowd heard her bid. And at once it seemed that Arin was worth something after all.

Arin forgot that he was sitting at his father's desk, two seasons later. He forgot that Tensen was waiting for him to say something. Arin was there again in the pit. He remembered staring up at the girl, feeling a hatred as hard as it was pure.

A diamond.

KESTREL DECIDED TO DRESS EXTRAVAGANTLY
for her meeting with the captain of the imperial guard. She
chose a snow-and-gold brocade dress whose long hem trailed.
As always, she strapped her dagger on with care, but this
morning she tightened the buckles more than she needed to.
She undid and redid them several times.

The captain called for her in her suite as she was finish-
ing her morning cup of spiced milk. He declined to sit
while she drank. When he blinked at her dress and hid a
brief smirk, Kestrel knew that she wouldn't like wherever
they were going. When he didn't suggest that she change
into something that wouldn't be so easily sullied, she knew
that she didn't like *him*.

"Ready?" said the captain.

She sipped from her cup, eyeing him. He was a hulking
man, face scarred across the lip. His jaw had been broken;
it jutted left. The captain had an unexpectedly fine, straight-
nosed profile, but she had caught only a glimpse of it when
he'd glanced around the sitting room to make certain they

were alone. He was someone who preferred to stare face-on. Then his features were all marred.

She wondered what he would do if he knew that she hadn't been an entirely unwilling captive in Arin's house after the Herrani rebellion.

She set the empty cup down on a small table. "Where are we going?"

His smirk was back. "To pay someone a visit."

"Who?"

"The emperor said not to tell."

Kestrel lifted her chin and gazed up at the captain. "What about hints? Did the emperor order you not to give hints, even little tiny ones?"

"Well . . ."

"What about confirming guesses? For example"—she tapped an arpeggio along the edge of the ebony table—"I guess that we are going to the prison."

"Not exactly a tough guess, my lady."

"Shall I try something more challenging? Your hands are clean, but your boots are dirty. Slightly spattered. The spots are shiny; recently dried. Blood?"

He was entertained now. He enjoyed this game.

"You've been up even earlier than I this morning, I see," Kestrel said. "And you've been busy. How incongruous, though, to see blood on your boots and to smell something so nice lingering about you . . . a subtle scent. Vetiver. Expensive. A dose of ambergris. The slight sting of pepper. Oh, captain. Have you been . . . *borrowing* the emperor's perfumed oils?"

He no longer looked amused.

"I'd think that such a good guess deserves a hint, Captain."

He sighed. "I'm taking you to see a Herrani prisoner."

The milk curdled in Kestrel's stomach. "Man or woman?"

"Man."

"Why is it important that I see him?"

The captain shrugged. "The emperor didn't say."

"But *who*?"

The captain shifted his heavy feet.

"I don't like surprises," Kestrel said, "any more than the emperor gladly shares his oils."

"He's nobody. We're not even sure of his name."

Not Arin. That was all Kestrel could think. It couldn't be him—Herran's governor was not *nobody*. Imprisoning him could trigger a new conflict.

Yet the prison held somebody.

The sweet taste of milk had soured in her mouth, but Kestrel smiled as she stood. "Let's go."

The capital prison was outside the palace walls, situated a little lower on the mountain, on the other side of the city, in a natural sinkhole that was expanded and fortified and spiraled with seemingly endless descending staircases. It was small—the prison of the eastern empire was rumored to be as large as an underground city—but its size suited the Valorian emperor well. Most criminals were shipped to a labor camp in the mines of the frozen north. Those that were left behind were the very worst, and soon executed.

Oil lamps were lit, and the captain led Kestrel down the first black, airless stairwell. The trailing fabric of her dress hissed behind her. It was hard not to imagine that she was a prisoner being led to her cell. Kestrel's heartbeat tricked her; it fumbled at the thought of being caught at some crime, of being locked up in the dark.

They passed a cell. Fingers curled like white worms through the bars of the cell's small window. A voice rasped something in a language Kestrel didn't recognize. It had a lisping quality she couldn't place until she realized that this must be the sound of someone who had no teeth. She shrank back.

"Keep away from the bars," said the captain. "This way," he added, as if there were any way but down.

When the staircase finally ran out of steps, it threw Kestrel off balance to stand on unstaggered ground. The corridor smelled like wet rock and sewage.

The captain opened a cell and ushered Kestrel inside. For a moment she hesitated, instantly and wildly sure that he meant to trap her here. Her hand went to the dagger at her hip.

The captain chuckled. The sound triggered a metallic rattle in the corner of the cell, and the captain lifted his lamp to illuminate a sitting man who strained at chains embedded in the wall. His bare heels scrubbed the uneven floor as he tried to push back, away from the captain.

"Don't worry," the captain said to Kestrel. "He's harmless. Here." He passed her the lamp, then dragged on a loose end of chain to draw the prisoner tight against the wall. The man shuddered and wept. He began to pray to all hundred of the Herrani gods.

She didn't recognize him. A relief. Then came a clammy shame. What did it matter if she knew him or not? The prisoner was going to suffer. She could see his suffering written in the captain's lamplit eyes.

Kestrel would not stay. She could not watch. She turned toward the door.

"That's against the emperor's rules," the captain told her. "He said that you have to be here for the whole of it. He said that if you became uncooperative, I should cut off this man's fingers instead of his skin."

The prisoner's prayer halted. Shakily, it started up again.

Kestrel felt like that thin, keening voice. Like the sound of a gear cranked tight and then let go. "I don't belong here," she said.

"You're my future empress," said the captain. "You do. Or did you think that ruling meant only dresses and dances?" He checked that the chain was taut. The man hung from his bonds. "The lamp, my lady." The captain beckoned her closer.

The prisoner lifted his head. Lamplight flared on his eyes, and even though Kestrel knew that this broken man wasn't Arin—the prisoner was too old, his features too delicate—her heart seized. They were ordinary eyes for a Herrani. But gray and clear, just like Arin's. And it suddenly seemed that Arin was the one stumbling over the name of the god of mercy, that *he* was begging her for something she had no idea how to give.

"The *lamp*," the captain said again. "Are you going to be difficult so soon, Lady Kestrel?"

She came forward. She saw, then, the outline of a bucket near the prisoner, filled to the brim with feces and urine, and that the man's right hand was a padded mitten of gauze.

The captain stripped it off. The prisoner choked on his prayer.

The skin on three fingers was missing.

Kestrel caught a glimpse of pink muscle and creamy, glistening bands of tendon. Her stomach heaved. The captain pulled a small table from a dark corner of the cell and flattened the man's hand across it, palm up.

"What is your name?" the captain asked him. When there was no answer, the Valorian drew his dagger and cut into the prisoner's fourth finger. Blood fountained up.

"Stop," Kestrel begged. "Stop this."

The prisoner thrashed, but was pinioned by the wrist. The captain raised his dagger again.

Kestrel caught his arm. Her fingers dug in, and the captain's face seemed to open—almost greedily, with a shine that said that he had awaited her failure. That's what this was. Kestrel had been failing the emperor's test even without knowing its criteria. Every hesitation was a black mark against her. Each ounce of her pity was being tallied by the captain, hoarded to be tipped out later before the emperor, spilled before him to say, *Look what a pathetic girl she is. How weak of will. She has no stomach to rule.*

She didn't. Not if this was what ruling an empire meant.

She wasn't sure what she would have done next if the prisoner hadn't gone still. He was staring at Kestrel. His eyes were wide, streaming. Stunned. He recognized her. She didn't know him. The urgency of his expression, however, was that of someone who has found a familiar key to a box he is desperate to unlock.

"My name is Thrynne," he whispered to her in Herrani. "Tell him that I—"

The captain shook off Kestrel's slackened grip and rounded on the prisoner. "You'll tell me yourself." The captain spoke Herrani with heavily accented fluency. "It's good that you're ready to talk. Now, Thrynne. What were you saying? Tell me *what*?"

The prisoner's mouth worked soundlessly. Blood welled across the table. The captain's blade gleamed.

Kestrel was calm now. It was the way the prisoner was looking at her—as if she were a stroke of good fortune. She couldn't betray that, even if she didn't understand it. She would make herself capable. She would handle whatever his expression was asking her to handle.

"I don't remember," Thrynne said.

"Tell me or I'll strip you bare."

"Captain," said Kestrel. "He's confused. Give him a moment—"

"*You* are confused if you think to interfere with my

interrogation. You're here to listen. Thrynne, I asked you a question. Stop looking at her. She isn't important. I am."

Thrynne's gaze jumped between them. He made a guttural sound, urgent and rough, with the slight whine of tamped-down pain. He focused on Kestrel. "Please," he said hoarsely, "he needs to know."

The captain peeled off a piece of skin and flicked it into the bucket.

Thrynne screamed. The scream broken by sucked breaths, it rang through Kestrel's head.

She reached for the captain. She tried to snag the hand that held his blade. He shoved her back easily, without even looking, and she fell.

"Don't refuse *me*, Thrynne," said the captain. " 'No' doesn't exist anymore. Only 'yes.' Do you understand?"

The scream was bitten off. "Yes."

Kestrel got to her feet. "Captain—"

"Quiet. You're only making this worse." To Thrynne he said, "What were you doing eavesdropping outside the doors of a private meeting between the emperor and the Senate leader?"

"Nothing! Cleaning. I clean."

"That sounds like a 'no' to me."

"No! I mean, yes, yes, I was sweeping the floor. I clean. I'm a servant."

"You're a slave," the captain corrected, though the emperor had issued a decree that emancipated the Herrani. "Aren't you?"

"Yes. I am."

Kestrel had quietly drawn her dagger. If the captain kept his back to her, she might be able to do something. It didn't matter that her combat skills were pitiful. She could stop him.

Maybe.

"And why," the captain said to Thrynne in a gentle voice, "why were you listening outside that door?"

The dagger in Kestrel's hand shook. She smelled the emperor's perfumed oil on the captain. She forced herself close. The breakfast milk swam up her throat.

Thrynne tore his gaze from the captain to glance at her. "Money," he said. "This is the year of money."

"Ah," said the captain. "Now we come to it. You were paid to listen, weren't you?"

"No—"

The captain's knife came down. Kestrel vomited, her dagger falling into the shadows. The sound of it hitting stone was lost in Thrynne's shriek. She wiped her mouth on her sleeve; she was not looking, she was pressing hands to her ears. She barely heard the captain say, "Who? *Who* paid you?"

But there was no answer. Thrynne had fainted.

Kestrel took to her rooms like someone sick. Infected. She bathed until she felt boiled. She left her ruined dress where it lay, balled up on the bathing room floor. Then she climbed into bed, hair loose and damp, and thought.

Or tried to think. She tried to think about what she

should do. Then she noticed that the feather blanket, thick yet light, quivered like a living thing. She was shaking.

She remembered Cheat, the Herrani leader. Arin had answered to him, followed him. Loved him. Yes, she knew that Arin had loved him.

Cheat had always threatened Kestrel's hands. To break them, cut off fingers, crush them with his own. He had seemed obsessed with them, until he became obsessed with her in a different way. She felt it again: that cold roll of horror as she began to understand what he wanted and what he would do to get it.

He was dead now. Arin had gutted him. Kestrel had seen it. She'd seen Cheat die, and she reassured herself that he could not hurt her. Kestrel stared at her hands, whole and undamaged. They were not peeled and bloody meat. They were slim, nails kept short for the piano. Skin soft. A small birthmark near the base of the thumb.

Her hands were pretty, she supposed. Spread against the blanket, they seemed the height of uselessness.

What could she do?

Help the prisoner escape? That would require a strategy hinged upon enlisting the help of others. Kestrel didn't have enough leverage over the captain. No one in the capital owed her favors. She didn't know the court's secrets. She was new to the palace and had no one's loyalty here, not for help with such an insane plan.

And if she were caught? What would the emperor do to *her*?

And if she did nothing?

She couldn't do nothing. Having done nothing in the prison had already cost too much.

This is the year of money, Thrynne had said. He had spoken the words as if they were meant for her. It was an odd phrase. Yet familiar. Perhaps it was as the captain had assumed: Thrynne was revealing that he had been paid to gather information. The emperor had many enemies, not all of them foreign. A rival in the Senate might have employed Thrynne.

But as the feather blanket stilled, transforming into a peaked field of snow over Kestrel's tucked-in knees, she remembered her Herrani nurse saying, "This is the year of stars."

Kestrel had been little. Enai was tending to her skinned knee. Kestrel hadn't been a clumsy girl, but she had always tried too hard, with predictable bruised and bloodied results. "Be careful," Enai had said, wrapping the gauze. "This is the year of stars."

It had seemed such a curious thing to say. Kestrel had asked for an explanation. "You Valorians mark the years by numbers," Enai had said, "but we mark them by our gods. We cycle through the pantheon, one god of the hundred for each year. The god of stars rules this year, so you must mind your feet and gaze. This god loves accidents. Beauty, too. Sometimes when the god is vexed or simply bored, she decides that the most beautiful thing is disaster."

Kestrel should have found this silly. Valorians had no gods. There was no afterlife, or any of the other Herrani superstitions. If the Valorians worshipped anything, it was glory. Kestrel's father laughed at the idea of fate. He was the imperial general; if he had believed in fate, he said, he would have sat in his tent and waited for the country of Herran to be handed to him in a pretty crystal cup. Instead he'd seized it. His victories, he said, were his own.

But as a child, Kestrel had been charmed by the idea of gods. They made for good stories. She had asked Enai to teach her the names of the hundred and what they ruled. One evening at dinner, when her father cracked a fragile dish under his knife, she'd said jokingly, "Careful, Father. This is the year of stars." He had gone still. Kestrel became frightened. Maybe the gods were real after all. This moment was a disaster. She saw disaster in her father's furious eyes. She saw it on Enai's arm the next day, in the form of a bruise: a purple, broad bracelet made by a large hand.

Kestrel stopped asking about the gods. She forgot them. Probably there was a god of money. Perhaps this was the year. She wasn't sure. She didn't understand what the phrase had meant to Thrynne.

Tell him, Thrynne had said. *He needs to know.* The captain had assumed that Thrynne had meant himself. Maybe that was it. But Kestrel recalled the prisoner's gray eyes and how he'd appeared to know her. Of course, he was a servant in the palace. Servants knew who she was without her knowing all their names or faces. But he was Herrani.

Say that he was new to the palace. Say that he recognized her from her life in Herran, when everything had been a series of dinners and dances and teas, when her greatest worry was how to navigate her father's desire for her to join the military, and his hatred of her music.

Or maybe Thrynne recognized her from when everything had changed. After the Firstwinter Rebellion. When the Herrani had seized the capital and Arin had claimed her for his own.

He needs to know, Thrynne had said.

Slowly, as if moving tiny parts of a dangerous machine, Kestrel substituted one word with a name.

Arin needs to know.

But know what?

Kestrel had questions of her own for Thrynne. She would seek a way to help him, and to understand what he had said—but this meant seeing Thrynne alone . . . and *that* required the permission of the emperor.

"I'm ashamed of myself," she told the emperor the next morning. They were in his private treasury. His note accepting her request to see him, and naming this room for the meeting, seemed to have been made with good grace. But he was silent now, inspecting a drawer pulled out of a wall honeycombed from floor to ceiling with them. He was intent on the drawer's contents, which Kestrel couldn't see.

"I behaved badly in the prison," Kestrel said. "The torture—"

"Interrogation," he said to the drawer.

"It reminded me of the Firstwinter Rebellion. Of . . . what I experienced."

"What you experienced." The emperor looked up from the drawer.

"Yes."

"We have never fully discussed what you experienced, Kestrel. I should think that whatever it was, it would make you encourage the captain in his proceedings instead of jeopardizing his line of inquiry. Or do we have a different understanding of what you suffered at the hands of the Herrani rebels? Do I need to reevaluate the story of the general's daughter, who escaped captivity and sailed through a storm to alert me to the rebellion?"

"No."

"Do you think that an empire can survive without a few dirty methods? Do you think that an empress will keep herself clean of them?"

"No."

He slid the drawer shut. Its click was as loud as a bang. "Then what have we left to address but my disappointment? My grievous disappointment? I had thought better of you."

"Let me redeem myself. Please. I speak Herrani very well, and my presence made the prisoner ready to talk. If *I* were to question him—"

"He's dead."

"What?"

"Dead, and whatever information he had with him."

"*How?*"

The emperor waved an irritated hand. "Infection. Fever. A waste bucket."

"I don't understand."

"The prison is designed to prevent suicide. But this man—Thrynne—was clever. Committed. Desperate. Any number of qualities that might make someone decide to infect open wounds by plunging them into a waste bucket."

Kestrel's nausea threatened to return. And guilt: a bad taste at the back of her throat.

The emperor sighed. He settled into a chair and gestured for Kestrel to sit in the one across from him. She sank into it. "You know his kind, Kestrel. Do you think that someone like him would resort to such measures to protect a Valorian senator who had paid him to learn which ways he should vote?"

"No," she said. Any other answer would seem false.

"Who do you think hired him?"

"The east, perhaps. They must have spies among us."

"Oh, they do." The emperor held her gaze in a way that didn't wait for an answer, but to see if she would voice what he already believed.

"He worked for Herran," Kestrel said slowly.

"Of course. Tell me, is their leader an inspiring sort of man? I've never met him. But you were his prisoner. Would you say that this new governor has . . . charisma? The sort of pull and power that lure people to take extreme risks on his behalf?"

She swallowed hard. "Yes."

"I have something to show you." He pointed at the drawer he had closed. "Bring what lies inside."

It was a gold coin stamped with the emperor's profile.

"I had this series minted in celebration of your engagement," he said. "Turn the coin over."

Kestrel did. What she saw left her frightened. It was a symbol of crossed knitting needles.

"Do you know what that is?"

Kestrel hesitated to speak. "It's the sign of Jadis."

"Yes. The perfect story, I think, to represent you."

Jadis had been a warrior girl from ancient Valorian legend. A lieutenant. Her army had been defeated, and she was taken prisoner by an enemy warlord who added her to his harem. He liked all his women, but developed a particular taste for the Valorian girl. He was not, however, stupid. He summoned her to his bed naked, so that she had no chance to hide a weapon. And he had her bound as well, at least at first. He didn't trust her hands.

But Jadis was sweet and easy, and as time passed and the warlord's camp traveled, he noticed that she had become friends with the other women in his harem. They taught her how to knit. Sometimes, when not at battle, he saw her outside the women's tent, knitting something shapeless. It amused him to know that the reputation of Valorian ferocity was nothing more than myth. How domestic was his little warrior!

"What's that?" he asked.

"It's for you," Jadis said. "You'll like it, you'll see."

The woolly thing grew over the months. It became a private joke between them. He would ask if it was meant to be a sock, a tunic, a cloak. Her answer was always the same: "You'll like it, you'll see."

One night, in the warlord's tent, long after he'd stopped

ordering her hands to be bound, he gazed upon her. "Do you know which battle comes tomorrow?"

"Yes," Jadis said. The warlord planned to strike at the heart of Valoria. He would likely succeed.

"You must hate me for it."

"No."

The word brought tears to his eyes. He wanted to weep against her skin. He did not believe her.

"My love," she said, "I have almost finished your present. Let me knit it here beside you. It will bring you luck in battle."

That made him laugh, for he couldn't possibly imagine how she expected him to wear that ugly, lumpy mass of wool. He was cheered as he remembered how dedicated she was to her hapless knitting. So what if she had no skill for it? It was proof of her devotion to him.

He went to the tent's opening and called for her knitting basket.

He set it beside the bed and enjoyed her again. Afterward, she knitted beside him. The warlord was made sleepy by the needles' quiet chatter. "Aren't you finished yet?" he teased.

"Yes. Just now I've finished."

"But what *is* it?"

"Don't you see? Don't you like it? Look closely, my love."

He did, and Jadis stabbed her needles into his throat.

The coin lay heavy on Kestrel's palm. All the breath had gone out of her.

The emperor said, "We were talking earlier about your captivity under Arin."

"It wasn't like this." She tightened her fingers around the coin. "I'm no Jadis."

"No? The governor, I hear, is an attractive man."

"I didn't think so." She hadn't, not at first. How miserable that she hadn't seen Arin for what he was, how worse when she did understand it, and how perfectly awful now, when he was lost to her and the emperor was asking for her secrets. "He was never my lover. Never."

That much was true. The sound of her voice must have convinced the emperor, or the way she clutched the coin. His response came gently: "I believe you. But what if I didn't? Would it matter if the slave had shared your bed? Oh, Kestrel. Don't look at me with such shock. Do you think that I'm a prude? I've heard the rumors. Everyone has." He stood, and came near to tap the fist she had closed around the coin. "That's why you need Jadis. This is a gift. If the capital thinks you favored the governor of Herran, let them think that it was for a purpose.

"You made a choice when you stood before me and pleaded for Herrani independence. You chose my son. You chose my cause." He shrugged. "I'm a pragmatist. I had no desire to mire myself in a battle with Herran when the east beckons. Your solution—Herran's new status as an independent territory of the empire—has been politically costly in some ways . . . but valuable in others. And militarily necessary. An added benefit? The military loves me now that its general's daughter will marry my son.

"I think we understand each other, don't we? I get a daughter intelligent enough to manage the empire one day, and in the meanwhile I can count on the goodwill of her father's soldiers. You get a crown and absolution from any past . . . indiscretions."

Kestrel lowered her hand, fist loose, but not loose enough to let the coin slip.

"Your dagger, please, Kestrel." He held out his palm.

"What?"

"Give me your dagger." When she still didn't move, he said. "It's too plain. My son's bride must have something finer."

"My father gave it to me."

"Won't I be your father, too?"

The emperor had just made it impossible for Kestrel to refuse without offending him. She drew the dagger, which she cherished. She pressed her thumb once against the ruby set into the dagger's hilt and carved with her seal: the talons of a bird of prey. She pressed hard enough for it to hurt. Then she gave her weapon to the emperor.

He placed it in the drawer that had held the coin and pushed it shut. He regarded Kestrel, his own dagger gleaming at his hip. He touched the golden line on her brow that marked her as an engaged woman. "I have your loyalty to the empire, don't I?"

"Of course." She tried to ignore the weightlessness of her scabbard.

"Good. And what's past is past, isn't it?"

"Yes."

The emperor seemed satisfied. "There will be no hint of any sympathy you might have toward Herran—or its governor. If you have any, rub it out. If you don't, you won't like the consequences. Do you understand?"

She did. Kestrel saw now that the emperor hadn't intended her visit to the prison to be a mere test or lesson. It had been a warning of what came to those who crossed him.

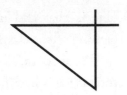

KESTREL CARRIED THE JADIS COIN WITH HER everywhere. It was in her pocket on the day she surprised the prince in her music room.

She was drawn up short by the sight of Prince Verex sitting at a table set with the pieces of an eastern game. He glanced at her, then down at the marble pieces. A blush seeped into his cheeks. He toyed with a miniature cannon.

"Borderlands is a game meant to be played by two opponents," Kestrel said. "Are you waiting for me?"

"No." He dropped the gaming piece and shoved his hands under his arms. "Why would I be?"

"Well, this is my room."

Within her first days in the palace, the emperor had given Kestrel a new piano and had had it installed here in the imperial wing, saying that this room's acoustics were excellent. This wasn't true. The room echoed too much. It sounded larger than it really was. Its stone walls were bare, the furniture stiff. Shelves were sparsely decorated with objects that had nothing to do with music: astrolabes, gaming sets, a clay soldier, collapsed telescopes.

"Your room," Verex repeated. "I suppose everything in the palace is here for your taking. My father is giving you the empire. You might as well have my old playroom, too." His shrug was tight-shouldered.

Kestrel's gaze fell again on the clay soldier. She saw its chipped paint, its place of prestige in the center of a shelf. The room was a cold, uninviting place for any child. She recalled that Verex, too, had lost his mother at an early age.

Kestrel went to sit across from him. "Your father didn't *give* me this room," she said. "He probably hoped we would share this space and spend more time with each other."

"You don't really believe that."

"But here we are together."

"You're not supposed to be here. I paid one of your ladies-in-waiting. She told me you planned to spend the afternoon in the library."

"One of my servants reports to *you*?"

"It seems that the general's daughter, despite her reputation for being so very clever, thinks she's immune to all the petty espionage a court is capable of. Not really that smart, is she?"

"Certainly smarter than someone who decides to reveal that he has her maid in his employ. Why don't you tell me which maid, Verex, and make your mistake complete?"

For a moment, she thought he'd overturn the table and send the Borderlands pieces flying. She realized then what he'd been doing as he sat alone in front of the Borderlands set, a game that was the rage at court. The pieces were organized in a beginner's pattern. Verex had been practicing.

It seemed that the hurt lines of his expression spoke in the clearest of words.

"You hate me," Kestrel said.

He sagged in his chair. His messy, fair hair fell forward, and he rubbed his eyes like someone woken too early. "No, I really don't. I hate *this*." He waved a hand around the room. "I hate that you're using me to get the crown. I hate that my father thinks it's a brilliant idea."

Kestrel touched a piece from the Borderlands game. It was a scout. "You could tell him that you don't wish to marry me."

"Oh, I have."

"Maybe neither of us has much choice in the matter." She saw his swift curiosity and regretted her words. She moved the Borderlands scout closer to the general. "I like this game. It makes me think that the eastern empire appreciates a good story as well as a battle."

He gave her a look that noted a sharp change in subject, but said only, "Borderlands is a game, not a book."

"Borderlands could be *like* a book, if one had constantly shifting possibilities for different endings, and for the way characters can veer off course into the unexpected. Borderlands is tricky, too. It tempts a player into thinking she knows the story of her opponent. Take the story of the inexperienced player. The beginner who doesn't see traps being set." Verex's expression had grown softer, so Kestrel arranged the Borderlands pieces into an opening gambit and moved them into different patterns of play for two opponents, explaining how a perceived beginner might win a game by deliberately falling for a trap in order to set one of his own. When the green general finally toppled the red, Kestrel said, "We could practice together."

Verex's large eyes were suddenly too shiny. "By 'practice,' you mean 'teach.'"

"Friends play games together all the time without thinking of it as practicing or teaching or winning or losing."

"Friends."

"I don't have many." She had one. She missed Jess terribly. Jess had gone to the southern isles with her family for her health. In the past, Jess would have gone to a charming little house her family owned by the sea on the warm southern tip of Herran, but the Midwinter Edict ordered Valorian colonists to surrender all property in Herran. The colonists were compensated by the emperor, and Jess's parents had purchased a new house in the islands. But Kestrel read the homesickness in Jess's letters. Kestrel wrote back. They wrote often, but letters weren't enough.

Verex nudged the fallen red general with his green one, listening to the rocking tap of marble on marble. "Maybe we could be friends, if you could explain why *you* don't tell my father that you don't wish to marry me."

But Kestrel couldn't explain.

"You don't want *me*," Verex said.

She couldn't lie.

"You claimed that you don't have a choice," he said. "What did you mean?"

"Nothing. Truly, I want to marry you."

His anger returned. "Then let's list the reasons." He ticked them off on his fingers. "You seek the empire, and a husband you can manipulate as easily as these game pieces."

"No," she said, but why wouldn't Verex believe his portrait of her: power-hungry, unfeeling? It was what Arin believed.

"You want a good laugh. So that at our engagement ball you can watch me lose at Borderlands while every single aristocrat and governor of the territories laughs with you."

"A ball? All the governors? Are you sure? No one's told me about this."

"My father tells you *everything*."

"He didn't. I swear, I knew nothing of a ball."

"So he plays games with you, too. My father is two-faced, Kestrel. If you think he adores you, you'd better think again."

Kestrel threw up her hands. "You're impossible. You can't blame me for his favor *and* claim that I'm no more than an amusing toy to him." She stood and went toward the door, for she saw that the brief peace between them had disintegrated, and her mind was reeling. An engagement ball. With all the governors. Arin was coming. Arin would be here.

"I wonder why my father didn't tell you," Verex said. "Could it be so that in catching you off guard, he could observe exactly what lies between you and the new governor of Herran?"

Kestrel stopped, turned. "There is *nothing* between us."

"I've seen the Jadis coin. I've heard the rumors. Before

the rebellion, he was your favorite slave. You fought a duel for him."

She almost reached out to a bookshelf to steady herself. It felt as if she might fall.

"I know why you're marrying me, Kestrel. It's so that everyone will forget that after the rebellion, no one put *you* in a prison, not like every other Valorian in Herran's city. You were special, weren't you? Because you were *his*. Everyone knows what you were."

Her vertigo vanished. She snatched the clay soldier off the shelf.

She saw instantly from Verex's expression that she held something he cherished. She would smash it, she would smash it against the floor. She would break Verex like his father had broken him.

Like she had broken her own heart. Kestrel felt the pieces of her heart suddenly, as if love had been an object, something as frail as a bird's egg, its shell an impossible cloudy pink. She saw the shock of its bloody yolk. She felt the shards of shell pricking her throat and lungs.

Kestrel set the soldier back on the shelf. She made certain her voice was clear when she spoke her last words before leaving the room. "If you won't be my friend, you'll regret being my enemy."

Kestrel retreated to her suite and sent her maids away. She didn't trust any of them now. She sat by a tiny window that gave a feeble light. When she took the Jadis coin from her pocket, it looked dull on her palm.

This is the year of money, she remembered. She had indeed planned on going to the library earlier today, as her maid had informed Verex. She'd hoped to research the Herrani gods, then thought better of it. The library possessed a paltry collection of books; it was mostly a glamorous room where courtiers sometimes met for a quiet tea, or where a military officer might consult one of the thousands of maps. The library would have suited Kestrel well if she had wanted to find a map or to socialize . . . or if she'd wanted members of the court to see her researching Herrani books.

She had turned away from the thick library doors.

Now she huddled in her velvet chair, trying to concentrate on the actual words of her conversation with Verex instead of on their emotional undertow. She flipped the coin, flipped it again. Emperor. Jadis. Emperor. Jadis. *He's two-faced,* Verex had said of his father. Kestrel thought about that phrase as she considered each side of the coin. *Two-faced:* the word dangled a hook into the dark well of her memory. It snagged on something.

The Herrani believed that a god ruled not just one thing, but a whole domain of associated ideas, actions, objects. The god of stars was the god of stars, yes, but also of accidents, beauty, and disasters. The god of souls . . . Kestrel's throat closed as she remembered Arin invoking that god, who ruled love. *My soul is yours,* he had said. *You know that it is.* His expression had been so open, so true. Frightened, even, of what he was saying. And she had been frightened, too, by how he had spoken what she felt. It frightened her still.

The coin. Kestrel forced her attention again to the coin.

There was nothing honest about the god of money. She recalled that now. This god was two-faced, like this piece of gold. Sometimes male, sometimes female. *He rules buying and selling,* Enai had said, *which means she rules negotiation. And hidden things. You can't see both sides of one coin at once, can you, child? The god of money always keeps a secret.*

The god of money was also the god of spies.

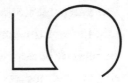

ARIN REMEMBERED.

It had been easy at first, the promise to be Cheat's spy. "I trust you most," the leader of the rebellion had murmured in Arin's ear after his sale to the general's daughter. "You are my second-in-command, lad, and between you and me we will have the Valorians on their knees."

Everything had slid and locked into place along well-oiled grooves.

Except . . .

Except.

The general's daughter had taken an interest in Arin. It was a gods-given opportunity, yet even in those early days as her slave, Arin had had the misgiving—uncomfortable, low, electric, like sparks rubbed off clothes in winter—that her interest would lead to his undoing.

And Arin was Arin: he pushed his luck, as he always did.

His habit was worse with her. He said things he

shouldn't. He broke rules, and she watched him do it, and said little of the breaking.

It was, he decided, because she didn't care what he did.

Then came an impulse whose danger he should have seen—*would* have seen, if he had been able to admit to himself what it was that made him want to shake her awake even though her eyes were open.

Why should she care what a slave did?

Arin would *make* her care.

Arin remembered.

How he couldn't sleep at night in the slaves' quarters for the music that needled its way through the dark, across the general's grounds from the villa, where the girl played and played and didn't care that he was tired, because she didn't know that he was tired, because she gave no thought to him at all.

He was whipped barebacked by her Valorian steward for some slight offense. The next day she had ordered him to escort her to a tea party. Pride had kept him from wincing as he moved. The fiery stripes on his back split and bled. She wouldn't see, he would not let her see, he would not give her the satisfaction.

Nonetheless, he searched for a sign that she'd even heard of the flogging. His gaze raked her face, finding nothing there but a discomfort to be so scrutinized.

She didn't know. He was certain he would have been able to tell. Guilt was an emotion she was bad at hiding.

Across the distance, where she was sitting on a brocade divan, teacup and saucer in hand, she dropped his gaze, turned to a lord, and laughed at something he had said.

Her innocence was maddening.

She should know. She should know what her steward had done. She should know it to be her fault whether she'd given the order or not—and whether she knew or not. Innocent? Her? Never.

He pulled the high collar of his shirt higher to hide a lash that had snaked up his neck.

He did not want her to know.

He did not want her to see.

But:

Look at me, he found himself thinking furiously at her. *Look at me.*

She lifted her eyes, and did.

The memories were strange, they were a network of lashes, laid one on top of the other, burning traces that might have resembled a pattern if it wasn't clear that they had been left by a wild hand with no restraint. The lashes were lit with feeling.

He was stinging, stinging.

"Arin," Tensen said during their meeting with the Herrani treasurer, who was even grimmer than usual, "where is your head? You've heard nothing I've said."

"Say it again."

"The emperor has had a new coin minted to celebrate the engagement."

Arin didn't want to hear about the engagement.

"I think that you should see it," Tensen said.

Arin took the coin, and didn't see whatever it was that Tensen thought he should see.

Tensen told him the story of Jadis.

Arin dropped the coin.

He remembered.

He remembered changing.

He saw Kestrel give a flower to a baby everyone else ignored. He watched her lose cheerfully at cards to an old Valorian woman whom society giggled about, not even bothering to hush their words, for she was too senile, they said, to understand.

Arin had stood behind Kestrel during that card game. He'd seen her high hand.

He saw her honesty with him. She offered it like a cup of clear water that he drank deep.

Her tears, glinting in the dark.

Her fierce creature of a mind: sleek and sharp-clawed and utterly unwilling to be caught.

Arin saw Kestrel step between him and punishment as if it meant nothing, instead of everything.

"Arin?" Tensen called through the memories.

Arin remembered the sunken days after he'd seen her last, after she'd handed him her emperor's decree of Herrani freedom and told him about her engagement. "Congratulate me," she'd said. He hadn't believed it. He had begged. She hadn't listened. "Oh, Arin," Sarsine said to him during the time when he wouldn't leave the rooms Kestrel had lived in. "What did you expect?"

Grief. It had all come to this.

"Arin," Tensen said to him again, and Arin could no longer ignore him. "For the last time, are you going to the capital or not?"

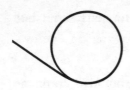

OFFICIALS AND ARISTOCRATS BEGAN TO arrive in the capital in preparation for the ball. Every day more sets of fine horses were brought into the imperial stables, limping from the bitter ride down winter roads. Although Kestrel had pointed out the difficulties of bad travel conditions for their guests, the emperor apparently thought this was unimportant. He had invited them; they must come. Fires were laid to warm palace guest suites that would be lived in for quite some time: after the ball, there would be parties and events right up until the wedding.

One afternoon, Kestrel took a carriage down through the city to the harbor, a maid shivering beside her. There was no reason why this girl couldn't be the one in Verex's employ, but Kestrel heaped furs on their laps and encouraged the maid to nudge her toes closer to the hot brick on the carriage floor.

Their progress through the city was slow. The roads

were steep and narrow, made less for the convenience of society and more for the purpose of slowing an enemy's progress up the slopes to the palace.

No new ships had arrived. Kestrel shouldn't have expected to see one Herrani-made anyway. It was green storm season. No sane person would sail between the Herran peninsula and the capital.

The harbor wind chapped Kestrel's lips.

"What are we doing here?" said the maid through chattering teeth.

Kestrel could hardly say that she was looking for a boat that had brought Arin. Time was running out for him to make the longer but safer trek through the mountain pass, which had been cleared after the treaty with Herran had been signed. The ball loomed at the end of the week. Most guests had already arrived. But not him.

"Nothing," Kestrel said. "I wanted the view." The girl blinked: her only sign of annoyance to have been dragged down to the harbor. But Kestrel wasn't allowed to travel without an escort. She had hundreds of engagement gifts— a pen made from the ivory of a horned whale, ruby dice from a colonial lord who had heard of Kestrel's love of games, even a clever collapsible tiara for traveling . . . The list of pretty presents was long, but Kestrel would have gladly traded them all for one hour of privacy outside the palace.

"Let's go," she said, and didn't return to the harbor.

She dined with senators. Over the rim of her wineglass, Kestrel watched the Senate leader, who looked oddly tan for winter, murmur something to the emperor.

What were you doing, she remembered the captain asking Thrynne in the prison, *eavesdropping outside the doors of a private meeting between the emperor and the Senate leader?*

It suddenly seemed that Kestrel's cup wasn't filled with wine but blood.

The emperor glanced up and caught Kestrel staring at him and the Senate leader. He lifted one brow.

Kestrel glanced away. She drank her wine to the bottom.

Her father sent his apologies. He couldn't come to the ball. He was mired in fighting near the border with the eastern plains. *I'm sorry,* General Trajan wrote, *but I have my orders.*

Kestrel stopped rereading the scant black lines of writing. Instead, she stared at all the blank space left on that one sheet of paper. The white of it hurt her eyes. She let the letter fall.

She'd never even considered it a possibility that her father would come—not until the moment that she had held his letter in her hands and ripped it open.

That blinding hope. That drop into disappointment. She should have known better.

She remembered the letter's last word: *orders.* Kestrel wondered how far her father's obedience to the emperor would go. What would the general have done in Thrynne's prison cell? Would his knife have cut as easily as the captain's, or worse, or not at all?

But when she thought of her father and imagined him in the captain's role, Thrynne wasn't there in the prison in her mind. She was the one in chains. *What were you doing,* the general asked, *bargaining with the emperor for a slave's life?*

Kestrel shook her head, and no longer saw the prison or her father. She was looking out a window in one of her rooms high above the palace's inner ward, facing the barbican, where visitors would enter.

She palmed away the window's frost. The barbican's gate was shut.

Come away from the window, she heard her father order.

She stayed where she was. The glass fogged.

'No' doesn't exist, Kestrel. Only 'yes.'

The view had clouded over.

She left the window. There was nothing to see anyway.

The days wore on.

There was a performance for the court. A Herrani singer. His voice was acceptable. But higher than Arin's. Thinner. Kestrel became angry at the way this unknown man's voice scraped the bottom of his register. This music was inferior, thready stuff. It had none of Arin's strength, his lithe resilience.

Kestrel hoarded the memory of Arin's song. It was honey in the hive of her heart. As the performance continued, Kestrel began to worry that the music she was hearing now was going to replace what she remembered of Arin's voice. He would never sing for her again. What if she could no longer even remember how he had sung for her once? She curled her fingers under the edge of her chair and gripped hard.

Finally the performance came to an end. The audience met the singer's silence with a dull silence of their own. No one clapped—not because everyone else had been able to judge the music's quality and found it wanting, but because they saw no point in applauding a slave, even after remembering that he no longer was one. And Kestrel, who had never forgotten what this man was and was not, certainly had no intention of applauding either.

Her music, too, was a problem. The piano brought little comfort—and what comfort it gave turned out to be false. Kestrel began to craft something that she thought was an impromptu, as difficult as she could make it. Then the notes nudged aside, twined together, and left spaces that she couldn't fill.

This was no impromptu. Impromptus were for soloists. This was a duet.

No, not quite a duet . . . only half of one.

Kestrel brought the lid down on the keys.

She invented a solitaire version of Bite and Sting. She played against a ghost. She played against herself. The boneyard—the stock of tiles left on the table after players drew their hands—dwindled until all the pieces were face-up like a final truth that she should have been able to decode. The tiger bared its teeth. The spider wove its web. Mouse, stonefish, viper, wasp . . . the black engravings on the ivory tiles became suddenly sharp in definition, then blurred before her eyes.

Kestrel mixed the tiles and tried again.

She invited Jess to the ball. Her letter practically begged Jess to come. Jess's reply arrived: she would be there, of course she would. She promised to stay with Kestrel for at least a week. Kestrel felt a terrible relief.

It didn't last.

She took tea in the palace salons with the daughters and sons of high-ranking military officers. She ate canapés on fashionable white bread that tasted awful because its color came from powdered chalk. Kestrel pretended to herself that the dry, tight quality of her throat had everything to do with the bread and nothing with the increasing disappointment of each day that did not bring Arin.

On the last morning before the ball, when the weather watchers in the palace predicted that a storm building above the mountains would close the pass to Herran with snow before the day was out, Kestrel stood on a block while the dressmaker pinned a panel of silver-threaded lace to her ball gown.

It was the final touch. Kestrel stared down at the layered fabric. The color of its satin base was uncertain. Sometimes it resembled pearl scraped from the inside of shells. Then light from the window would dim and the dress became dark, full of shadows.

Kestrel was tired of the long hours on the dressmaker's block, tired to think of all the eyes that would watch her enter the ballroom, of all the gossip that swirled through the palace about details so minute as her choice of dress. Bets had been laid, she'd heard. Entire fortunes might be won or lost based on what she wore.

She lifted her gaze from the dress to watch the snow-heavy clouds build in the sky. She watched as if the window were her last exit, each cloud a stone laid to wall it off.

The dressmaker was Herrani. She'd been freed with the rest of her people when the emperor had issued his edict almost two months ago. Why Deliah stayed in the capital instead of returning to Herran, Kestrel didn't know. She didn't ask, and Deliah rarely spoke. She didn't say anything that day, either—not at first. She pinned in silent precision. But her gray eyes glanced up once to peer at Kestrel.

Kestrel saw a certain curiosity in the way they lingered. A waiting, a wondering.

"Deliah, what is it?"

"You haven't heard?"

"Heard what?"

Deliah fussed with the hem. "The Herrani representative has arrived."

"What?"

"He arrived this morning on horseback. He came through the pass in the nick of time."

"Take this dress off."

"But I'm not finished, my lady."

"Off."

"Just a few more—"

Kestrel tugged the fabric from her shoulders. She ignored Deliah's small cry, the pricks of pins, the thin chime of them scattering onto the stone floor. Kestrel stepped out of the dress, pulled on her day clothes, and rushed out the door.

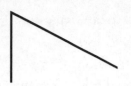

HE WAS WAITING IN THE RECEPTION HALL, A lone figure lost in the vast, vaulted chamber. The Herrani representative was an elderly man whose thin frame leaned heavily on his walking stick.

Kestrel faltered. She approached more slowly. She couldn't help looking over his shoulder for Arin.

He wasn't there.

"I thought the barbarian days of the Valorian empire were over," the man said dryly.

"What?" said Kestrel.

"You're barefoot."

She glanced down, and only then realized that her feet were freezing, that she'd forgotten even the existence of shoes when she'd left her dressing chamber and hurtled through the palace for all to see, for the Valorian guards flanking the reception hall to see right now.

"Who are you?" Kestrel demanded.

"Tensen, the Herrani minister of agriculture."

"And the governor? Where is he?"

"Not coming."

"Not . . ." Kestrel pressed a palm to her forehead. "The emperor issued a *summons*. To a state function. And Arin *declines*?" Her anger was folding onto itself in as many layers as her ball gown—anger at Arin, at the way he was committing political suicide.

Anger at herself. At her own bare feet and how they were proof—pure, naked, cold proof—of her hope, her very need to see someone that she was supposed to forget.

Arin had not come.

"I get that disappointed look all the time," Tensen said in a cheerful tone. "No one is ever excited to meet the minister of agriculture."

She finally focused on his face. His green eyes were small but clever, his wrinkled skin darker than hers. "You wrote me a letter." Her voice sounded strained. "You said that we had much to discuss."

"Oh, yes." Tensen waved a negligent hand. The lamplight traced the plain gold ring he wore. "We should talk about the hearthnut harvest. Later." His eyes slid slowly to glance at the Valorian soldiers lining the hall, then met Kestrel's gaze again and held it. "I could use your insight on a few matters concerning Herran. But I'm an old man, my lady, and very saddle sore. A little rest in the privacy of my rooms is in order, I think. Perhaps you could show me where they are?"

Kestrel didn't miss his message. She wasn't blind to the way he had indicated that their conversation could be overheard, nor was she deaf to his coded invitation that they could speak more freely in his guest suite. But she struggled against the pain in her throat, and said only, "Your ride here was hard?"

"Yes."

"And the snow. It's falling already?"

"Yes, my lady."

"The mountain pass will close."

"Yes," Tensen said gently, and he saw too much. Kestrel could tell that he heard that horrible note in her voice, and that he recognized it as the sound of someone fighting tears. "As expected," he added.

But she hadn't expected this: this stupid hope, this punishing one, for who would long to see someone who was already lost? What good would it have done?

None.

Apparently Arin knew this, too. He knew it better than she, or his hope would have been equal to hers, and would have driven him here.

Kestrel drew herself up straight. "You can find your rooms by yourself, Minister Tensen. I have more important matters to attend to."

She strode from the hall. The veined marble floor was icy beneath her feet: a frozen lake with fractures she did not care to see.

She walked, she did not care.

She did not.

Jess adjusted Kestrel's ball gown, stepped back, cocked her head, and peered. "You're anxious," Jess said, "aren't you? Your face looks pinched."

"I didn't sleep well last night." This was true. Kestrel had asked Jess to come early from her house in the city, and spend the night before the ball in Kestrel's palace rooms. Kestrel and Jess had shared a bed, like they sometimes did when they were little girls in Herran, and talked until the lamp had burned all its oil. "You snored," Kestrel said.

"I did *not*."

"You did. You snored so loudly that the people in my dreams complained."

Jess laughed, and Kestrel was glad for her silly little lie. Laughter softened Jess's face, filled the hollows of her cheeks. It drew attention away from the dark rings beneath her brown eyes. Jess never looked well. Not anymore, not since she had been poisoned on the night of the Herrani rebellion.

"I have something for you." Jess opened her trunk and lifted out a velvet bundle. "An engagement present." Jess unwrapped the bundle. "I made this for you." The velvet held a necklace of flowers strung on a black ribbon, the petals large, blown open, fashioned from sanded shards of amber glass and thin curls of horn. The colors were muted, but the flowers' size and spread made them almost feral.

Jess tied the ribbon around Kestrel's neck. The flowers clicked against one another, sliding low to rest against the dress's bodice.

"It's beautiful," Kestrel said.

Jess adjusted the necklace. "I understand why you're nervous."

The crackle of flowers went silent. Kestrel became aware that she was holding her breath.

"I shouldn't say this." Jess's eyes met Kestrel's. They were hard, unblinking. "I hate that you're marrying into the emperor's family. I hate that you're going to walk straight from this room to your engagement ball. With the *prince*. You should be my sister. You should be Ronan's wife."

Kestrel hadn't seen Ronan since the night of the First-winter Rebellion. She'd written letters, then burned them. She'd sent an invitation to the court. It was ignored. He was in the city now, Jess had said. He'd fallen in with a wild crowd. Then Jess had gone tight-lipped and wouldn't say any more—and Kestrel, who had loved Ronan as much as she could, and missed him, didn't dare ask.

Slowly, Kestrel said to Jess, "I've told you before. The emperor made the offer of marriage to his son. I couldn't refuse."

"Could you not? Everyone knows the story of how you brought the wrath of the imperial army to Herran. You could have asked the emperor for anything."

Kestrel was silent.

"It's because you do not *want* to refuse," Jess said. "You never do anything you don't want to do."

"It's a political marriage. For the good of the empire."

"What makes you think that *you* are the best thing for it?"

Kestrel had never seen such resentment in Jess's eyes. Quietly Kestrel said, "Ronan wants nothing to do with me now anyway."

"True." Jess seemed to regret her hard words, then to regret her regret. Her voice stayed stony. "I am glad that he won't be here tonight. How could the emperor invite *Herrani* to the ball?"

"Just one. One Herrani."

"It's disgusting."

"They're not slaves anymore, Jess. They're independent members of the empire."

"So we reward murder with freedom? Those rebels killed Valorians. They killed our *friends*. I hate the emperor for his edict."

Dangerous words. "Jess—"

"He doesn't know. He didn't see the slaves' savagery. I did. *You* did. That so-called governor kept you as some kind of toy—"

"I don't want to talk about that."

Jess scowled at the floor. Her voice came low: "You never do."

Kestrel stood next to Verex outside the closed ballroom doors, listening to the swell of the emperor's voice. Kestrel couldn't distinguish the words, but heard the sure rhythm. The emperor was a skilled public speaker.

Verex's head was lowered, hands stuffed in his pockets. He was dressed in formal military style: all black, with gold piping that echoed the glittering horizontal line drawn above Kestrel's brows. His belted, jeweled dagger matched hers. The emperor had finally given Kestrel the dagger he'd promised, and it was indeed fine—set with diamonds and exquisitely sharp. It was too heavy. It dragged at her hip.

She wished the emperor would stop talking. Her

stomach dipped and rose with the sound of his voice. Her nails curled into her palms.

Verex scuffed his boot.

She ignored him. She touched a glass petal on her necklace. It felt frail.

The emperor's voice stopped. The doors flung open.

It was like a hallucination: the crowd in a splash of colors, the heat, the applause, the fanfare.

Then the crash of sound faded, because the emperor was speaking again, and then he must have stopped speaking, because Kestrel heard the breathless silence that came just before Verex kissed her.

His lips were dry. Polite.

She had known it was coming, it was all planned, and she had done her best to be as far away from herself as possible when it happened. But her mind couldn't stay asleep forever. It told her to stay put, don't shrivel away, this is not so bad, the kiss is a thing, an empty thing, a scrap of blank paper. Yet Kestrel was awake, and she knew the taste of her own lies.

"I'm sorry," Verex said quietly when he pulled away. And then they were dancing before everybody.

The kiss had numbed her. Verex's words didn't register at first. When they did, they seemed like her own words, like she'd been saying them to her old self, the one who had given up Arin. *I'm sorry,* she told herself. *Forgive me,* she'd said. Kestrel had thought she'd known what her choices had cost her, but when the prince had kissed her she sharply understood that she was going to pay for this for the rest of her life.

"Kestrel?"

"Sorry," Kestrel repeated as they spun across the ballroom floor. The prince's feet had no natural talent, but he was grimly capable, the way someone might be if his dancing master came to lessons armed with a switch.

"I've been unforgivable," Verex said. "Is that why you look so miserable?"

Kestrel studied the piping on his jacket.

Verex said, "Maybe there's one final reason you are determined to marry me."

The violinists' bows sank down across the strings.

"My father is holding something over you," Verex said.

Kestrel glanced up, then away again. Verex drew their clasped hands to his chest. The crowd murmured and sighed.

He shrugged. "It's how my father is. But what does he—?"

"Verex, am I so bad a choice for a wife?"

He smiled a little. The dance was ending. "Not so bad."

"Let's agree, then, to make the best of things," Kestrel said.

Verex bowed, and before Kestrel could decide whether this was his *yes* or simply meant to mark the dance's end, he passed her hand to a senator's. Then there was another dance, and another senator, and she was whirled into the exchequer's arms.

After that, faces and titles no longer held much meaning.

Finally, she stepped deliberately wrong so that someone trod on her toes. She soothed her partner's horrified apologies, but begged for a rest and made certain she limped a little as she went to sit in the corner of gamers.

Kestrel chose a gilt chair set apart from the others, but it wouldn't be long before someone pulled a chair near, and she would have to talk and smile even though the muscles in her cheeks felt as if someone had pinched them.

She needn't have worried. All eyes were focused on the crown prince, who sat across a Borderlands table, facing a highly ranked lieutenant of the city guard.

The game was careening toward a humiliating end for the prince. The lieutenant had already captured many of Verex's key game pieces, lining up the green figures in a row. Verex's general was isolated from his troops and flanked by the lieutenant's. The marble pieces tapped out their paths, knocked each other down.

Verex's eyes lifted to meet hers across the room. He set a tentative finger on his green infantry.

It was just a game. What did it matter if Verex made the wrong move, and lost?

Yet Kestrel thought of Arin, who hadn't answered the emperor's summons, and wondered what he would lose because of it.

She thought of the possibility of peace with Verex.

She held the prince's gaze and shook her head—the slightest of gestures, a mere tip of her chin.

He lifted his hand from the infantry and settled it on the cavalry.

Kestrel used two fingertips to brush invisible lint from her dress, flicking her hand forward, away from her body.

Verex moved the cavalry two paces forward.

So it went, the smugness draining from the lieutenant's face as Verex's army made significant advances and crucial kills. Verex looked to his father, who had appeared on the edges of the crowd. When the prince's asking eyes turned again to Kestrel and she saw how hope made them luminous, she couldn't look away. She offered her silent suggestions. He took them.

The green general toppled the red one.

The crowd roared for their prince. The emperor folded his arms and rocked on the balls of his feet, his expression amused, pinned to his son's.

But not disapproving.

Kestrel heard Verex decline to play another game. Now that the spectacle was over, the crowd's attention would soon turn to her. There was a Borderlands game at another nearby table between a senator's daughter and Risha, the eastern princess who had been kidnapped as a small child and raised in the imperial palace as a pampered hostage. Kestrel had expected that Risha would be a good Borderlands player, but from everything Kestrel had seen, the princess possessed (or cultivated) a decided mediocrity at the game. There was no excitement to be had at *that* table. A bit farther over was a match between the Herrani minister— Tensen, she remembered his name—and a very minor Valorian baron who had probably condescended to play with Tensen only for the pleasure of beating him before a crowd. Many were watching, widening mirthful eyes when Tensen forgot how a gaming piece moved, or seemed to doze off between his turns. That farce might hold people's interest, but not for long.

And then they would come for her.

Kestrel's throat closed when she thought of faking joy at her engagement. Yet she would have to do it. She would have to dance all night long and into the gray hours of morning, until the last reveler had left the ballroom and her shoes were worn out and her heart was in shreds.

Kestrel stood. The emperor wasn't watching her, at least not for now. His eyes were on his son. She threaded through the crowd, telling each person who stopped her that she had promised a dance to someone else. The ballroom was thick with people. Faces clustered around her like children's puppets on sticks.

Somehow she dodged them, and slipped down a hallway where the air was cooler. No one lingered here. There was nothing to see, nothing to do. This area was used only in fine weather when the balconies lining the hallway were open to the palace gardens below. Each balcony was now curtained off from the hallway, and Kestrel knew that the glass shutters attached to each balustrade had been drawn and fastened for the winter. Despite every attempt to ward off the cold, it seeped beneath the velvet curtains. It lapped over Kestrel's slippered feet.

With a quick glance behind to make certain that no one was near and no one saw her, she dove through a curtain and pulled it shut behind her.

The balcony was a box, its glass walls like black ice: sheer slices of the night outside. Light from the hallway lined the seam of the curtain and glowed at its hem, but Kestrel could barely see her own hands.

She touched a glass pane. These windows would be

open on the night of her wedding. The trees below would be in bloom, the air fragrant with cere blossoms.

She would choke on it. Kestrel knew she would hate the scent of cere flowers all her life, as she ruled the empire, as she bore her husband's children. As she aged and the ghosts of her choices haunted her.

There was a sudden sound. The slide of wooden curtain rings on the rod. Light brightened behind Kestrel.

Someone was coming through the velvet.

He was pulling it wide, he was stepping onto Kestrel's balcony—close, closer still as she turned and the curtain swayed, then stopped. He pinned the velvet against the frame. He held the sweep of it high, at the level of his gray eyes, which were silver in the shadows.

He was here. He had come.

Arin.

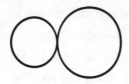

KESTREL HAD FORGOTTEN. SHE HAD THOUGHT that she remembered only too well the lines of his face. The restless quality to how he would stand still. The way he looked fully into her eyes as if each glance was an irrevocable choice.

Her blood felt laced with black powder. How could she have forgotten what it was like to burn on a fuse before him? He looked at her, and she knew that she had remembered nothing at all.

"I can't be seen with you," she said.

Arin's eyes flashed. He raked the curtain shut behind him. The closed-off balcony became deeply dark.

"Better?" he said.

Kestrel backed away until the heel of her shoe met the balustrade and her bare shoulder blades touched the glass. The air had changed. It was warm now. And scented, strangely, with brine.

"The sea," she managed to say. "You came by sea."

"It seemed wiser than riding my horse to death through the mountains."

"*My* horse."

"If you want Javelin, come home and claim him."

She shook her head. "I can't believe you sailed here."

"Technically, the ship's captain did, cursing me the entire time. Except when I got sick. Then he just laughed."

"I thought you weren't coming."

"I changed my mind." Arin came to lean against the balustrade beside her.

It was too much. He was too close. "I'll thank you to keep your distance."

"Ah, the empress speaks. Well, I must obey." Yet he didn't move except to turn his head toward her. Light from the curtain's seam cut a thin line down his cheek in a bright scar. "I saw you. With the prince. He seems bitter medicine to swallow, even for the sweets of the empire."

"You know nothing of him."

"I know you helped him cheat. Yes, I watched you. I saw you play at Borderlands. Others might not have noticed, but I know you." His voice grew rough. "Gods, how can you respect someone like that? You'll make a fool of him."

"I wouldn't."

"You're a bad liar."

"I *won't*."

Arin went quiet. "Maybe you won't mean to." He edged away, and that line of light no longer touched him. His form was pure shadow. But her sight had adjusted, and she saw him tip his head back against the window. "Kestrel . . ."

An emotion clamped down on her heart. It squeezed her into a terrible silence. But he said nothing after that, only her name, as if her name were not a name but a question. Or perhaps that wasn't how he had said it, and she was wrong, and she'd heard a question simply because the sound of him speaking her name made her wish that she were his answer.

Something was tugging inside her. It yanked at her soul. *Tell him,* that part of her said. *He needs to know.*

Yet those words had a quality of horror to them. Her mind was sluggish to understand why, so caught it was in the temptation to tell Arin that her engagement had been the bargain for Herran's freedom.

"I don't want to talk about your fiancé." Arin pushed away from the balustrade and stood tall enough to cast a shadow over her if there had been any light. "I seek information."

"Gossip, Arin?" she said lightly, and toyed with her necklace in the dark until its fretful clicking made her let go.

"I'm looking for a Herrani servant. He's missing."

The memory of Thrynne welled up. *Tell him. He needs to know.* Those had been the tortured man's words. "Who is he to you?" Kestrel asked.

"A friend."

"You could ask the palace steward."

"I'm asking you."

She couldn't believe it. The mere *fact* of Arin's asking

was so reckless. No matter that his trust didn't extend quite so far as to admit the truth of the situation: that Thrynne had been a spy sent to gather information on the emperor, and must be assumed caught. It was nevertheless clear that Arin was the sort of person who would dash safety to pieces. No one with any sense of self-preservation would inquire after the whereabouts of his spy from the emperor's future daughter-in-law, who had already betrayed Arin once.

But self-preservation had never been Arin's strong suit.

What would he do with the truth of Kestrel's engagement?

Where is my honor in all this? he'd asked her once. She didn't know what honor was to him. She thought that it wasn't the same as her father's: monumental, marble-cut. No, Arin's honor was alive. She sensed the way it moved. She couldn't see its face—maybe it had many faces—but she believed that Arin's honor was the kind that would hold its breath and bite its lip until it bled.

If she told Arin the truth, he'd wreck the peace she'd bought. It almost didn't matter whether he loved her. Arin wouldn't let someone imprison herself so that he could go free. He'd find a way to end her engagement . . . and she would let him.

She'd felt it before, she felt it now: the pull to fall in with him, to fall into him, to lose her sense of self.

There would be scandal, and then there'd be war.

Kestrel must keep her secret. She was going to have to lie with her whole self. She could be cold. She could be distant. Even with him.

As for Thrynne . . . she had a plan.

"Very well," Kestrel said. "Tell me your friend's name. I'll share what I know in honor of the protection you gave me after the Firstwinter Rebellion. A Valorian remembers her debts."

Arin stayed very still. "I hadn't realized I had done anything that begged repayment. What I did, I did for you."

"Precisely. So ask. I will answer. We will be even."

"Even? If you insist on seeing things that way, you and I will never clear our debts."

"Do you want your information or not?"

"What I want . . ." He muttered the words. Then his voice steadied and came clear. "My friend's name is Thrynne. He cleans. Floors, mostly." Arin described the man's features.

Kestrel pretended to think. "No. I'm sorry. I don't recall seeing someone like him."

"Maybe if you took more time to consider—"

"Doubtful. There are hundreds of servants and slaves in the palace. How am I to know each one?"

"So you give me nothing."

"When have I ever given you anything?"

Softly, Arin said, "You gave me much, once."

"Well," said Kestrel, "as cozy as this little chat has been, I'd like to get back to my party." She stepped toward the curtain.

His movement was swift. He blocked her path, hands coming down on either side of her to brace against the balustrade. He didn't touch her, but was close enough now that she could see the dark shape of his mouth and the angry glimmer of his eyes. He said, "That's not all I came for."

She could smell the sea on his skin, stronger now: salty and sharp.

"Kestrel, this isn't you."

She pressed back against the chill glass. "I don't know what you mean."

"This voice you've been using, that bright one . . . do you think I don't recognize it? It's the sound of you laying a trap. Of you hiding behind your own words. And I know that the way you've been talking is *not you*. Say what you want about me, about what happened between us, about the shape of the sun and the color of the grass and any other truths in this world you want to deny. Deny everything until the gods strike you down. But you can't say that I don't know you." He was now close enough that the air between them was alive against Kestrel's skin. "I . . . have thought about you." His voice dropped. "I have thought about how I have never known you to be dishonest with me."

Kestrel's laugh was robbed of breath. It was short, incredulous.

"Let me rephrase that," Arin said. "You may have tricked me. But you were true to yourself. Sometimes even to me. You have never been *false*."

"Are you forgetting that I sent my father's army to crush yours?"

"I knew you would. You knew that I knew. Where is the lie? I've never felt that there was a lie on your lips. Please, Kestrel. Please. Don't lie."

She gripped the cold stone of the balustrade's railing.

He said, "Do you know anything about Thrynne?"

"No. Now let me pass."

"I'm not done. Kestrel . . . do you really want to marry the prince?"

"I thought you didn't want to talk about him."

"Want and need aren't the same." His mouth hovered near hers. "Tell me. Is this engagement really your choice? Because I don't believe it. Not unless I hear you say so."

The glass against her back was a blaze of cold. She shivered. He was so close. All she had to do was uncurl her fingers from the balustrade and lean forward into him. It felt inevitable, like an overfull cup ready to spill.

The rasp of his unshaved cheek brushed hers. "Do you?" he said. "Do you want him?"

"Yes."

"Prove it," Arin murmured into her ear. The heat of him settled against her. His palm squeaked against the glass by her head.

"Arin." She could barely speak. "Let me pass."

His lips caught at the base of her neck, slid upward. "Prove that you want him," he said into her hair. His kiss traveled across her cheek. It brushed her forehead, then rested right on the golden line that marked her engagement.

"I do," she said, but her voice sounded like she was drowning.

His kiss was there, waiting near her lips. "Liar," he breathed.

Her hand came between them, and pushed. She was

shaken, startled by the way she had shoved him. She felt suddenly, cruelly starved—and angry at herself for this hunger of her own making. "I said, *let me go*. Or will you hold me here against my will?"

He recoiled. His boots scraped back. She couldn't see his expression, only the way he snatched his arms to his sides and stood stiff. He covered his face as if it weren't already hidden by the dark. He muttered something into his palms, then they fell away.

"I'm sorry," he said. He tore open the curtain, and was gone.

The light hurt Kestrel's eyes. She blinked, her lashes wet, her vision too bright, blurry.

When her pulse had steadied and she could see and breathe and think again, she tentatively stepped into the hallway.

It was empty. She could hear music now. She hated to hear it. Her whole future was in that airless ballroom. She wondered if this ache inside her would ever go away—and if she might feel even worse when it did.

She had to return to the ball. Surely she'd already been missed. The emperor would be wondering where she was.

Kestrel slowly walked down the hall toward the ballroom.

She had almost reached it when someone came out of its open doors. Tensen took one look at her. His eyes widened, and he shook his head, striding toward her with an urgency that defied his age and made his cane seem purposeless.

"You can't go in there," he said.

"I must."

"No, you must find a mirror. A private one. Because Arin just stormed through the ballroom. His mouth was shiny. Maybe people will think it was from wine and not glittered oil, but they won't if they see you, too."

Kestrel's fingers flew to her forehead and the engagement mark Arin had kissed moments ago. She touched her hair, its loosened tendrils.

How did she look?

Like someone who had had an illicit liaison?

"That's right," Tensen said grimly.

"Come," Kestrel said, turning to retrace her steps back down the hall, away from the ball.

"With you?"

"You and I need to talk."

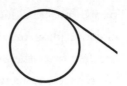

KESTREL LED TENSEN TO A SMALL, EMPTY salon where lamps and a fire burned. Tensen shut the door behind them.

"Block it with your cane," Kestrel said, pointing at a tapestry hook that was about level with the doorknob. "Since you don't need it anyway."

Tensen glanced ruefully at her before setting the curved end of his cane around the doorknob and latching the straight end into the hook. "That won't hold. Not if someone really wants to get in."

She ignored him. She came close to the mirror above the fireplace's mantel, which held a wide-bottomed vase of hothouse flowers.

Maybe it was the roses, the way that they covered her neck in the mirror's reflection, reaching up to her chin. Maybe it was the hurried escape down the hallway.

Kestrel looked breathlessly in bloom. Color was high in her cheeks. Her lips, though Arin had not in fact touched them, were bitten red. The blacks of her eyes were wide pools. The necklace Jess had given her was broken, the cracked glass petals hanging limply from their ribbon, crushed from the pressure between her and Arin.

Kestrel's reflection stared back. She had the air of something that has been opened and cannot be shut again.

She looked like pure scandal.

Her hair wasn't the worst of it. Yes, the upswept arrangement was coming loose, a lock slipping here and there, but her hair was too short for intricate braids, which meant that it often came undone. Kestrel was in the habit of appearing a little disheveled, and pinning her hair back in place herself.

The real problem was the mark. The golden line on her brow had become a smear.

"Do you have extra oil and glitter with you?" Tensen said.

Kestrel gave his reflection in the mirror an exasperated glance. She wasn't carrying a purse. Where did he think she'd keep such items? The cosmetics were on the dressing table in her suite.

"I'll find one of your ladies-in-waiting in the ballroom," Tensen said. "Or do you have a trusted friend? Someone who can fetch what you need and bring it here?"

Kestrel thought about how long that would take. She thought about how one of her maids reported to Verex. She thought about Jess, and what her friend's reaction would be if the Herrani minister of agriculture approached her at the ball to request her assistance in making Kestrel look respectable again.

"No," Kestrel said. "Bring me a lamp."

Tensen's expression was disapproving. It said that he didn't see how a lamp could serve, and that time was being wasted. But he did what she asked.

Kestrel blew out the lamp and set it on the mantel to cool. With her dagger, she cut fabric from the hem of her inner slip, grateful for the dress's many layers. She took the roses from the heavy ceramic vase, set their dripping stems on the mantel, and tipped the vase's water onto the silk rag. She used it to scrub her forehead clean. She remembered Arin's kiss there, and scrubbed harder. She tossed the rag aside. She untied her necklace, found the brightest amber glass petals, and hammered them against the mantel's surface with the vase's bottom. She ground the petals into dust. Dipping one finger into the lamp's oil, Kestrel hissed at the burn, yet didn't wait for the pain to fade. She drew an oiled, horizontal line above her brows.

Now for the glitter. She tapped her finger into the glass dust.

"You'll cut yourself," said Tensen, but his disapproval had vanished.

"I'll be careful," she said, patting the dust over the oiled line. She tucked loose tendrils back where they belonged and pinned them more securely in place. The roses returned to their vase, the vase resumed its place in front of the mirror, and Kestrel wiped the remaining glass dust off the mantel with her wet silk rag. She threw the rag and necklace into the fire. "Well?" she asked Tensen, turning to face him.

"Excellent."

She shook her head. "Optimistic." The mark shimmered, but was barely golden. "Are you always so optimistic?" she asked. "I think you must be, or you wouldn't have written that letter to me, or hinted that we have information to share."

"Am I wrong?"

"You forget that I outrank you. *I* will inquire. *You* will answer. Minister Tensen, what were you before the Herran War, ten years ago?"

Slaves had never liked that question. She'd seen teeth clenched at its asking. If an emotion could have a sound, Kestrel thought that the one produced by that question might sound like the glass petals had, ground beneath the heavy vase.

But Tensen only smiled. "I was an actor."

"I suppose that's good experience for a spymaster."

Tensen wasn't at all put out by having that title pinned on him. He seemed positively delighted by this conversation. "I hope I'm not so obvious to everyone."

" 'Hope' is the operative word here, since your governor gave all signs that he wouldn't be here tonight, and if he sent someone to the capital in his stead it must have been a person of political value to him, someone he trusts, someone intelligent and observant. You've taken some pains to appear weaker than you are, but you're no old man ready to doze off."

"Well, I *am* old. That much is true."

Kestrel made an impatient noise. "Are you even really the minister of agriculture?"

"I like to think that I'm able to play many roles."

"And you are very optimistic indeed if you believe that the emperor won't notice, especially when he knows full well that Herran has spies in the palace."

Tensen lost his smile. "What do *you* know, my lady?"

"That this conversation will end now unless you make me a promise."

He raised his brows.

"Promise that Arin will never learn that you and I spoke," she said. "I can offer information. You can give it to your governor. But it can't be linked to me."

Tensen considered her. He passed a gnarled hand over the carved back of a chair and pursed his lips as if there was something wanting in the chair's design. "I know that your presence in Arin's house after the Firstwinter Rebellion was . . . complicated."

"I didn't want to be there."

"Maybe not at first."

Slowly, Kestrel said, "I never could have stayed."

"My lady, it's not for me to know what you wanted or what you could or could not do. But your condition surprises me. If you're sympathetic enough toward my governor—or his cause—to share something with me, why can't Arin know? I swore by the god of loyalty to serve him. You would make me break my oath."

"Do you know how I escaped from your city's harbor?"

"No."

"Arin let me go," she said, "even though letting me go was the same thing as inviting the Valorian army to break down his city's walls. So promise me, because it is in *your* interest that Arin can't know. You can't trust that he'll always choose the safety of his country—or even of himself."

Tensen was silent.

"Do you see?" Kestrel pressed. "Do you see that the

very reason you stopped me from entering the ballroom is why you can't tell Arin that your information comes from me? Let's not pretend that you don't know how I came to look like I did, and why I can't look that way when I return to the ballroom." Kestrel's gaze dropped to her hands. She wished she had something to do with them. She imagined that she held one of those roses on the mantel. She could almost feel the bloom's texture, its curled velvet as sinkingly soft as the balcony's curtain.

"Arin and I are impossible," she said quietly. "Dangerous. It's best that we keep our distance from each other."

"Yes," said Tensen. "I see."

"Do you promise?"

"Would you trust me to keep that promise?"

"I trust my ability to ruin you if you don't."

He laughed. It wasn't quite a disbelieving laugh, only the kind that the aged sometimes have for the young. "Then speak, my lady. You have my word."

Kestrel told him about Thrynne and what the tortured man had said.

The minister pressed a palm to his mouth, thumb rumpling the wrinkles near one eye. As he heard more, his hand shifted into a fist, still covering his mouth. He had the look of someone trying not to be sick.

His hand fell away. "You think that Thrynne had something important to tell Arin. What did Thrynne overhear during the emperor's meeting with the Senate leader?"

"I don't know."

"You could find out."

But Kestrel was already walking toward the door. "No."

Tensen spread his hands. "Where's the harm?"

She shook her head at the obvious absurdity of such a question.

"Are you afraid of the risk of finding out more?" said Tensen. "I hear that you love a gamble."

"This isn't a game."

"Yet you've played it well so far. You're playing it now."

Kestrel set her hand on the cane blocking the door. "This kind of conversation won't happen again. I am not one of your people. I have my own country and code . . . and no reason to become your spy."

"Then why tell me anything at all?"

Kestrel shrugged. "Valorians see little point in the sacred, but we honor the last request of the dying. I've told you what I know for Thrynne's sake."

"Only for him?"

Kestrel handed Tensen his cane. "Good night, Minister. Enjoy the remainder of the ball."

Verex found Kestrel in a corner of the ballroom pouring a glass of iced lemon water with floating sprigs of mint. "Where have you been? And why are you serving yourself? Here." He took the cut-crystal dipper from her and poured.

But Kestrel wasn't really watching him. Her mind was a curtained balcony. It was filled with the memory of warm movement. Of almost coming undone. Coming close, pushing away, letting go . . .

Verex set the cold cup in her hand. The lemon-mint water tasted alien: piercingly sweet and clear.

He took his time pouring a cup for himself. His movements were tense. He seemed constantly on the point of saying something.

"Thank you," he finally murmured.

"For what?" Kestrel's heart was made of treason. Didn't Verex sense that? Couldn't he tell? Why would he ever thank her?

"For the Borderlands game. You helped me win."

She'd forgotten about that. "Oh. It was nothing."

"I'm sure to *you* it was," he said bitterly. His eyes roamed the ballroom, then settled on the emperor. Verex drank. "I couldn't find you earlier. I looked everywhere."

Kestrel's cup was cold and sweating in her hand. She ran a quick thumb through the condensation. She was aware that some courtiers lingered nearby, as close as politeness would allow. They were drawing closer.

"Did a senator corner you?" Verex asked. "They'll do that. They'll try to worm their way into your good graces for a chance to influence my father. Well, Kestrel? Where *were* you? And what . . ." He frowned, peering closely at her. "Your mark has faded."

"Oh," she said. "I have a headache." As the courtiers watched, she rubbed at her forehead, smudging the mark. She hoped the gesture seemed casual, absentminded, as if she had been doing it all evening.

Arin rambled around the palace suite he was to share with Tensen. It was not small or large, neither luxurious nor spare. Arin had thought that the palace steward would assign the Herrani contingent an insulting set of rooms, but this suite seemed chosen to send the message that the Herrani didn't matter one way or the other.

He shrugged off his shirt. It was early in the evening, not yet midnight. The ball was still whirling on its giddy axis. Tensen hadn't returned.

Arin could smell Kestrel's perfume on him. It exhaled faintly from his shirt, mingled with the scent of the sea. Folding the fabric—or not really folding it, more smoothing it out over the back of a dressing room chair, as if the cloth were a living thing that needed soothing—Arin found a hole in the seam where the shoulder met the body. He worked a finger through the rip and swore.

Well, it was an old shirt. He had worn his finest clothes. He'd torn them out of the trunk upon his arrival in the palace and flung them on, fumbling with the cuffs, knowing he was late for the ball. Maybe the hole had happened then, in his haste.

It would have happened sooner or later. All of his best garments were ten years old. They had been his father's.

They fit Arin badly. Even after alterations, it seemed that there wasn't enough room anywhere. His father had been an elegant man, his proportions artistic. If he stood here now next to Arin, a stranger would never guess they were related.

Arin pressed a hand to his face. He felt the bones that

made him look so different. There was the prickle of a beard.

How ridiculous he must have looked next to those polished courtiers, with his ill-fitting clothes and unshaven face.

How rough, how thuggish.

How wrong.

Arin flicked open a straight razor, filled the washbasin, and lathered soap. He tried to shave without looking too closely at his face in the washbasin mirror.

A nick pinkened the lather with blood.

He kept at it, more attentive this time, until he had finished, wiped off the lather, and poured water over his bowed head. He looked up again, dripping. His face was clear.

Sometimes Arin could see the boy he had been before the war. When he did, he usually felt a tenderness for that child as if he were wholly other than Arin, not part of himself at all. That boy didn't blame Arin, exactly, for existing when he did not, but when Arin caught a glimpse of the child, usually lingering about the eyes, Arin always looked away. He would feel a small sharpness, like the nick of the razor.

Arin's face was wet, his hair black with water. He shivered, suddenly aware of the winter. He searched for something to wear, and pulled on a nightshirt and robe.

Arin felt again his nervousness as he'd stood outside the balcony curtain. The curtain had swung after Kestrel had closed it behind her, and he'd gingerly touched its sway. He remembered that hunted expression she had thrown over her shoulder before disappearing behind the velvet.

And then there, in the dark, with her . . . it made Arin's throat tighten as if he were thirsty. *Prove it,* he'd told her, words thick with desire, full of a traitorous kind of confidence, one that came and then abandoned him and then returned and left in such rapid tides that he couldn't keep his footing. *Prove that you want him.* Kestrel had pushed him away.

He could have sworn that he had sensed in her the same wish that was in him. It had been on her skin like a scent. Hadn't it? But then Arin remembered how she'd escaped his house in Herran. He saw her again on the harbor: her hand on a weapon, that flash in her eyes. It had wrecked him. *He* had done this, he had made this, had lied to her, tricked her, killed her people, killed whatever it was that had made Kestrel open up to him on Firstwinter night . . . before she knew his treachery.

Of course she had chosen someone else.

There was a knock at the dressing room door.

"Arin?" Tensen called. "Can I come in?"

No, Arin wanted to say, and had he still been in front of the mirror and seen his face he *would* have said it, because his reflection would have shown something vulnerable and uncertain, and he would have despised it. He wouldn't have let anyone see him then.

Tensen knocked again.

Arin's wet hair was cold. A chilly rivulet crept down his neck. Arin dried himself off, rubbing a towel at his short hair as he kept his back to the mirror. He went to open the door.

Tensen scrutinized Arin, which made the younger man's

jaw go tight. But Tensen gave him an easy smile, pulled up the dressing room chair, and sat gustily down. "That," he said, "was exhausting. And profitable."

"What have you learned?" Arin asked.

Tensen told him about Thrynne.

"Gods," Arin said.

"No, Arin. I won't have that look on your face. Thrynne knew what he risked when he came to the capital. He did it for Herran."

"I asked him to."

"We all make our choices. What would you choose: Herran's sake, or yours?"

Arin's answer was quick. "Herran's."

Tensen said nothing for a moment, only gazed up at him with the pensiveness of someone considering a question not so easily answered. Arin didn't like that expression, he bristled at it, but before he could speak, Tensen said, "What would you have *me* choose?"

"I can't tell you what to choose for yourself."

"No, what would you have me choose for *you*? Say that you were in Thrynne's position—imprisoned, worse—and my intervention could help you but hurt our country. What should I do?"

"Leave me there."

"Yes," Tensen said slowly. "That's what I thought you'd say."

Arin threaded fingers through his damp hair and tugged until his scalp hurt. "Are you sure of this news?"

"My source is good."

"Who?"

Tensen waved a hand. "No one important."

"But who?"

"I promised not to tell. Don't make an old man break his promises."

Arin frowned, but said only, "This isn't the year of money. And what *did* Thrynne overhear the emperor and Senate leader say?"

"I don't know."

"I'll find out."

"Caution, Arin. I myself might have a way."

"Oh?"

Tensen smiled. "A new recruit." He refused to say anything more. He found a comfortable position in his chair and changed the subject in a way that spun Arin's head. "Well, I think they make a charming couple."

"What?"

"The prince and Lady Kestrel."

Arin had known whom Tensen had meant.

"Their kiss was sweet," said the spymaster. "One would assume their marriage was just a political alliance—*I* certainly did, until I saw them kiss."

Arin stared.

"You must have missed it," Tensen said. "It was at the beginning of the ball. But of course you were late."

"Yes," Arin said finally. "I was."

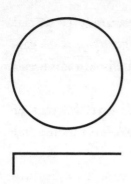

KESTREL CREPT INTO BED AT DAWN, FOOT-
SORE FROM DANCING. SHE HUNG HER UN-
BUCKLED DAGGER ON ITS HOOK ON THE
bedpost. She shivered, more from fatigue than cold, as she
got beneath the blankets next to Jess. The other girl lay
sleeping, curled on her side.

"Jess," Kestrel whispered. "I broke your necklace."

Jess gropingly stretched out her hand and caught Kestrel's. "I'll make you another one," she murmured. Eyes
still shut, she frowned. "I saw him at the ball."

"Who?" But Kestrel knew who, and Jess slipped back
into sleep.

An elite group of courtiers and visiting dignitaries were invited to join Kestrel for hot chocolate in the Winter Garden the morning following the ball. White and gray furs
muffled the ladies, while the men favored sable, except for

the occasional rakish youth who sported the rusty striped fur of an eastern tiger. Braziers burned throughout the garden's open patio, which was bounded at the southern end by an evergreen hedge maze.

Kestrel had arrived late, and alone. Despite the meager rest, she'd woken up a few hours after dawn because her body knew that she needed to. Jess still slept. Kestrel dawdled in her preparations, changing her dress twice, hoping that Jess might stir. But she didn't, and Kestrel was reluctant to wake her. Finally, she left the suite.

Although the footmen in the Winter Garden should have announced Kestrel's presence upon her arrival, she bribed them not to. She pulled her white furs more closely about her face and walked alone through a pathway of trees with sprays of pink and red berries. They were poisonous—yet beautiful, sprinkled like bright musical notation against the black bars of branches. Through the trees, Kestrel watched the party and listened.

Many complained about their dancing blisters. "I'll plunge my bare feet right into the snow, to numb them!" cried a colonial lady from the southern isles.

"Oh no," smiled a naughty young man. "Let me warm them instead."

The entire scene looked pretty and fun . . . and fake. Who knew if that flirty young man even liked the lady—or if he liked ladies at all. Kestrel wasn't the only person at court who planned to marry someone she didn't want.

Kestrel could see the emperor seated in the patio's center next to the largest brazier, surrounded by senators. At the far end of the patio, near the hedge maze, Verex hunched over a Borderlands table. His back was to Kestrel. The eastern princess sat across from him, her expression gentle as she executed a merciless move.

The Herrani hadn't been invited to this exclusive event. Kestrel needn't worry about meeting Arin's gaze . . . or not meeting his gaze.

Then again, he might come anyway. It would be like him to turn up uninvited.

Wouldn't it?

Kestrel found that she had come close to a tree. Her hands were on its bark. It was silver; smooth and papery in places, rough in others. She had been running fingers over the bark's striations and knots the way she'd seen blind people come to understand an object. When she thought of this, she realized that she was trying to understand whether she wanted to see Arin here in the Winter Garden or not. And that was a fool's question. It was pure, punishing foolishness, the mere consideration of either possibility, when she had already decided that neither should matter.

So it did not matter that her short nails had found a split in the bark. It did not matter that she was nervous as she peeled away a strip of bark in one long curl. Or that she was unhappy, unrolling the strip like a scroll with a blank message she couldn't read.

Then she looked at the bark and thought of Thrynne's stripped skin. She dropped the bark. It fluttered to the ground. Kestrel lifted her eyes and saw the emperor again.

She emerged from the poison trees. Her footfalls were

quiet on the path. The first group of courtiers, clustered around a brazier, didn't notice her arrival.

Lady Maris, the Senate leader's daughter, was murmuring something that unleashed flurries of breathless giggling from her friends.

"—they all looked like that, I'd free them, too," Maris was saying. "Or make him *my* slave."

Kestrel deliberately stepped on a fallen twig. It snapped.

Maris glanced up. Her friends went pale and their laughter died, but Maris's eyes were defiant. "Chocolate, Lady Kestrel?" she offered. "It's hot."

"Yes, thank you." Kestrel joined the ladies. They made room, edging away.

Maris lifted the chocolate pot from its stand over the brazier and poured for Kestrel, who accepted the tiny cup and sipped. It wasn't until the chocolate scalded her tongue that Kestrel knew the exact degree of her anger. It simmered: dark and bitter and somehow even sweet. Kestrel smiled. "Lady Maris, your father is looking very well. He's so tan. Has your family been somewhere sunny?"

"Oh, don't talk to me about it!" Maris gave a little dramatic mew. "It is too, too horrible!"

The other ladies relaxed, relieved that Kestrel seemed to have no interest in being vengeful. And why should she? their expressions seemed to say. It had been a bit of harmless gossip. In fact, Lady Kestrel ought to be pleased to hear compliments about the Herrani governor. It couldn't have been so bad being his captive, now could it? The ladies saw quite another side to that Jadis coin.

Kestrel watched them think this through, and shrug their furred shoulders, and drink their chocolate.

"Can you believe that my father sailed to the southern isles without me?" Maris said. "A luxury trip to blue skies while his only child languishes here in winter. Though you can be sure that if *I* had gone, I would never have let the sun darken my skin. It makes one look so coarse! Like a dock-worker! Really, what was my father thinking?"

Kestrel shouldn't have asked Maris about the Senate leader. She should steer clear of everything to do with him. She had sworn not to embroil herself any further in Herran's affairs.

And yet, she had gotten angry. She was angry still.

And yet, the Senate leader was tan.

And yet, this was unusual.

Her mind kept returning to this detail, like a thumb rubbing a flaw in a bolt of silk, or that papery bark of the poison berry trees.

But so what if the Senate leader was tan? A trip to the southern isles explained it. She told herself once more to leave the matter alone.

Yet she didn't.

"The southern isles have many delights," Kestrel said. "Surely your father brought you gifts?"

"No," said Maris. "The wretch. Oh, I love him, I do, but couldn't he have spared one little thought for me? One little present?"

"He brought you nothing? But the southern isles have linen, perfume, sugar, silver-tipped tea . . ."

"Stop! Don't remind me! I can't bear it!"

"Poor thing," one of her friends said soothingly. "But just think, Maris. Now your many suitors have more choice in gifts to please you."

"They do, don't they? And they *should* please me."

"Is that what fashionable young men do in the capital?" Kestrel asked. "Give gifts?"

"Oh, yes . . . though they often ask for something in return."

"A kiss!" cried a lady.

"Or an answer to a riddle," said another. "Riddles are very popular. And the answer is always love." Which made sense, given that the court was full of young people who had chosen to marry rather than serve in the military. By the time they turned twenty, every Valorian had to fight for the empire or begin giving it babies. *Future soldiers*, her father would say. *The empire must grow*, he'd add, and Kestrel would wonder if this was the working of every general's mind, or only her father's: to see something as soft as a baby and imagine it grown hard enough to kill. And then Kestrel would shrink from the thought of becoming like her father, and he would know that he had said the wrong thing, and then they would both say nothing.

"No, I've heard other riddles," said a girl, drawing Kestrel back to the conversation. "Ones with different answers: a mirror, a candle, an egg . . ."

"I like riddles," said Kestrel. "Tell me one."

"There is a riddle that I simply cannot figure out," said the lady sitting next to Maris. "It is: *I leap without feet to land, my cloth head is filled with sand. I have no wings, yet try to fly . . . what am I?*"

Kestrel helped herself to some cream. She wasn't angry anymore. The truth was that she, like her father, knew how good it felt to cut with certain weapons. She took a whitened sip of chocolate, the cream cool and pillowy against her lips. "Maris knows the answer to that riddle," she said.

"I?" said Maris. "Not at all. I cannot guess it."

"Can you not? The answer is a fool."

Maris's smile wilted. There was a silence broken only by the delicate clink of Kestrel setting her cup on the tray. She gathered her white furs about her and swept away.

She noticed the eastern princess making a move at Borderlands. Her rider hopped over Verex's pieces to kill an engineer. Verex laughed. The sound surprised Kestrel. He sounded so happy. Kestrel would have gone to their table, to find out once and for all just what kind of player the princess was, and why Verex had laughed as he had. But the emperor caught Kestrel's eye. He beckoned her toward him.

"We have a problem," the emperor told Kestrel as she approached. "Come help us." The senators surrounding him were high-ranking, all with seats in the Quorum. Kestrel joined them, grateful that the Senate leader had his back to his daughter's coterie.

"Problem?" said Kestrel to the emperor. "Don't tell me you've run out of chocolate already."

"A more serious matter," he said. "The barbarian plains."

Kestrel glanced at the eastern princess, but Risha was engaged in her game with Verex, and the emperor's voice had been pitched not to carry. Risha possessed a grace perfectly proportioned to her beauty. Her black hair was braided like a Valorian's. She wore rings when a true easterner would have kept her fingers bare, and the contrast of gold against Risha's richly dark skin was striking. She was about Kestrel's age. Maybe Risha didn't remember much of her life in the east before her kidnapping. Maybe she had grown accustomed to the capital and thought of it as her home. Kestrel couldn't say what the girl would have thought about the emperor referring to her country as a problem, and to her people as barbarians. Uncomfortably, Kestrel remembered that she'd called them barbarians before, too, just because that's what people she knew did. Kestrel wouldn't do that now. This seemed at once a meaningful difference and yet also worth very little.

"Your father writes that the plainspeople prove tricky," the emperor said. "The eastern tribes at our borders are skilled at stealth attacks. They vanish when the general musters his army against them."

"Burn the plains," said a senator, a woman who had served under Kestrel's father. "They're dry this time of year."

"It's good land," said the emperor. "I'd like to turn it into farms. A fire would spoil my prize."

And kill the plainspeople, Kestrel thought, though this was a factor no one raised. The plains were vast, and north enough in Dacra that it didn't rain much there this time of year. Valorian soliders would set the fire while the plainspeople slept. They would wake, and they would flee to the river, if they could make it. But a fire would rage fast and fierce through the dry grasses, and by the time the plainspeople woke it would likely be too late. They'd be burned alive.

There was some debate about whether a fire might endanger Valorian troops. But if not, it would be a significant victory, argued the Senate leader. The plains lay north of the delta where the eastern queen ruled. If Valoria captured the plains, it would squeeze the savages into the southeastern corner of the continent. "And then it's only a matter of time," said the emperor, "before Valoria rules the entire continent."

"Then burn the grasses," said the senator who had been in the military. "Fire is good for the earth anyway. Eventually."

Kestrel watched Risha knock over one of Verex's pieces, an unimportant one. Risha shivered in her furs. It was never cold in the east. Did this knowledge live in Risha's memory, or had it been given to her as it had been to Kestrel, as a piece of someone else's information? The princess was young when she'd been captured, as young as Kestrel when her family had moved from the capital to the newly conquered territory of Herran. Maybe Risha didn't remember her home at all.

Kestrel saw Herran, and her garden there, and seeds beneath her childhood fingers as her nurse pressed them into the soft earth.

She saw a plain of fire. Flames waving and snapping, horses running wild, tents burned to their frames, then crackling down. Parents would snatch up their children. The air would choke hot and black.

"Kestrel?" said the emperor. "What do you think? Your father wrote that you've advised him well on the east before."

She blinked. The sky was white over the Winter Garden. The trees dripped their deadly berries. "Poison the horses."

The emperor smiled. "Intriguing. Tell me more."

"The plainspeople rely on horses," Kestrel said. "For their milk, their hides, their meat, to ride for hunting . . . Kill the horses, and the tribes won't be able to live without them. They'll trek south to take refuge in the delta. The plains will be yours. You'll mow the grasses and send it to feed our own horses. You can plant the earth as soon as you like."

"And how do you propose to poison the horses?"

"Water supply," suggested the military senator.

That might poison people as well. Kestrel shook her head. "The river is wide and rapid. Any poison would be diluted. Instead, have my father send scouts to determine where the horses graze. Spray those grasses with the poison."

The emperor leaned back in his seat. His cup of chocolate steamed, veiling his face as he tipped his chin and studied Kestrel with a slanting gaze. "Very neat of you, Lady Kestrel. You solve all my worries. You hand me the unravaged plains for the low price of poison. How nice that you minimize our enemy's civilian casualties at the same time."

Kestrel said nothing.

He sipped his chocolate. "Have you ever witnessed your father in battle? You should. I'd like to see *you* fight under a black flag, just once. I'd like to see you truly at war."

Kestrel couldn't quite return the emperor's stare. She

lifted her eyes and noticed the prince and Risha leave their gaming table. They disappeared into the hedge maze. Kestrel understood now why Verex seemed so happy. She wondered if the whole court knew about him and the princess. She suspected it must.

"Oh," the emperor drawled, "the Herrani wish to speak with you, Kestrel. They've made a formal request."

His words seemed to linger in the air longer than possible. Kestrel had the odd impression of the emperor playing a piano, and striking a dissonant chord that caught the fascination of everyone listening.

"Hardly surprising," she said coolly. "The Herrani are bound to want to speak with me from time to time. I was named their emissary."

"Yes, we should correct that. You're too busy for such a dull job. They'll be notified that you have given up the position. There's no need for you to meet with either of the Herrani representatives again."

When Kestrel returned to her suite, the bed was empty and made. Jess's trunk was gone.

But Jess had promised. Her visit was supposed to last longer than this. They'd barely seen each other, and for Jess to *leave*, to leave now, so soon . . .

Kestrel tugged on a silken bellpull. When her ladies-in-waiting arrived in her sitting room, she asked, "Where's my letter?"

The maids looked quizzical.

"From my friend," Kestrel said. "For me. It's not like her to leave. Not without saying something."

There was a silence. Then one of the maids offered, "The lady had her trunk sent to her townhome in the city."

"But *why*?"

A silence made clear that no one knew why. Kestrel pressed her lips shut.

"It's late," a maid said. "Shouldn't you change into a new dress for the afternoon? What will you wear?"

Kestrel waved a hand in a gesture very much like one she'd often seen the emperor make. She hadn't meant to do that. It upset her. "I don't care," she said curtly. "You choose."

Her ladies-in-waiting bustled into action, putting away her furs and parading gowns. While the maids tutted over some fabrics and fingered others approvingly, Kestrel wondered what Jess would have chosen. She shoved that thought away.

But this was like discarding a Bite and Sting tile only to draw a series of worse ones. Because there was Arin, in the velvet balcony of her mind, and there was the Winter Garden, cold with his absence, and there were the pink and red berries and her awful advice to the emperor.

Kestrel knew what would happen after the eastern horses died.

She imagined the yellow-green waves of grass. The ticking zizz of grasshoppers. Horse carcasses rotting in the sun.

The plainspeople would starve. Their children would grow hollow. They would cry for horse milk. The plainspeople would move south on foot to their queen's city in the delta. Many would fall in their tracks. Some would not get up.

This would happen. It would happen because of Kestrel. She had done this.

But wasn't this better? Hadn't the alternative been worse?

The alternative almost didn't matter. It didn't keep Kestrel from feeling a sick horror at what she'd done.

One of the maids shrieked.

The maid had opened another wardrobe. Masker moths were flying out. They beat against the lamps and spun up in panicked, gray spirals. Their dusty wings began to wink orange and rose as they blended into the tapestries.

"They've ruined the clothes!" A maid slapped moths out of the air. One hit the carpet and lay still. Its wings went red, tipped with white to match the carpet's design exactly. Masker moths had the property of camouflage even in death.

Kestrel stooped and picked it up. The furred, lifeless legs clung to her. The red wings changed to match her skin.

The maids hunted the moths ferociously. Masker moths were a common household pest in the capital, and this wasn't the first time they'd eaten into a wardrobe of expensive clothes. Judging by the number of moths, the larvae must have been fattening themselves on Kestrel's silks for at least a week. The maids killed every last moth, crushing them against the walls. Masker moths left behind smears of no discernible color. Damaged wings lost their camouflage.

"Go, all of you," Kestrel told her maids. "Fetch servants to clean out the wardrobe."

None of the ladies-in-waiting thought to question why they *all* must go. No one asked why Kestrel couldn't simply summon servants with the pull of a bell. They glared with satisfaction at the carnage of dusty wings, and left.

When she was alone, Kestrel opened the wardrobe wider and found a pelisse crawling with moth maggots. Using her dagger, she cut a swath of fabric where the larvae squirmed most thickly. She brought it to her dressing table, which was stacked with bottles of perfumes and oils and jars of cream. She took a pot of bath salts and dumped its entire contents out a window, then dropped the cloth and its larvae into the pot and stoppered it, but loosely, so that air would flow. To be sure, she hatched a cross into the cork's center with her dagger's point. Kestrel set the pot at the back of her dressing table and arranged the bottles to hide it.

She sat back in her dressing chair, thinking about the creatures feeding on the cloth in the pot. They were fat already. They'd become moths soon.

And when they did, she had a plan for them.

Kestrel went to her study, and wrote a letter to the Herrani minister of agriculture.

KESTREL SET HER CUP ON ITS SAUCER. "I DIDN'T ask to see *you*," she said.

"Too bad." Arin claimed the chair across from her table in the library in a manner unbearably familiar to her. It was as if the chair had always been his.

He slouched in his seat, tipped his head back, and looked at her from beneath lowered lids. The morning light fired his profile. "Worried, Lady Kestrel?" He spoke in Valorian, his accent roughening his voice. He always pronounced his *r*'s too low in his throat, so that when he spoke in her tongue everything came across as a soft growl. "Dreading what I'll say . . . or do?" He smiled a grim little smile. "No need. I'll be the perfect gentleman." He tugged at his cuffs. It was only then that Kestrel noticed that they came too short on his arms and showed his wrists.

It pained her to see his self-consciousness, the way it had suddenly revealed itself. In this light, his gray eyes were too clear. His posture had been confident. His words had had an edge. But his eyes were uncertain. Arin fidgeted again with his cuffs as if there was something wrong with them—with him. *No,* she would have said. *You're perfect,* she wanted to say. She imagined it: how she would reach out to touch Arin's bare wrist.

That could lead nowhere good.

She was nervous, she was cold. Her stomach was a flurry of snow.

She dropped her hands to her lap.

"No one's here anyway," Arin said, "and the librarians are in the stacks. You're safe enough."

It *was* too early for courtiers to be in the library. Kestrel had counted on this, and on the fact that if anyone did turn up and saw her with the Herrani minister of agriculture, such a meeting would excite little interest.

One with Arin, however, was an entirely different story. It was frustrating: his uncanny ability to unsettle her plans—and her very sense of self. She said, "Pressing where you're not invited seems to be a habit with you."

"And yours is to put people in their place. But people aren't gaming pieces. You can't arrange them to suit yourself."

A librarian coughed.

"Lower your voice," Kestrel hissed at Arin. "Stop being so—"

"Inconvenient?"

"Frankly, yes."

His smile came: quick, true, surprised by itself. Then changing, and slow. "I could be worse."

"I am sure."

"I could tell you how."

"Arin, how is it for you here, in the capital?"

He held her gaze. "I would rather talk about what we were talking about."

She arranged her fingers along the studs that pinned green leather to the tabletop. She felt each cool, small, hard nail. The silence inside her was like those nails. What it held down was something sheer: a feeling like fragile silk, billowing up at the sound of his voice.

If she and Arin were to talk about what they had been talking about, that silk could tear free. It would float up. It would catch the light, and cast a colored shadow.

What color would it be, Kestrel wondered, the silk of what she felt?

What would it be like to let it go, let it canopy above her?

"It wasn't a false question," she said quietly. "I think the capital must be strange for you."

Arin studied her, thoughtful now. "Is it that way for you?"

"It shouldn't be."

"You were raised in Herran. This isn't your home."

"It's my country."

Arin's face closed along lines she knew well. He shrugged, the movement small and short. He helped himself to tea.

Hesitant, Kestrel asked, "Are they good to you here?"

A rising ribbon of steam curled around his face. He drank from the cup and lowered it, the gesture as fluid as that of any courtier. But his hand was a laborer's hand, and the porcelain cup, painted with flowers and dipped in gold, looked out of place. Arin frowned at the cup. "Sometimes I think it was easier to be ignored. Here, no one ignores me. Even if they ignore me they *don't*, not really. The way they *don't* look feels like they're staring. When I was a slave in Herran, no one ever looked at me. No one looks at a slave." Arin set the cup on its saucer with an abrupt *click*. "Kestrel, when did I do it? I keep asking myself when I did the thing that was beyond your understanding. Was there one thing that made too many for you to forgive me? The lies—"

"I would have lied, too."

"The Herrani rebellion. I plotted for months. I plotted against *you*."

"I understand why."

"Your friends, then. Your people. The poison. Benix's death. Jess's sickness. It was my fault. You blame me."

Kestrel shook her head—not to deny his words, but because it wasn't as simple as he'd said. "Sometimes I imagine that I'm you. I imagine your life. What we did to it. And I know what *you* did back. So yes, I blame you . . . and I don't. If I'd been you, I would have done the same. I might have done worse."

"Then what *can't* you understand?" His voice grew hoarse. "Was it . . . the kiss? In my kitchen. Was *that* the unforgivable thing?"

"Arin."

"I shouldn't have."

"Arin."

"I'm sorry, Kestrel. I'm sorry. Tell me what I can say."

It wasn't the misery that gave her pause. It was his voice.

It was what lay beneath his voice: that underground river of song that was always there, that he tried to dam and block and bury. It had been his secret. When she had bought him, she'd felt the strain of this secret even then. Arin was a singer. Yet he had disowned it, he hid it. His secret had seemed so vital, so fiercely kept, that Kestrel had never forced its fact to the surface, and hadn't thought to question whether Arin hid anything else.

He was waiting for her to speak. A library clock chimed. The sound woke her from her memory. A new thought made her skin prickle with fear.

Even if Arin didn't know her secrets, he sensed them. It was as if he could hear them rustling in her dark heart. Kestrel had decided she would never tell him. Yet a mere moment ago she'd spoken too openly, like someone who hoped he would guess exactly what her secrets were.

She met his anxious eyes. She thought of the nails in the table and the force it had taken to drive them in. She thought about temptation, and the smart thing, and how in the seventeen years before she'd met Arin, she'd always known which to choose. "I forgive you." Kestrel made her tone offhandedly kind, even bored. "There, do you feel better? My choice to marry the prince isn't about blaming you. It's not about you at all. I simply want something else."

He stared.

"Really, Arin. I have the chance to rule half the known world one day. That isn't too difficult to understand."

He turned to look out the window. The light was stronger now. It bleached his face.

"Since we are being so honest," she said, "I'd like for you to tell me why you're here instead of Tensen. Did he send you?"

"He never read your note," Arin said to the window. "I saw your seal. I opened the letter."

"I suppose I should scold you for it." She lifted one shoulder in an elegant shrug. "Though I might as well tell you as him."

Arin looked at her then. "Tell me what?"

"That I am no longer the imperial ambassador to Herran."

"But you agreed. It was part of the treaty the emperor signed. That I signed. It's *law*."

"The law is written by the sword. The emperor holds the sword, not you, and if he says that I am not to be burdened by a tiresome post, who are we to disagree? Come, let's not quarrel. The tea is nice, isn't it? A little too steeped, though. I might not finish my cup."

Arin's expression was turning dangerous. "So we're to talk about *tea*?"

"Would you prefer chocolate?"

"And when I see you next, shall I compliment your dazzling shoes and doeskin gloves? Because what else will you have to discuss? Doesn't the life of an empress-to-be bore you?" Arin had switched to speaking in his own language, but she'd never heard him sound like this before. His voice was mincing and sharp. It was a mockery of the way courtiers talked. "Maybe we can discuss the latest crimes of your beloved empire over tea. I can admire the cunning little shapes of hardened sugar and pass you a tiny sweet swan on a spoon. You can set it to swim in your cup while you pretend that the massacres in the east aren't happening. And maybe I will note how the people of the southern isles are still slaves, and the tribes of the northern tundra were wiped out long ago. You will say that the southern slaves have it better under the empire than when they were free. Look at all that clean water piped down from the mountains through the imperial aqueducts, you'll say. Isn't that lovely? As for the northern tribes, there were never very many of them anyway."

His voice tightened. The mockery was gone. "And I might tell you that Herran is thinned to the point of starvation. We are poor, Kestrel. We eat through a meager supply of grain and wait for the hearthnut harvest, and for news of how much your emperor will seize of it. What if I ask if you know how much? You'll probably say that you remember how your Herrani nurse used to bake hearthnut bread for you. Maybe you've even been to the southern tip of Herran's peninsula where the hearthnut trees grow, and remember how the sun there is hot year-round. You'll say all this in a cozy tone as if we share something, when what we share is what your people steal from mine.

"I will say *tell me*. Tell me how much we'll have to live by after the emperor's tithe. You'll say you don't know. You have no intention of knowing."

Kestrel had risen from her seat.

"Then I will be silent," Arin said, "and you will stir your tea. You will drink and I will drink. There. Is that how it will be?"

Kestrel was light-headed. "Go away," she whispered,

though she was the one standing. Arin didn't move from the table. He stared up at her, jawline tight, and she didn't understand how it could still be there in his face: that hard expectation, that angry faith. *Don't fail me,* his eyes said. *Don't fail yourself.*

She quit the table.

"You're better than this," he called after her. A librarian stepped from the stacks to shush him. Kestrel walked away.

He said, "How can the inconsequence of your life not shame you?"

He said, "How do you not feel empty?"

I do, she thought as she pushed through the library doors and let them thud behind her. *I do.*

Kestrel was shaking when she sat down in front of her dressing table. Curse Tensen. Curse him for not collecting his own letters, or for sleeping in late while Arin had rifled through them. She'd been discreet in what she had written—this was the imperial court, and the only secrets put down on paper were *meant* to become gossip—but what if she hadn't been?

She'd better reconsider her plan. Tensen couldn't be trusted to keep Arin in check. She was a fool even to consider becoming the minister of agriculture's new spy. What kind of spymaster allows his letters to be read?

Then again, what kind of would-be spy stamps a letter with her own seal? What a stupid mistake.

Kestrel looked at the bottles on her dressing table and imagined how it would sound if she sent the whole lot of them crashing to the stone floor. A great, glorious smash. But a moment passed, then another, and she calmed, reaching carefully for a pot set back behind the others.

Kestrel seemed to see the pot in her hand as if it were far away.

You're better than this, Arin had said.

Her fingers tightened around the pot. She brought it close. She smiled a hard smile, one as thin as the glass beneath her nails.

The masker moth larvae had cocooned. There were bulging, pellet-like cases all over the silk.

Kestrel returned the pot to its place. She would wait for the moths to hatch. It wouldn't take long. Then she would make her move.

She pled a minor illness: a cold caught from sitting too long in the Winter Garden after the ball. Verex didn't visit, but sent a kind note along with a vial of medicine.

The emperor sent no word.

Kestrel wrote to Jess: a teasing letter filled with merry turns of phrase that chided Jess for abandoning her in her hour of need. There were too many parties, too many boring people. Jess had left her defenseless.

I need my friend, Kestrel wrote. Then she saw the anxiety in her spiky cursive. Kestrel felt the nibbling fear that she *had* been abandoned, that she had unknowingly offended Jess.

I saw him, Jess had said. She had seen Arin at the ball. But then she'd clung to Kestrel's hand in the dark. Jess wouldn't have done that, surely, had she guessed what Arin and Kestrel had been doing while the dancers danced?

Maybe the sight of Arin had frightened Jess. Kestrel couldn't blame her. Jess had witnessed things Kestrel hadn't the night of the Firstwinter Rebellion. And Jess knew they were Arin's doing.

Kestrel blacked out her last line of writing.

I miss you, little sister, she wrote instead.

Jess's reply was slow in coming. It was short. Jess was tired, the letter explained, her health worse than thought. *By the time you receive this, we will have left for the south again,* Jess wrote. The entire family would go. Jess was sorry.

It was an explanation of sorts. But Kestrel found herself rereading the letter in her empty receiving room, searching for signs of love as if it could be captured in a double-dotted *i*, or in the decorative slash through the last word of Jess's last sentence. The paper in Kestrel's hand felt thin.

Uneasy, Kestrel crumbled the letter's wax seal between her fingers. She tried not to think about how she hadn't even been able to see Jess one more time. She tried not to think about how the empty room felt suddenly emptier.

Kestrel kept to parts of her suite that were unquestionably private: her bedchamber and dressing room. And one day, even though she couldn't have possibly heard the flutter of such small wings, Kestrel lifted her head, came quickly to the dressing table, and cleared a path through the bottles to see masker moths hatching in their pot. Some were struggling out of cocoons. Others clung to the glass, their wings clear, or they clustered upside down on the bottom of the cork and turned a stippled light brown.

Kestrel lit a candle. When the moths had all hatched and the candle had burned down, Kestrel poured molten wax over the stopper of the moths' pot. She sealed it thoroughly, so that no air would leak into the pot.

It took a day for the moths to die. Afterward, Kestrel announced to her maids that she felt much better.

THERE WAS A RECEPTION IN THE PALACE
gallery. Everyone was invited to admire the emperor's collection of stolen art. Kestrel's father had once told her that
the military had a standing order to spare art during the
sack of a city. "He didn't like that I razed the Herrani palace when we invaded." The general had shrugged. "But it
had been the right military move."

Her father had never feared the emperor, so Kestrel told
herself that neither should she. This was why, in full view
of a crush of guests milling about the statues and paintings, Kestrel made her way toward Tensen.

A few amused eyebrows were raised—*Can't seem to
keep away from the Herrani, can she?* Kestrel practically
heard—but the emperor's back was to her for now, and she
would need only a few moments. She slipped a hand into
her dress pocket.

Tensen stood before a landscape stolen from the southern isles. Arin wasn't with him. He was late. Perhaps he
wouldn't come at all, given their last conversation.

The painting of Tensen's choice showed bleachfields, where fabric had been stretched out to whiten in the sun, and crops of indigo flowers grown for dye. "Lady Kestrel," Tensen began, pleased, but she cut him off.

"I see you appreciate a fine landscape," she said. "Did you know that these flowers are painted with actual indigo? They represent the thing and *are* the thing at the same time." Kestrel began to talk, long and loud, about art. She watched as nearby courtiers, once interested in eavesdropping on this conversation, grew bored and turned away. Kestrel let her voice gradually lower as Tensen waited, green eyes curious—and bright with cautious hope. Even if he'd never seen the note Arin had stolen, it couldn't be hard for him to guess that Kestrel wanted to discuss more than art.

She removed her hand from her pocket. "Such exquisite detail," she said, pointing. "Look, you can practically see each petal." With a brush of her fingers, she set a dead masker moth at the bottom edge of the painting where it met the frame. The moth clung. It deepened to purple. It became part of the painting.

Tensen looked at the moth, then looked at her.

Quietly, she said, "I will find out whatever it was that Thrynne overheard. And when I do, I will leave another moth here for you. Come to the gallery every morning. Develop a fondness for this painting. Look for the moth. That's how you will know to meet me."

"Where?"

"Outside the palace." But her knowledge of the city was meager, and she wasn't sure how to be more specific.

"There's a tavern in town that serves Herrani—"

"Then they serve the captain of the guard's spies, too. The emperor must know what you are, Tensen. He does nothing to get in your way at the moment because he's waiting to see what you know and what you'll do with it." Kestrel glanced again at the emperor. Prince Verex had approached him and was saying something heated, his face flushed. The emperor's profile showed sardonic boredom.

"Then where?" asked Tensen.

Kestrel watched the emperor take a glass of wine from a servant who then faded into the background as if she, too, were a masker moth. *No one looks at a slave,* Arin had said. This gave Kestrel an idea. "How is fresh food brought into the palace?"

"The kitchen staff buys it in the city market, from the grocers' stalls and the Butcher's Row."

"Yes. There. We'll meet in the Row. If you dress as a servant, no one will give you a second glance."

"The prince's bride is bound to draw more than a few stares."

"Let me worry about myself." She was anxious to sort out the trickier detail of meeting: *when.* "Look." She pointed to the bottom edge of the painting's frame and explained how he was to imagine the line was the rim of a clock's face straightened, and that time moved along the frame from dawn to dusk. Where the moth rested would indicate the hour of their meeting the following day.

"What if someone else notices the moth?" Tensen asked.

"It's just a moth. A common pest. It doesn't mean anything."

"A servant might find it before I do and sweep it away."

"Then that's what I'll assume has happened, if I don't see you in the Row at the appointed hour. Really, Tensen. Do you want my help or not?" She understood his doubt, yet it rankled, and bothered her all the more because she had the uneasy feeling of playing a doomed game. The winner knows her whole line of play. But Kestrel saw only one move, and maybe the next.

Verex was getting louder. Kestrel couldn't hear what he was saying to the emperor, but heads were starting to turn even before Verex stormed from the gallery.

"Rumor has it that the prince doesn't approve of what's happening in the east," Tensen murmured.

Kestrel didn't want to think about the east.

"Slaves say that the eastern princess is like a sister to Verex," Tensen added. "They were raised together—at first—after her kidnapping."

Kestrel's eyes automatically sought Risha then, and when she saw her, standing at the other end of the long hall, Kestrel's blood seemed to pale. She felt her pulse quiet. Kestrel imagined the blood it pushed through her body growing pink, then clear. Thin, trickling water.

It wasn't Risha that made Kestrel go cold, or the tiny eastern painting the princess gazed at as if it were hung on the moon. Kestrel told herself it wasn't the clear loss on Risha's face.

But there was nothing else in this gallery that could strike Kestrel with such guilt.

"There's been a Valorian victory in the eastern plains," Tensen said. "Have you heard? No? Well, you've been ill.

Your father poisoned the tribes' horses and seized the plains. It was swift."

She tried not to hear him. She looked at the princess standing alone.

Kestrel would go to her. She would leave Tensen and the indigo moth and cut a path through the courtiers, passing between the soapstone sculptures plundered from the northern tundra, because if Kestrel didn't go to Risha now, she was sure that she would become just like the statues: smooth, cold, hard.

Before she could move, someone else appeared at the princess's side.

It was Arin. He spoke softly to Risha. Kestrel had no real way of telling that his voice was soft, not from so far away, not with the din of courtiers talking. But Kestrel knew. She *knew*, she could see compassion in his eyes, in the tender curve of his mouth. Arin would say nothing but soft words to this young woman. He leaned toward her. Risha answered him, and he touched three fingers to the back of her hand.

And why wouldn't Arin grieve with Risha? He had lost his family. He had lost everything to the Valorians. Of course that drew him to her loss. Their shared sorrow created a shelter around them that Kestrel could never enter.

What would she have said to Risha anyway?

It was my fault.

Or: *It could have been worse.*

That was as stupid as telling Arin the truth. Kestrel

would have to swallow her words, and be silent, and swallow again until her belly was heavy with everything she couldn't say.

She wondered if Arin would lift his gaze and see her watching them. But his eyes remained on Risha.

It seemed to Kestrel that her life had taken the shape of a folded knife, her heart a blade inside a body of wood.

"You'd better go," Tensen said suddenly. She had forgotten that he stood next to her, that they were surrounded by the court, and that she had meant her conversation with Tensen to be as brief as possible. She had meant to avoid the notice of the emperor.

Who was staring across the gallery at them.

His fury boiled. The courtiers nearest to him sensed it. They edged away.

"Wait," she told Tensen, though the emperor was bearing through the crowd toward them.

"I don't think so."

"*Wait.* Why did my father poison the eastern horses?"

"Why do you Valorians do anything? To win, obviously. Now, if you'll excuse me—"

"Was it his idea? The emperor's? Or—what do people say?" How widely known was her role in seizing the plains?

"The court doesn't care how or why General Trajan did it. They rejoice in the result."

"Thank you," Kestrel said, but Tensen had already gone.

The emperor closed in on her. She tried not to reach for

her new diamond dagger, or wish for the one her father had given her and the emperor had taken. The crowd gave them a wide berth.

"I told you to stay away from the Herrani," the emperor hissed.

"No, you didn't." Her voice was a miracle. Calm. Steady. It couldn't possibly be her own. "I don't remember those exact words."

"I was perfectly clear." The emperor's hand came down on her arm. To the rest of the court, the gesture might have looked affectionate. They didn't see how he worked his thumb into her inner elbow and pinched the flesh there.

At first, the pain was small. Mean-spirited, almost childish. It didn't seem serious, which gave Kestrel the courage to lie. "That's what I told Minister Tensen. That I'm no longer the imperial ambassador to Herran. Isn't that what you wanted? I thought it only polite to tell the minister in person."

"I'm surprised you didn't tell the governor."

"I don't want to talk to the governor."

"No? You haven't spoken with Arin?" The emperor's nails were sharp.

Kestrel almost saw her error, but another part of her insisted that there could be no error, not with him. Her mind filled with lead. It said *deny*. And although the knowledge of what she had done wrong suddenly fizzed through her, fear corroded her thoughts, and lied to her, and told her to lie hard enough to make the lie true. "No," she told the emperor. "Of course not."

"That," whispered the emperor, "isn't what my librarians say."

He pinched harder. The pain deepened. It drove into her fear. It pinned her feet to the floor.

"You disobeyed me, Kestrel. You disobeyed me twice."

"I'm sorry," she said. "I'm sorry."

The emperor released her, his thumbnail bloody. "No, you're not," he said. "But you will be."

YET THE EMPEROR DID NOTHING.

Kestrel's dread grew. There was a half-moon scab and a stormy bruise on her inside elbow. That couldn't be her only punishment.

Kestrel's letters to Jess, filled with false cheer, went unanswered. It occurred to Kestrel that the emperor had intercepted the letters. But this, though it hurt, wouldn't be enough for the emperor's revenge. Something worse must come.

She'd seen the way he was with others. A soldier had recently been found guilty of desertion, and his high-society parents had pled for leniency. Desertion was a form of treason. The punishment for treason was death. Courtiers gossiped that maybe, just this once, the soldier would "go north"—meaning, to the tundra's work camp. But the parents clearly hoped for even better than that. Their gold made its way to certain pockets. They regularly petitioned the emperor to release their son. The emperor had smiled and said he would see. It amused him to wait, and watch people twist on the knife of his waiting.

Kestrel felt the shame of her mistake. The instinctive guilt of being caught. And worse: a slippery, eel-like uncertainty in herself. What did she think she was doing, with her moths and treasonous promises to Tensen?

She thought about what her father would say if he knew.

She thought about the prison and Thrynne's skinned fingers.

But maybe the emperor planned a punishment fit for a child, like barring Kestrel from the piano.

Maybe he would humiliate her at court.

Maybe the stolen letters *were* enough.

Kestrel's bruise faded. The scab flaked away.

Uneasy, Kestrel finally decided that the emperor wouldn't risk doing anything extreme to General Trajan's daughter.

She dined with the emperor every day. He was slyly kind, even solicitous. He acted as if nothing had happened.

Kestrel stopped tensing herself for a blow that didn't come.

Maybe it never would.

To Arin, the imperial palace was a big box of architectural tricks. It didn't matter, though, how many dead-end hallways there were. He didn't care about the dizzying array of chambers for leisure. He ignored the way that tight, winding staircases could split into several directions.

In the end, the palace was really just a building, and in every building servants were housed in the same place: the worst.

So when Arin went looking for Kestrel's dressmaker, she wasn't hard to find. He took staircases down. He went into the dark. He followed musty air. Insufferable heat. The kitchen's fires. Sweat and fried onion smells.

The Herrani servants were helpful. Too helpful. Their eyes were shining. They would have shared anything with him. Their faces fell to be asked so little as the whereabouts of a dressmaker. Even the slaves from various conquered territories, whose languages Arin didn't speak, and who worked in tense and arcane hierarchies with the newly freed Herrani, watched Arin with expressions approaching awe.

Arin's failure felt hot within him. It was a kind of poison, steeping steadily. The Herrani servants asked to be told the story of how Arin had brought a mountain down on Valorian troops. How had he saved Minister Tensen during that assault on a country estate? Was it from a crossbow quarrel, or a thrown dagger?

The stories were worthless. Everything Arin had done, from the Firstwinter Rebellion to his last stand against the Valorian general, had changed nothing. His people still belonged to the empire.

"Deliah," Arin reminded the Herrani gathered in the largest kitchen. "Where is she?"

Her workshop was in a nicer section of the palace, on the ground floor in a room with enough light to make the bolts of fabric glow. When Arin entered, Deliah was sewing, her lap heaped with rich, wine-dark cloth. Her mouth was full of straight pins. She removed them slowly, one by one, when Arin asked his question.

"I want to know who's been bribing you," he said.

"That's not what I thought you'd ask."

"I've been to the city." Arin hated being in the palace. He felt better in the city, though he didn't like that either, and never shook the feeling of being in enemy territory. He prowled it, and kept to the alleys. "There's a tavern—"

"I know the one you mean. It's the only place that serves Herrani."

"They serve everyone—especially bet-makers and book-keepers. If *I* were to bet on something, it'd be on the fact that you must have every courtier in the palace hounding you for a tip on what your lady will wear to her wedding. The payout could be huge."

Deliah had been stabbing pins into the small cushion strapped to her wrist. Now she stopped and ran a finger over the stiff silver grass of clustered pins. "I don't tell anyone anything about the wedding dress. I don't take bribes. Not even from you."

"I'm not saying that you do. That's not what I want. Just tell me who's been asking."

"If you want a list, it'll be long."

"So tell me who *isn't* asking."

She was still wary. "Why?"

"Because that's the person who already knows."

Deliah touched the pins again. "The Senate leader," she said. "Most of the courtiers ask in person, even the important ones. They don't want to risk that somebody else might learn what they think I'll tell. But I've never seen the Senate leader. Even his daughter, Maris, wants to find out. Her bribe was the promise that I could work for her." Deliah gave a short laugh. "I dress the imperial family. The emperor would never let me go." Her eyes challenged Arin, daring him to promise that something would change, that he could make it change for her.

His hot feeling of shame cooled into a black lump: a hard, burnt thing.

He moved to leave.

"Something happened to her," Deliah said suddenly.

He stopped. "What do you mean?"

"Before you came—weeks before you came—Lady Kestrel's maids brought me a dress. It was white and gold. And filthy. The hem had been dragged through something, I'm not sure what. It was on the seat of the dress, too. The knees. There was vomit on one sleeve. Some seams had split."

Arin's mouth went dry.

"The maids wanted to know if I could salvage it," Deliah said. "Impossible. It was ruined. I tore that dress into rags."

Arin made himself speak. "When?"

"I told you when."

"Was Kestrel with someone the day she wore that dress?"

Deliah spread her hands helplessly. "I have no idea *exactly* when she wore it, or the company she might have kept. You'd have to ask her ladies-in-waiting, and I don't recommend that. At least one of them is in the pocket of the prince, and only the gods know how many report to the emperor."

"You must know something more."

"I've told you everything."

"You see her. When you fit her to a dress . . . you see her skin. Was there . . . damage?" He had a gut-wrenching memory of Kestrel's face after Cheat had attacked her. "Bruises. Scars. Anything. Anything around that time. Anything since."

"No," said Deliah, which was a deep relief to him until she added, "not that I could see. I haven't fitted her in the past week, though."

"Watch her."

"I can't do that. I can't keep reporting to you. The emperor . . ."

"*I* am Herran's governor."

She gave him a pitying look. "We both know how much that's worth."

He covered his eyes. He shook his head. "At least let me know if there's been anything else . . . strange."

She shrugged. "The usual. Orders for a new day dress. Minor repairs. Complaints about pests getting into the wardrobes and eating the fabric. That sort of thing." Deliah still had that look on her face, and Arin wanted to defend himself, to say that the only reason she should report on Kestrel's doings was that the general's daughter was obviously up to something, that the ruined dress was evidence of what he couldn't see and *must* see, because Kestrel had a knack for working her fingers through schemes, and sometimes she pulled the strings, and sometimes she tugged at the edges until she uncovered something she shouldn't.

Arin wanted to insist that if a secret concerned Kestrel, it concerned the emperor, and that concerned Herran. This was why he asked for Deliah's help. It was for his country. Only for that.

It was not out of worry for Kestrel.

Not out of love.

Not because the description of that dress made Arin try to imagine every possible thing that had been done to Kestrel while she wore it, or everything she might have tried to do.

In the end, none of this was easy for him to say. He was silent as he made to leave Deliah's workshop.

"She cares for you," Deliah said suddenly. "I know that she does."

It was so blatantly untrue that it almost seemed like a cruel joke.

Arin laughed.

Arin's mind had gone dark, which was perhaps why he didn't notice that the hallway had, too. All the lamps but one had burned down. The last sputtered in its oil.

He hadn't been paying attention to where he was going. He'd intended to return to his rooms, but this hall was nowhere near that wing. He found himself in a disused part of the palace hung with frayed tapestries that—as far as he could tell in the dim light—glorified Valorian conquests from a century before, when Herran was at its height and Valoria was a speck of a country with unwashed warriors who liked the sight of blood so much they'd cut their own flesh to get it.

The tapestries were crude. It might have amused him, if he were in the mood to be amused, how bad Valorians were at beauty. They stole it. They forced it. They had never been able to bring beauty to life.

Yet this made him think of Kestrel's hands springing from piano keys, and coming down again, and running wild, and this made him think of the ruined dress, and this made him stride farther into the shadowed hall as if he could escape his own thoughts, and that brought him smack against a blank wall.

He swore. He looked up at the scrolled woodwork of the ceiling and tried to be very careful not to insult the god of the lost. Instead, he focused on the woodwork carvings of his dead end, and noticed an odd, rigid line cutting through the swirling pattern. Narrowing his eyes in the light of the dying lamp, he caught a gleam in the ceiling. Metal. There was a metal strip running horizontally across the ceiling—no, not *across*, not exactly. It was set *into* the ceiling.

Arin was so distracted by wondering what that thing was that he didn't see a shadow slip toward him and then behind.

He heard a metallic cranking sound. That line burst into full being—an iron gate hurtling down from its slit in the ceiling.

It hit the stone floor. It trapped Arin into the dead end.

And even though he was already turning, adrenaline punching through his veins and singing high in his brain, he didn't quite see the shadow behind him become a man. He didn't see a face.

There was a rush of air. Arin was shoved back against the grate, and then he didn't see anything at all.

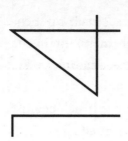

ARIN LAY ON STONE. HIS NECK CROOKED
painfully against something hard and cold. It took several blurry seconds before he thought *gate*, and then *ambush*.

He didn't move. He didn't open his eyes. He couldn't
have been knocked out for long, because hands were patting him down for weapons. Arin wore no dagger at his
hip. That was too Valorian. But his knife was pulled from
one boot. His attacker came down on him, kneeling on his
chest. Heavy. The air squeezed out of him.

Arin's head throbbed. It took everything he had not to
be sick.

The weight on his chest shifted. "Let's make you
pretty," the man said, and set the tip of a blade against
Arin's lips.

Arin's fist cocked up and slammed into bone. He
shoved the man off him. He was awake now, he was on his
feet. He wouldn't go down again.

His attacker shook away the stun of Arin's blow, his

hair catching the lamplight. The man was blond. Valorian. Dressed in military black.

And well armed. A knife in each hand, a short sword at his waist. One of those knives was Arin's.

He'd have to get it back.

Arin was still trapped between the man and the gate. A bad position. The man swung the hand that held Arin's blade, and Arin ducked. The knife raked the gate behind him, shot sparks. Hitting metal instead of flesh seemed to throw Arin's opponent off balance, and Arin drove into the opening made when the man's swing had gone wide and wrong. Arin thrust a knee up, sank it into the man's gut, seized a wrist, and wrested back his knife.

But not before the man sliced through the air with his own.

That dagger was beautiful. Arin saw its flash. It arrested him somehow, it started him thinking when he had absolutely no business thinking. Arin didn't flinch away fast enough. The blade cut into his face.

Pain seared from forehead to cheek. Red flooded Arin's left eye. He was blinking, he was half-blind, he was desperate to know if someone can still blink if an eye has been gouged out. He wept blood. His face had split. He could feel air inside the parted flesh, and his hand instinctively went to it.

That saved him. Without meaning to, Arin had blocked a second blow, which caught him in the forearm. It tipped him sideways, and in his shock Arin didn't fight the momentum, which knocked him against the long wall of the hallway.

He had dropped his knife. But his hand was scrabbling the wall even as his mind screamed at it not to be stupid, there was no weapon there.

Arin's hand wrapped around a dead lamp set into the wall and ripped it free. He smashed it against the man's head. He heard a cry. He ground the shards in.

And now the fight was his. Now Arin was remembering every nasty trick he'd ever learned with his fists, elbows, and feet, and he was forgetting that he'd never really been trained to hold a weapon, except as a boy, and that boy's arm had trembled under the weight of a child-size sword, and little Arin had begged not to be made to do it, and so what did his grown self know about the sword, which he yanked from the attacker's scabbard? What did Arin know about the Valorian dagger that appeared in his hand as if a god had set it there? What could he do even as both of his blades were hurtling through the darkness, and the Valorian cried, "Please," and Arin stabbed into him as if this was an art, this was *his* art?

With all the grace in the world, Arin's body said *mine*, and cut the man's soul right out of him.

Where was Arin's breath?

He gasped. With one good eye, Arin looked down at the bloody mess of the Valorian at his feet. He dropped the sword. He tried to wipe away the red-black blindness from the left side of his face. Blood streamed. No matter how Arin pawed at the flowing wet curtain, he couldn't see through it.

He gave up.

He was still holding the Valorian dagger. He was holding it strangely, as if it belonged to him, which was impossible. Yet his fingers clutched it and refused to let go.

His breath still shuddering through him, the pain still hot, Arin lifted the dagger into the weak light.

He knew this blade.

How could he know it?

The dagger was light, well balanced. It hadn't been made for a strong hand. Arin had been a blacksmith; he knew quality when he felt it. The tang was simple yet strong. The hilt had been chased in gold, but not overly so—nothing gave the dagger too much weight or interfered with its clean efficiency.

And it was loved. Someone had taken very good care of the blade that had carved Arin's face open.

None of this explained why Arin's hand held the weapon so tightly. He frowned, then rubbed at the blood on the hilt. There was something red beneath the red. A ruby.

It was a seal.

The dagger's seal showed the hooked talons of a kestrel.

ONCE TENSEN HAD RECOVERED FROM THE sight of Arin dripping blood on the carpet of their suite, the old man was remarkably matter-of-fact. "Let me see," he said, and gently pushed Arin down into a chair.

Arin kept the sodden cloth to his face. In that dark hallway, he had ripped the sleeve from his inner shirt and pressed it against the pulsing cut. He hadn't lifted it away since. He was afraid to know what lay beneath. Everything hurt too much to tell exactly how badly he'd been injured.

"Arin." Tensen tried to peel Arin's fingers away from his face. Arin sighed, and let him. He thought about things like depth perception, and how it would be to fight if he had one eye. He thought about a monster's face.

The cut bled freely. Blood ran into Arin's mouth and down his neck as Tensen inspected him.

"Open," Tensen said.

Arin's lashes were sticky with blood. "Open," Tensen said again, and when Arin still didn't, the minister fetched a pitcher of water from the bathing room and poured it onto Arin's face.

Arin hissed. He choked on the water. He pressed back into the chair, soaked, and trembled like an animal as Tensen's fingers went to the corner of his eye and pried the lids apart.

Arin caught a glimpse of light, then the blood ran in again.

"It missed the eye," Tensen said. "You're cut from the middle of your forehead down through the brow and into the cheek. Your eyelid's even scratched, just a bit. But the bone of your brow caught the worst of it."

Relief flowed through Arin.

Tensen produced a clean handkerchief and padded it onto the left side of Arin's face. "You need stitches. And"—he looked more carefully at Arin's right hand, curled against his thigh—"tweezers."

The shards from the lamp. They had embedded deep into his palm when he'd hauled up the iron gate to escape his trap.

Tensen said, "The god of luck must love you."

"Don't talk like that."

"Give the gods their due, Arin, or they might not look kindly on you during the next assassination attempt."

"I'm not sure he meant to kill me. At least not right away." *Let's make you pretty,* the man had said. Arin had the sense that his face had been a piece of paper meant to be scrawled with a message. Arin told Tensen as much, including that the dead man had worn the insignia of the palace guard. But Arin said nothing of the dagger and its seal.

He had slipped it inside his boot, where it fit badly to the sheath for his own knife. He felt the Valorian blade rattle whenever he shifted his feet. The pommel peeked out over the top of Arin's boot, but he had tugged the legs of his trousers down to hide it.

Tensen went to work on him. The cut to Arin's forearm had been a glancing blow muffled by the wool of his jacket. Tensen cleaned the wound, bound it tightly, and left it alone. Then he began to rub soap into a froth in his hands until they held a quivering white cloud, bubbles popping lightly. It was lovely, this cloud. It smelled of summer flowers; it was an airy poem. It looked very innocent. But Arin knew what Tensen meant to do with it.

"This," Tensen said, "will feel very pleasant." He patted the foam into the slash on Arin's face.

Murderous. The soap ate into the wound. It licked a burning tongue into Arin's flesh. He couldn't breathe. If he breathed, he would scream.

Tensen rinsed it all away. Then more soap. More water. By the time he finished, Arin was limp in his chair and desperately grateful when Tensen pressed a new cloth to the cut. The fire in his face throbbed down. Arin kept his eyes closed and slipped back into the old, familiar, seeping pain as easily as into a warm bath. How much better that old pain seemed now. How comforting, how like a friend. Arin was half in love with it.

But Tensen was moving around in the suite, and Arin knew what would happen next. He opened his good eye to see Tensen sterilizing a needle in the flame of an oil lamp.

"No," Arin croaked. "Get Deliah."

"You're not a dress."

"Do it," he said, though he'd seen Tensen patch wounds together on a battlefield. It was why he had agreed to take an elderly man on every military mission in Herran—that, and the fervency in Tensen's green eyes, the truth in his voice when he had sworn to do anything for his country. Tensen had an actor's knack for becoming whatever he wanted to be. If it was a doctor, he would be one. He used to joke that it was because he had once played the role of a doctor in a theatrical production. Arin didn't much care where Tensen's skills came from. He appreciated them. But he wouldn't let Tensen sew his face.

"I'm not sure it's wise for Deliah to know," said Tensen.

"Do you think *this* can be kept a secret?"

Tensen gave a slight smile to show that a point had been made. Arin would never look the same again.

The minister left.

When he returned with Deliah, the cloth on Arin's face was seeping blood and he felt almost sleepy. Deliah gave him a grim look edged with weariness, as if Arin were a child who had gotten himself hurt doing exactly what she'd told him not to do. The expression made her look a little like his mother. That's what Arin imagined as she threaded the needle and put her cool hands on his hot face. It wasn't hard to see his mother when he squinted through one eye that watered. The needle went in. It pushed out. There was the grating tug of the thread. A tightening pain. Tensen blotted away blood so that Deliah could see better, and it began again. A bolt of lightning stitched down his cheek.

Maybe it was because half of his face no longer felt like his face. Maybe it was because he wanted so very much to forget what Deliah was doing, or needed to believe that things could be worse. Arin thought of the beating he'd received the day before Kestrel had bought him. He had been shoveling gravel with other slaves put to laying a new Valorian road. He'd been keeping his head down. He was being good . . . until there came a scuffling sound.

Arin had looked up. Two Valorians were dragging an easterner toward the other slaves. A murmur went through the Herrani working on the road. From what Arin heard, the eastern slave had managed to escape several days before. He had just been caught.

The Valorian law on runaway slaves was clear.

Arin had lunged forward. He shouted at the Valorians. He cursed them.

His masters that day didn't understand Arin's language well, or his punishment would have been worse. The overseer punched Arin in the face. The Valorians ordered the Herrani to hold Arin down. They did. They shoved him into the gravel. The overseer hit again, and even from where Arin lay he could see the other masters preparing the eastern runaway. They dragged the slave's head back by the hair.

The easterner caught Arin's gaze as a Valorian drew his dagger. "Don't worry," the slave called to Arin in Herrani, which wasn't very different from the eastern language of Dacra. "The emperor will get what he deserves."

Then the Valorians cut off his ears and nose.

"There," Deliah said, snipping the thread. "Thirteen

stitches, two separate seams: forehead and cheek. I left the eye alone."

The blood merely oozed now. Arin opened his stinging left eye. With both of his eyes open and clear, Deliah didn't look like his dead mother at all. She washed her red hands in a bowl.

"Nicely done," said Tensen.

"Don't ask me to do this again," she told them, and left.

Tensen pulled a chair up to Arin's, sat, and began to dig the glass out of his right hand. After everything else, the sensation of this was oddly satisfying.

"Deliah had some interesting things to share earlier today," Arin said. Tensen's tweezers caught a big piece and dragged it out.

"Oh?" Tensen dropped the glass onto a nearby end table.

Arin told him what she had said. The older man listened. The bloodstained shards grew into a little heap.

"This is worth looking into," Arin said.

"I don't think Lady Kestrel's choice of dress is Herran's greatest priority."

Arin tightened his hands, then winced as this drove the glass deeper. Tensen, his tweezers lifted, gave him a cool look that told Arin he got what he deserved. "You're wrong," Arin said. "The fact that the Senate leader must know about the dress is important. The winnings from a correct bet could buy the Senate leader a small island, and none of the money would come from imperial coffers. Thrynne overheard something between the Senate leader and the emperor. What if the emperor was collecting a favor, and repaying the Senate leader with a tip for the perfect bet? We need to find out what that favor was."

Tensen prodded a tiny shard to the surface of Arin's palm. He inspected it.

"And the ruined dress," Arin continued. "Something dangerous is going on with Kestrel."

"Vomit on a sleeve and dirt on the knees? Let's not be dramatic. So the lady drank too much wine and tripped during a tipsy stroll through the Winter Garden. It's none of our concern."

"She's scheming," Arin insisted. "I can feel it."

Tensen set down the tweezers. "You're seeing what you want to see."

"No, I'm not. That makes no sense. I don't want her to be in trouble."

"But maybe you'd like her to be *troubled*. Unhappy with her new life. What would you do then, Arin? Rescue her from it?"

Arin said nothing.

"She seems happy to me," said Tensen.

"The dress's seams were ripped. The skirts were filthy. There's no mud in the Winter Garden. The garden has flagstones. Where did the stains come from?"

Tensen stared at him. "Arin. I don't mean to be unkind, and I know you feel that what Deliah said is important, but all I am hearing is an obsession with the prince's bride and what she likes to wear."

Arin closed his mouth. He shivered, suddenly chilled by doubt.

"Please," said Tensen. "Leave the spying to me."

"But you've learned nothing. Not since you told me about Thrynne."

"All in good time."

"Is it your new recruit? Has he learned something?" Arin saw Tensen's expression change slightly. "Or *she*?"

"Not yet. I'm encouraged that we'll hear something soon."

"I don't like this. I don't like how happy you seem about nothing at all from somebody whose name I don't know."

"I think of my informant as the Moth."

"I want a *name*."

"I see. You're concerned about whether we can trust this person. Don't be. The Moth is highly motivated to give us what we need."

Arin slammed his good hand down on the end table. "I will send you back to Herran. I swear that I will pack you onto the next ship there if you don't tell me who your informant is. *Now*."

Tensen swept the scattered shards back into their pile. He relaxed into his chair. His small green eyes were bright. "I noticed you speaking with Princess Risha the other night."

He fell silent, and the silence began to speak to Arin.

"Yes," Arin said slowly. "She was upset."

"Of course. What happened in the plains was tragic. Its people are refugees in the eastern capital. Hundreds died during the trek from the plains."

"Are you telling me—?"

"It can't be easy to be a knife held to the throat of one's own people. That's why Risha was kidnapped as a child.

The emperor can make the eastern queen grieve at a moment's notice. I'm surprised the emperor hasn't killed the queen's little sister already—but then again, that's a card he can only play once. He must be waiting for the right moment. I wonder what Risha thinks, while he's waiting."

Arin absorbed what his minister was saying—or what Arin *thought* he was saying. It occurred to him that it might be wise to suspect one's own spymaster, who'd been employed to traffic in deceit. And Tensen had been an actor before the war. But Arin could see no reason for Tensen to pretend that Risha was his Moth. Arin *could* see why she would work against the empire.

The old man looked at him, his expression kind. Arin suddenly craved kindness. He was seized by a horrible feeling, a familiar one. He'd been caught in its fist for ten years. He was sick of it. Why couldn't he outgrow it? He was no child. He had no business feeling lonely.

Loss of blood made Arin light-headed. His thoughts seemed to float and drift.

Tensen rose and brought a fresh bowl of water to Arin, who sank his right hand into it.

"Risha is very beautiful," the minister commented.

"Yes," Arin said. "She is." It was hard to think. Arin was so tired.

"Well, I'm going to bed," Tensen said. "Unless I need to pack for an abrupt departure over the tempest-tossed winter sea?"

"No. Go to sleep."

Tensen smiled and left him.

Arin sat for a long time in that chair. He considered

what he knew, what he thought he knew, and what he knew he didn't know. Then he reconsidered everything.

His thoughts began to take strange shapes. They beat their wings and fluttered away. Arin found himself borne on those wings and flown into sleep.

He had dreams where moths were crawling on his face. Their legs became black stitches. They laid eggs in a long line down his forehead and over his cheek. The eggs hatched.

He dreamed of Kestrel. He dreamed of Risha.

He dreamed that Kestrel had become Risha, that the sun had become the moon, and he couldn't tell whether he was blinded by the light or the dark.

An infection set into the wound. Arin's fever raged high.

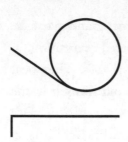

NO ONE LOOKS AT A SLAVE, ARIN HAD SAID.
Kestrel began to look very closely at hers. She settled on
one. This particular woman was in fact not a slave but a
paid servant, one of the Valorians selected to be a lady-in-
waiting to Kestrel. It was a mark of high status to be served
by one's own people; in return, the Valorian ladies-in-
waiting were decently paid and their blue servant dresses
trimmed with white.

Kestrel couldn't remember the woman's name. But she
was about Kestrel's height and size. She would do.

One morning not long after the reception in the imperial gallery, Kestrel contrived to be alone with the servant
and spill a large glass of water on her.

"I'm so sorry!" Kestrel cried. "Oh, I *am* clumsy."

"No matter, my lady," said the flustered woman. "It's just
water."

"But water is very *wet*. You must be uncomfortable.
Here, change into this." Kestrel offered one of her dresses,

carefully selected for being simply cut, without ornament, yet made from a rich fabric.

"I couldn't," said the maid.

"Of course you can! And you will keep it. Do you think I would miss it? Now, you'll insult me if you believe that. Go on, you may use my dressing room."

The maid was reluctant, but Kestrel placed the dress firmly in her hands. The woman's expression changed as she began to think things through. Kestrel saw her thoughts. If the maid worked for an entire year, she could still never afford a dress like this. It was a treasure. She could wear it and be stunning. Or maybe she would sell it. The fabric was velvet. It would fetch a fine price.

The maid went to try on Kestrel's dress.

When the woman emerged into the sitting room, Kestrel could tell that it took all of her control not to spin around and feel the skirt swing. "It fits perfectly," the woman said. "Are you sure I may keep it?"

"Of course." Kestrel took the woman's work dress from her crooked arm.

"Oh. I have to take my work dress back to the housekeeper."

"I'll take care of that."

"But I can't let you—"

"I insist." Kestrel smiled. Later, she would apologize to the housekeeper. She'd explain that she had no idea where she'd put the dress. She'd cover any cost.

After the maid had left, Kestrel took the damp work dress into her bedroom and dried it before the fire. She hid it in the back of a wardrobe filled with summer clothes that would remain packed away for the next two seasons.

It was possible that this maid reported to Verex— or worse, to the captain of the palace guard, or the emperor. But Kestrel didn't think that an exchange of dresses would seem noteworthy. It was only the whim of a kind mistress.

Kestrel waited for a night when she wasn't called upon to appear at a function. This took some time. There were dinners, game nights, and friendly, bloodless swordfights performed for an applauding audience. The prince's bride was expected to attend everything.

The governor of Herran, however, seemed to feel no such pressure.

Arin never came. More than a week had passed since she'd seen him in the art gallery. Kestrel didn't dare to ask for any news of him. When she met Tensen's eyes once across a crowd of courtiers, he shook his head.

Unless she had information to give Tensen, she should keep her distance—especially after what happened the last time. Kestrel could still feel the emperor's nails digging into her skin.

He hadn't carried out his threat to her—or so she thought. But his mood had soured. The entire court felt it. Kestrel wasn't the only one relieved when finally a night arrived when no one was expected to put on finery and gather in the emperor's presence. A holiday-like atmosphere ruled the palace. There were rumors of lovers who would meet for frosted kisses in the Winter Garden's hedge maze. Some courtiers swore they would crawl into bed early with hot bricks at their feet.

Kestrel had plans of her own. That night, she wiped her forehead clean of its engagement mark and tied a scarf over her hair. She pulled on the rough blue-and-white work dress and searched for a pair of comfortable shoes.

When she caught a glimpse of herself in a mirror she hesitated. Her features looked somehow smaller. She was too pale.

You disobeyed me, she heard the emperor say.

"No" doesn't exist anymore, only "yes," said her father and the captain of the guard in one voice.

But:

You are better than this, Arin said, and then she heard her own voice, calling out the highest bid to buy him. She heard the calm, cultured tones she had used to persuade the emperor to poison the eastern horses. Guilt swelled inside her.

Kestrel left her suite. She kept her head down and her pace brisk.

No one saw Lady Kestrel. Aristocrats in the halls didn't even glance at her. Servants did, but saw someone familiar yet unrecognizable, which wasn't strange in a palace staffed with hundreds of servants and slaves.

She was only a maid. If her step was a little too proud, it went unnoticed. If she occasionally looked lost in the servants' quarters, it was shrugged off as the problem of a new girl.

The maid tightened her scarf. She found her way out

one of the back kitchen yards. She stepped past palace guards, who ignored her. Though women not in the military weren't supposed to walk alone, few people cared if a maid broke the rules. She was beneath notice.

Kestrel walked into the frozen city.

"At last," Tensen said. "A night with nothing to do." He turned an appraising eye toward Arin, who lay on a divan near the sitting room fire. "You look better. Almost fit for society."

"I doubt that."

"Well, you're no longer feverish, are you? And the swelling in your face has gone down. You don't look quite so puffy. One more night of rest, Arin, and then it's back into the fray. You can't avoid the court forever. Besides, the reactions could be telling."

"Yes, stifled gasps and open disgust will be very informative."

"You'll cause a stir. Stirs are good. They churn up all kinds of gossip and conjecture . . . and the occasional truth."

"I'm surprised you need *me*. I thought you had the perfect access to information. Where's your Moth, Tensen?"

The minister said nothing.

Arin stood and went to the fire. He was weak from the fever, his movements disjointed. The heart of the fire was as red as the ruby set in the hilt of the dagger Arin kept in his boot. "Still no word about who arranged for the ambush?"

Tensen shrugged. "The emperor isn't happy. I can think of a good reason why. You're alive, and your assailant isn't."

"There's no proof that the emperor's behind it."

"The palace guard's insignia on that dead man isn't good enough proof for you?"

"If it was the emperor, why does he do nothing? Say nothing?"

"I think," Tensen said, "that he wouldn't want to acknowledge a failure." His green eyes narrowed. "What makes you believe that the emperor *wasn't* behind it? Do you have other enemies I don't know about?"

"No. It was him."

"So you're just being difficult."

"One of my enduring qualities."

Tensen rose from his chair. "I'm going to visit the art gallery."

"You go there a lot."

"I played an art connoisseur once, in the Herrani theater festival fifteen years ago. Old habits die hard."

"Then you must enjoy looking at all of the emperor's pretty things."

Tensen paused with his hand on the doorknob. He glanced back at Arin. "You might not believe me, but certain people will respect you more for how you look now. The emperor is going to regret making his mark on you. Be ready for tomorrow, Arin. It's time you left this suite. You're well enough, and there's no excuse to avoid the world."

Arin mulled over Tensen's words long after the minister

left. He thought about his fevered dreams, which he couldn't quite remember, though they had filled him with a nameless urgency. A restlessness.

In Arin's boot there was a sheath, in his sheath was Kestrel's dagger, and in the dagger's groove was his dried blood.

In the capital city was a tavern, in the tavern was a bookkeeper, and in the bookkeeper's hands was a book of bets.

Arin pulled on his winter coat, made sure he had everything he needed, and set out for the city.

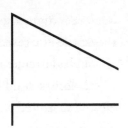

THE COLD WAS EXHILARATING. IT PINCHED
Kestrel's cheeks and chased her down sloping streets. She
wanted to laugh. The palace was at her back, high on its
hill, and she was here, winding through the city's wealthy
quarter with its haughty town houses and blazing oil
lamps. The cobblestone streets were marbled sheets of ice.
Carriages moved slowly, but Kestrel didn't. She skidded
through this quarter. She wanted no part of it.

She wanted the tight, dirty streets of the Narrows, the
fishy smell of the wharf. And she would have it.

I wanted to feel free, Arin had told her once in Herran.
She breathed in the cold, and it felt free, so she felt free,
and it felt alive, so she felt alive.

Kestrel wondered what would happen if she never went
back to the palace.

She hugged her arms to her chest. She had entered a
darker quarter of the city. Streetlamps were few. Soon there
were none. Kestrel took any street that went down, for that

was the way to the sea. The streets became a network of alleys: the Narrows.

She sidestepped a cat that streaked into the shadows. The cold was loud here. It rang off the jam-packed buildings. It shattered with noise tumbling from the flung-open door of a tavern. Kestrel saw its sign, which showed a broken arm, and watched as a man with the looks of a Valorian aristocrat stumbled outside the tavern and was sick in the street. He lifted his head, wiped his mouth, and blearily stared at Kestrel without really seeing her.

Then he squinted. His gaze was fuzzy, but gaining focus. "Do I know you?" he said.

Kestrel hurried away.

"You don't look so good," the bookkeeper said. She had her hands stuffed in her trouser pockets and her boots up on the table. She studied Arin over the steel-toed tops of them.

It was early for the Broken Arm to be this lively. But a ship had come in, and its sailors were already drunk. In a corner, Valorian soldiers argued over a game of Bite and Sting.

The bookkeeper, however, was calm—tipped back serenely in her chair, surveying the scene, smoking, waiting. People came to her.

"Want to place a bet?" she asked Arin. About his age or a bit older, the bookkeeper was only part Valorian. Her loose hair was a color that turned up sometimes in Valorians, who called it "warrior red," but her flat black eyes and light brown skin hinted at a northern heritage.

Arin smiled. The smile tugged painfully at his stitches. "What I want," he said, "is a word."

"Just that? You strike me as the type to want more than what's good for him. That mark on your face is fresh."

"I want to see the bets."

She exhaled a cloud of smoke. "I was right. You *are* a mad one. No one sees the bets . . . unless they ask very nicely."

"I can be nice."

She nodded at the empty chair beside her.

Arin sat. "I can share information."

She shrugged. "I've got no call to trust it."

"I could work for you."

"What I need you can't give. I'm a one-woman business. I've got thugs, sure, to remind people when they need to pay up. You'd fit that part. But—no offense—that's not worth what you're asking."

Arin hesitated, then reached into his pocket. He opened his hand. On his palm lay an emerald earring, its stone the size of a bird's egg. It had been his mother's.

"Would this do?" he said.

Kestrel's delight in the cold wore off around the time she reached the wharf. She'd worn as many layers as would fit under the work dress, but she shivered as she neared the harbormaster's house. Rocks and oyster shells crunched beneath her boots.

The house's entrance faced the sea and its torchlit promenade. Kestrel kept to the building's back and the shadows gathered there. She heard sailors joke as they entered the house to leave their names with the harbormaster, who recorded them in his ledger. He noted everything that entered and left the harbor—sailors, come ashore for leave in the city, and ships that docked. He wrote down the ships' point of origin and the goods they carried.

In his ledger should be written what Kestrel needed to know about the Senate leader's ship. He'd brought back no luxuries from his voyage to the southern isles for his daughter. Perhaps he had felt stingy, or angry with Maris . . . or his ship had brought back no such luxuries at all—which was strange indeed, since usually the sole purpose of a trip to the isles was for their goods.

What if the Senate leader *hadn't* been to the isles? He could have traveled elsewhere, to another place where the sun shone hot even in winter, hot enough to tan his skin. What if he'd gone to the very southern tip of the Herran peninsula, where hearthnut trees grew? She remembered Arin's anxiety over the harvest, and how much of it the emperor would seize. Maybe the Senate leader had been secretly estimating the crop's worth.

Kestrel waited until the sailors left the house and took the curve of the promenade that led up into the city. Then she reached for a rock encrusted with tiny shells, weighed it in her hand, and broke a back window of the harbormaster's house.

A thump came from inside the house: a chair, tilted back, had been dropped down on all four legs.

The sound of heavy boots. A sea-weathered door whining on its hinges. Feet on rocks, crunching closer.

Kestrel could be sure his dagger was drawn. Hers was, too. She'd chosen the plainest scabbard she owned and had wrapped the dagger's jeweled pommel with a scarf, but she still seemed to see the diamonds' sharp eyes through the cloth.

The harbormaster rounded the back corner of the house. He was large—a former soldier, like all harbormasters. He held a sword, not a dagger. He didn't see her yet.

If Kestrel played this wrong, she was likely to lose. A fight with this man could mean death . . . or arrest. She would be brought before the emperor.

She would be asked to explain.

The freezing sea was in Kestrel's blood. Her veins ran with it.

She grabbed another rock and pitched it into the shadows. It hit farther up the beach.

The harbormaster instinctively turned to see what had made that sound.

Kestrel swung the pommel of her dagger at the back of his head.

The bookkeeper whistled. "You *do* surprise a girl." She touched the emerald on Arin's palm. "How do I know it's real?"

"That's your risk. My offer's good for tonight only.

Take it and give me what I want . . . or doubt me, and I'll walk away." He closed his hand around the earring. Arin could tell the bookkeeper was hungry for the sight of it again. She looked exactly how he felt.

"Earrings come in pairs," she said. "Where's the other one?"

"Gone."

"Got any more surprises like these?"

"No."

Her black eyes were bright in the rushlights. Even though the Broken Arm tavern had in fact grown louder since they'd started speaking, Arin had the sense of things quieting: a muffling of the world, a breath held as the bookkeeper made her decision. He desperately hoped she would say yes. He desperately wanted her to say no.

"Give it here," she said.

Arin's hand didn't move. Then, slowly, he loosened his hold on the jewel. He let it slide, green and glowing. He held the memory with the bare tips of his fingers: his mother's face in the nighttime, hung with twin green stars. She rested her palm on his forehead and said the blessing for dreams. She lifted her hand away, and Arin opened his, and dropped the earring into the bookkeeper's waiting grasp.

Kestrel dragged the harbormaster's unconscious body. Her arms burned, her bad knee screamed in protest, but Kestrel dug her heels into the rocks and pulled until the man was hidden behind the house where the shadows were darkest. Then, her breath sharp and thin in her throat, she stepped inside, locked the door, and went to the ledger open on the man's desk.

She flipped back to entries from earlier that winter. She found the Senate leader's ship—the *Maris*.

Point of origin: the southern isles. Goods: none.

Kestrel let go of the page. It sighed down.

She'd been wrong to suspect that the Senate leader had traveled to Herran instead of the isles. Here was the proof of it.

What else might she have gotten wrong? Her pulse sped with fear of herself, fear of her choices, her certainty. Kestrel's heartbeats flew, one right against the other, like flipped pages of a book.

Were all her lies to Arin worth it, if she couldn't see the truth? Kestrel had thought she'd known what was best for Arin. Perhaps her greatest lies were the ones she'd told to herself.

But then . . .

Kestrel paged again through the ledger.

What if the Senate leader had lied to the harbormaster? What if the harbormaster had lied to his book?

She found the latest entries. The *Maris* was docked in the harbor now. The ledger listed the number of its pier.

Kestrel left the book open on the desk exactly as it had been. She riffled through desk drawers until she found a purse filled with silver. She pocketed it, pulled out the drawer, and dumped it and its contents on the floor.

Did you hear that the harbormaster was attacked? she imagined city guards saying. *A case of petty thievery.*

Kestrel left the house and headed for the piers.

"You understand," the bookkeeper said as she tucked the emerald away, "that you can't make any bets after you look in my book. Not with me, not ever." She sat more seriously now, all business, the four legs of the chair firmly on the floor. She pulled a slim book from her inner jacket pocket. "Got something in particular you'd like to see?"

"Show me the entries about the wedding."

The bookkeeper raised one brow, which made Arin wonder if she knew who he was. She found the list and held the book out to Arin, her thumb wedged in its open seam.

These bets concerned the wedding night. They went into great detail. The wagers showed a breadth of curiosity and imagination that made Arin wish he'd never looked.

"Not that," he said. "That's not what I meant. I want to see bets about the dress."

Both of the bookkeeper's brows were arched now, this time in disdainful boredom. She turned a few pages and offered the book again.

Arin saw the Senate leader's bet. It was in the middle of several entries that concerned the dress. Others had guessed the same color the Senate leader had wagered on—red—but no one else had bet on the number of buttons, the neckline, the length of the train, the style of the scabbard . . .

Arin examined the pages again. He'd been mistaken about something. He'd gone through the dress wagers too quickly before, racing to find the Senate leader's name and to escape the memory of the first set of bets he'd seen. He saw now that the Senate leader wasn't the only one to have gone into careful detail about the wedding dress. Another person had bet in the exact same way, and more recently.

Arin tapped the name. "Who's that?"

The bookkeeper peered. "A palace engineer. She works on water. Aqueducts. Canals. That sort of thing."

Arin closed the book and handed it back.

"That's it?" she said.

"Yes." He added, "If you want a tip, that bet's the correct one."

The bookkeeper drew up her boot so that it was planted on the seat of her chair as she sat, one leg dangling down, the other bent into the perfect position for her to prop an elbow on the knee, drop her chin onto her fist, and look up at Arin. "I think you've overpaid me. How about I give you something extra before you go?"

Sailors strolled the wharf. Kestrel hung back, chafing her arms for warmth. Waves slapped the sides of large merchant ships docked at piers that reached out into the black, glassy sea.

She kept her eyes on one ship in particular. She saw several sailors from the *Maris* clatter down its pier, ready for shore leave, but she let them go.

Then Kestrel spied the perfect target. He walked alone,

cheeks ruddy from the cold and drink. His merry steps wavered a little. He was humming.

"Sailor," she called as he passed, "care for a game of cards?"

He stopped. He came close, and Kestrel could see that he wasn't drunk after all. His eyes were alert, his expression a mix of friendly and sly. The sailor reached into his coat pocket for a pipe, and the slow, deliberate way he packed it told Kestrel that he wouldn't be an easy opponent.

She would enjoy the game all the more.

"Well?" she said. "Will you play?"

He gave her an appreciative grin. "Absolutely."

They stepped off the promenade and onto the rocky beach, where they found a few wooden crates dragged together. There were signs of an earlier, abandoned game: an empty bottle of wine and scattered tobacco ash.

Kestrel sat. "I trust you have a deck."

"A sailor always does." He joined her. He lit his pipe, sucked until the tobacco crisped and glowed, and reached for his purse.

Kestrel said, "Let's play for something else."

"I was hoping you'd say that."

"Mind out of the gutter, seaboy. The stakes are questions and answers."

"Can I ask the sort of questions that belong in the gutter?"

"*If* you win."

"I warn you, I'm pretty good."

Kestrel smiled. "I'm better."

The bookkeeper climbed onto Arin's lap. She settled her knees at his hips, lifted smoke-scented fingers to his jaw. She tipped his head back. Her black eyes glinted down at him, and her red hair slipped over his cheek. Her hair lay cool against his stitches. He thought about his ruined face, and how, in this moment, it was to not feel so ruined.

"*I'd* like to make a bet," she said, and leaned to whisper in his ear.

Arin's hands went to her waist.

"You look disappointed," Kestrel said.

The sailor tossed his cards onto Kestrel's winning hand spread out on the crate. "I did hope for something more exciting than telling you that yes, the *Maris* sailed to southern Herran about a month ago. Can't I at least lose in an *interesting* way?"

Kestrel's laugh was white in the cold. "We could gamble for your coat."

"Ah, love, why don't we skip to the part where you win and I give it to you?"

Arin lifted the bookkeeper off his lap. He set her gently down on her chair.

"It's sad," she said, "to see someone act against his best interests."

Sometimes, it was as if Kestrel still owned him. Arin thought about the silver she'd paid for him. He felt its terrible weight. He couldn't forgive it. It lay hard and shiny inside him. As he'd grown to know her, in Herran, the silver sank slowly down through uncertain waters. Then came a current's warm push. He'd floated up. That silver lay deep below, and the thought of diving for it had felt like drowning. But sometimes—especially since the treaty, especially in this damned city, and especially now—the silver seemed close. Bright as treasure.

Yet Arin knew the pull of his blood. He turned away from the bookkeeper. "I know my own best interests," he told her.

She smiled, propping her boots back on the table. "Someday you'll know better."

Arin quit the table. He stepped out of the tavern and into the night.

The sailor stood and offered Kestrel a flourished hand. She let him lift her to her feet. He wrapped his coat around her shoulders and bunched the loose fabric together in an almost fascinated sort of way. "Sweet palace maid, won't you come to sea with me?"

"I'd sink the ship. Can't you tell? I'm bad luck."

"Just my kind." He gave her a hearty kiss on the cheek. Then he took off over the rocks, running up onto the promenade. "I'm freezing!" he shouted. He ran in the direction of the city. He opened up, and began to sing the melody he had been humming earlier. He sang it full and loud. The song was more or less on pitch, and Kestrel liked to hear it leaping over the wavebreaks, jagged with his runner's breath.

It was not beautiful. It was not Arin's voice: rich liquor poured to the brim. But it was happy. Kestrel was happy to hear it, and thought about being grateful for what one can get.

KESTREL HAD WHAT SHE NEEDED. IT WAS TIME to return to the palace. But her feet were slow on her way through the city. They dragged up the hill.

She didn't want to go back. Refusal rose up within her: stony in her throat, hard and hurting. She stood before a high bridge over the river that ran down from the mountain and switchbacked through the city. Kestrel should have crossed it. She should have come down on the other side and made her way up through the aristocratic quarter with its diamond-paned oil lamps.

But she didn't.

Kestrel touched the wrought-iron railing that ran the length of the river. The cold metal burned. Kestrel skimmed her palm along it as she walked—slowly, then quickly, racing along the river's edge for no other purpose than to see where it would lead her . . . so long as it was away from where she was supposed to be.

A water engineer. Arin took a skinny set of stairs that led up out of the Narrows. At the top, he turned to look down at the city. Lamplights scattered over the darkness: jewels across a black velvet lap.

To Arin, the bets about the wedding dress were clear. Though Tensen had doubted him, Arin had been right: the Senate leader was being paid with lucrative information. He had done the emperor a favor. But what?

And if the water engineer had been paid in kind, what had *she* done?

Arin heard the sound of rushing water. The river.

There was a canal, he remembered, where the river thinned and gentled. A series of locks, crafted by the water engineer herself.

Arin found the river and followed it.

Kestrel stopped at the sight of the locks. At first, she marveled at their design, at the way a series of gates could open or close to raise or lower the water level so that a barge could deliver its goods.

Such an invention. What a sharp mind had made these.

When Arin came to the locks, someone else was there. A palace maid, her back to him. She was Valorian; through the faint light of a far-off lamp, he could see the white-trimmed hem of her blue skirt peeking out from beneath a large coat. Her hair was covered with a work scarf. She was all shadow, a small huddle of it.

Somehow his heart caught at the sight. The boy he had been, the one that Arin caught glimpses of sometimes in the mirror, spoke up shyly within him to say *lonely*. He said *beautiful*.

But this was not a painting. This was a person. This was a Valorian stranger he wanted no part of, with her palace dress that reminded Arin of everything the empire had cost him.

He told that boy to go away.

Arin kept walking. He followed the canal until it curved. Even if he looked back, he would no longer be able to see the maid.

The more Kestrel stared at the locks, the more she began to feel like that river. She sensed her staggered self. The things pent up behind the floodgates. The iron lies she herself had swung into place and locked tight.

Kestrel heard footsteps: another late-night wanderer. They slowed, but didn't stop. They carried on, became far-away echoes, then gone.

She, too, should leave. Kestrel couldn't avoid the palace forever.

Something made Arin turn back. The hand of a god? He couldn't say. But his feet were retracing their steps before he even realized it. His body was alight, alive, insistent.

Arin's mind buzzed with the puzzle of it even as he quickened his pace. Why did he feel the urge to return?

There was no great mystery in a palace maid standing alone by the canal. There was nothing more to see.

But:

Hurry, said his feet.

Hurry, said his heart.

The maid, however, had gone.

He kept searching. As the canal expanded into the river and a bridge arched its back in the gloom, he remembered the maid's shoes: black dueling boots. Why would a maid wear boots that were part of the ceremonial garb for a Valorian duel?

Unless she had nothing more practical to wear. Arin had a very strange image of a faceless maid sorting through piles of glamorous shoes for a comfortable pair.

Why would he think that?

Her dagger, too, hadn't been quite right. It wasn't unusual for a maid to wear one—all Valorians did—but they didn't wrap their hilts with cloth. That changed the grip. Arin couldn't think of any reason that someone would cover a hilt like this . . . unless it needed to be hidden.

He was running now. Sweat stung the cut on his face.

Although he hadn't seen the maid's hands, he kept imagining a memory of them.

He saw pale, lithe fingers. He remembered them reaching for his own. He felt them slide under his shirt, over his skin. He saw them strike music from black and white keys, storm down, then quiet the melody, lull it, and trick it into dreams.

When Arin truly did see the girl's hand in the darkness, resting on a railing near the bridge, he thought it was a phantom of his imagination. The maid's fingers rippled along the railing. They played an unheard song.

He knew that gesture.

He knew that hand.

Arin slowed. She was lost in thought. She didn't hear him coming, or if she did it didn't matter to her. The river mattered. The music in her head mattered. She stared into the dark.

Arin was quiet as he came close, quiet when he said her name, and quiet when he touched her cold, bare hand. He touched her little black star of a birthmark, near the base of her thumb.

He didn't want to startle her. At first, he thought he hadn't. He felt the stillness in her before she turned to look at him. He felt the recognition. But when Kestrel finally glanced up at Arin, she recoiled as if she didn't know him. She snatched her hand from his and lifted it—to ward him off, he thought. To block the very sight of him.

He'd frightened her after all. There was a cry on her lips. Horror in her eyes.

A monster stood before her. Arin remembered that now.

The monster was him.

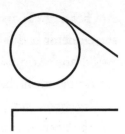

KESTREL SAW ARIN FLINCH AWAY, HARD, FROM the hand she'd lifted to touch him. It fell as if burned.

She seemed to feel the knife that had done this to him. It went into her. It hit something vital, and she hunched inside herself. Shock made it impossible to speak. Pain scooped the air from her throat.

Arin's fingers touched the two seams that cut a long broken slash down the left side of his face.

"What happened to you?" she whispered.

He covered the wound. But Kestrel had seen its length. The livid skin straining at black stitches. The way it had changed him. The way he hid it.

"Arin, tell me."

He stayed silent.

"Please," she said.

Arin crouched down, and Kestrel didn't understand the movement until he had pulled a dagger from his boot.

Her dagger. Her beloved dagger, with its perfect weight

and her seal carved into the hilt's ruby. Her dagger, which the emperor had taken weeks ago.

"This," Arin said, and gave it to Kestrel.

I'm sorry, she had told the emperor.

No, you're not. But you will be.

She dropped the dagger to the ground.

Arin retrieved it. "Take care. You'll damage the blade. I happen to know that it keeps a nice, sharp edge. I made sure that the palace guard I took it from knew it, too. You'd think that a Valorian would have more courage than to hire someone to attack me in a dark corner."

"Arin, it wasn't me."

"I didn't say it was." But he was angry and rough.

"I could never."

Arin must have sensed that she was ready to weep, that the dagger in his hands was warping in her blurred vision. He spoke more gently. "I don't think that you did."

"Why?" Her voice wavered and broke. "I could have arranged for it. That's my dagger. That's my seal. Why do you believe what I say? Why would you believe in me at all?"

He moved to lean forward on the railing, forearms folded with the blade dangling down over the river, his face in profile. Finally, he said, "I trust you."

"You shouldn't."

"I know," he muttered.

She heard the strain in his voice. His eyes cut to her, and she saw that he knew she had heard it. His body shifted into a position of determined nonchalance. "Logically speaking," he said lightly, "the idea that you hired someone to attack me doesn't make much sense. I'm not sure what your motive would be."

"I could have wanted to put an end to the rumors."

"That would be a shame. I like the rumors."

"Don't joke. You should blame me. You must."

He shook his head. "It's not like you to send someone else to do your dirty work."

"I could have changed."

"Kestrel, why are you trying to convince me of your guilt?"

Because this is my fault, she wanted to say.

"A moment ago, you insisted that you had nothing to do with this," Arin said, "and that's what makes sense. Do you want to tell me why the emperor took your dagger? Whom did he want to punish with it? Just me . . . or you, too?"

Kestrel couldn't speak.

"I might even be flattered," Arin said, "if the emperor's form of flattery didn't hurt so much." He straightened, and offered her the dagger again.

"No," she said sharply.

"It's not the blade's fault."

She choked on her anguish. On her guilt, her fault, and his trust. "If you give that dagger to me, I will throw it in the river."

Arin shrugged. He tucked the dagger back into his boot, then he faced her. The slash curved slightly in his cheek like half a smile, but his mouth was flat as he watched her take him in. "I'm sure that my new appearance is fascinating in all sorts of ways, but I don't want to talk about it anymore. I'd rather talk about *this*." He pointed at Kestrel's work scarf and dragged his finger down through the air to her black boots. "Kestrel, what are you doing?"

She had forgotten what she wore. "Nothing."

He lifted his dark brows.

"It was a dare," she said. "A senator's daughter dared me to sneak out of the palace without an escort."

"Try harder, Kestrel."

She muttered, "I was tired of being closed up inside the palace."

"That I believe. But I doubt it's the whole truth."

Arin's eyes were narrow, inspecting her. His hand slid along the railing as he came close. He reached for the collar of the sailor's coat. He drew it away from her neck.

The world went luscious, and slow, and still.

He bowed his head. Stitches scratched against her cheek. Arin buried his face in the hollow between her neck and the coat collar and breathed in. Warmth flooded her.

Kestrel imagined: his mouth parting against her skin. The teeth of his smile. And she imagined more, she saw what she would do, how she would forget herself, how everything would slip and unloop, like rich ribbon off its spool. The dream of this held her. She couldn't move.

She felt him feel how she didn't move. Arin hesitated. He lifted his head and looked down at her. The blacks of his eyes were huge.

He released her. "You smell like a man." He put some distance between them. "Where'd you get that coat?"

Kestrel's voice wasn't quite as shaky as the rest of her. "I won it."

"Who was your victim this time?"

"A sailor. At cards. I was cold."

"Flustered, Kestrel?"

"Not at all." She firmed up her voice. "To tell the truth, he gave it to me."

"Quite an evening you're having. Sneaking out. Taking coats off sailors. Why do I feel, though, that that's not the whole of it?"

She shrugged. "I enjoy a good card game. Courtiers provide few."

"What were the stakes of your late-night gamble?"

"I told you. The coat."

"You said he *gave* it to you. You also said that you won. What *did* you win, then, at cards?"

"Nothing. It was merely for fun."

"A game against you with nothing at stake? Never."

"I don't see why. I once played against you for matches."

"Yes, you did." He briefly closed his eyes. Kestrel saw the thin, almost vertical red line that marked his left lid. It scratched at her heart.

He looked at her. His gray eyes hunted her face. She fell prey to them as she always did. Arin smiled. It wasn't a real smile, and it dragged at the left side of his face. "I challenge you to a game of Bite and Sting, Kestrel. Will you play?"

She turned back to the river. "You should leave the capital."

"A stormy journey across the sea with no one to keep me company? How tempting."

She said nothing.

"I don't want to leave," Arin said. "I want to play with you. One game."

There was temptation, and there was the smart thing, but it was becoming increasingly hard for Kestrel to make the right choice. "When?" she managed.

"The next available opportunity."

There was hardly a Bite and Sting set lying at their feet. Kestrel would have time to prepare . . . though she had no real notion of what such preparation could be.

Wasn't it just a game? Just one? "Very well," she heard herself say.

"Winner take all," said Arin.

She looked at him. "The stakes?"

"The truth."

Kestrel couldn't agree to that. She couldn't even say no, for that would admit that the truth was something she couldn't afford to give.

"Not enticing?" said Arin. "I see. Maybe such stakes aren't high enough. Not for you. That's it, isn't it? I'd give you *my* truth for the asking. You know that. You don't want to win something that's free." His eyes measured her. "Kestrel. You're hiding something. And I want it. Let's say this. If you win, I'll do whatever you ask. If you tell me to leave the capital, I'll go. If you want me never to speak with you again, I won't. You name your price." Arin offered his hand.

"Give me your word that you'll pay properly. On your honor, as a Valorian."

She tried not to look at Arin's outstretched hand. She held the collar of her coat closed tight against the cold.

To lose was unthinkable. But if she won . . . she could send Arin home. It would be for the best. It had become too dangerous for him to stay. Too hard.

"Kestrel." He touched her bare wrist. Slowly, he slid his fingers into the warmth of the coat's large cuff. Her pulse shot beneath his thumb. "One last time?" he asked.

Her fingers loosened, almost like they didn't belong to her. They opened, and they found his.

It suddenly seemed that Kestrel had been an empty room, and that all of her wishes came crowding in. They thronged: delicate, full-skirted, their silk brushing up against each other. "Yes," she whispered.

Arin's eyes were bright in the darkness. His hand was hot. "Swear."

"A Valorian honors her word."

"Come." He drew her toward a descending alleyway.

"Now?"

"Would you rather play in the palace? I wonder where would be best, my rooms or yours?"

She dropped his hand. She rubbed her palm, trying to rub away the feel of him.

He watched her do it. His expression changed.

"We'll play later," she said, and that was when she knew for certain that she might have agreed for the simple pleasure of playing against him, or even for the poisoned prize of sending him from the capital, but some weak part of her had also agreed out of the sneaking hope that she might lose. "Later," she said again.

"No. Now."

"We can't wander around the Narrows waiting to stumble upon a Bite and Sting set."

"Don't worry," said Arin. "I know a place."

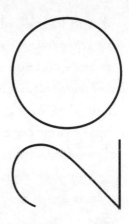

ARIN WONDERED IF THE FEVER FROM THE
wound had truly left him. He felt wild.

It was the confusion.

He led the way back down into the Narrows. His stride
was longer than Kestrel's. He shortened it . . . and moments later, was practically loping.

Arin didn't know what was real anymore. What was
real? Kestrel's look of disgust when she'd first seen him?
But then the wan lamplight had caught her face more fully.
He'd seen shock and grief.

Or he thought he had. *You're seeing what you want to
see,* Tensen had told him.

When Arin had pulled that stolen—borrowed? won?—
coat away from Kestrel's throat, a sensation had sparked
the air between them. Hadn't it? But then she'd turned to
stone. Like she had before on the balcony, that first night.
Maybe those sparks had been in Arin's head. Maybe they
were the kind you get when someone punches you in the
face.

Arin hadn't lied when he said that he trusted her. But that trust always came with a wrench of the gut. Trusting her made no sense. Arin knew all the reasons it didn't. His trust was foolish. Unhealthy. To be honest, Arin didn't understand his own trust. He wasn't even sure if this stubborn impulse came out of real hope or was the habit of a beggar, fallen asleep with his hand held out for small coins.

Arin shot a glance behind him. Kestrel was casting worried looks around the skinny alley—at the sick and waste in the gutter, the wavy orange light from torchlit gaming houses, the crumbling stairs. Mean-looking slicks of ice.

She caught his glance. She tugged at her work scarf to hide her cheek as if he were a stranger. Like he didn't already know who she was, and she might succeed in tricking him with her disguise.

Her disguise! Arin stopped in his tracks and marveled at the sight of her dressed as a maid. Her bright hair was hidden. Her face bare. Brow clean. That godsforsaken gold mark was gone.

He felt something buoyant. Practically giddy. It filled his lungs. It made him spin a story. A pure fantasy that exposed just how far his mind had gone.

Arin imagined her as Tensen's Moth.

Yes, Arin mocked himself, surely that was it. Everything was explained.

Amazed at his powers of self-deception, Arin told himself his absurd little story. Tensen's hints about Risha as the Moth had been mere insinuation. Tensen had said nothing straight. And Kestrel was in a good position to gather information for Arin's spymaster, wasn't she? Beloved by the court. Daughter of the general. Close to the emperor. Promised to his son. Tensen would never tell Arin if *she* was his source.

It fit perfectly. Look at her now. The maid's uniform. That coat. Something hidden in her eyes. Oh, yes. Kestrel would make a fine spy.

And let's not forget that ruined dress Deliah had described, with the ripped seams and vomit and mucky hem.

Wouldn't it be like Kestrel, to risk herself?

For what? Herran?

Him?

Gods of madness and lies. Arin was insane.

He laughed out loud.

Kestrel had stopped, too. She'd seen his face fill with a strange, hard mirth even before he'd laughed. "Arin," she said. "What's wrong?"

"Nothing." He shook his head, still smiling. "Everything. I don't know."

"What is it?"

"A joke. Something stupid. Not real. Never mind."

She was reluctant to press him. She didn't want to hear that joyless laugh again.

They continued on for a few paces beneath the wooden signs that hung over establishments' doors like rigid flags. Kestrel stopped when she realized where Arin was leading her. She eyed the tavern across the street, the one with the sign of the broken arm, under which that sick lord had almost seen through her disguise. "I can't go in there."

"Not grand enough for you?" Arin still had that satirical light in his eyes.

"Someone might recognize me."

"They won't."

"Do I look so different in plain clothes?" She heard the self-conscious note in her voice, and was embarrassed.

"Kestrel, I'm going to suspect that you think yourself too fine a lady to enter the Broken Arm. Or that you're afraid to lose to me, which is really quite understandable."

She scowled at him, then led the way.

The tavern was all wild noise and light. There was a press of people. The air lay thick with tobacco smoke, the meaty smell of cheap tallow candles, and a yeasty, humid odor that seemed due to a mix of alcohol and sweat. Kestrel threaded through the crowd.

"Do you know where you're going?" she heard Arin say near her ear, amused.

Kestrel pushed ahead. She could breathe a bit better closer to the bar, though when she came nearer she saw three disheveled courtiers, drunk and loud. She knew one of them by name. He ranked highly, and had been a part of the emperor's inner circle at the Winter Garden party.

Kestrel ducked her head, afraid to be recognized.

She wasn't quick enough. His gaze fell on her . . . and slid away. She saw him *not* see her, or at least not see anything worth his attention. One of his fellows laughed at something the other said. The senator turned to them.

There was a merry call for another round. They didn't glance her way.

"You've stopped," Arin murmured in her ear.

Her heart still hammering, Kestrel spun so abruptly to face Arin that she jostled into him. His hand caught her shoulder.

"I'm leaving," she said.

"You promised. One game."

"Not here. Not now."

Arin's grip tightened. "Then you forfeit. I win."

Her heartbeat changed in her ears. It rode high at his touch. There was temptation, and then there was . . . something else, that might have been the smart thing if she hadn't forgotten it.

That something else shape-shifted. It hardened inside her. It pushed for *yes*, spurned *no*, and called Kestrel a coward. It joined hands with temptation.

"I never forfeit," she said. He smiled. She led him to a far corner with a cluster of tables. The tables were all occupied. A pair of Valorian merchants sat at the one farthest from the senators. Kestrel went up to the merchants. "Give us your seats," she said, and dropped the purse she'd stolen from the harbormaster onto the table. The merchants looked at it, looked at her, and decided to drink on their feet. They took the purse and left.

"Blunt, but effective," Arin commented as Kestrel claimed a chair, her back to the courtiers. Arin remained standing. She thought he might say something teasing. That steely mirth hadn't quite left him, but it had softened during their push through the tavern. He looked a little tired, like a runner done running. Whatever thought had seized him in the alleyway was gone . . . or had gone away enough. She couldn't see it anymore on his torn face.

His dear face, dear to her, dearer still. How could she love his face more for its damage? What kind of person saw someone's suffering and felt her heart crack open even wider, even more sweetly than before?

There was something wrong with her. It was wrong to want to touch a scar and call it beautiful.

Arin wasn't looking at her anymore. He'd been distracted.

Kestrel followed his gaze to see a black-eyed redhead at a nearby table giving Arin a cool look. His expression didn't change, but something inside him did. Kestrel felt it. It twisted her heart.

When Arin's attention returned to Kestrel, she examined the splintery surface of the table. "I'm going to get a Bite and Sting set," he said. "And wine. Should I get wine?"

The answer to that was a clear no. Kestrel needed all her wits about her for a game she shouldn't—*couldn't*—lose. But she felt suddenly miserable, and realized that she'd been nervous ever since Arin had found her by the river. She said yes.

He hesitated, like he might counsel her against that choice. Then he left the table.

The crowd swallowed him. Kestrel couldn't see where he had gone.

Arin didn't like to leave her for long. She was going to attract attention. It was her nature. But when he returned with wine and a game set, she was alone and quiet: an almost eerie silence in the tavern's storm.

He saw her before she did him. He saw that she was unhappy. He realized that this was what had arrested him by the canal when he'd thought she was a nameless maid: the sense that this stranger had lost something as precious to her as what he had lost was to him.

In his mind, Arin lost to Kestrel at Bite and Sting, and let all of his questions slip away.

In his mind, he said, *Tell me what you want.*

And she said, *Leave this city.*

She said, *Take me with you.*

Kestrel lifted her gaze. As he met her eyes—an extremely light brown, the lightest shade before brown becomes gold—Arin knew that he was a fool. A thousand times a fool.

He must stop. They were painful, these waking dreams. Why did he allow himself to think them? They skewed everything. Arin was ashamed now, remembering how he'd pretended—even if for a moment—that Kestrel was the Moth. He shoved that lovely little lie from his head. He refused to think of it again. Thoughts like this made him feel split in two, just as his face was: one side fine and the other sore and throbbing.

He sat, and set the game, wine bottle, and glass on the table. He poured.

"Only one glass?" she said.

He handed it to her. "I've no head for wine. How is it?"

"Terrible." But she drank deeply.

Arin upacked the set. Kestrel picked up one of the tiles, which was made of rough wood, and turned it over in her fingers. Her thumb rubbed at some grime. He watched her drink again.

Arin thought of the ruined dress Deliah had described. Tensen had dismissed it with an impatient wave of the hand, a gesture that told Arin it was ridiculous to imagine anything dire. Vomit on the sleeve of a dress? Well, don't courtiers like wine? Arin had seen scores of Valorians drunk until sick. As for the dirt on the dress and split seams . . . anybody can trip. The Winter Garden had no mud, true, but Arin hadn't seen all of the palace grounds. There were places he wasn't allowed to go. Kestrel could have tripped anywhere.

Neither tripping nor drunkenness seemed like Kestrel. But he watched her drain the glass.

I could have changed, she'd said by the river.

Arin took the game piece from Kestrel. He mixed the tiles with unnecessary force. They drew their hands.

Arin's was pitiful. The only thing that saved this game from being a lost cause was a pair of mice, and mice held almost the lowest value. The rest of his hand was an assortment of Sting tiles—which Kestrel delighted in playing, and played well. He, less so.

And Kestrel had a high hand. He knew it. She had no tells—not exactly. It was more that she had a concentrated *lack* of tells. She changed without giving any clear sign that she had changed. She gathered intensity.

"Kestrel."

She discarded a tile and drew another. She didn't look

at him. He'd noticed—of course he had—how she avoided looking at him now. And no wonder. Arin's face stung. The stitches itched. He was tempted to rip them out. "Look at me," he said. She did, and Arin suddenly wished she hadn't. He cleared his throat. He said, "I won't try anymore to convince you not to marry him."

She slowly added the new tile to her hand. She stared at it, and said nothing.

"I don't understand your choice," Arin said. "Or maybe I do. It doesn't matter. You want it. That's clear. You've always done exactly what you wanted."

"Have I." Her voice was flat and dull.

He plunged ahead. "I was wondering . . ." Arin had an idea. He'd had it for some time now. He didn't like it. The words lay bitter on his tongue, but he had thought about it, and thought about it, and if he said nothing . . .

Arin made himself study his tiles again. He tried to think which Sting tile would profit Kestrel least. He discarded a bee. The instant he set the tile down, he regretted it.

He pulled a high Bite tile. This should have encouraged him, yet Arin had the sense of flying toward the inevitable moment when Kestrel won and he asked her what she wanted.

"I thought . . ."

"Arin?"

She looked concerned. That decided him. Arin took a deep breath. His stomach changed to iron. His body was girding itself in a way he knew well. Arin was tightening the muscles needed before a plunge into deep water. A punch to the gut. The lift of the hardest, lowest, highest notes he could possibly sing. His stomach knew what he'd have to sustain.

"Marry him," Arin said, "but be mine in secret."

Her hand lifted from the tiles as if scorched. She sat back in her chair. She rubbed at her inner elbow. She drank the dregs of her wine and was silent. Finally, she said, "I can't do that."

"Why?" Arin was hot with humiliation, hating himself for having asked. The cut burned in his cheek. "It's not so different than what you would have chosen before. When you kissed me in your carriage on Firstwinter, you thought to keep me your secret. If you thought of anything. I would have been one of those special slaves, the ones called for at night when the rest of the house is sleeping. Well? Isn't that how it was?"

"No." She spoke low. "It wasn't."

"Then tell me." Arin was damning himself with every word. "Tell me how it was."

Slowly, Kestrel said, "Things have changed."

Arin jerked his head to the side, chin up, stitched left cheek tilted to catch the light. "Because of *this*?"

She replied as if the answer was obvious. "Yes."

He shoved back from the table. "I think I'll have that drink."

Arin began to walk away, then glanced back over his shoulder. He made sure his words were an insult. "Don't touch the tiles."

Kestrel didn't understand. His anger made no sense. Wasn't it clear that Arin's wound was her fault? And that worse could happen?

He didn't return.

She thought about what she didn't understand. She thought about how Arin's wound might run deeper than the flesh. She remembered his question and her answer. She remembered them again.

Slowly, she began to see the misunderstanding. For her, *yes* was the emperor's message carved into Arin's face. For Arin, *yes* was the scar itself, not what it meant. His anger was for how he looked . . . how he thought he looked to her now.

A horror sank into her. She couldn't wait until he returned. She must find him. She must set things straight.

Arin had forced his way up to the bar, where he waited to ask for a second glass. The Valorian barkeep ignored him. She served everyone else first. When new Valorians came up to the bar, she served them, too. She wasn't going to glance at Arin unless he made a scene—which he was very ready to do. In his head, he heard Kestrel say *Yes*.

The surface of the bar was sticky and smelled sour. Arin stared at it and thought of the emerald earring, how it had shone: enchanted, his. Sarsine had found it hooked into a thick, patterned carpet that had been rolled up and shoved into storage in a disused quarter of his house in Herran. The emerald had been like one of those tales where a god is revealed. Arin had sworn he would never part with it.

Yet he had, and he understood now that it hadn't really been information he wanted to buy. It had been trust. Arin could no longer trust himself. Arin had believed the bets in the bookkeeper's hand were important. The emerald had seemed to promise that if this belief could be proven true, then Arin could trust his every belief.

Arin's palms were sticky now, flattened against the bar. His temper slowed. He remembered the Kestrel he'd known in Herran. He didn't think about who she'd been lately. And he didn't make his increasingly frequent mistake of reimagining this new Kestrel—so fully Valorian, so nicely set in the court and capital—as the person he wanted her to be.

He simply remembered the person she'd been. Arin asked that Kestrel the same question he'd asked the Kestrel dressed as a palace maid, and she gave the same answer. But this time, her *yes* was also a *no*. This time, her answer was a box with a false bottom, and the meaning of it went deeper than he had seen.

He had misunderstood her.

Arin began to think he shouldn't have walked away from that table. He should go back. He should go back right now.

And he would have, if he hadn't been distracted by a snatch of conversation from a nearby table.

A group of senators were drinking. The Broken Arm had a very mixed crowd that night, more than its usual share of courtiers. These were talking about the east.

". . . an impressive victory," said one. "Exactly the sort of thing I'd expect from General Trajan."

"He can't take all the credit," said another. "The idea was his daughter's."

"Really?"

"I was there. There was a gathering in the Winter Garden the morning after the engagement ball. Only the most important members of the court were invited, of course. A group of us discussed how best to take the eastern plains. The emperor even asked *my* advice. If I say so myself, my idea was very good. Yet let no one believe that I am ungenerous. I understand why the emperor preferred Lady Kestrel's plan. It was she who suggested that the general poison the horses. The eastern savages won't be able to live without them, she said. We all knew that would do the trick. And didn't it just?"

Laughter.

"To Lady Kestrel." The senator raised his cup.

"To Lady Kestrel!"

Kestrel had stood to leave the table and find Arin when she heard the cheer.

Had she been recognized?

No one was looking at the maid in the corner. Still, Kestrel grew even more anxious.

She couldn't see Arin. He was lost in the swarm of people by the bar.

Or had he left the tavern entirely? Had she offended him that much?

Kestrel was reassuring herself that Arin wouldn't leave their game unfinished, when he emerged from the crowd empty-handed.

He dragged his chair back from the table.

"Arin . . . what I said earlier, about the wound—"

"I don't want to talk about that." He sat, and repositioned his tiles.

"But I need to tell you. Arin, your face—"

"I don't care about my face!"

Kestrel shut her mouth. Arin refused to look up at her. With a nauseating dread that she didn't yet understand, she sank into her chair. "Why were those senators drinking to me?"

He didn't answer.

"Do you know why?"

Arin met her gaze with an unflinching stare. "Play."

"You've no glass after all." She poured wine into her own. She spilled a few drops. She wiped them away with her thumb, rubbing hard at the glass, and offered it to him. He ignored her.

So Kestrel played, and watched Arin toss down tiles and claim others. She felt the pulse of his fury. It was worse than when he'd left the table. It had grown fierce, practically solid. It was the kind of anger that comes close to trembling. The game slipped from Kestrel's control.

In the end, she welcomed the loss. She would tell Arin the truth. She swore to herself that she would. Everything could be explained. She was afraid of it, afraid of the anger in him now, and of what he would do with the truth. But she would give it to him. She could no longer bear not to.

Arin said, "Did you tell the general to poison the horses of the eastern plainspeople?"

"What?"

"Did you?"

"Yes," she said haltingly, "but—"

"Do you realize what you've done? Hundreds of people—*innocent* people—died in the exodus to the queen's city."

"I know. It was a horrible thing—"

"Horrible? Children starved while their mothers wept. There are no words for that."

Guilt swelled in her throat. "I can explain."

"How do you explain murder?"

"How do *you*?" she said with a flash of her own anger. "People died because of you, too, Arin. You have killed. Your hands aren't clean. The Firstwinter Rebellion—"

"This is not the same."

He seemed to choke on his words, and Kestrel was appalled at how everything she said went so wrong. "I meant that you had your reasons."

"I can't even speak of my reasons. I can't believe that you'd bring them up, that you would *compare* . . ." His voice shook, then dropped low. "Kestrel. The empire's only reason is dominion. And you have *helped*."

"I had no choice. My father would've—"

"Thought you weak? Disowned you for not being his warrior girl, ready with the perfect plan of attack? Your father." Arin's mouth curled. "I know you want his approval. I know that you'd marry the prince to get it. But your father's hands run with blood. He is a monster. What kind of person feeds a monster? What kind of person *loves* one?"

"Arin, you're not listening. You're not thinking clearly."

"You're right. I haven't been thinking clearly, not for a long time. But I understand now." Arin pushed his tiles away. His winning hand scattered out of line. "You have changed, Kestrel. I don't know who you are anymore. And I don't want to."

Later, when Kestrel remembered this moment, she said the right things. In her imagination, he understood.

But that was not what happened.

Arin's anger curdled into disgust. He was sick with it. She could tell. She could tell from the swift way he stood, as if escaping contamination. She saw it in the set of his shoulders when he turned his back, even as she called to him. Arin walked away. He let the tavern door slam behind him.

It was silent in the palace gallery. Bones must be silent like this, Kestrel thought, when they lay deep in the earth.

She stood in front of Tensen's painting longer than she actually looked at it. Finally, she set a moth on its frame. She told herself the kind of lie that knows itself for what it is. Kestrel decided that it was better that Arin think this way of her.

Yes. It had all been for the best.

"AND WHAT," SAID THE EMPEROR, "IS SO UR-
GENT THAT YOU MUST RETURN TO HERRAN
now?"

"My duty to you, Your Imperial Majesty," said Arin.

"He speaks so handsomely," the emperor said to the
court, and the senators and lords and ladies hid their smirks
in a way that showed them all the more. There was no longer anything handsome about the governor of Herran.

Risha didn't smile. From across the room, Arin caught
the easterner's gaze: somber and steady.

"I'm not sure what to think about this request for my
permission for you to leave," the emperor said. "Governor,
have you been . . . treated *badly* here?"

Arin smiled with the cut side of his face. "Not at all."

The courtiers whispered delightedly. It was as good as a
play. The disfigured face. The emperor's slippery mockery.
The pretense that nothing was wrong.

"What if we enjoy having you at court?" said the emperor.

Arin stepped more fully into the light. He saw, as if outside himself, the way he stood before the emperor in this echoing state room. Arin hadn't slept since he'd left Kestrel in the city the night before, but he felt extremely lucid. He knew how the morning sun caught the dust motes around him. It cast a harsh glare on his slashed face. It picked out the frayed threads of his clothes. And it paused, lingering, over the dagger strapped to his hip, and the way Arin's hand was curled around the hilt and covered its seal. The blade was unsheathed. It had two cutting edges. The crossguard was short, meant to protect a much smaller hand than Arin's, and was hooked in the Valorian style. Everything about the dagger was Valorian.

The courtiers buzzed.

His face.

Who did it?

That blade.

Whose is it?

That's a lady's dagger. How did he get it?

Stole it, maybe.

Or . . . could it have been a gift?

Arin almost heard the whispered words.

"Your welcome has been so much more than I could expect," Arin said. The emperor smiled a little. His eyes didn't leave Arin's hand on the dagger's hilt. Arin was glad. He thought that the emperor was quite pleased with his son's engagement to the military's favorite daughter. The marriage would make General Trajan part of the imperial family . . . and would renew the soldiers' loyalty to the emperor.

But there were those rumors. Even the minting of an

engagement coin hadn't laid them to rest. It was the first time that Arin thought of the rumors about him and Kestrel coldly. He thought about them as something he could use. Yes, Arin bargained that if he lifted his hand to reveal the hilt and seal of Kestrel's dagger, it would be recognized. Courtiers would gasp.

Arin could make rumor look real.

A Valorian always wore her dagger, except in the bath or bed. Whether the courtiers judged it a theft or gift, they would think very hard about how close Arin must have been to Kestrel in order to take her blade.

"As much as I would dearly love to stay," Arin said, "if I'm to govern your territory in a way that will please you, I must return to it."

"A serious young man, aren't you?"

"Yes." Arin shifted his grip on the hilt—not so much as to reveal the seal, but to show that he would.

The emperor didn't like that. Neither would Kestrel if she were here, or Tensen, who had gone to his beloved gallery at dawn and was probably there still. The minister wouldn't like anything at all about what Arin was doing. Blackmail the emperor? In front of the court?

Arin wasn't supposed to be in possession of that dagger. He was supposed to be dead, or mutilated beyond recognition. Or both. It felt good to remind the emperor of his mistake. It felt good to threaten him with having to explain to the court why the dagger of his son's bride was strapped to another man's hip.

"Am I free to go?" Arin asked.

"My dear governor, what a question! We'll miss you, of course, but we would not hold you here."

Arin thought that he was going to leave the state room without any mention made of the prickling red-and-black wound that crawled down his face. But the emperor said sweetly, "Those are very neat seams," and then Arin was dismissed.

"Fair tides to you," called a voice behind him in the empty hallway outside the state room.

Arin turned and saw Risha. Her words had a warm but stilted quality that suggested that her farewell was an eastern one, translated into Valorian.

"I'm glad to see you go," Risha said. "You don't belong here. People who don't belong pay for it."

Arin instinctively touched his cut cheek and winced. Then he grit his teeth. His face wasn't his face anymore, but so what? Maybe it suited him. Maybe Arin had been too soft, too trusting, too baby-skinned, too much like that boy he'd been before the war, the one who had made him turn back to find Kestrel standing by the moonlit canal.

Arin was glad that boy was gone. He was glad to be someone new.

"I don't know how you bear it," he told Risha in Valorian. The words came slow and heavy. He hated the feel of that language on his tongue.

Risha frowned. "Bear what? Living in the imperial court?" She shook her head. "My place is here."

It was dangerous to mention Tensen, or the information Arin's spymaster had suggested Risha might give them. They were alone for now, but the state room doors could open at any time. Quickly, in his own language, Arin said, "Thank you."

A look of confusion crossed Risha's face. "I don't speak Herrani," she reminded him in Valorian.

Arin might have said more, but then the state room doors *did* open. The court began to file out and look at them. He turned away. He left with his unsaid words burning inside him. *Thank you*, he wanted to say again, with wonder at the thought that Risha would risk herself for a people not her own.

How different she was, Arin thought as he walked away. His mouth was tight and tasted metallic, as if he'd bitten his tongue.

How different Risha was from Kestrel.

A fish thrashed against the board. Kestrel saw the fishmonger bring the mallet down hard. She flinched, though she knew that a palace maid wouldn't be bothered by this sight. A maid wouldn't glance twice at the pink slush of frozen blood at the base of the stalls in the Butcher's Row. A palace maid wouldn't stare at the slick organs in the gutter and realize that she'd never seen the inside of a chicken, or paid any thought to it.

Kestrel made herself look hard at the slurry that ran down the Row. When her throat closed up, there was a reason right before her. It was there in the disgusting street. It was on the damp wood of the fishmonger's mallet. It wasn't in the Broken Arm tavern last night, or in Arin's wounded face turning away from her. It wasn't in what she'd done to deserve it.

She pulled the sailor's coat tight around her, and lifted the blue-and-white hem of her work dress as she walked down the Row.

A little Valorian girl ran ahead of her, braided ropes of white-blond hair bouncing against her shoulders. The girl gripped a cloth doll by the arm. Something about the doll caught Kestrel's eye, and she wasn't sure why until the child caught up to her mother and begged for another toy the woman carried in her basket. It was a boy doll dressed in black. Then Kestrel noticed the golden thread stitched across the girl doll's brow and realized who these toys were supposed to be.

Kestrel pushed past the girl and her mother. She tried to forget the doll. She looked for Tensen.

She found him inspecting a gutted suckling pig that hung from a hook in a stall. "Oh, good," he said when he saw Kestrel. "Just in time. I might have had to buy a pig to keep up appearances, and who knows how I would have smuggled *that* back into my rooms."

They merged into the crowd of shoppers—servants, mostly, sent to get the morning meat while it was fresh. Kestrel and Tensen worked their way to the end of the line of stalls and up the slope of a hill, where there were few people.

"The Senate leader has been to southern Herran," Kestrel told him. "I can think of only one reason. The emperor asked him to inspect the hearthnut harvest and gauge how large the crop will be. The emperor must plan to take it all from Herran. He'll know if you try to hold back any for yourselves."

Tensen looked older in the outside light, his wrinkles deeper, his eyes nearly lashless. "This will mean famine."

Slowly, Kestrel said, "I have an idea."

Tensen waited. When she remained silent, he raised his brows.

"It might not be a good idea," she said.

"It must be better than nothing."

"I'm not so sure." She thought of the horses of the eastern plains. She heard Arin saying *murder*. That word had raked claws through his voice. It had sunk them deep into her.

Tensen placed one hand on her shoulder. For all that his hand was light while the general's was heavy, the gesture reminded Kestrel of her father. "You could harvest the crop early and hide it," she told Tensen, "but leave some hearthnuts on the trees. Then infect them. Choose your favorite pest. Gull wasp, beetles, caterpillars . . . whatever will breed quickly. When the emperor asks for the crop, it won't be your fault if you've nothing to give him." Tensen's smile warmed. Kestrel wondered what her father's father had been like, or her mother's, and whether if she had had a grandfather, he would look at her like this. "If the emperor believes you're lying, he can see the wasted fields for himself. But . . . it might ruin the trees. You might starve next year when nothing but worms grow in your fields."

"We'll worry about next year if we come to it," said Tensen. He squinted at a few pinpricks of snow. They were just starting to come down. "Arin's been pressing me to say who provided the information about poor Thrynne."

Her heart jumped. "What did you tell him? You can't tell him it was me. You promised."

"Don't worry. We both know what it means to lie for the right reasons. I won't share your secret. I insisted on my informant's anonymity. I called her the Moth. That doesn't bother you, does it? Being named after a lowly household pest?"

The corner of Kestrel's mouth lifted. "I don't mind being a moth. I would probably start eating silk if it meant that I could fly."

The sleeve's cuff had finally frayed. Arin pitched the shirt into the trunk. He unstrapped the sheathed dagger, whose almost slight weight made him uneasy. He didn't like to have Kestrel's dagger on him. But he also didn't like the idea of packing it away, or leaving it behind. He glanced back at the openmouthed trunk. The unraveling shirt rested on top of its contents.

Arin set the dagger aside. He reached for the shirt again and tugged on a thread. It spun free, a spider's line that Arin wrapped around one finger until it cut off the circulation. He gave a sharp yank. The thread broke from the shirt. He stared at it.

It was crazy, the thought that a simple string could help

Herran. But Arin left his rooms, sought Deliah, and asked her for spools of thread in many colors.

"You smell like fish," Arin told Tensen when the minister entered the suite.

"My shoes, I think. I stepped in something." Tensen glanced up and saw the closed trunk with its tightened straps waiting by the door. "Arin, are you leaving me?"

"I'm no good here."

"Do you think you will do more good in Herran? I hate to be rude, but surely you understand by now that being a governor means little more than giving the emperor whatever he wants. Your cousin's been able to manage that just fine in your absence."

"I'm not going to Herran. I'm going to the east."

Tensen blinked, then frowned. He passed a palm over the trunk. He fiddled with the straps. "What could you hope to find there?"

"Allies."

"The east doesn't make allies. The east is the east. They don't like outsiders."

"I'm not asking for your advice."

"Apparently not. Because if you were, I would remind you that people who go to that country rarely return, and those who do aren't the same."

"I could use a change."

Tensen studied him. "You were out all night. I wonder what has inspired this decision of yours."

"Tensen, we're already at war. We need to face facts. Herran will have to fight free of the empire, and we're no match for it. The east might be."

"It's illegal for a foreigner to enter Dacra."

"I'm no ordinary foreigner."

Tensen cupped his hands and opened them wide as if scattering seeds to the floor. It was the Herrani gesture of skepticism.

"Don't doubt me," Arin said.

"It's not you I doubt, but the idea. It's not safe."

"Nothing's safe. Staying here isn't safe. And going home is useless. You asked me when we first came here what I would choose, myself or my country."

"That's true," Tensen said slowly. "I did."

"*This* is my choice."

"A choice like that is easy when you don't really know what it will cost."

"Whether it's easy or not doesn't matter. What matters is that it's *mine*."

Tensen pursed his lips. The loose flesh of his neck sank gently beneath his lowered chin. Abruptly, he leveled his gaze and met Arin's. Tensen pulled the gold ring from his finger. "Take this."

"I can't take that."

"I want you to."

"It was your grandson's."

"That's why I want you to take it."

"Tensen. No."

"Am I not allowed to worry for you?" Tensen didn't look at the ring in his outstretched hand. He kept his eyes on Arin. "You'll go east no matter what I say. If you won't take my advice, the least you can do is honor an old man's gift by accepting it."

Still reluctant, Arin took the ring. It fit on his smallest finger.

"Off you go, then." Tensen patted the strapped trunk with deliberate lightness, in a way that avoided the emotion of the moment and yet also didn't, because the avoidance was evidence of Tensen's difficulty. He no longer looked at Arin directly. It made Arin wish he hadn't accepted the ring. It made him remember his mother's emerald. It made him wonder which pain was greater: to give up something precious, or to see it taken away. In a flash that he would have resisted if he could, Arin remembered Kestrel in the tavern, her lips bitten white as he'd accused her. She had looked cornered. She had looked trapped.

No, *caught*. That's how the guilty look.

"Stop in Herran on your way east," Tensen said, and Arin was glad to be torn away from his thoughts. "I have a job for you." The minister told Arin about the hearthnut harvest.

"Where'd you get this information?" Arin asked.

Tensen smiled.

"You met with the Moth," Arin said. "Outside the palace. That's why your shoes smell like fish."

"I should have cleaned them," Tensen said mournfully.

Arin tried to imagine Risha talking with Tensen on the wharf, or maybe in the Butcher's Row, but failed. "When was this meeting? It's almost noon. You weren't in the state room this morning." Neither had been Kestrel.

Arin was suddenly furious with himself. He knew exactly which way his thoughts were going. He couldn't believe it. Even now, even when he *knew* what Kestrel had done, even when he'd heard her *admit* it, heard it from her very lips, Arin's mind kept playing its favorite sick game. It noted that Risha certainly hadn't smelled like fish. Not like Tensen. How conveniently Arin's imagination ignored the possibility that Risha might have spoken with Tensen and then changed her shoes before going to the state room. No, Arin's unruly mind didn't care for that logical explanation. Instead it presented Arin with the image of Kestrel in her maid's dress. Meeting with Tensen. Telling him secrets.

"Stop," Arin snapped. Tensen closed his mouth, his expression puzzled. "Just stop." Arin pressed his fingers to his temples. He rubbed hard. "You don't have to tell me where you were or when. I don't need to know."

"Arin, have I made you angry?"

"No."

"Why are you angry?"

"Only at myself." Arin's hand shifted to pinch the bridge of his nose, his thumb digging into the corner of his closed left eye. He ignored how it made the scratched eyelid smart. He wanted that image of Kestrel to go away. "It's stupid." Arin felt worn out. He'd been ill, hadn't slept. His body was very heavy.

"Gods, Arin, sit down. You look ready to fall asleep on your feet."

Yes, the tired mind plays tricks. Arin knew that. His hand dropped from his face. He found a chair, sat, and felt better. More focused. "I went into the city last night," he told Tensen. "I asked the bookkeeper about bets on the wedding dress. The chief palace engineer knows how to play the odds."

Tensen listened to Arin explain what he had learned from the bookkeeper. "So if the emperor paid the senator for his secret trip to Herran with a golden bet," Tensen said, "it's possible that the water engineer is profiting from some similar favor."

"Look into it."

"I will, but what would you have me do with what I learn? Sending a message to you in the eastern queen's city is impossible."

"There's the temple island," Arin said. Dacrans worshipped one god, and since all were free to worship her, foreigners were allowed to dock at a holy island off the country's southern coast. It was a great center of trade. "You can send a message there."

"Even so, we'd risk the message falling into unfriendly hands. Messenger hawks can be captured, codes broken—"

"First someone would have to realize he's looking at a code." Arin produced the sack of spooled threads. "Do you remember Favor-Keeping?"

The hours lengthened. The time for the midday meal came and went, and Arin and Tensen ignored their gnawing hunger as they sorted out the threaded code, how each color would represent a person, as did the Favor-Keeper's ball of strings throughout the years of slavery. Arin tied a different number of knots for each letter of the Herrani alphabet. He braided meaning into the way one color would cross another, and in the end he held something that looked like a piece of trim that could be sewn on the cuff of a sleeve and worn openly. A new fashion. To most eyes, it would look like nothing more than decoration.

Black was the emperor. Yellow, the prince. Tensen chose green for himself. "Here." Arin had handed him the spool of gray. "For your Moth." He added, "For Risha."

Tensen smiled.

It wasn't until they had assigned a color for almost every key courtier that Tensen said slowly in a way Arin would remember, "Don't you want a thread for Lady Kestrel?"

"No. I don't."

From Kestrel's windows that day, she saw banners on the barbican rise and blow toward the sea with a wind that must have been warm. A fine rain—not snow—blurred the view. Firstspring would come sooner than Kestrel wanted. Then Firstsummer, and the wedding.

Alone, she shook dead masker moths from their envelope of paper onto a mosaic marble table. She'd given half of her moths to Tensen in the market, in case he wanted to leave one for her on the painting in the gallery.

Kestrel watched moths change to match the mosaic. Then she pushed one with a delicate finger and watched it change again.

She felt a surge of anger at the moths for hiding so well. She resisted an urge to crush them.

Couldn't she try to explain herself to Arin? Last night, Kestrel had been ready to tell him everything. She still could.

Uncertain, Kestrel swept the moths back into their packet.

Deliah came. Kestrel had forgotten that she was supposed to be fitted for a day dress. The Herrani woman pinned around her. Kestrel watched the window mist with rain.

Deliah paused in her pinning. "I think you should know that Arin left today. He sailed when the wind rose."

Kestrel's gaze flinched away. She looked again toward the window as if she would be able to see the harbor, and beyond that, the waves, and on the waves, a ship. But all Kestrel saw were the battlements of the palace. The rain had stopped. It had lifted its gray veil. The sky was clean now, and brutally clear.

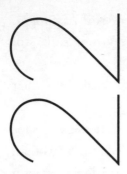

YOUNG COURTIERS WERE MAKING KITES FOR the city's war orphans. Waxed black parchment was glued to stick frames and painted with the golden eyes and feathers of birds of prey. Kestrel and Verex would bring them to the orphanage on Firstspring.

In the large solarium, which had been added to the palace after the Herrani invasion as if the emperor had seized the whole history of Herrani architecture along with its country, Kestrel made a paper chain for a kite's tail. At other tables, courtiers talked quietly. Kestrel sat alone. Her fingers moved quickly, but she felt as if someone else was making them move, and that she was no more than that cloth doll she'd seen carried through the crowd of the Butcher's Row.

Kestrel thought of visiting the children. She thought of telling them how their parents had brought honor to the empire. She thought of a ship sailing far away from her.

Her fingers stopped. Her throat closed. Kestrel summoned a new set of paints. She began to cover her kites with swirls of green and blue and pink.

Kestrel heard a rustle of silk as a woman claimed a nearby chair.

"Very pretty," Maris commented. "But not military colors."

Kestrel dipped her brush in a jar of water, rang it noisily around, and then set it in a pot of violet. "They're children, not soldiers."

"Why, you're right, of course. This is much more cheerful! Here, let me help."

Kestrel eyed her briefly, but Maris contented herself with painting in silence. After making her second kite look like a gaudy butterfly, Maris said, "Your friend has a delicious brother. Tell me all about him. Is he taken?"

Kestrel lifted her brush. Paint dribbled down her sleeve. "What?"

"Lord Ronan. Very lucky, isn't it, that the conquering of Herran gave us so many more titled young men? All that new territory, so nicely portioned out by the emperor ten years ago, with lovely titles to go with it. Too bad the land is gone. But a lord is a lord forever. And he is *such* a lord! Just the other day, I saw Ronan fight in the city, and—"

"You didn't. You can't have."

Maris's eyes flashed. "He's not yours to keep or give."

"That's not what I meant."

"We can't all be empresses. I must marry. I am nearly twenty." Maris's voice dropped. "I don't want to go to war."

"I meant that you must have seen someone else in the city." Kestrel tried to speak evenly, but she already didn't believe her own words. "Ronan isn't in the capital. He went with Jess and their parents to the south."

"I assure you, he didn't."

"They went away." Kestrel's lips had gone numb. "For Jess's health."

Maris's expression changed. Kestrel saw it shift from confusion to a curious understanding before it settled, finally, into a kindness that made Kestrel's stomach clench. "Lady Kestrel," said Maris, "you are mistaken. I have wondered why their family avoids the court, but Jess and Ronan attend many functions in the city. I have seen them several times. They've been in the capital ever since your engagement ball."

Kestrel went to Jess's townhome in the city. Jess's footman took her card, embossed with her personal seal, and accepted her into the receiving room, which was lined with polished, crossed spears. There was no trace of dust. The house showed no signs of having been closed up for a family journey south.

"The lady is not at home," the footman said.

"But the family's in residence?" Kestrel pressed. "Is Jess *usually* here?"

The footman shifted, and was silent.

"Is her brother home?" Kestrel asked.

When the footman still said nothing, Kestrel said, "Do you know who I am?"

The footman confessed that Ronan kept odd hours. "He's often not here. And his sister—"

"If she's not here, then I'll wait in the parlor until she

returns," Kestrel said, though this proposal risked seeing Ronan.

The footman fidgeted. "I wouldn't recommend that, my lady. I believe that both brother and sister will be out for a great deal of time."

"I'll wait."

And she did. She was determined to sleep on the parlor divan if she must.

The fire throbbed low. Her tea grew cold.

She remembered Jess frowning in her sleep. She remembered crushing the glass petal of Jess's necklace against the marble mantel.

Was Jess's silence her absence, her lies—because of that broken gift? Maybe that was Kestrel's offense. But she had told Jess, and Jess had forgiven her. Hadn't she?

Or . . .

What had Ronan told Jess? Kestrel had thought his pride would keep him from ever telling his sister about his marriage proposal to Kestrel on Firstwinter night—and his rejection, and whom Kestrel had preferred over him.

Dread ate at her. When the clock struck the third hour, she shifted against a cushion. It released a trace of Jess's perfume. A white flower from Herran. It bloomed behind Kestrel's eyes.

The scent was fresh.

The parlor had a view of the road. Kestrel could see her own carriage, and her escort waiting inside it.

Kestrel fought the realization. She didn't want to understand. But she did . . . she envisioned so clearly how Jess had been sitting on this very sofa when Kestrel's carriage had pulled up. Jess had left word with a footman. Then she'd retreated to another part of the house. She was waiting there. She was waiting for Kestrel to leave.

The perfume watered Kestrel's eyes.

"I'll return another day," she told the footman on her way out, but when she stepped into the carriage, Kestrel glanced up over her shoulder and caught a flutter of fabric in a high window of the town house. A curtain had been drawn aside. Someone was watching her.

The instant Kestrel looked at it, the curtain fell.

As Kestrel walked through the barbican, she overheard palace guards laughing.

"Where's he disappeared to these days?" one of them said.

"The kennels," answered another. "He's been playing with puppies in the muck. The perfect place for our illustrious prince, if you ask me."

Kestrel stopped. She returned, and approached the guards. They weren't afraid, which meant they thought she shared their contempt.

She looked at the guard who had spoken last. Kestrel slapped his face. In the shocked silence that followed, Kestrel clenched her stinging hand and walked away.

Verex was holed up in one of the kennel's pens, sitting on a nest of filthy straw and nursing a puppy with a rag sopped in milk. The puppy was peacefully floppy in Verex's hands, its skin wrinkled and loose, eyes closed.

When Verex saw Kestrel, he almost looked like an animal himself, cornered and wary. "Don't say it," he told her.

"Say what?"

"Whatever you're going to say."

She leaned over the barrier of the wooden pen. "Will you show me how to do that?"

The hand holding the rag lifted in surprise. Milk dripped onto the puppy.

Kestrel entered the pen, sat next to Verex on the straw, and held out a cupped hand.

"No." He brought her left palm up to meet her right and form a bowl. "Like this." He eased the little animal into her hands. It was a yielding warmth, soft and boneless. Its whole body moved with its breath. Kestrel wondered if she'd been like this, as a baby in her father's arms, and if he had been quieted and comforted to hold her as she held this creature.

"It's a runt," Verex said. "Its mother won't nurse it." He showed her how to nudge the milk rag into the puppy's mouth.

"There's something I have to tell you."

The prince fiddled with a bit of straw. "Oh, I figured it out. It's not hard to guess what my father holds over you." He caught her startled look. "Not when you know him like I do. He'd have this hound's neck snapped even if its dam nursed it after all. He doesn't like weaklings. But he loves to discover a weakness. And now your governor is gone."

She kept her blurred eyes on the puppy. "That's not what I meant. That's not what I wanted to say."

"But it's the truth. You love him. That's your weakness. One way or another, it's why you agreed to marry me."

Kestrel smoothed a thumb over the soft flip of one tiny ear. She looked at the puppy, blind and asleep even while sucking at the milk.

Verex said, "No one likes to be used."

"I'm sorry. I didn't mean to use you."

"Honestly, I *expect* to be used. This is the court. I never thought . . . well, I'm my father's son, aren't I? Of course my marriage would be arranged. Of course I wouldn't get to choose. I know that I've been angry. I know that I *am*, and that it eats at me, but . . . I would have understood, Kestrel, about the engagement. I understand you now. You could have told me *why*."

"Do you think that *why* really matters?"

"Don't you?"

"Verex, I've done something horrible." The puppy's ribs rose and fell as Kestrel told Verex about her plan to poison the horses of the eastern plains, and why she'd suggested it.

He was silent. One hand twitched in the straw. Kestrel thought he meant to take the puppy away from her, but he didn't.

She said, "I've heard that you don't agree with the war in the east."

"My father says I'm soft. He's right."

"You must blame me all the more."

"For being hard?" He brushed his fair hair out of his eyes so that he could see her better. "Is that what you think you are?"

"If I hadn't suggested poison, maybe the plains wouldn't

have been burned after all. Maybe our army would have done nothing."

He gave a cynical laugh.

She said, "If I'd never talked with your father, at least whatever *did* happen wouldn't have been my fault."

"I'm not sure that not knowing is the same thing as innocence." He leaned back into the rustling, smelly straw. "I think that you did the best that you could. Risha will think so, too, when I tell her."

"No. Don't tell her. Please."

"I tell her everything," he said simply.

Kestrel's gaze fell again to the puppy. She wondered what it would be like to be able to tell someone everything. She stroked the soft creature. "Will it live?"

"I hope so."

A quick, hot liquid streamed through Kestrel's fingers. She yelped. The puppy's urine trickled down her sleeve.

Verex widened his already large eyes. "*That* was lucky."

"Lucky?"

"That's not all puppies do, you know. It could have been worse."

Kestrel smiled. "That's true," she said. "You're right." Her smile grew, and became a laugh.

Her maids were horrified. They ran a bath and practically stripped the clothes from her. But Kestrel nursed that floating feeling of forgiveness Verex had given her. It buoyed her in the warm bath.

She asked to be alone.

The bath cooled. Her hair, water-dark, lay flat and sleek over her breasts like armor.

Arin had changed her. It was time to admit that.

Kestrel stood in the bath. The water sheeted from her. She wrapped herself, oddly and unreasonably shy with her own nakedness.

What kind of change had Arin wrought?

She thought back to last summer, and how it had felt as if he were thumbing her eyes wide open to see her world. She thought about the puppy, velvety blind, and her wish never to have heard any plan for the eastern plains, so that she wouldn't bear any responsibility for what had been done.

Kestrel thought that she needed to open her eyes wider. She looked.

There was the plush robe around her, for the prince's bride must have comfort. She saw stained glass set in the bathing room windows, for a Valorian must have beauty. Gold rings glimmered wetly on Kestrel's wrinkled fingers. The general's wars had won luxury for his daughter.

And there were the rules. They hung invisible in the humid air. But who had decided them? Who had decided that a Valorian honors her word? Who had convinced her father that the empire must continue to eat other countries whole, and that slaves were Valoria's due right of conquest?

Her father held his honor so firmly, like a solid thing, something that couldn't twist free. It occurred to Kestrel that she had wondered before what her father's honor was like, and Arin's, but she didn't know the shape of her own.

There was dishonor, she decided, in accepting someone else's idea of honor without question.

Kestrel bent to touch the faucet and pipe of the bath. There was running water in Herrani houses, for fountains, mostly, but the imperial palace was veined with an ingenious system of pipes that pumped in warm water from thermal sources in the mountain, heated it further with a furnace, and swept it up to the highest floors. This system had been invented by the chief water engineer, the one who had designed the canals.

On the day after Arin had left, Tensen had asked Kestrel to investigate something. "The chief water engineer has done the emperor a favor," he'd said. "Could you find out what it was?"

Kestrel lifted her hand from the still warm bath pipe that led to the floor and vanished into it. She went to the window, and stood in the light of its brilliant stain. Her hands glowed blue and deep pink. She unlatched and swung open the window. Everything went clear. The air was raw. Kestrel could scent it on the wind: that thing that was going to blow her forward in time, to warmth, flowers blooming, trees in pollen and then spread green.

Spring.

ON THE SIXTH DAY AT SEA, ARIN STOPPED being seasick. That night, there were no clouds. Stars frosted the sky. The ship was becalmed.

Arin was on deck, turning Kestrel's dagger in his hands. In the end, he'd decided to take it with him. It was his now, by his own blood. Or so he told himself.

He sheathed it. He tipped his head back and gazed at the wide band of stars that arched over him in a glittery smear.

Sarsine had seemed so tired when Arin had seen her on his way from the capital. He'd worried over her wan face and shadowed eyes.

She'd snorted. "It's the food."

"What's wrong with it?"

"There's too little of it." She'd sighed then, and said that all of Herran was tired.

"That will change," he told her. He explained how to save the hearthnut harvest. Sarsine had touched the back of his hand in gratitude. Then she'd looked at him hard.

Her eyes were bright. She said, "Look at what they did to you."

"It's nothing."

But she wept over his changed face, which made him feel worse about it. Arin let her. He didn't know what else to do.

Later, Sarsine said, "Now tell me what you haven't told me."

So he had told her about Kestrel. Arin recalled it now as he shifted to look out over the black mirror of the sea.

Sarsine had been quiet. They'd been in the library of his family home, not the salon. Kestrel's piano was in the salon. Though out of sight, the instrument had loomed in his mind: large, shining. Intrusive. He wanted to rid himself of it.

Sarsine said, "This doesn't sound like her."

Arin shot her a cold glance.

"You know her better than I do," Sarsine admitted.

He shook his head. "I've been lying to myself."

It seemed that he'd been confused for a long time, that the last clear thing he'd done was to declare that the emperor's treaty was a trick. Arin knew that his army would have lost that day. The Valorians had already breached the city walls. But the fight would have been vicious. The Herrani would have fought to the death. They would have killed as many as they could. The treaty ended up being a bloodless victory for the emperor: a way to drain Herran's resources without losing another Valorian soldier.

It could be a trick, Kestrel had said, *but you will choose it.*

It had been snowing then. Snow had caught in her eyelashes. He used to wonder what would have happened if he had reached to brush it away. He used to imagine the snowflakes melting beneath his fingertips. It shamed him to remember this.

Arin hadn't fallen asleep on the deck of his strangely still ship, yet it felt as if he'd been dreaming. As if dreams and memories and lies were all the same thing.

He startled at the sound of a fish breaking the water. He had no idea how long he had been standing there. The stars had moved in the sky.

Chilled, tired, Arin went below.

He left winter behind him. The wind had picked up. It luffed the sails. It filled their canvas bellies. The Herrani captain, who had been somewhat of a legend before the war, was pleased. The ship sped over the waves.

The sun became melted butter. Arin stripped away his father's hot, threadbare jacket. He didn't want to wear it again.

The sea sheered into green: marvelously clear. Arin saw whole worlds in the water below. Fish broke away and came together and rearranged themselves like pieces of a colored puzzle.

Once, a creature leaped out of the water. Its dorsal fin was scalloped and pink. It made a strange, whistling cry, then dived under again.

Arin's wound finally healed. He tugged out the stitches himself.

He was truly in eastern waters now. The wind and sea and sun made it easier not to think.

Though not always. There was a shining hot day when the sun was high over Arin's head and he saw what he thought was the shadow of the ship in the water. Then the large shadow shifted and slid in a way that made no sense. Arin stared, realizing that the shadow was in fact an enormous sea creature swimming far below the ship. He hadn't understood what he'd seen.

He heard Tensen's words again: *You're seeing what you want to see.*

Arin thought of Kestrel, and wondered if some wounds ever heal. His heart thumped in his ears. He was stunned all over again by his anger.

But what does Tensen want you to see? whispered a voice inside him. The very thought was an insult to Tensen, who had warned Arin from the first about his obsession with Kestrel.

Arin could now appreciate—in a gritty, unpleasant way—that Kestrel had been honest with him. For a long time, she'd tried to make things clear. She'd sent troops to attack Arin's forces after she'd fled Herran. She'd told him of her engagement. She had not once—Arin cringed to think of it—responded to his advances. And when he'd asked her about the Valorian attack on the eastern plains, she hadn't denied her involvement. The guilt had been plain on her face.

The noon sun beat down on Arin's head. He hammered his thoughts into a kind of nonthinking: smooth and burnished like a shield.

Arin spun Tensen's ring around his finger, but didn't take it off.

The ship swam through the jade waters of the delta toward the eastern queen's city. Then the vessel could go no farther. Arin gave Tensen's ring to the captain. Arin had wrapped it in a handkerchief edged with a stitched, coded message.

The message told Tensen that Arin had arrived safely in the queen's city. A white lie. It was almost true. Arin didn't want the old man to worry. As for the ring—

I couldn't bear to lose such a gift, Arin had sewn onto the handkerchief.

Then he had strapped on Kestrel's dagger, which he rather wished he *would* lose.

Arin was lowered alone in a launch. He rowed away from the ship, which would sail back to Herran. The captain would pass the ring and message into other hands. There was a slight risk the ring wouldn't make it to Tensen. It could be intercepted by a Valorian. But Arin trusted himself with it less, and wasn't worried that the ring itself might be identified. It was very plain.

Arin faced the ship as he rowed away. When he rowed up a thin river fringed with reeds, he could no longer see the ship. Twice, tempestuous bursts of rain came out of nowhere, soaked him to the skin, and vanished.

The river gave way to winding canals. The city had begun. It was made from white, slick stone, with little bridges over each canal like bracelets on a lady's arm. Somewhere, a bell began to ring in its tower.

Arin was just beginning to navigate the city's watery labyrinth . . . but not the stares. The canal glided with sleek vessels that made his launch look like a duck. Even if that hadn't marked him as a foreigner, his skin would have. People stopped what they were doing to look at him. A child washing laundry in the canal was so startled that he let go of the shirt in his hands. It floated out into the canal, then was sucked under.

Word must have traveled ahead of Arin, or loped along the banks of the canals.

Grappling hooks spun out over the water and snared Arin's launch. One bit into his arm and tore a small red line.

Arin's boat was dragged to a pier, where he was quickly seized.

THE PRISON WASN'T TERRIBLE. HE HAD A TINY window with a view of the sky.

Arin had tried to explain when they'd hauled him off the boat, but even though his language felt close to Dacran, like a thin skin was all that separated them from understanding him, the easterners regarded him with the same uncomprehending frustration Arin felt.

Their black eyes were lined with sunset colors. Both men and women had closely cropped hair, and wore the same loose white trousers and shirts. When a sudden rainfall plummeted down with a violence that bounced raindrops off the paved bank of the canal, it soaked through the white fabric, revealing trim muscle.

Kestrel's dagger was taken. At the sight of an imperial weapon, something hardened in the air between Arin and them.

A woman had asked him a curt question.

"Look at me," Arin had said. "I'm no Valorian." The

Dacrans could see his dark hair, the gray Herrani eyes. They must know that he had been their enemies' slave.

But his last word had made matters worse. The tension tightened.

"Please," he said then. "I need to speak with your queen."

That was understood.

There was a sudden surge toward him. His arms were wrenched behind his back. His hands were bound, and he was dragged away.

In his cell, Arin passed his hand over the rectangle of blue sky. He blocked it, revealed it, blocked it again. Then he let the color fully in. The walls of his schoolroom in Herran had been painted this shade. Arin thought of the times when his father came to listen to his lesson in logic, and told the tutor to leave. He would take over from there.

The quiet pleasure of that memory tried to keep Arin company. When it slipped away, Arin knew that he was afraid.

A foreigner armed with an imperial dagger, asking to see the queen?

Arin had been so stupid. But not quite stupid enough to be able to ignore what might lie in store for him once someone opened that prison door.

Arin rubbed at his cheek, felt the raised and tender scar. He was no stranger to pain. The Valorians had shown him the ways a body can betray you.

When Arin was a slave in the quarries, Cheat had tried to teach him about it, too. It was for Arin's own good, he'd said. Arin should learn to resist it. Cheat had cut Arin's inner arm with a sharp stone. Arin had gasped at the blood. He'd dragged at Cheat's grip. "Stop," he'd said. "Please."

"All right, all right." Cheat finally let go. "I don't want to do this, either. What can I say? I'm too fond of you."

And Arin, who had been twelve years old, felt ashamed and grateful.

There were various ends to the story of this eastern prison cell, this window. Most of them weren't good. Arin didn't know how he would do under torture.

He remembered telling his plan to Tensen. He'd travel to the east. He'd gain the queen's sympathy and help. Easy. In his memory, Arin's own voice sounded almost blithe.

No, not quite.

Arin had been *eager* to leave the capital. Desperate. He had needed to escape, and he knew whom he was fleeing. How could Arin ever trust his instincts, when Kestrel had proven him so grievously wrong? Arin should have known that sailing to the east was a bad idea. He swore that from now on, he would doubt everything he was tempted to believe.

There were footsteps, multiple ones, approaching the other side of his solid cell door.

Logic is a game, came the memory of his father's voice. *Let's see how you play.*

There was a window in his cell.

A prisoner would be drawn to it, like an insect to light. Like he had been.

Whoever was coming would expect to see him near it.

Arin moved away.

He positioned himself in the path the door's swing

would take. When it opened, and someone began to step forward, Arin slammed the door back against him. Arin hauled the man close and choked an arm around his neck.

The guard cried out in his language.

"Let me go," Arin said, even though it was he who held the man tight. "Get me out of here."

The Dacran wheezed. He scratched Arin's arms, his face. He spoke again, and Arin remembered only then that he'd heard more than one set of footsteps.

The other set belonged to a man standing in the doorway.

"Do something!" Arin thought the guard in his grasp must be trying to say. Because the second Dacran was oddly still. Arin peered, not understanding what kept him back from the fray, or from bargaining for the safety of his friend.

The silent man took one step into the cell. The light caught his face. Arin's grip on the guard tightened.

The man in the doorway had a skull's face. The tip of his nose was gone, the nostrils unnaturally wide slits. A scar that grazed the upper lip showed that the knife had gone downward to cut off the nose. The man's ears were nothing but holes.

"You," the man said to Arin in Herrani. "I remember you."

THE DAY BEFORE KESTREL HAD BOUGHT HIM.

The eastern slave who had tried to run away.

The emperor will get what he deserves, he had told Arin.

"I see that you, too, have earned your marks," said the Dacran as he stood in the cell's doorway. "But you still aren't as good-looking as me."

"Who are you?"

"Your translator. Are you going to let him go?" He nodded at the guard, who had gone unconscious in Arin's grip.

"What will happen to me if I do?"

"Something nicer than if you don't. Come, youngling. Do you think my queen would have bothered to send someone who speaks your language if she meant you harm?"

Arin let the guard slide to the floor.

"Good boy," said the skull-faced man, and lifted a hand. Arin thought it was to touch his scar, or maybe to place a palm to his cheek as Herrani men did. That gesture wasn't appropriate with a stranger, let alone someone from another country, yet Arin decided to allow it.

The man wore a heavy ring, and the hand went not to Arin's face but his neck.

The ring stung Arin. It drove in a little needle that fuzzed the blood.

Arin's limbs became lead. Darkness climbed up his body, opened its wide mouth, and swallowed him whole.

Someone was weeping. Her tears fell warm on his brow, his lashes, his mouth.

Don't cry, he tried to say.

Please listen, she said.

He would, of course he would. How could she think that he wouldn't? But when Arin tried to answer her, there was only a rustling of air in his throat. He thought of leaves. He remembered the punishment of the god of music, how he had been cast into the body of a tree for one cycle of the pantheon: one hundred years of silence. Arin felt his skin splitting into bark. Twigs burst from him. Leaves grew. They stuffed his mouth with green. The wind swayed his branches.

Arin opened his eyes. Water dropped in. He blinked, and realized that no one had been weeping over him after all. He was on a boat beneath the rain. He was trussed up and flat on his back in a slow-moving, narrow vessel not very different from a canoe.

The rain stopped. A dragonfly with wings as large as a bird's swept over him. It shimmered red against the suddenly blue sky.

Arin strained against his bonds.

The boat shifted, and a face leaned over him. The eastern man's mutilations were starker in open daylight. He tsked. "Didn't it occur to you, little Herrani, that the queen might have sent me to translate an interrogation of a not-so-friendly nature? You're too trusting."

With a fingernail, he flicked open a tiny compartment on the underside of his ring. He touched Arin, and the skull and the sky and the red dragonfly were gone.

The emperor was furious. He showed it in certain ways.

To the Herrani minister of agriculture, who had been the one to break the news of the infested hearthnut crop, the emperor sent a personal invitation to a theatrical performance of the conquest of Herran. Tensen had a front row seat and was spattered with animal blood during the killing of the Herrani royal family.

The court used flattering ways to soften the emperor's mood. This irritated him with disastrous consequences. Many aristocrats found that their sons and daughters had abruptly "decided" to enlist in the military, and were sent east.

"Just stay out of his way," Verex told Kestrel.

"It's no one's fault that gall wasps ruined the crop. He can't blame me."

"He blames everybody."

But to Kestrel the emperor was unfailingly kind—doting, even, until the day that he announced that she was to attend a military parade at the end of the week. "Your father is coming home."

In her mind, Kestrel was a girl again, clambering onto her pony to ride out to meet her father, to be the first to see him so brave on his horse, gloriously grimed by battle. She wore a child-size sword he'd had made for her. He smiled to see her. He called her his little warrior.

"Careful, Kestrel," said the emperor. "You can of course be yourself around *me*. There is no need to hide anything. But society won't understand such obvious happiness on your face, not when your father's been injured."

"He's hurt?"

Kestrel asked, she asked what felt like a hundred times, a thousand times, how her father was, how badly he'd been hurt, where, how. Was he coming to Valoria to rest or die?

The emperor shrugged and smiled and said that, really, he didn't know.

A black snake wound through the city. From the palace battlements, Kestrel could see the snake flash little scales of gold. She strained hard to discern the front line of the black-clad soldiers. It felt as if someone had clamped a hand down over her nose and mouth. Her fear had an airless quality.

Verex gently touched her arm.

The emperor noticed. His expression was unreadable. Verex stared back, defiant, and Kestrel felt a little better.

The battalion marched up the mountain, the boots of more than a thousand soldiers striking down on the stone road. Black flags and gold swallow-tailed pennants snapped in the wind. Kestrel took a small spyglass from her skirt pocket.

"Undignified," the emperor said. "Do you think your father will want you to see his face before he sees yours? Is he an enemy, that you would peer at him? You will show respect for my friend."

Kestrel flushed. She put the spyglass away.

They were the only three on the battlements: the emperor, the prince, and the lady. The rest of the court had collected in the inner yard, filed according to their rank, stiff and silent. Many of them knew what it meant to fight. The rest thought that they did. They all stood to attention.

Then Kestrel heard the shifting black troops march closer, and she could see, at the head of the line, one man on a horse, leading the rest.

Kestrel's heart seemed to hatch inside her and let go something that soared. Her father must be well. His injury couldn't have been bad, or he would have been borne to the palace on a litter.

Kestrel no longer cared for dignity. She ran for the stone steps leading down from the battlement. She raced down the staircase, tripping over the hem of her dress, catching at the railing, cursing her heeled shoes.

She burst into the yard just as brass horns sounded their fanfare. The barbican gates heaved open, and the battalion marched in.

The general rode his horse straight toward Kestrel. That winged feeling inside her faltered. Her father's face was gray. A wide bandage wrapped around his lower torso leaked blood.

The general halted his horse. The battalion stopped behind him, and the walls of the yard rang silent.

Kestrel stepped toward him.

"No," said her father. She stopped. He dismounted. It was agonizing to see how slow he was. Blood streaked his saddle.

Again Kestrel would have gone to him. Once he stood on the paved ground, she would have offered her arm. Not in an obvious way. Couldn't a daughter walk arm in arm with her father? But he raised his gauntleted hand.

She came close anyway. "Let me help."

"Don't shame me."

The general's words were said low, through clenched teeth. No one heard their exchange. But Kestrel felt as if everyone had, and that every single person gathered there knew everything there was to know about her and her father as he led the way inside the palace, and she was forced to follow behind.

HE REFUSED MEDICINE. "THERE'S A FINE LINE between medicine and poison," he said.

The cup was in the healer's hand, not Kestrel's, but she reacted as if she had been the one accused. "No one would poison you," she told her father.

"That's not what he means," said Verex.

Everyone looked at him, including the emperor, whose expression was like when Verex had comforted Kestrel on the battlements. The face of the imperial physician, however, showed a clear respect for the prince. Kestrel's father simply squinted and looked worn, and leaned back on the bloodied bed. Kestrel had no idea what her face showed.

"Almost anything that heals can also hurt . . . depending on the amount," said Verex. "Even in the right amount, the general might not like the side effects."

"It's only to fight infection," said the physician, "and to make you sleep."

"Exactly," said Kestrel's father. The way he looked at the cup made clear what he would do if it came any nearer.

"I need to clean the wound."

"You can do that just as well while I'm awake."

"Please, Father," said Kestrel. He ignored her.

"Old friend," said the emperor, "you've proved yourself a thousand times over. There's no need for this stubbornness."

"It could be forced down," Verex suggested. Everyone gave him a look of horror.

"You'll drink it," the emperor told General Trajan. "I order you to."

Kestrel's father sighed. "I hate being outnumbered," he said, and drank.

He blinked heavily. He turned his gaze toward Kestrel. She didn't know whether he meant to speak or only to look, and if it was to look at her, she didn't know what he wanted to see, or did see. But she held her breath, waiting for a word. A gesture. A gesture would be enough.

He closed his eyes. His face seemed to slow. He slept.

Kestrel realized that she had never seen her father sleep. Somehow that was what made the tears finally fall.

"It's not so serious," said the emperor, but the expressions on the physician's face—and Verex's—disagreed. "Come. No more tears." The emperor offered her a handkerchief, and his voice was gentle.

Verex looked away.

When the emperor had left, the physician said to Kestrel, "You should leave, too, my lady."

"No."

The physician tried to hide his impatient disapproval.

"I won't faint," she said, though she didn't trust her own promise.

"Would you mind if I stayed with you?" Verex asked her. For all that the question was meek, it managed to decide things. The healer went to work.

Verex talked to her the entire time. He described what each of the healer's tools did, and the antiseptic properties of the wash. "Abdominal wounds are dangerous," he said, "but the blade didn't damage any internal organs."

"How do you know?" asked Kestrel.

"He'd be dead by now," the healer said shortly.

It was a gash, long and deep. It exposed pink layers of flesh and went down right to yellow fat. The healer's antiseptic fizzed in the wound, and blood ran out.

Kestrel felt sickeningly light. She was going to faint after all. Then she looked at her father's sleeping face and wondered who would protect him while he slept, if not her. She kept her eyes open. She kept her feet on the ground.

"Too deep for stitches," muttered the physician.

"He's going to pack it with wet, sterile gauze instead," Verex explained. "It will heal slowly, from the inside out." The prince's voice was strong and sure. He was turning the grim words of the physician into something hopeful. "Really, that's the best way to avoid infection, because the wound can be cleaned out daily."

The physician gave him a sidelong look. "I'm not sure I need the commentary." But Kestrel did, and Verex knew that she did.

When it was finished and the gore was cleaned away, the wound hidden below swaths of gauze, Kestrel's father looked both larger and smaller than he ever had to her. His face had always seemed to be cut from stone. It was softer now. The sun lines that fanned from his closed eyes were as white as thin scars. His light brown hair held no trace of gray. He had been young when she was born. He wasn't old now. Yet he looked ancient.

The physician left. He would return, he said. Verex brought a chair so that Kestrel could sit by her father's bedside. Then he became awkward again. His stooped shoulders hunched a little more as he asked whether she needed him to stay with her.

She shook her head. "But . . . thank you. Thank you for helping me."

He smiled. There was a touch of surprise in his smile. Kestrel thought that he was probably not used to being thanked.

Then she was alone with her father. His breath was slow and even. His hand lay palm up on the bed beside him, fingers slightly curled.

Kestrel couldn't remember when she had last held his hand. Had she been a child then? Surely she had held his hand before.

She hesitated, then she let her palm rest upon his. With her other hand, Kestrel made his loose fingers hold hers close.

He woke during the night. The lamp had been turned down low. His eyes opened just slightly, and gleamed in the feeble light. He opened them wider. He saw Kestrel, and didn't smile, not exactly, yet the set of his mouth changed. His hand tightened around hers.

"Father." Kestrel would have said more, but he closed his eyes briefly in the way of someone who wants to say *no* without speaking, yet hasn't the strength to shake his head. Softly, he said, "Sometimes I forget that you aren't a soldier."

He was thinking about when he'd entered the palace yard, and the way she had greeted him. Kestrel said flatly, "You believe I don't know how to behave around you."

For a moment, he was silent. "Maybe I'm the one who doesn't know." There was another silence, long enough for Kestrel to think that that was all he would say, but he spoke again. "Look how you've grown. I remember the day you were born. I could hold you with one hand. You were the world's best thing. The most precious."

Aren't I now, to you? she wanted to say. Instead, she whispered, "Tell me how I was."

"You had a warrior's heart, even then."

"I was just a baby."

"No, you did. Your cry was so fierce. You held my finger so tightly."

"All babies cry. All babies hold on tight."

He let go of her hand to lift his, and brush his knuckles across her cheek. "Not like you."

He had fallen asleep again. When the physician came at dawn to clean the wound, the pain woke him.

"More?" The physician nodded at the empty cup that had held the medicine. The general gave him a dark look.

When the physician had left again, her father rubbed

his eyes. His face was slack with pain. "How long did I sleep?"

"About four hours after the healer first cleaned your wound. After you woke in the night, another three."

He frowned. "I woke in the middle of the night?"

"Yes," said Kestrel, confused, but already feeling wary, already tensing as if some blow was about to fall.

"Did I . . . say something I shouldn't have?"

Kestrel realized that he didn't remember waking, or the conversation. She could no longer tell if he had meant what he had said to her then. Even if he had meant it, had he meant to say it?

He had, after all, been drugged.

An emotion leaked away. It came from a small cut that Kestrel couldn't close.

"No," she told her father. "You didn't."

ARIN WOKE WITH THE MOVEMENT OF BEING heaved up onto something hard. His head thumped, and the world was a weird, jigsawed thing of sky and stone and water. Then his vision cleared, and Arin realized that he was lying on a stone pier. The skull-faced man was stepping out of the narrow boat anchored to the pier. He muttered something.

"What did you say?" Arin croaked.

The man hunkered down and gently slapped Arin's cheek twice. "That I need a wheelbarrow."

Wherever Arin was going, he wanted to be on his feet. "There's been a misunderstanding."

"Foreigners are illegal in Dacra. You broke our laws by entering the country. You'll have to pay the price."

"Just let me tell you *why*—"

"Oh, reasons. Everyone has reasons. I don't care to know yours." The easterner stared down at Arin, and although it wasn't the man's eyes that had been mutilated, it was hard to hold his gaze. Arin remembered seeing him for those few bare minutes in Herran. How the runaway eastern slave was being dragged past the road Arin was forced to pave. A Valorian dagger had flashed. Arin had cursed his masters. He had been beaten down. The man's face was whole, and then it wasn't.

"You ran away again," Arin said. "You got free."

The man straightened. He stared down at Arin from a height. "Do you think you did something for me that day?"

"No."

"Good. Because I think that you liked your chains, little Herrani. Otherwise, you would have fought with everything you had. You would look like me." He bent to grasp the ropes wound around Arin's chest, and Arin realized that he meant to drag him.

"Let me walk."

"All right." The easy response surprised Arin until the man pulled Kestrel's dagger from the satchel slung over his shoulder, cut the ropes binding Arin's ankles, and watched him with a smile.

It was then that Arin realized that he couldn't quite feel his feet. Standing up was going to be hard. Walking no longer seemed like a great idea.

Arin's wrists were bound in front of him. Rope coiled around his upper body at the biceps. He decided to take that as a healthy amount of respect for the way he'd attacked the prison guard.

The easterner was still smirking.

Arin inchwormed to his knees. He struggled to his feet. He nearly fell back down.

The soles of his feet stung with a thousand little

knives. He wobbled. Arin saw, again, Kestrel's blade in the easterner's hand. He was suddenly furious at her, as if *she* had drugged him, tied him, and watched him try to walk when he couldn't.

He clenched his teeth until it hurt. He took a step.

The Dacran said something in his language.

"What?" said Arin. He took another wavering step. He bent his arms at the elbows, lifting his bound wrists. It helped him balance. He flexed his fingers. The feeling in them was fine. He could open and close his hands. "What did you say?"

"Nothing."

"Tell me what you said."

"You want to know? Learn my language for yourself." The man was unsettled, apparently by whatever he'd said as Arin tried to walk. He looked down and opened the satchel to place Kestrel's dagger inside.

Arin knew an opportunity when he saw it.

He shouldered his weight into the man, toppling them both down. The dagger hit stone. The man was shoving Arin off him, but Arin jerked a knee up into the Dacran's stomach and rolled to claim the dagger.

Later, Arin would realize how lucky he'd been. But for now he thought nothing at all. The dagger was in his hands, he was flipping it by its hilt. That exquisitely sharp edge sliced through the ropes at his wrists.

The Dacran gasped on the ground, clutching his gut. Arin loomed over him and couldn't quite remember when or how he'd gotten to his feet. When had he yanked the ropes that had bound his chest up over his head? Ropes lay in a heap on the pier. Arin stared at them. He stared at the man, who stared back.

No, not really.

The Dacran wasn't really looking at Arin. His gaze was going over Arin's shoulder.

Arin turned. For the first time, he truly saw where he was: on a large island in the middle of the river. The pier was grand, edged with low, scalloped walls of translucent stone. A path traveled from it up onto the island, to a castle with steeply pitched roofs and walls that gleamed like glass.

But the pier didn't matter, or the path, or the castle.

What mattered were the ranks of white-clad guards who had trained their small crossbows, wound and notched, at Arin.

"Good," said the skull-faced man. He stood, and held out his hand for Kestrel's dagger.

Arin hated that he always hated to let it go.

The man took it. "Good."

Defeated, Arin muttered, "You said that already."

It began to rain. The Dacran looked at him through the bright gray of it. "No. It was what I said earlier, when you got to your feet and walked."

The castle had looked like glass because it had been made from that odd, translucent stone. Through the rain, Arin could see dark shapes of people moving behind its outer walls. But other figures seemed to stand *inside* the stone.

Arin wiped water from his eyes. "Does it always rain so much here?"

"Wait till summer," said the Dacran. "It gets so hot that some of the city canals dry up and we walk in them like deep roads. Then you'll wish for rain."

"I won't be here in summer."

The other man said nothing.

As they passed through the castle gate, Arin tried to peer into the wall. "Are those . . . statues inside?"

"They are the dead." When Arin shot him a startled look, the man said. "Our ancestors. Yes, I know that *some* people from other countries set the people they loved on fire or dump them in a hole in a ground. But Dacra is a civilized nation."

They entered the castle. Arin was so wet it felt as if the rain was still drumming down on him. His boots squelched. Inside the castle, some walls were built from solid white marble, and others from that glassy rock. It had a dizzying effect. Arin found it hard to judge the space and shape of things.

"Well?" said the Dacran. "Where do you keep *your* family dead?"

"I don't know where they are," Arin said shortly. The other man went silent, and that made Arin uncomfortable, resentful. He wondered when he would stop sharing things he shouldn't. It was a bad habit.

It had begun with her. He could swear that she was the start of it all.

"The ground," Arin said, though he had not in fact seen what had been done with the bodies of his parents and sister. "We bury our dead, as I'm sure you know if you

lived in my country long enough to learn its language."
The Dacran didn't admit to it, or that he might have been
needling Arin with questions whose answers he knew. This
made Arin angrier. "You're no more civilized than I am."

"You asked to walk. Here you are, walking. You asked
to speak with my queen. You will. You've broken our laws
three times—"

"Three?"

The man ticked them off, starting with his smallest
finger. "You entered our country. You bore the weapon of
our enemy. And you struck a member of the royal family."

Arin stared at him. The man gave a slow smile. "But we
have been polite," he said.

"Who are you?"

The man led the way down a hall lined with palm-size
paintings.

"Wait." Arin caught the man's arm.

The Dacran glanced down at Arin's hand on him, then
gave a look that made Arin let go. "You are also not supposed to *touch* a member of the royal family. It's not so
grave an offense as *striking* me, but still. I don't know what
my sister is going to do with you. The queen can hardly
sentence you to death more than once."

"Your sister?"

"That last offense bears a lesser punishment, though I
don't think you'll like that one either."

Arin had stopped, only vaguely aware that they had entered a high-vaulted chamber. "But if you're the queen's
brother, that means you're Risha's brother, too."

The Dacran stopped as well. "Risha?"

There was a silent energy in this new room that kept Arin from saying anything else.

It was wariness. It was the watchful eyes of guards.

It was the hard expression of the young queen, who looked at Arin as if she had already pronounced his death.

"DON'T SAY THAT NAME AGAIN," MUTTERED
the skull-faced man to Arin.

The queen asked a sharp question. Her brother's answer was slow, complicated. It was marked by pauses. Each
pause gave life to a new tone of voice.

The rain must have stopped. The peaked ceiling, made
from that sheer stone, glowed with sudden sun. Prismatic
light lit the room. Arin watched the queen's changing face
as her brother spoke. Her black eyes, lined with elaborate
patterns of color, narrowed. She stopped him.

"This is the part where I translate," the Dacran told
Arin, "and you hope that I tell the truth."

The queen said, "You've broken three of our laws"—
here, her brother stopped his translation to hold up four
fingers—"what keeps you alive is our curiosity. Satisfy it."

Arin said, "I have a proprosal—"

"No," the man told him. "Don't start there. We don't
even know your name."

So Arin gave it, and his rank.

"*Governor* is a Valorian title," said the queen. "You are Valorian."

The insult went bone deep.

"You cannot deny it," said the queen. "We have heard of you. Arin of the Herrani, who once bit his masters' heels, is a tame dog once more. Did you not swear an oath of loyalty to the emperor?"

"I'm breaking it now."

"Do you so easily break your oaths?"

"Wouldn't you, for your people?"

"I'm not translating that," the skull-faced man told him. "It's insulting. You're a little self-destructive, aren't you?"

Impatient, the queen interrupted. She told Arin to explain his possession of the Valorian dagger.

"It's a reminder," he said.

"Of?"

"What I despise."

The queen considered this. Her face was leaner than Risha's, but much like her younger sister's. It was easy, looking at the queen, to feel again his admiration for Risha, the way it had grown from the first moment Tensen had revealed her to be his Moth. Arin said to the queen, "I know that your country has suffered. I know that my own is too small to stand alone against the empire. If I had a choice, the empire or the east, I'd choose you. Let Herran be your ally."

She cocked her head. "What exactly would we do with you?"

"Let us fight for you."

"In exchange for our protection of your little peninsula, no doubt. As you have pointed out, Herran *is* small. Your soldiers would hardly swell our ranks. Do you *want* your people to be our cannon fodder? Even if you did, how would that work? We do not even speak the same language."

"We'll learn yours."

The queen raised a skeptical brow.

"I'll prove it to you," Arin said.

"I would like to see you try."

"Good," Arin said, using the one Dacran word he knew, the one that the skull-faced man had said to him on the pier.

The queen's surprise was clear. But she didn't smile, and what she said next made Arin wonder if he hadn't just somehow deeply offended her.

"Let us turn," she said, "to the subject of your punishment."

For bearing an enemy's weapon, Arin was forbidden to carry any at all.

For entering Dacran territory, Arin was not allowed to leave it.

For his crimes against Roshar, the queen's brother, the injured party was given permission to exact his choice of punishment.

"I'll have you killed later," Roshar told Arin after bringing him to the room where he would stay. "I need time to decide the very best method."

Arin looked at him. The mutilations made it hard to see any resemblance to Risha or the queen. Roshar must have caught the quality of Arin's gaze. The way it examined. Roshar sneered. "Or maybe I'll find a punishment better than death."

Arin glanced away.

Roshar began unpacking Arin's things—with the exception of the dagger—from the satchel onto a table. Food, water, clothes. "What's this?" Roshar held up the packet that contained spools of thread.

"Sewing kit."

Roshar tossed it on the table. Then he stared down at all of Arin's things as if they could add up to the answer to a hard question. "You've come a long way."

"Yes."

"All the way from the imperial capital." Quietly, Roshar said, "Is my little sister well?"

"Yes. She—"

"I don't want to talk about her. I just wanted to know how she is."

"Did you discuss her with the queen when we first entered that room?"

Roshar looked at Arin as if he were insane. "Of course not."

"Then what took so long to tell the queen?"

"Your crimes. In loving detail."

"No," Arin said, "it sounded like a story."

Roshar prodded a flask of water. "Clearly you didn't know *anything* about our country, if you bothered to bring *this*."

"Why won't you tell me what you said?"

Roshar kept poking at the flask, making it rock against the table. Slowly, he said, "Maybe I did tell a story. Maybe it was about two slaves in a faraway land, and how one helped the other."

"But I didn't." Arin remembered it again. He tasted the dirt in his mouth, felt the gravel under his cheek. He heard the cries. He felt his shame.

"You saved me," Roshar said.

Arin was confused. At first he thought this was sarcasm. But there had been something open in Roshar's voice, like yearning. Was Roshar reinventing what had really happened? Maybe he was imagining a version of the world where the Valorian's knife had never cut his face. A fiction. A story with a happy ending.

"I'm sorry," Arin said carefully. "I tried. But I couldn't do anything."

"You did. You saved the thing in me that decided I would run away again."

"I WANT YOU TO DO SOMETHING FOR ME," Kestrel's father said.

Firstspring had come and gone. Kestrel had missed most of the celebrations to be with her father in his rooms, as she was every day. The only event she'd attended was the one at the orphanage, where the children had looked dubiously at the bright kites she offered. "They're not the right color," a little girl had said. "I want a black one." Afterward, Verex had gone through the leftovers. "May I keep this?" He lifted a pink-and-green kite. "It's my favorite," he said. Kestrel had smiled.

Now she looked warily at her father as he lay in his bed. She waited to see what he would ask.

"I want you to go to the battling clubs in the city," he said, "and recruit people to the military."

Kestrel edged her chair away from the bed. The wooden squeak was loud. She toyed with a bit of embroidery on her sleeve and imagined that her disappointment was a thread that could be tied into knots and stitched down tight.

During all the hours she had sat by her father, this was the first time he'd asked her for anything. What had she hoped he would ask?

Perhaps to be brought a glass of water. Or to be told what had happened to the dagger he'd given her. He couldn't have missed its replacement. The emperor's gaudy blade was right there in full view, strapped to Kestrel's waist.

It seemed impossible to tell her father certain things unless he asked for them.

But some words came easy, because they were angry and had been said many times before. "I want nothing to do with the military."

"Kestrel."

"Look at what it's done to you."

"I will heal."

"And the next time? You are going to keep fighting until the day you're killed, and I have to set an empty plate at the table for my father's ghost."

"We don't believe in ghosts."

"Then you'll leave me with nothing at all."

"We need more soldiers," he said. "The army is stretched too thin."

"Then stop trying to take new territory."

"That isn't what the emperor wants."

"What do *you* want?"

"That," he told her, "is a foolish question."

Was it because he had known her all her life that he knew exactly which words would hurt most? But no, it couldn't be time that gave someone that power. Arin had it, too. *I don't know you anymore,* he'd said. *And I don't want to.*

If she went to the battling clubs and signed more soldiers into the army, did that mean that their deaths would be her fault? Would the blood of the people they killed be on her hands? And the grief and anger of those who were left behind—was that her doing, too? She remembered how the war orphans had wanted black kites.

"Recruit them yourself," she told her father.

He was silent as she strode to the door. It was that silence that ultimately stopped her. Though Kestrel's back was to him, she still saw him as he lay wounded on the bed. Pale and drawn. Tired in a way she'd never seen.

If she recruited more Valorians . . . it might help him when he returned to the field. More soldiers could mean that he'd be kept safe for another year. Maybe two.

Kestrel sighed. Her back still to him, she said, "I don't know why you think that *I* could persuade anyone to sign up."

"The people love you."

"They love *you*. I'm just your daughter."

"You escaped from Herran. You alerted us to the rebellion. And by now everyone must know how I won the eastern plains."

"I wish you'd claimed that idea for your own."

"I would never do that."

Kestrel turned, set her shoulders back against the door, and crossed her arms. She thought of Tensen's latest request for information. "Do you know the chief water engineer?"

"Elinor?" From his bed, the general looked at Kestrel

with eyes narrowed in pain. This conversation had exhausted him. His breath was uneven. If he'd been anyone else, he would have already asked for medicine. "I know her a little."

"From your campaigns in the east?" With the exception of the plains, the lands there were watery, especially farther south, though Valorian soldiers had never reached the queen's city in the delta.

"Yes, and in Herran. Why?"

"She has a townhome here. I thought that maybe . . . after I go to the battling clubs, you'd like for me to pay her a call. I could ask her to join the regiment when it returns east. You might need someone to build bridges, or dams—"

"Yes." If he'd had more energy, the general would have looked amused. "I do. But she's the emperor's now. He doesn't like to share. Don't waste your time visiting her."

Kestrel paused, then said, "I'm going to the battling clubs under one condition."

"Ah." His head leaned back into the damp pillow. "A bargain. What must I do now?"

"Drink your medicine."

The battling clubs were not-very-secret societies. There were four in the city, and they each served young aristocrats with luxurious headquarters designed for private parties, sultry moments in hidden rooms—and, of course, fighting.

Each club came equipped with an impressive variety of weaponry. There were keyed rooms for combatants who wished to be alone, and arenas for matches meant to be seen.

Everybody knew the few club rules. Clean up your own blood. Money up front for gambling. Members only. Even Lady Kestrel would have had problems at the door if she hadn't shown her father's signet ring.

The clubs unsettled her. It didn't matter how much dark wainscoting lined the walls, or that the furnishings were backed by southern isle silk. The rooms still smelled like wine and sweat and blood. It made her think of fighting Irex in Herran. His boot cracking against her knee. She remembered Cheat's weight flattening her against the floor.

Kestrel's mouth was chalky.

She asked for water. She was served. Then she went about her business.

After three clubs, she had collected about twenty names. It wasn't much. Several Valorians who signed were wild-eyed and laughing. Some were flattered. Others—especially those closest to twenty years old—were resigned, because the empire would soon make them choose between marriage and the military anyway. If a citizen wouldn't make babies to boost the imperial population, she would have to make war.

In one club, two young women signed up together. They insisted on writing their names on the same line. This made Kestrel realize that they were a couple. People who loved that way—or who otherwise didn't want to marry against their desires—often joined the military. Kestrel watched the women sign, and thought of her own marriage, and felt even worse than before.

Kestrel reclaimed the list. She shoved it inside her skirt pocket.

In the last club, a fight was on.

The small arena was packed and loud, the air heavy. Kestrel was a latecomer and had to stand at the back of the crowd. Peering over someone's shoulder, she caught a glimpse of the fighters, both men, both with blond hair tied back. The one whose back was to her was slender but quick.

It was a fistfight. Kestrel couldn't see any weapons either in the combatants' hands or strapped to their bodies, so this wasn't a duel fought over honor, but for pleasure.

The larger man crashed a fist into the face of the thinner one. He cried out. The crowd surged forward.

Kestrel did, too. She knew that cry. She would swear that she recognized that voice. But the gap that had given her a view of the fighters had closed. She could see nothing now, and people were shouting, and she couldn't even tell if they were shouting someone's name.

She did. She called out a name. The noise swallowed it.

Kestrel elbowed her way forward. She pushed her way to the front. The slender man was coming up from the ground. He delivered a series of uppercuts to his opponent's gut, yanked on an ear, and punched his face.

The big fighter went down. He wasn't getting up.

The crowd began shouting again, and this time they clearly *were* shouting a name. It was the same one on Kestrel's lips, the one that she said again as the winner turned around, wiped blood from his mouth, and saw her.

Ronan.

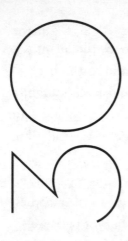

AFTER THE CROWD CLEARED, KESTREL TOLD the club owner to find her a private room. Ronan was a member, and could have arranged this himself. Instead, he watched and listened to Kestrel's instructions with something like amusement, or the air of someone pleasantly surprised by the appearance of an old friend. But his smile was bitter.

He ordered a carafe of cold wine. Once he and Kestrel were alone, he drank half of it down at once.

"A private audience with the future empress," Ronan said, unwinding bloodied linen strips from his knuckles. "I'm honored." He settled his long frame in a chair and looked up at her. He had a split lip. His blond hair was loose and sweaty, his finely drawn face purpled with bruises. He ran a finger along the rim of his glass until it hummed.

When Kestrel was little, Jess's older brother had ignored her. Then one evening, when Kestrel was perhaps fifteen, she and her father had been invited to a society dinner at his house. Over the third course, she asked a senator whether he'd marry all of his mistresses if he could have more than one wife.

Kestrel hadn't meant to upset the senator. She'd just been curious. She wasn't aware that his wife, also at the dinner, hadn't known about the mistresses.

Kestrel was sent from the table to sit alone in Jess's suite.

Ronan smuggled her dessert. They ate white powdered cakes together, sugar dust all over their faces, and she laughed as Ronan imitated the senator's reaction, puffing out his cheeks and holding his breath until his face turned red.

After that, Ronan noticed her.

Kestrel missed her friend. She missed him right now as he sat before her, everything about him playful and careless except for his eyes, which cared very much, and were cold.

He drank his cup dry. "What do you want, Kestrel?"

"Did you tell Jess?"

Ronan arched one brow. "Did I tell Jess." He twirled his glass by its stem. "Let's see. Did I tell Jess that those rumors were true, that all autumn long you had a lover—"

"I didn't."

"That's right. It began in summer, when you bought him. Did I tell Jess *that*? Did I tell her that you'd rather buy someone to bring to your bed than love her brother? Maybe we wondered out loud what was so repulsive about marriage to me that you chose a slave instead.

"Maybe I told Jess, 'I know, I know. You loved her, too. But on Firstwinter night she wasn't there when you drank the poisoned wine. She wasn't there when you gagged and choked and I dragged you behind a curtain to hide while slaves stabbed our friends. Kestrel wasn't there when I held my dying sister. Because Kestrel left the ball with *him*.'" Ronan set the wineglass down on a table with infinitely delicate precision. "No, I didn't tell Jess that. One broken heart in the family is enough."

Kestrel tasted the memory of those sugared cakes. Their lost sweetness made it impossible to speak.

"Troubled, Kestrel?"

Though she knew he didn't really want to hear her answer, she couldn't help telling him. "Jess won't answer my letters. When I pay her a call, servants say she's out. She's not. She's in her rooms, waiting for me to leave. I thought that maybe . . ."

"I had been telling her some hard truths." Ronan laced his fingers and then spread them wide, shrugging. "Have you considered that whatever has come between you two is *your* doing?"

I saw him, Jess had said when Kestrel had slipped into bed beside her the night of her engagement ball. What exactly had Jess seen?

"What's this?" Ronan quickly leaned forward to tug on a corner of the folded paper peeking out of her skirt pocket. He pulled the recruitment list free.

"Nothing." She reached for it.

He jerked the page away and unfolded it. "Ohhh. I know what *this* is. Look, you even got Caris to sign up. Now, where's a pen?"

"No. Ronan, don't."

Holding the list of recruits high above Kestrel's reach as if they were children, Ronan rummaged one-handed around the room.

"Stop." Kestrel yanked on his arm. She tried to snake her way into his path. He ducked, and twisted, and laughed. He opened a secretaire and found a jug of wine where papers should be. "Nice, very nice, but not exactly what I was looking for . . ." He pulled out drawers. He crowed when he found ink and a pen.

Ronan, sent to war. Ronan, bleeding into the dirt.

She was near tears. "Please," she said, "don't sign that paper."

He inked the pen and held the list down on the secretaire with both hands as if it might fly away.

"I beg you," Kestrel said.

Ronan smiled, and signed.

Kestrel's escort was waiting patiently by the club door. The maid said nothing as they stepped into the carriage and Kestrel gave the order to return to the palace. But the girl watched as Kestrel unwrapped the balled sheet of paper and let it fall to her lap.

With a shuddering jolt, the carriage pulled forward. It trundled up the mountain.

"It's dirty," the maid said. She was looking at the list.

It was splotched with ink. Kestrel had knocked the bottle over when she finally snatched the list back from Ronan. The page had rusty smears right by his name; Ronan's knuckles must have been still bleeding. And although the maid wouldn't have been able to tell, not after the way the page had been crushed, the paper was a little warped, the way paper gets when exposed to water, or sweat—or tears.

Kestrel gently folded the page. Destroying it would change nothing. It wasn't the signature that was important, but the act of signing. The recruits would still report to the city barracks. They'd given their word, witnessed by Kestrel. A Valorian honored his word.

"What is that?" said the maid.

"A guest list." Kestrel imagined a long, empty table set with bare white plates. *She* had set them.

Suddenly, Kestrel leaned forward and rapped at the glass that separated her from the carriage driver. She had changed her mind, she said.

Kestrel gave the driver a new destination.

"I didn't realize you were interested in water engineering," said Elinor as a southern isle slave served them a rare liquor that tasted like burnt caramel. It was very expensive.

Kestrel sipped from her cut-crystal glass. Elinor's townhome was modest. The walls were painted instead of papered. A long crack ran through the lacy white plaster molding in the ceiling.

But the water engineer had expensive liquor. There were pale, sweet, imported berries heaped in a bowl on the low table near the divan where she and Kestrel sat. Of course, Elinor *would* set out her finest food and drink for a visitor of Kestrel's rank. But the liquor and berries seemed too much for someone of her means, judging by the state of her house. Tensen had told Kestrel about the bets placed on her wedding dress. She thought that the berries, liquor, and even the crystal glasses could have been acquired on credit by someone expecting a large windfall in a matter of months. The Firstsummer wedding was, after all, not so far away.

Kestrel forced a smile. "The emperor thinks I should be interested in anything that concerns the empire. And my father valued your skills during war."

The engineer's plain face went pink with pride.

"Didn't you serve with the general in the east?" Kestrel said.

"Years ago." Elinor's face lost its pleasure. When she caught Kestrel's questioning look, she said, "The east is a savage land. Engineers might technically be members of the military, my lady, but I wasn't ready. The Dacrans are devious fighters. I was supposed to build bridges and dams, not fight, but the reeds by the rivers were high. They were infested with tigers. They hid barbarians with poisoned crossbow quarrels. Your father kept me safe. He kept me alive."

If the emperor had rewarded the engineer, could it have been for a favor she had done in the east? Maybe it had nothing to do with Herran.

The southern isle slave refilled the engineer's cup. Kestrel watched her. She was a young girl, younger than Kestrel. The southern islands—the Cayn Saratu, as their people had once called them—had been one of the first territories Valoria had conquered. Kestrel's father had been a lieutenant then. This girl was young enough to have been born into slavery. She'd never known another life. She might not have ever known her mother tongue—or even her mother.

Suddenly Kestrel no longer cared whether the emperor's secret was about Herran, or the east, or some other territory. She wanted the empire to be that long table that haunted her mind. She wanted to flip it over and send all those empty plates crashing to the floor.

The slave stirred uneasily. Kestrel realized that she was staring at the girl, who said, "More, my lady?"

"No, thank you."

The engineer said to Kestrel, "I suppose you don't remember me. You were a little girl when I saw you last. It was just after the colonization of Herran."

Kestrel looked at Elinor again, at the solid, intelligent way of her. Kestrel had a faint memory of kneeling by the fountain in her Herran villa and tipping red dye filched from the slaves' workroom into the fountain. She'd been curious. She had overheard a word at dinner the night before, while her father talked with his guest. *Dilution*. It was a word she didn't know.

"I dyed our fountain pink because of you," Kestrel told the engineer.

"Really?"

"I was trying for red, but I didn't have enough dye." Kestrel pressed her thumb into the pattern cut into her crystal glass and said, "Why were you in Herran then? Did you live there?"

"No, I designed the city aqueducts. The Herrani system of running water was too primitive."

"Have you been to Herran recently?"

"No," said the engineer, but she was looking away. "Why would I?"

"Oh, I don't know. Maybe I wish that you had, and that we could talk about it. Sometimes I'm homesick."

Elinor frowned. "Herran is a colony. *This* is your home."

"Herran *was* a colony. Now it's an independent territory."

"By the grace of our emperor."

Quietly, and helplessly, the way one reaches for a lost thing that had always been there before, Kestrel said, "I miss the birds that sing there this time of the year. They carried straw in their beaks and built nests under the eaves. I miss the flickering light of the horse paths." The engineer was staring with disapproval. Kestrel didn't care. The words were said to Arin, who wasn't there, and Jess, who wouldn't listen, and Ronan, who was leaving, and her father, who had shared her home. She spoke to the southern isle slave, who had probably been born and sold and raised in the capital, and had never known her home, and so had been robbed, along with everything else, of homesickness. "There was a hill in the orange grove," Kestrel said. "When I was little, I would lie there in summer and look at the fruit hanging in the trees like party lanterns. Then I was old enough to go to parties, and my friends and I would stay up until even the fireflies went to sleep."

"How nice." Yet the engineer's voice was cold.

"Herran is beautiful."

"The problem has never been Herran. It's the Herrani."

Then, as if neither of them noticed the great fault line

that had opened up with their words to split the ground between them, Elinor said, "Do try the berries, my lady. They are very sweet."

When the general was well enough to leave his rooms, the emperor insisted on a celebration. A mock sea battle was staged at night on the man-made pond in the Spring Garden. Two small boats were painted to look like ships of war and loaded with courtiers who shot off fireworks.

"You don't like it?" the emperor said when General Trajan remained silent during the applause.

"Fireworks are a waste of black powder."

"Valoria has more than enough. Our enemies will never be able to compete with our cannons. Our stores of black powder are vast."

"Every resource has its limits."

"He's always like this in the capital," the emperor told Kestrel cheerfully. "He's never happy unless he's in the field."

Kestrel wanted to say that he had been happy in their home in Herran. In truth, though, he'd rarely been there, and she'd never dared to ask after his happiness.

The general shifted in his wrought-iron chair. The walk to the garden had exhausted him, Kestrel could tell. Though the court physicians packed his wound with less gauze every day, it hadn't yet closed.

"Where's Verex?" Kestrel wished he were there.

The emperor shrugged.

A firework popped into a shower of gold. It illuminated

the crowd gathered around the pond. Its light glimmered on Risha's face, and on Verex, who sat next to her on the other side of the pond.

The emperor saw them, too. Kestrel was coming to understand that the emperor's anger tended to coil itself tightly. It was the kind that could seem to sleep. Inevitably, though, it lashed out.

"I hear that you paid a call to my water engineer," he said to Kestrel.

Another firework went off. It seemed to thud inside Kestrel's chest. The emperor was looking at her in the same way he had looked at his son: as if he didn't like what he now.

Kestrel said, "I thought that maybe I could convince her to return to the east with my father."

A firework lit the emperor's face with exploded light. "That is *my* decision."

"It was just an idea. In the end, I said nothing about it to her."

"She tells me, however, that your conversation was nonetheless interesting."

The smell of sulfur was strong. The smoke burned Kestrel's lungs. And she knew, from the threat in the emperor's voice, that she *had* been prodding at a secret about the water engineer.

She looked at her father. He was staring straight ahead, watching as a drunk gentleman stood in one of the boats, teetered, and fell into the water. The crowd laughed.

Kestrel held her breath. The fireworks cracked and burst inside her. She waited for the emperor to speak again.

She worried that her father would say that he had told Kestrel not to go to the engineer's house.

"Perhaps the capital isn't entertaining enough for you," the emperor said to Kestrel. "I hear that you long for Herran."

"Why wouldn't she?" General Trajan said curtly. "She grew up there."

The sky rained green and red. The two men looked at each other. Kestrel knew that expression on her father's face.

Her fear slowed. She breathed again. Though the spring night was chilly, she felt suddenly warm. She felt the cloak of her father's protection. She pulled it tightly around her.

"Of course," the emperor said silkily, and turned to watch as another fuse was lit.

WHEN THE GENERAL'S WOUND FINALLY
closed, the emperor gave him a gold watch.

Kestrel stood with her father and the emperor on the
pale green lawn of the Spring Garden. Archery targets had
been set up, and courtiers took their turns. The sky was
heaped with whipped-cream clouds. The wind blew soft
and warm. Kestrel's maids had packed away her winter
clothes and brought out dresses of lace and toile.

She thought of Arin in his twinned rooftop garden in
Herran. She wondered what bloomed for him there now.

The watch struck the hour.

General Trajan raised his brows. "It chimes."

The emperor looked pleased, and Kestrel supposed that
it might have been easy to mistake her father's expression for wonder. But she saw the uncomfortable line of his
mouth.

"Don't be jealous, Kestrel," said the emperor. "I haven't
forgotten that your birthday is coming up."

She would turn eighteen. Her birthday was near spring's

end: right before the wedding. "It's more than two months from now."

"Yes, not so far away. Trajan, I insist that you stay in the capital right through until the wedding."

The general shut the watch. "We just seized the eastern plains. If you want to hold them—"

"Your lieutenants can manage. You're barely healed. You can't expect to lead a regiment in battle, and quite frankly, you're no good to me dead. You'll stay here. We'll celebrate Kestrel's birthday together." With the air of someone presenting the best idea in the world, he added, "I thought that she could perform for the court."

There was the soft, faraway thump of an arrow hitting canvas.

The general said nothing. Kestrel watched his mouth harden.

"She has such a gift for music," said the emperor, "like your wife did."

The general's hatred of Kestrel's music had always been clear. It embarrassed him: her love for an instrument that one bought slaves to play. Sometimes, though, Kestrel thought that it wasn't just that. The piano was his rival. He had wanted her to enlist in the military. She wouldn't. He wanted her to stop playing. She wouldn't. The piano became her way of refusing him . . . or at least this was how she had thought he saw it. Only now did it occur to her that he hated to hear her play because it hurt.

"I confess," the emperor said, "that I want to show Kestrel off. I want everyone to see what talent my future daughter has." With a smile, he excused himself to speak with the Senate leader.

General Trajan's hand closed around the watch.

What a silly gift to give a man who led nighttime assaults where stealth could mean the difference between life and death. "Give it to me," Kestrel said. "I will find a nice convenient rock to drop it on."

The general smiled a little. "When the emperor gives you a gift, it's best to wear it." He glanced at the new dagger at Kestrel's hip. "Sometimes what he gives is actually a way of saying what's his."

I'm not his, she wanted to say, but her father was already gone, walking slowly across the lawn to greet an off-duty naval officer.

Someone must have struck a target's center. She heard a smattering of applause.

"Are you going to shoot?"

It was Verex. He had approached without her noticing.

"Not today." The wind was tricky and her father was here. She didn't want to miss.

Verex offered her his arm. "Let's see who wins."

As they walked together, Kestrel said, "You seem to know a good deal about medicine."

He shrugged.

"Would you rather be a doctor than an emperor?"

Verex peered down the low slope. He didn't say anything. Kestrel wasn't sure if it was because he had been offended by the question or because he didn't know how to answer it. Then he said, "The Herrani minister of agriculture is looking at you."

Kestrel glanced to see Tensen sitting in a chair under the trees, folded hands resting on the cane planted into the grass in front of him.

"No, don't look back," said Verex. "Be careful, Kestrel."

Her step faltered. "I'm not sure what you mean."

"You know why my father keeps him at court, don't you?"

Slowly, Kestrel said, "To watch him."

"What will my father think if he watches that minister watch *you*?"

Kestrel swallowed a bubbling nervousness. Her hands, though lightly gloved, were very cold. But she strove to sound confident and careless. "People look at me all the time. I can't help it."

Verex shook his head and turned to eye the archers.

"I assure you," she said, "I care nothing for Herran's minister."

He gave her a sidelong, reproachful look. "Kestrel, I know what you care about."

She tried for a teasing tone and change of subject. "Since we're gossiping about who watches whom, don't you think it's time you told me which of my maids is in your pay?"

"What would that change? Don't you realize by now that *all* of them are watching you? I bribe one, but who bribes the others?" Verex faced her fully now. "You asked me whether I would have liked to become a physician. Yes. I would have. Once. I even had books on the subject. My father burned them. Kestrel, I know you think that you've hidden your heart where no one can see it." Verex's dark eyes held hers. "But you need to hide it better."

An arrow flew high above its target, its feathers whistling.

"Verex, what has my maid told you?"

"Not much . . . so far." He must have seen the worry she was trying to hide. His expression softened. "Let's keep it that way, shall we?"

Kestrel mustered a bright, tense smile.

Verex sighed. "Come on," he said. "I want to see Risha shoot."

Kestrel let him lead her to the archers. She was glad that she'd made no promise to enter the archery contest. Her fingers would tremble on the bowstring.

Risha notched an arrow. She had a fine, strong line. Kestrel focused on watching the eastern girl. If she watched Risha with the same intensity that Verex did, she might be able to forget, if only for a moment, Verex's warning.

Risha let the arrow go. It soared lazily and hit the target's edge. All of her arrows in the target were badly placed. Kestrel would have thought from the way Risha held her bow that she would have been able to do better. Then again, the day was full of sneaky little breezes.

Risha aimed again.

". . . born first?" Kestrel heard someone saying. "A baby prince or princess?"

Verex went still beside her. Kestrel spotted the gossiping courtiers. She realized they were looking right at her and Verex. Their words came clear on the wind. It shouldn't have taken so long for Kestrel to understand what they meant. When she did, her cheeks burned.

Risha let the arrow fly.

It drove deep into the target's very center.

LEARNING THE EASTERN LANGUAGE MADE Arin feel like he was remembering something he didn't know he knew. Dacran was very similar to Herrani. It had some of the same patterns, and though the vocabulary was different, the words didn't sound completely alien, either. Arin learned quickly.

If the eastern language felt familiar, much in this new country was strange. Dacran cuisine focused far more on color than taste. Clothes were plain but cosmetics were not, and men as well as women used them. Roshar in particular liked to line his eyes with vivid, dramatic flair, as if to show that he knew this drew attention to his mutilations, and he didn't care.

Arin was allowed to roam the castle and city. "Everyone knows who you are," Roshar had said with a shrug. "If you wander too far away, the city militia will happily shoot you."

"What exactly is 'too far'?"

Roshar told him to figure it out for himself.

The queen, meanwhile, kept her distance.

At first, Arin stayed inside the castle, thinking that the structure was a shell that housed not only the queen, but her internal self. If he knew its hallways and alcoves and chambers, he might be able to guess at what would persuade her to an alliance with Herran.

But the dizzying mix of transparent and opaque walls gave him no clues. He wandered. Sometimes he heard distant music played in other rooms. There was an instrument like the Herrani violin, except with a flatter bridge, and here the strings were tuned more sharply and played with a percussive quality: lots of plucked notes and aggressive bow strokes.

Arin rarely saw the queen. When he did, she ignored him in an icy way that never failed to remind him that he had no weapon. His parents had thought that openly carrying a blade was the height of barbarism. Now, though, Arin felt strange without Kestrel's dagger at his hip. Its lack made him uncomfortable . . . and even more uncomfortable about what that discomfort might mean.

The easterners were always well armed. They favored small weapons. Their crossbows were smaller than Arin had ever seen. From Roshar, he learned that they weren't as powerful as a western crossbow, but more accurate and easier to load quickly.

The eastern love for the miniature was everywhere within the castle. Paintings no larger than a handspan adorned the walls. Basins collecting rainwater that funneled down from the roofs were decorated with tiny mosaics of dragonflies. Shelves in rooms meant for smoking held clocks the size of watches, and porcelain eggs that, when opened, showed coiled snakes made from jointed green glass. Some eggs hatched tiny tigers that gnashed their mechanical teeth.

Once, Arin strayed far into the recesses of the castle and found a model of the castle on a pedestal. Inside, suites had details that made Arin wish for a magnifying lens. With a fingernail, he turned a faucet in a bathing room. Water filled the teacup-size bathtub. It all made Arin feel too large: thuggish and fumbling.

"I was told that you were here," said a voice behind him. It was Roshar.

Arin turned off the bathtub's water.

"That was my sister's." Roshar's tone made clear which sister he meant. He stared at a suite of rooms that looked fit for a little princess. A chest sat at the foot of a canopied bed. Arin moved to open it. He expected Roshar to snarl an objection, but Roshar simply looked at him, black eyes curious and narrow, like the eyes of the snakes in the porcelain eggs. With one finger, Arin reached inside the chest.

He snatched his hand back. Blood speckled his finger. It felt as if he'd been bitten by a host of tiny fangs.

Roshar took the chest from the small room. He tipped its contents onto his palm, which he held out for Arin to see.

Miniature weapons. Swords the size of matchsticks. Daggers like sharp, steel filings. Roshar squeezed his hand around them, then flung the bloody little weapons into Risha's dollhouse suite.

"Let's get out of here," he said.

"A beheading would be spectacular," Roshar said as Arin steered up the canal. It was a clear day. "Don't you think? You're too heavy for a good hanging. Your neck would break the moment you dropped."

"Beheading's quick, too."

"Not if the ax is dull."

It was a typical conversation between Arin and Roshar, who had very helpfully taught Arin his country's words for various deaths by execution and reminded Arin on a daily basis that his life was in the prince's hands. Usually, this kind of talk cheered Roshar, who lay settled into his end of the canoe, his arms crossed over his chest. One leg draped over the side of the boat. His eyes were on the blue sky. But the lazy posture looked like a lie today. Roshar's body was set with hard lines.

Then his gaze lowered and cast out over the city. Something caught his attention. It changed his face. It stole all the pretending from it, and left nothing but the same naked anger that had made him clench a fist around Risha's toy weapons.

Arin saw what he saw.

A woman wandered near the edge of the canal. She wore the tapered trousers of the plainspeople. Nestled in her arms was a cloth bundle of blue, the color worn by Dacran children. She held the bundle like a baby. But it had no face. It had no hands. It was nothing more than a rag wrapped around itself. She touched it tenderly.

Arin stopped rowing. The water swirled away from his still oar.

Sometimes, Arin almost understood what Kestrel had

done. Even now, as he felt the drift of the boat and didn't fight its pull, Arin remembered the yearning in Kestrel's face whenever she'd mentioned her father. Like a homesickness. Arin had wanted to shake it out of her. Especially during those early months when she had owned him. He had wanted to force her to see her father for what he was. He had wanted her to acknowledge what *she* was, how she was wrong, how she shouldn't long for her father's love. It was soaked in blood. Didn't she see that? How could she *not*? Once, he'd hated her for it.

Then it had somehow touched him. He knew it himself. He, too, wanted what he shouldn't. He, too, felt how the heart chooses its own home and refuses reason. *Not here*, he'd tried to say. *Not this. Not mine. Never.* But he had felt the same sickness.

In retrospect, Kestrel's role in the taking of the eastern plains was predictable. Sometimes he damned her for currying favor with the emperor, or blamed her for playing war like a game just because she could. Yet he thought he knew the truth of her reasons. She'd done it for her father.

It almost made sense. At least, it did when he was near sleep and his mind was quiet, and it was harder to help what entered it. Right before sleep, he came close to understanding.

But he was awake now. He was staring as the glassy-eyed woman cradled her cloth baby. He saw her caress the blue folds. He saw the end of understanding.

Arin wished that Kestrel could see what he saw. He wished that he could make her pay for what she had done.

SPRING PINCHED THE WORLD OPEN. TIGHT buds split along their seams and spilled out their colors.

Kestrel stayed indoors. It didn't help. Thoughts, too, have their seasons, and she couldn't stop what worked its way up through the underground of her mind. And what were her thoughts? What did she gather in secret, in guilt? What did she hold, and lift to the light to see better, and what did she drop as quickly as she could, as if it were hot to the touch?

That last kind of thought grew like flowers with fire for petals. They blackened the grass around them. They burned from root to stamen. Kestrel avoided them.

Except when she didn't. Sometimes, she went to them first. Sometimes, she lied to herself along the way.

She thought about the piano she had left behind in Herran. And it was allowed for her to think about that, because why wouldn't she miss the instrument she'd grown up playing, and had been her mother's? There was nothing wrong with thinking that the palace piano had a rich, ring-ing sound, that it was probably the finer instrument, but that it made her long for the one she'd played almost all her life. She could practically feel the cool keys.

Her piano was in Arin's house. She knew the house well. It had been her prison. It had become—almost—her home.

But then she thought that this was not true. She didn't know Arin's house all that well, and her insistence on this truth made it clear that she had told herself that earlier lie only so that she could correct herself. Because wasn't there a part of Arin's home that she had never seen?

This was her correction:

This was the burning flower:

Kestrel had never been in Arin's rooms. Yes, she'd visited his childhood suite. She'd been there once with him. But that wasn't where he had slept during her time there. That wasn't where he passed his private hours, where he bathed and dressed and read and looked out windows. No, she'd never seen those views.

Arin had lived on the other side of the twinned rooftop gardens that joined his suite to hers. He'd given her the key to its door. In her mind, Kestrel held the key. She fitted it to the lock. She eased the door open.

She imagined what she would find. Maybe the hall that led into Arin's rooms from his garden would have a tiled floor that had been glazed so that it glittered in the dark like the scales of a magic creature. In her imagination, night had fallen hours ago. The darkness felt ripe.

Arin wouldn't burn lamps in every room, especially the rooms he wasn't using. That was something Kestrel would do. No, Arin would light one lamp and turn it down low, in the way of someone who had long been forced to conserve what little he had. There'd be one light to follow. When she found it, she would find him.

Sometimes, she found him in his bedroom.

Sometimes, this was too much to think. It made her heart flinch. It stole her courage. So she found him in other places: in a chair by the sitting room fire, or crouched by the fire itself, feeding kindling into the flames.

Once she found him, what happened next was always the same. Her imagination gave him something to hold so that he would set it aside when he saw her. The kindling. A book.

He was surprised to see her. He didn't think she would come.

He straightened. He stood. He came close.

Arin had won the truth from her that night in the capital city. He'd won it fairly. This time he would collect what she owed. This time, he demanded all her reasons. She would pay them fully. The truth lay on her tongue. But not just there. Kestrel felt the truth in her throat, too. It stemmed down deep inside her. She wondered if this was how it felt to sing. Was this the moment before song, the way the body set and readied itself?

She could ask Arin. He would know. But she was afraid of speaking.

But he was listening. He was waiting for his answers.

This was the moment. This was when it always happened. And this was what it was: Kestrel lifted her mouth to his, and sang the truth into him.

She could no longer bear Jess's silence. Too many letters had gone unanswered. Kestrel had been turned away from Jess's door too many times. Kestrel hated to force a meeting . . . but in the end, that's exactly what she did. She sent an announcement embossed with the imperial seal. The heavy paper proclaimed the day of Kestrel's arrival at Jess's townhome. It appointed the hour.

And Jess was there.

Kestrel was ushered into the parlor, where Jess sat on a needlepoint sofa near a fire stoked high even though the day was fair. Kestrel stood awkwardly, twisting and untwisting the ribbon of her purse. Jess looked even thinner than before, her hair dull, her eyes not quite meeting Kestrel's. They were focused a bit higher—on the engagement mark on her brow, Kestrel realized.

Jess's gaze flicked away. "What do you want?"

Kestrel had been queasy in the carriage the whole way here. That feeling was worse now. Her insides screwed into a wormy knot. "To see you."

"Well, I'm here, just as you commanded. You've seen me. And now you may leave."

"Jess." Kestrel's throat closed. "I miss you."

Jess picked at the needlepoint image stitched into the sofa's seat cushion. It showed a warrior girl hunting a fox. Jess's nails tugged out a thread.

"Was it the necklace?" Kestrel asked. She'd been quick—unfeelingly, cruelly quick—to crush the glass petals of Jess's gift into dust. She caught herself hoping that a broken gift was all that had made their friendship go wrong.

"The necklace." Jess's voice was flat.

"I didn't realize how much it meant to you. I—"

"I'm *glad* it's broken." Jess leaped to her feet and went to a crystal tray set on a side table. It held a cut-glass pitcher of water and a small vial filled with a murky liquid. Jess poured water into a glass, splashing a little. She tipped the vial over the glass. Several drops fell into the water and clouded it. Jess drank deeply, her brown eyes too shiny, and hard.

Kestrel's father would recognize that look, because it was made for war.

But he wouldn't see Jess's unshed tears. Or if he did, he'd pretend they weren't there.

Kestrel's own eyes stung. "Tell me what I've done."

"You know. You're the one who knows everything. *I* know nothing. I'm a little innocent, struggling to keep up. Why don't *you* tell *me*? Tell me that I'm slow. Laugh at how I fell asleep in your bed, how tired I was, how I had looked for you at your wretched ball and you never spoke with me there, not once. How I hid in the crowd and drank glass after glass of lemon water, just to have something to do. Tell me how I saw that slave of yours, pushing through the crowd. He looked dirty. He wore rags. He was dark and disgusting.

"Yet he glittered." Jess's voice came low, ferocious. "His mouth glittered. His jacket did, too. Why don't you explain *that*, Kestrel? I'm too stupid to figure it out on my own."

Kestrel felt herself go slowly, icily pale.

"I didn't think anything of the way his jacket caught the light," Jess said. "Like crystals, I thought. Or bits of glass. Strange. But I didn't want to look at him. I would *not* look at him. I turned away.

"And then I went to sleep. You woke me, you told me about the broken necklace. I'm so *slow*. Can you believe that it wasn't until morning, when I was alone in your bedroom, that it occurred to me that there was a very simple explanation for everything?" Tears trembled on Jess's lashes. "Why don't you tell me what it is, Kestrel? Tell me the truth."

Kestrel didn't understand how the truth could be so two-sided, like a coin. So precious—and ugly. She stood in the center of the parlor: silent, trapped by her own silence . . . and by how her silence became her answer.

Jess wept freely now. "He took everything from me."

Kestrel stepped toward her. Jess threw up her hands as if in defense. Kestrel halted. "Jess," she said quietly, "he didn't."

Jess gave a short, hard laugh. She swiped at the tears on her cheeks. "No? He took my home."

"Not for himself. It was part of the emperor's treaty to give the colonial homes back."

"Which *he* signed."

"It wasn't your house to begin with."

"Listen to yourself! We won that land. It was ours. That's the rule of war."

"*Whose* rule, Jess? Who says that this is the way it must be?"

Jess's eyes narrowed as if seeing something from far away. "*He* has done this to you."

"No, he hasn't."

"You've been my friend for more than ten years. Do you think I can't tell when you lie?"

"No one has *made* me change."

"But you have."

Kestrel was silent.

"He took Ronan," Jess said. "Ronan's joined the Rangers, did you know that?"

No. Kestrel had known only of his enlistment. The Rangers were an elite brigade. They vied for the deadliest missions. A bright shard of fear entered Kestrel's heart. "Ronan took himself away," she said finally. "No one made him enlist."

"No one?" Jess's voice was hoarse with fury.

"I begged him," Kestrel said. "I begged him not to."

"What does it matter what you begged? Ronan knew. I would bet anything that he did. He knows what I know. That slave took *you*. That was *my* gift on his clothes. That was *your* engagement mark on his mouth. And that was what *you* wanted. It was what you wanted when I lay dying on the floor of the governor's palace. And even before that: when I chose your dress and asked you to be my sister. You wanted it all along."

Kestrel's gaze fell to the needlepoint sofa. She stared at the unraveling hunter girl.

"Deny it," Jess said.

If Kestrel pulled on the loose thread, the embroidered face would come undone. If she pulled hard enough, maybe the needlepoint girl would disappear altogether.

"Deny it!"

"I can't," Kestrel said miserably.

"Then leave."

But Kestrel couldn't move.

"Go away, Kestrel. I don't want to see you again."

Kestrel sat before the piano in the stark palace music room. The row of keys looked blankly back.

Jess knew.

Kestrel sank one hand down into a violent chord. And there it was again, that odd, troubling echo, the one that always made her music sound as if it were listening to itself. She took her hand away. Her body became rigid, her bones grimly set. Maybe she would have been able to do what she usually did, which was to forget the echo. Maybe she would have stormed right into the music. But she was held tight by a feeling she'd never had.

She didn't want to play.

Kestrel left the piano. She considered the room. What would make the acoustics sound right? Tapestries on the walls? Kestrel thought about this. She thought hard, hard enough to ignore how desperately she had wanted Jess to understand.

Kestrel was inspecting a shelf and wondering whether the acoustics would be better if she filled the shelves with more books when she saw it. At the back of one of the high shelves set into the wall, there was no wooden panel. The other shelves had wooden backs.

This one had a screen. A cunningly painted screen, with realistic knots of wood and darker grain.

Kestrel came close. She stood on her toes and shifted a barometer out of her way. She tapped the metal screen.

Echo.

There was some kind of chamber on the other side of

the wall. Behind the painted screen was a place where someone could see what Kestrel did, could hear what she played, could hear anything she said to someone else in this room.

This room, which had been Verex's, and which the emperor had given to her.

Kestrel came down on her heels.

The emperor loved his games.

Kestrel frantically revisted every moment she'd spent in the music room. Had she ever made a mistake? Let slip something she shouldn't have? She didn't think so. No, no one could have seen anything wrong.

Deviant.

Treasonous.

Kestrel backed away. Someone could be watching her even now.

She left the room. She scoured the hallway outside for a way inside the hidden space. She ran fingers over the hallway's carvings until the center of a wooden flower gave way under her touch, and a panel slid aside.

The secret room was empty and small and dark and cold. The screen gave a view of her piano and most of the brightly lit room, but not the door. Kestrel stared at where she had been sitting.

She turned once more to face the hidden room. It looked almost ordinary. Plain, clean. Not dusty. But it smelled airless and dank. Like a prison.

KESTREL STAYED CLOSE TO HER FATHER. HE could walk well enough but tired easily, so she challenged him to Borderlands games played in his suite, though most of the court spent whole days out of doors in the blue weather, opening parasols against the sun. There had never been such a spring, the courtiers exclaimed. The Firstsummer wedding was sure to be glorious.

When Kestrel played Borderlands with her father in his suite, they usually moved their pieces in silence. But one day, not long after she had seen Jess, her father shifted his infantry forward in reckless fashion.

"Why are you exposing your soldiers?" Kestrel asked.

His brows lifted. "Are you criticizing my line of play?"

"You should use your cannon."

He had the beginnings of a smile. "Have I foiled some strategy of yours?"

"I could decimate your front lines. I could do it right now."

"Well, if you must."

Kestrel was growing angry. She made no move.

Her father said, "Are we arguing?"

"No."

"What are we arguing about?"

Kestrel thought of Ronan, fighting in the east. She thought about how she'd crushed the necklace Jess had given her because it had been expendable. It was the kind of choice her father had raised her to be able to make. She thought about how when they were little girls, she and Jess had walked hand in hand, Jess's palm fresh against hers. Kestrel thought about Arin, in Herran's city, and what he must think of her now. And finally, Kestrel thought about herself as if she were two people, and one self stood behind the screen in the music room, watching her other self, and judging.

"You are sacrificing them," she told her father.

"It's just a game."

Kestrel said nothing.

"You worry about my methods," said the general. "You think I don't know how to go to war."

"You're wasting lives."

"I protect my soldiers as best as I can. And I *do* use cannon. The Valorian army is well-gunned. We have significant stores of black powder. Our arsenal outstrips anything an enemy can offer. I rarely even need much cannon."

She imagined Ronan at the very front of an army. "So you let our people fight hand to hand instead."

"That's what we do. It's who we are. If we can't take what we want with our own hands, we don't deserve to win it."

Kestrel leaned away from the gaming table. She sat back in her chair.

He said, "Would you rather I line up my cannon barrel to barrel and raze the eastern forces?"

No, of course not. That wasn't what she'd meant.

"You accuse me of wasting lives. I could, Kestrel. I could waste them in the thousands, the tens of thousands. I don't. I try to minimize enemy casualties."

"Only so that you can enslave people afterward."

His mouth thinned. "I think we should finish our game."

He won.

Verex stopped her in the hallway. "I've been looking for you."

"Maybe you bribed the wrong lady-in-waiting. You should choose one who keeps a closer eye on my whereabouts."

He laughed. "Or maybe *you* should bribe one of my valets, so that we'd be even. Then again"—he shrugged good-naturedly—"my whereabouts aren't very interesting." He tugged her hand. "Come. I have something to show you. Give you, actually."

"A gift?"

"A wedding present."

The word *wedding* stopped her heart. "It's too early for that."

"It's never too early for presents."

"I don't have anything for you."

"Oh, just come. You'll like it, I promise."

It was a good-size puppy. A black, squirming creature with folded ears and a tail that had been docked for hunting. It was chewing the leg of one of the ornate chairs in Verex's sitting room. It had left a yellow puddle on the wooden floor.

"The runt," Verex said proudly. "She survived."

Kestrel bent low, her organza skirts rustling. She offered a hand to the animal, who snuffled it, then pushed beneath so that Kestrel could properly scratch behind her ears. Her stubby tail beat back and forth. Delightedly, the puppy nipped Kestrel's wrist.

Kestrel felt suddenly quiet and warm, as if she had just come inside from a long walk on a day chillier than anyone had predicted.

She straightened. She went to Verex and kissed his cheek.

"Oh," he said, and awkwardly patted her shoulder. "Well." He smiled.

They played with the puppy, whom Kestrel didn't yet want to name. They tossed velvet cushions for the dog to catch. She savaged them. Feathers flurried over the floor.

This moment was simple, smooth, like a pebble lifted from a riverbed. Kestrel could have asked Verex about the screen in the music room. She could have talked about that Borderlands game with her father, or how her oldest friend was no longer her friend. But Kestrel didn't want to. Nothing should spoil this moment. She played tug-of-war with the dog until the animal dropped her cushion, which no longer bore even the vaguest resemblance to a cushion. The puppy collapsed in a black heap and fell asleep.

Kestrel wondered what Jess would name her, then shoved that thought from her mind.

But . . .

Something had been troubling her. Something about that day in Jess's parlor that she should be able to figure out. A mystery that Kestrel thought could have a clear answer when so much else seemed bewildering, like how she understood Jess's anger—and didn't.

"You know a lot about healing," she said to Verex.

"Not really." He sat on the floor by the sleeping puppy, who had huddled on Kestrel's feet. "I studied it a bit. I told you: my father didn't like it. I didn't get far."

"But you know some things."

He shrugged. "I suppose."

"Is there a brownish medicine one might take with water?"

"*Diluted* with water?"

"Yes, that's what I mean. The medicine leaves a residue at the bottom of the glass."

He pursed his lips. "That could be a few different things. You should ask the palace physician. He's developed many medicines made in concentrated form to be diluted later with water. He's excellent at calculating dilution. He trained as a water engineer." When he saw Kestrel's surprise, Verex said, "Yes, he even served in the military with the palace water engineer. But that was long ago. He had a gift as a medic on the battlefield and changed professions." Verex ran a hand down the back of the puppy, who sighed heavily. "Don't you wish it were that easy? To change who you are?"

For a moment, Kestrel didn't quite hear his question. Her mind was sparking with the connection between the palace physician and its chief water engineer, who had been bribed for some unknown thing.

She'd promised Tensen she would discover what that thing was.

She'd promised herself to live by her own ideas of honor. She would help Tensen. Because it was right. Because it mattered.

How can the inconsequence of your life not shame you?

Kestrel's memory was so full of Arin's voice that she didn't realize that Verex was peering at her. What had he asked?

If she wished to change herself.

"No," she lied. Then she decided that what she'd said was the truth. "No," she said again, "I don't."

"THIS CAME FOR YOU," THE DACRAN QUEEN
said in her language, handing Arin a parcel. "A Herrani
ship brought it to the temple island."

He tucked the package under his arm. It couldn't be
simply a package. It was news. Arin hid his eagerness.

And he hid his surprise. At the queen, delivering something to him. At her standing in his room, which was only
one room, not a suite. The bed—much higher than Arin
was used to, and narrower—was in a corner, neatly made.
The light was soft and gray. It haloed a geometric star of
small, triangular windows clustered into a radiant pattern.
The queen's black eyes, lined with streaks of blue paint that
swirled greenly down to her brown cheekbones, seemed to
glow. She was tall; her gaze was almost level with his.

"Open it," she said.

Arin rubbed a palm against his scarred cheek.

"Do you understand me?" she said. "You seem to.
You've learned my language quickly."

"So could Herrani soldiers. We could fight together."

"And yet you cannot obey even a simple command."

Arin opened the package. It was a shirt edged with intricately woven trim in colors he knew well. He shouldn't have stared and begun to decode the knots and colors beneath the queen's gaze, but he did. The Moth—

"That cloth is too heavy for our weather," said the queen.

"I'll send it back." Arin would cut away the woven trim and sew on a message of his own for Tensen.

He draped the shirt casually across the back of a chair, reading in the threads that the imperial water engineer was living beyond her apparent means, and was unfriendly to Herran. The Moth believed that the engineer *had* made a bargain with the emperor. There was no proof, but—

It began to rain. Arin heard water rushing through the castle pipes. The queen had been silent, watching him. He forced himself to turn away from the shirt.

Maybe it was because his mind was full of the Moth, and the way the gray thread that represented her wove throughout the entire trim. Arin looked at the queen and saw Risha instead. The queen had those straight brows, the same shape of the mouth, and the same—he began to suspect it, the idea grew—generosity.

"I am sending my brother outside the city," she said. "You will go with him." She paused, then added, "You are good for him. He is restless."

"Was he with your sister when she was captured by the empire?"

The queen's face closed.

Arin said, "I think he blames himself."

"He blames me."

"I don't understand."

The queen went to the kaleidoscopic windows and watched the rainfall. She pretended his words had meant something else. "It can't be easy to learn another language so quickly. Do you have a gift for it?"

He wasn't sure. Even now, he didn't recognize every word she used. His mind darted meaning into the blank moments and made sense of what he didn't know, crafted whole sentences from understood parts. It felt like a game . . .

As this last thought occurred to him, he saw its danger. He felt the kick in his gut that told his mind to stop, and he snatched at that half thought about words and meaning and games. He tried to drag the thought back. It spun away. It began to think for itself, about Bite and Sting, and about how he could beat someone without knowing each tile in play. Yes, he had won, even when playing against Kestrel made it feel like all the tiles were blind on both sides.

He slammed that thought down. Because the truth was that guessing at what he hadn't known about Kestrel had served him badly. He had believed in things that weren't there . . . or weren't there anymore.

"No," he bluntly told the queen. "No gift."

"Perhaps Dacra and Herran shared some common ancestor, thousands of years ago," she mused, "and that is why our languages are close. But no. We are too different."

"We don't have to be."

She turned to face him. "Stop asking for an alliance."

"I won't."

"Fool."

"I prefer to think of myself as an optimist."

She clicked her teeth: a Dacran way to say *no*. It was an impatient noise. Arin had heard it used with children. "Herran has nothing to offer us but lives," the queen told him. "I would pack your people into the front lines. When we win, I would take your country and make it mine. The word we want for you is not *optimist*. Nor, I think"—she appraised him—"*fool*. It is *desperate*."

The rain must have stopped. The pipes hushed.

She said, "I would be, too. I would ask what you ask. But I would offer more. Then I would negotiate better terms of an alliance."

He thought of that emerald earring he'd paid into the bookkeeper's hand. He thought not about what it was, but what it had meant. He held the value in his mind, its pricelessness, and he cast about for an idea of what could match it. "Tell me what I can give you."

She lifted one shoulder in a delicate shrug. "Something more."

"Tell me what that is."

"I will know," she said, "when you give it to me."

Arin and Roshar rowed up the river. Soft dawn hardened into bright day. The castle was at their backs, then gone. Reeds on the banks tapped a light tattoo against each other, and swarms of enormous dragonflies rippled like flags alongside the canoe.

Roshar steered. When they'd set off from the city, Arin had noted the crossbow slung across Roshar's back, and a set of throwing knives at his hips. Arin had asked if Roshar expected resistance from the plainspeople who had made camp upstream. Roshar had blithely said, "Oh, this is for river beasties," and looked coy. Then, though Arin hadn't pressed him, Roshar added, "If you must know, I'm going to hunt a nice poisonous snake and make you eat it. You *do* like to ruin a surprise."

The canoe slowed. Roshar had paused, so Arin lifted his oar, too, and glanced behind him. Roshar was looking into the reeds. His mutilated nose made his profile jarringly flat.

The current started to push them downstream. They took up their oars again.

There was something about the day—the tempo of the reeds, the dipping of the oars, the dragonflies' *brrr*, and even Roshar's stunted profile—that opened something inside Arin. If he had had to put what he felt into words, he would have perhaps said that it was a kinship with the moment.

He began to sing. For himself, for the day, for the way it made him feel. It had been a while. It felt good to push that music up and into the world, to feel how the initial heft of it lightened on his tongue. The song floated out of him.

He wasn't thinking. He wasn't thinking about her. But then he thought about how he wasn't thinking about her. The song became lead. He shut his mouth.

There was a silence.

Finally, behind him, Roshar spoke. "Don't let my sister hear you do that, or she won't let me kill you."

Arin didn't look back. Then he said, "When I was leaving the capital, I saw Risha."

The canoe angled its direction. Roshar had stopped rowing again. "Does everyone there call her that, or just you?" When Arin glanced questioningly over his shoulder at the prince, Roshar said, "Her name is Rishanaway. That's what strangers should call her. Risha is her little name."

Arin wasn't sure if this was what Risha had asked to be called by the court, or what they had decided to call her. He remembered what she'd said to him on his last day there. Reluctantly, but firmly, because he thought Roshar should know, Arin said, "She told me that her place was in the palace."

Arin saw regret on Roshar's face, and loss . . . but also relief. Arin didn't understand it. As he found himself questioning whether the queen and her brother *wanted* their stolen sister returned, he realized that some furtive part of him had been wondering whether *that* would have been enough to secure the alliance his country needed. If he had brought Risha with him to Dacra, would that have been the queen's "something more"? How would Risha have been most valuable to Herran—as Tensen's Moth, or as a bargaining chip with the Dacran queen?

Arin checked himself. These were questions Kestrel would ask. Kestrel knew exactly how to calculate what someone was worth. His lips curled in sudden disgust.

"Pleasant thoughts for both of us, I see," said Roshar.

"Oars in the water now, little Herrani, or we'll never make the camp before nightfall."

The day had gone orange. It hadn't rained once.

"Nearly there," Roshar said.

"Why do the plainspeople have to move camp?"

"They don't *have* to, but this particular tribe has camped upstream of an agricultural village with crops. The villagers have complained that the water flowing downstream to them is contaminated. My sister wants these refugees to move into the city with the rest."

A fist squeezed Arin's heart. He remembered the woman with the cloth baby. He thought about being forced from his home, and how it would be to build a new home, and to be forced from that one, too. "So they suffer yet again."

"Arin, do you think I *want* to ask them to move? My sister always gets me to do her dirty work." Roshar sighed. "I suppose my face must be good for something." When he caught the startled quality of Arin's silence, Roshar said, "Yes, poor prince, maimed by the empire. Don't you want to do what he asks of you, ye people of the plains? Look at him. Look at his face. He has lost something, too." Roshar swore under his breath.

Arin looked back, even though he knew that Roshar wouldn't want him to see his expression then. It was in moments like these, when the emotion in Roshar's eyes matched his mutilations, that the prince looked most damaged.

Roshar spoke again, clearly this time. "Dacra will take the plains back. General Trajan is in the imperial capital now. It's the right time. We'll take back what they stole."

"No. Don't."

"What?"

"Burn the plains."

"*What?* Never."

"Curse the empire," said Arin. "Curse them. Burn that godsforsaken army out of your land. If they want it so badly, let them burn for it."

"But we can take the plains back. I know we can."

"And when the general returns to the front? What do you think he'll do? *He* will set *you* on fire. You're lucky he didn't do that to begin with." Something twinged inside Arin. Something that had to do with Kestrel. And he was so sickeningly furious with himself, for the way his mind kept reaching for her, at the way his body remembered her, even now, even here, half a world away, that he ground whatever thought he had been about to think into dust.

"Arin." Roshar was still horrified. "That's our *land.*"

"Sometimes you think you want something," Arin told him, "when what you need is to let it go."

The sky was dusky pink when Roshar announced that they'd reached their destination. Arin didn't see an encampment, only a rust-colored screen of reeds. Beyond it, Roshar said, were grassy fields and the refugees.

They paddled to shore and slid into the mucky shallows

to drag the boat into the mud and reeds. Roshar loaded his crossbow. He caught Arin's glance. "Just a precaution."

"I thought you were joking about the snake."

Mournfully, Roshar said, "And *I* thought you believed every little word I said." He pushed ahead through the reeds.

Arin wasn't sure what worried Roshar—he hoped not snakes; a crossbow wasn't a practical weapon against them—but he, too, was worried now. Roshar, a good distance in front of him, looked small in the reeds. Arin moved to catch up. Mud sucked at his heels. "The queen shouldn't have sent you alone."

Roshar turned. "I'm not alone," he said simply. "You're here."

Arin was about to ask for a weapon. He was closing the gap between them.

There was a ripple in the reeds. A prowling wave.

The beast surged from the reeds and spread its claws.

THE TIGER SLAMMED INTO ROSHAR. ROSHAR flung an arm up just as it struck him down. The beast bit the limb, snarling low, its muzzle wet with blood. Its jaws opened to reach for the neck, then closed again on the arm that got in the way.

Arin turned and ran for the canoe. It rocked under the heave of his body against its side. He snatched an oar from its well, stumbled back through mud and bent reeds, and cracked the oar down on the tiger. He beat its face aside.

A roar. The massive striped body recoiled. Roshar rolled away, crimson with his own blood. His hands were empty. He made a gasping sound that was, for one split instant, the only thing Arin heard.

Then the tiger came down on Arin.

He was shoved onto his back into the mud. He sank down. He was swallowing mud, straining the oar up between him and the tiger, who bared broken teeth. Its breath was hot. Its snarls ripped through Arin's body as if he were the one making that sound. Claws were in his shoulders. Pain curled in. He tried to push back with the oar and block the jaws, but he knew how this would end. His arms would give out. The oar would splinter. The tiger would finally get the right angle and close in on his neck.

Black nose. Pulsing stripes. Wild amber eyes. The colors of Arin's death.

But he remembered Roshar's empty hands.

He remembered a crossbow.

And although he knew that a crossbow was no good (how could he aim it *and* keep the tiger at bay? Gods, was it even still loaded?), he risked a glance. He looked away from the tiger's teeth. He looked into the reeds. He saw a snapped crossbow quarrel, its leaden tip sticking out of the mud.

An arm's length away.

"Roshar," he choked out.

Arin heard the reeds rattle. He couldn't see Roshar move, but the prince did, and that was enough.

The tiger's attention lifted from Arin.

Arin reached out, yanked the quarrel from the mud, and drove it into the tiger's eye.

He felt the tiger roar. He dug in deeper. Hot liquid spilled between his fingers. He pushed the quarrel in.

The body heaved onto him. Claws slackened.

Somehow that was when fear set in. The tiger was dead, but Arin was struggling against it, half drowning in the mud as he beat against the striped fur and stared, horrified, into one amber eye, and one ruined and leaking.

Then Roshar was there, and they worked together until Arin slid out from under the body.

He lay gasping in the mud. Roshar sat heavily beside him. The prince's forearm was shredded, held gingerly at an angle. Blood ran from the elbow.

Arin closed his eyes. He saw the tiger's eyes. He opened his. He saw a labyrinth of reeds, the slick of mud beneath his cheek.

Roshar inhaled. For one bizarre moment, Arin thought that the sound he heard next had come from the prince.

A scratchy cry. A mewl.

No. Arin knew what that was. He screwed his eyes shut. He wouldn't look.

"A cub," Roshar said.

And then Arin had to see. A little tiger clambered through the bent reeds. Its forelegs sank into mud. It looked at its slumped mother and cried piteously.

Arin was stricken. He tasted mud in his mouth.

He saw, in his memory, a boy. Begging and weeping. Pulling at his mother's dead hand. Tugging her long, bloody black hair. Arin's hands had been small then. But they'd had a terrible strength. They'd clung hard. Then his mother's murderer had dragged him away.

Arin breathed through the memory. He choked on air as if it were knotted rope. He wiped mud from his face. Spat it out.

"Now, what to do with *you*," said Roshar, looking at the cub. It floundered in the mud. It sank in past its haunches.

"Leave it alone."

Roshar ignored Arin. He slogged through the boggy reeds until he reached the cub. With his good arm, Roshar lifted the tiger free.

"Brother, you are mad," said the queen.

"He loves me," Roshar protested. The cub was sleeping, huddled against Roshar's leg.

"And when it has grown, and is large enough to eat a man?"

"Then I'll make Arin take care of him."

Arin had had enough. He moved to leave Roshar's suite.

"Wait," said the queen.

Arin was sore. His raked shoulders were padded with gauze, and he was tired, achingly tired from the journey back, from the shock of the plainspeople when he and Roshar had stumbled to the camp with a tiger cub, from how easily they had agreed to move camp once they saw the danger of tigers breeding nearby. How they'd fed Arin when he hadn't wanted to eat. And then there had been Roshar's fascination with the tiger's carcass, the way the prince had inspected the slack jaws to pronounce that the broken teeth were an old injury, and thank the goddess for that, he'd said, or they would have had no chance at all. "I would have lost my arm at the very least," Roshar had said. As it was, his arm was a bloody mess. It had been cleaned, stitched, and dressed in the camp. "Looks like you'll have to get me and the cub home all by yourself," Roshar had said cheerfully. So Arin had paddled downstream while

Roshar slept, having numbed his arm with a lighter dose of the same drug he'd once used to knock out Arin. The drugged ring was a cunning thing. He'd pricked himself with it, then eyed Arin's torn shirt and raked shoulders. "Sorry," he'd said. "None for you. You've got to row."

Arin swore at him.

Roshar smiled. "Watch your mouth," he'd said, and closed his eyes.

Arin's shoulders had burned and bled as he paddled. The cub unhappily paced the canoe the entire way to the queen's city. The boat wobbled as the animal moved, and moved again, and found its uncertain footing, and cried.

"Wait," the queen said again to Arin. She left Roshar's side, crossed the room, and offered something. It gleamed on her uplifted palm: Kestrel's dagger. "Thank you," said the queen. She tried to give it to him.

"I don't want it."

The hand that held the dagger faltered.

Arin said, "You know what I want."

The queen shook her head. "No alliance."

Arin remembered the suffocating fear as he lay trapped beneath the tiger's paws. The fear had squeezed his gut. It had robbed his breath. It was the *familiarity* of that fear, not just the fear itself, that had done it. This was how he had felt for months, for *years*: pinned down by the empire.

In his mind, Arin shrank the dagger on the queen's palm. He made it the size of a needle. Easy to ignore. Easy to lose.

He saw again how Roshar had tossed Risha's tiny weapons into the castle dollhouse.

He saw an eastern crossbow, so small compared to a Valorian one.

The tiger cub, its little teeth bared.

His own country, helpless before the empire's massive army, their engineers, their black flags, their black rows of cannon, their seemingly limitless supply of black powder.

Arin saw, suddenly, an idea.

It took shape inside him. It was small. Compact, hard, mobile. It grew behind his eyes until he blinked, and saw again what was actually there before him in Roshar's suite. Not a memory, or a fear, or an idea. Just a dagger on the queen's palm.

How much damage, really, could one dagger do?

"Get that thing away from me," Arin told the queen. "I want a forge, and I want to be left alone."

KESTREL'S FATHER INSPECTED THE PUPPY. HE gripped the scruff of its neck and held it stock-still. He lifted the surprisingly big paws. He held the muzzle and peeled back the pink-and-black lips to see the teeth.

"That's a good dog," he said finally. "You'll have to train her."

No, Kestrel decided. She didn't.

Kestrel had a gift. It lay in a small box tucked into her skirt pocket. It tapped against her thigh as she walked through an arcade and into the Spring Garden. The wind was warm and soft. It made the puppy beside her sniff the air. The dog caught the scent of something and bolted for the trees. Kestrel didn't call her back.

The palace physician was known to tend to his own plot of medicinal herbs. Kestrel found him there by a shrub with a peppery scent.

He straightened at the sight of her. Immediately concerned, he asked if her father had worsened.

"He's well," she said, "though I *am* here because of him." She offered the small box. "Thank you. You saved his life."

He was pleased. There was a slight flush to his lined cheeks, and his hands, dusted with earth, accepted the box carefully. Then he became awkward, fumbling with the box in his haste to clean his hands on a handkerchief, which he didn't have. Kestrel gave him hers.

He smiled apologetically. "I'm not used to appearing presentable to society." He opened the box and caught his breath. Inside lay a golden pin: a flowering tree, the sign of the physicians' order. It bore jeweled fruit. "This is too much."

"For my father's life? It is not enough."

His eyes grew moist. Kestrel felt a little guilty, as if she'd sat down to play Bite and Sting with someone who had no head for the game.

Yet there might be a connection between the physician and the water engineer. She'd promised Tensen to discover what the water engineer had done for the emperor. And then there was that long table set with empty plates in her mind. The eastern plains. The slaves who cleaned the imperial palace. Arin's stitched face.

"Will you show me your garden?" Kestrel asked.

They walked the green rows.

"I'm worried about a friend of mine." Kestrel described Jess's vial of dark liquid. "Is it safe?"

"I think I know who this friend of yours is. A colonial

girl from Herran? No need to worry. I gave her the medicine myself. It's just something to calm the nerves."

Kestrel was relieved. "So it *is* safe."

"Well, in the right dosage." Quickly, he added, "But she would never have access to enough to do her harm. Even city apothecaries aren't allowed to sell it. I oversee the making of that medicine in the palace, and I give out very small supplies."

"Is it addictive?"

"No. The body doesn't crave it. But the mind might. Your friend might come to rely upon it to sleep. If used for too long, it could be dangerous."

"*How* dangerous?"

His expression spoke the answer. "But that would take months of use."

Kestrel's voice rose. "Why would you give my friend a medicine that could kill her?"

"My lady." His voice was respectful but firm. "Every medicine has its risks. We use a medicine because its benefit outweighs potential harm. Your friend needs peace and sleep. Not forever. Just long enough for her to feel that peace is possible. She's weak. I worry that if she doesn't rest, she could fall prey to a serious illness." When he saw Kestrel's uncertainty, he said, "When you saw her, did your friend tremble? Did her hands shake?"

"No."

"Then there's no need to worry. Trembling is a sign of overdosage—not that this would even be possible in the case of your friend. I gave her very little."

The puppy bayed in the distance. "Don't give her any more." Kestrel twisted her fingers together. "Please don't."

"I wouldn't." The physician was affronted. "There's no need to even ask that. I would never risk a Valorian's well-being."

Kestrel tried not to worry. With years of practice at pretending that what really mattered was nothing, she asked the physician about his garden. They discussed his herbs and the earth and the weather.

In war, her father said, *the best feint is the one that you mean. If you want to distract your enemy and make him miss a key move, your ruses must be real.*

This was Kestrel's line of play.

She truly wanted to thank the physician.

She truly wanted to know about Jess's health.

The truth of things, she was coming to understand, has a weight that people sense. She'd given these truths to the physician for him to hold so that while his mind was heavy with them, she could make a move that wouldn't seem like a move at all.

"I'm amazed at how well your garden is doing," she said. "The weather is so fickle. Warm one day, chilly the next. I hardly know what to wear anymore."

"You always dress exquisitely."

"I do, don't I? But it's hard to settle on the right choice. Why, I've even changed the plans for my wedding dress."

He paused midstride. He started to say something, but she carefully missed it. She was helped in ignoring him by the puppy, who came bounding toward Kestrel. It carried a stick in its teeth. The puppy laid it at Kestrel's feet and barked.

"But . . . but it's too late to change your wedding dress," said the physician. "A new one would never be ready in time. Lady Kestrel, you must reconsider . . ."

She ignored him as he continued to talk. The puppy looked at her expectantly, wagging its short tail, wuffling with excitement. Kestrel stooped to pick up the slobbery stick. She threw. The stick soared into the blue sky, whipping over itself. The dog raced across the lawn to fetch it. Kestrel smiled, and waited for the stick to be brought back.

"Sneaky," Arin teased her.

Kestrel shrugged a little helplessly at her imagination. She'd come to accept the way her mind would conjure up Arin. She'd come to need it.

She'd left the physician in his garden to walk the lawn alone with her dog. The day had grown warm. Kestrel sat on the lawn. The green scent filled her senses. She seemed to even taste it.

The puppy settled beside her. Kestrel took off her tight shoes. The grass prickled through her stockings. The palace was too large to appear distant. Still, Kestrel felt far from it, at least for now.

"Not far enough." Arin spoke as if he could read her mind.

She faced her pretend Arin. His scar was healed. His

gray eyes were startlingly clear. "You're not real," she reminded him.

"I *feel* real." He brushed one finger across her lower lip. It suddenly seemed that there were no clouds in the sky, and that she sat in full sunshine. "*You* feel real," he said.

The puppy yawned, her jaws closing with a snap. The sound brought Kestrel to herself. She felt a little embarrassed. Her pulse was high. But she couldn't stop pretending.

Kestrel reached beneath her skirts to pull down a knee-high stocking.

Arin made a sound.

"I want to feel the grass beneath my feet," Kestrel told him.

"Someone's going to see you."

"I don't care."

"But that someone is *me*, and you should have a care, Kestrel, for my poor heart." He reached under the hem of her dress to catch her hand in the act of pulling down the second stocking. "You're treating me quite badly," he said, and slid the stocking free, his palm skimming along the path of her calf. He looked at her. His hand wrapped around her bare ankle. Kestrel became shy . . . though she had known full well what she was doing.

Arin grinned. With his free hand, he plucked a blade of grass. He tickled it against the sole of her foot. She laughed, jerking away.

He let her go. He settled down beside her, lying on his stomach on the grass, propped up by his elbows. Kestrel lay on her back. She heard birdsong: high and long, with a trill at the end. She gazed up at the sky. It was blue enough for summer.

"Perfect," she said.

"Almost."

She turned to look at him, and he was already looking at her. "I'm going to miss you when I wake up," she whispered, because she realized that she must have fallen asleep under the sun. Arin was too real for her imagination. He was a dream.

"Don't wake up," he said.

The air smelled like new leaves. "You said you trusted me."

"I did." He added, "I do."

"You *are* a dream."

He smiled.

"I lied to you," Kestrel said. "I kept secrets. I thought it was for the best. But it was because *I* didn't trust *you*."

Arin shifted onto his side. He caressed her cheek lightly with the back of his hand. That trailing sensation felt like the last note of the bird's song. "No," he agreed, his voice gentle. "You didn't."

Kestrel woke. The puppy was draped across her feet, sleeping. Her stockings lay in a small heap beside her. The sun had climbed in the sky. Her cheek was flushed, the skin tight: a little sunburned.

The puppy twitched, still lost in sleep. Kestrel envied her. She rested her head again on the grass.

She closed her eyes, and tried to find her way back into her dream.

Later, in the Butcher's Row, Kestrel told Tensen to find out if the water engineer changed her bet on the wedding dress. If she did, then it meant that Elinor and the physician were working together.

Kestrel plucked at her work scarf. She tugged it low. Her disguise felt very thin. "There's something else . . ." The weather remained warm, but she shivered. "I was wrong to make you promise not to tell Arin about me."

Tensen raised his white brows.

"I want him to know," she said.

"I'm not sure that's wise."

"Of course," she said hastily, "a letter sent to Herran would be too risky. But maybe you know of a way . . ." She heard the pleading in her voice, and stopped.

Tensen's expression shifted. It showed a flash of something—what, Kestrel couldn't quite tell, it had come and gone too quickly—and then settled into sympathy. "Oh, Kestrel," Tensen said. "I would tell him, but he's not in Herran. I don't know where he is."

"You're his spymaster. How can you *not know*?"

"No one does." Tensen spread his hands. His gold ring caught the light. "If you don't believe me, you can certainly ask around. But"—his voice grew concerned—"given your . . . history with Arin, I'm not sure such inquiries would be safe. They could come to the attention of the emperor. Or your father."

Kestrel felt horribly trapped and robbed, though she hadn't known it was possible to feel robbed of something she had already given up. She struggled not to show this. Already, that dream on the grass had faded in her memory. It was as if she'd worn it out by thinking too much about it. But in the moment, it had felt so real. Kestrel couldn't quite believe that it hadn't been.

She looked numbly at Tensen's ring. He hadn't worn it in a while. She supposed that it had been lost, and found again. Sometimes things happened that way. But sometimes, Kestrel knew, what's lost stays lost forever.

KESTREL WASN'T SURE HOW, BUT GENERAL
Trajan had learned about the deserter: the well-bred son
who had left his post in a brigade fighting in the east.

"And he's here." Her father's voice was flat. "Living in a
palace suite."

"I haven't decided what to do with him." The emperor
reached for his fork and knife and suggested that they
begin the third course. He caught Kestrel's eye. She began
to eat.

Her father did not. "What is there to decide?"

"Trajan, he's just a boy. No older than Verex." The emperor smiled fondly at his son, who looked down at his
plate.

"He betrayed you. He betrayed me. He betrayed *himself.* Where is his honor now?"

"I imagine it's with his parents' lucrative mills in the
southern isles. Maybe it's been ground along with their fine
grain and baked into delicious bread."

"The law on desertion is clear."

The emperor drank his wine. "To be honest, I was saving him for you. Go see him if you like."

"I will," her father said, "and then I'll return to the east."

"You can't even walk the length of the Spring Garden without catching your breath. Would *you* follow such a commander into battle?"

Her father's eyes squinted as if narrowed against a sudden glare of light. Kestrel brought her fork clattering down on her plate. Anger boiled up her throat. She opened her mouth to speak, but her father's eyes cut to her, and it was the same as when he'd stood in the palace courtyard, his blood on his horse, and she had moved to help him.

"All in good time, old friend," the emperor said gently. His voice had an almost smoky sound, a quality that might have been love if love were like cured meat: hung, dried, and stored to be eaten a little at a time in hard conditions.

Verex pushed his food around his plate. Kestrel's father didn't move.

"I'm sorry," the emperor told him. "I'm not ready to lose you yet."

The general wanted her to come with him. "One day you'll rule the empire," he said. "You need to know what to do."

This was what he did.

He went to the young soldier's palace suite. He watched the young man, not much older than Kestrel, grow pale. The general brought Kestrel into the sitting room with him, then drew the soldier to the side, one firm hand on the shoulder. The general murmured in his ear. The boy sank in on himself, and turned his face so that Kestrel couldn't see.

The general's voice took the tone of a question. The boy inhaled a shuddering breath. Kestrel's father said something that sounded soothing. Safe. She'd heard him like that before, when she was small.

"Forgive me," the soldier said in a strangled whisper.

"I will," the general said. "After."

Then he told Kestrel that it was time to go.

The deserter used his dagger. An honor suicide.

For a few days, the gossip was on every courtier's lips. Then news came from the east. The barbarians had burned the plains, said the report. The empire's latest prize was black, barren, smoking.

The names came later. A much longer list of casualties than usual.

One name was passed around the court like a pearl. It was said slowly, in appreciation of its luster, its smooth weight, the way it rolled into the well of a palm and warmed.

When Kestrel heard it, she realized that she had been expecting this since the day Ronan had snatched the recruitment list from her. The discovery of that expectation cracked some brittle thing inside her. She had known. She had known this would happen. And yet it was now clear that she hadn't *believed* that she did, that she had shunted thoughts of it away into a part of her mind where things were kept but never looked at.

How could she have hidden from that knowledge?

How could she have known that Ronan would die, and yet not know it?

It had been so clear.

In her rooms, alone, Kestrel covered her mouth. The pearl of Ronan's name lodged in her throat. She swallowed. It hurt.

She had dreams that shamed her in the morning, dreams where Ronan gave her a white powdered cake, yet spoke in Arin's voice. *I made this for you,* he said. *Do you like it?*

The powder was so fine that she inhaled its sweetness, but always woke before she could taste.

Kestrel wrote to Jess. She was afraid to visit.

The next day, Kestrel's maid brought her a letter. Kestrel's heart leaped to see Jess's handwriting on the outside, and that familiar wax seal. Instantly, she blamed herself for that surge of relieved hope. It was wrong for her to feel this way when Ronan was dead.

But she hadn't thought Jess would answer her. And this letter—Kestrel weighed it in her hand before she broke the seal—was just as thick as the one she had sent Jess. Surely Jess wouldn't write so much if she wanted nothing to do with Kestrel.

Kestrel opened it. She felt again that strange mixture of knowing and not knowing, of shock and resignation.

She unfolded the envelope. Hadn't she seen this coming? Hadn't it been obvious?

The envelope contained the letter Kestrel had sent to Jess: unopened, unread.

Kestrel hadn't played the piano since discovering the music room's hidden screen, but she no longer cared who heard her. She wanted someone to listen to her grief.

Her music was angrier than she had expected. A sweet prelude that twisted away from her, and darkened, and knitted its way down into the lower octaves. She played until her wrists hurt. She played until she fumbled. The room vibrated with dying chords.

Kestrel rubbed her hot wrists. There was a ringing silence. Then, just as Kestrel was about to go over her mistake, she heard a faint chime.

She knew that sound.

There *was* someone behind that screen. A person likely to know about the palace's hidden listening chambers. And why wouldn't the emperor share such a secret with this man? The emperor valued him. The proof? Consider the emperor's gift: a golden watch. It showed the phases of the moon. Its hour and minute hands were tipped with diamonds. It chimed the hour.

Kestrel didn't know what had made her father hide behind the screen. She didn't know if he was still there, or if he'd left the instant after his watch had chimed and Kestrel had lifted her head at the sound.

All she knew was that he had listened to her play. He'd never done that before.

A memory came to Kestrel. Deep into her seventh year,

when Kestrel was still weak from the same disease that had killed her mother, the general had decided to ride with his daughter out of the city. She had nearly fallen asleep on her pony. The Herran countryside was crisp. The chill had made her nose run. He had taken her hunting. He helped her notch the bow. He pointed out the prey. He shifted her elbow into the right position. When she missed, he didn't say anything. He shot a pheasant, plucked it, and built a fire. She dozed before it, and woke to find herself covered with furs. It was dark. Her hair smelled like smoke and roasted fowl. When her father saw that she was awake, he reached into a saddlebag for a loaf of bread, which he broke. He gave her the larger half.

In the listening silence of the music room, Kestrel lowered her hands to the piano keys and played the memory of that day. She played the sway of her pony beneath her, the phlegm in her lungs, the tension in the bowstring, the glowing heart of the fire. She played the way that her father, when he thought that she was still asleep, had brushed hair from her forehead and tucked it behind her ear. He had drawn the furs up to her cheek. She was young enough then to call him papa.

Kestrel played the moment when she had opened her eyes, and he had looked away. She played the feeling of the bread in her hand.

Not long after, Kestrel went to the gallery. She was brought up short to see her father there. He was looking out one of the slender windows, his back to the art. He turned when she entered.

"I heard that you come here every day," he said. "I hoped to speak with you alone."

They'd been avoiding each other since she'd heard his watch chime. "You could have come to my suite," she said.

"I was curious. I wondered what you like so much about the gallery." He came to meet her. His boots echoed in the vast space.

"You know what I like." How many times had he called her love for music a weakness? He had warned her: the Herrani had admired the arts, and look what had happened to them. They'd forgotten about the sword.

A frown dented his brow. He lifted his gaze from the collection of sculptures and paintings and focused again on Kestrel. His voice low, he said, "Your mother played beautifully."

"And I?"

"You, even more so."

"I was glad that you listened to me play."

He sighed. "That watch."

"I like your watch. You must continue to wear it. It'll keep you honest."

"Listening like that was beneath me."

"What if I had invited you?" Kestrel asked.

"You didn't."

"I did, over and over, for years."

He was silent.

"It was always an open invitation," Kestrel said. "It still is."

Her father gave her a small smile. "Would you show me your favorites?" He gestured at the gallery.

Kestrel had almost forgotten why she was here. She'd pushed thoughts of Tensen, the water engineer, and the palace physician away. Now they came back. She felt a stitch of fear, a thread of guilt pulled tight.

She couldn't really see the painting she now thought of as Tensen's. It was farther down the gallery. From the entrance, it was a mere square of purple.

She kept her father from it. She showed him an alabaster bowl she admired, and a bronze fisherman lifting a fish scaled with lapis lazuli. There was an eastern porcelain egg that opened to show an armed girl.

But her father noticed the painting. "I remember that," he said. "I took it for the emperor."

He approached it. Kestrel, silent with dread, had no choice but to go with him. If she tried to turn him away from the painting, she would only call more attention to it.

A masker moth lay on the painting's frame. Kestrel's pulse leaped.

Her father studied the landscape. "It looks different here than it did in that southern mansion." He didn't appear to notice the camouflaged moth. If he did, what would he make of it? Nothing? It seemed impossible that something that meant a great deal to her could mean nothing to him. Carefully casual, she said, "Do you like the painting?"

He shrugged. "The emperor does." His gaze lifted from

the canvas. Kestrel felt a terrible relief. Then her father spoke again, and as she listened, that relief shriveled into shame. "I know that you don't want me to return to the east. I won't lie, Kestrel. I need to fight. But the need . . . has been different over the years. It hasn't been just for honor." His light brown eyes were fixed on hers. "You were born a few months after Verex. I wouldn't have made you marry him. But I hoped. On the battlefield, I hoped you'd inherit the empire. When you chose Verex, it felt like fate."

"You don't believe in fate."

"I believe that the land I won was for you. You are my fate."

Guilt swelled in her throat. It made it hard to breathe, and she couldn't hold his gaze any longer. But the instant her eyes fell from his, they darted quickly, helplessly, toward the moth.

Her father saw. He blinked. He peered at the painting's frame. He frowned.

It was just a moth, Kestrel tried to tell herself. He couldn't possibly guess what it meant.

She thought her father might say something. She readied herself to answer him. But in the end, all he did was silently flick the moth to the floor.

"The water engineer changed her bet," Tensen said. "She and the emperor's physician *are* working together."

"I can't meet with you again like this," Kestrel said. "I'm going to be caught."

Tensen was instantly worried. He asked for her reasons,

but it wasn't so simple as her father seeing the moth on the painting's frame, which Tensen dismissed. It was that feeling of skating close to ruin. She'd felt this before, or something like it, when she had first begun playing Bite and Sting and didn't know when to leave the table, or stayed because she needed to know what would happen next. She needed to see all the tiles turned, the play played, the final measurement of who had what and who had come short. She'd lost easily at first, especially against her father. Then she had learned.

"I just can't," she told Tensen.

He tried to flatter her. He appealed to her sense of good. He questioned her courage. He did everything but mention Arin, which he seemed to sense would end everything.

Tensen was a skilled player, too.

"Well," he sighed, "you could keep your ears open, couldn't you? If there's something I need to know, tell your dressmaker."

Kestrel was eager to leave the Butcher's Row. She agreed to pass anything of note on to Deliah. She hurried away, the hem of her maid's dress catching on her boothooks.

TEMPTATION WAS THE COLOR WHITE.

It was black ink, quivering at the point of a pen's nib.

It was Kestrel, writing in her study. She wrote a letter to Arin. She wrote her reasons. She wrote her heart. Everything was inked in quick and heavy lines. Nothing was crossed out. It looked up at her: bare, black-and-white honesty.

That was temptation. But this was reality: the fire that burned low on the grate, despite the high spring weather, despite the nearing end of spring and the climb of days toward the Firstsummer wedding.

Reality was red. It was hot, hungry, snapping. It ate whatever Kestrel fed it. She burned the letter. Soon there was nothing left of the fire but cold, scaly black wood, lightly furred with ash. The letter lay in flakes. One page curled like a black shell.

Kestrel thought of the emperor. She thought of her father.

There was nothing left to read in the dead fireplace.

Still, Kestrel took a poker and raked it through the ash to make sure.

Kestrel's eighteenth birthday was fast approaching. Her birthday—and the piano recital the emperor had commanded—was less than a fortnight away. It would be the last official court gathering until her wedding two days following. She played ferociously for hours on end. Sometimes she heard her father's watch chime: a light sound, as light as a smile. It always soothed her music. When Kestrel played for him, the melody ran sweet, sheer, and strong.

She had a dress fitting for the recital. The gown was a delicate affair of creamy lutestring silk, the lace sleeves short and loose. Kestrel stood still on the dressmaker's block. Fleetingly, it occurred to her that the block was about the height of an auction block. She remembered Arin standing on one.

Kestrel wondered what it would be like if time could be unsewn, the threads ripped out and redone. She went back to the day of the auction, that first day, that sight of a slave stepping onto the block. She imagined everything differently. This time, she didn't bid. He wasn't for sale. Her father had never won the Herran War. Kestrel grew up in the capital instead. Her mother didn't sicken, didn't die. Kestrel saw the baby in her father's arms, the one that she had been. In Kestrel's reimagining of the world, that baby was exactly as her father had described.

Deliah knelt, floating the hem up. The silk puffed,

then fell in scalloped folds. Deliah fussed with it. Kestrel's maids grew bored and drifted into other rooms.

Then, quickly, quietly, Deliah said, "Do you have any news for me?"

Kestrel sharply glanced down at her. "No."

"Tensen hopes that you will—soon."

Kestrel said nothing, but Deliah nodded as if she'd spoken. The dressmaker looked somehow both disappointed and relieved. "Well," Deliah said, "I'm sure you know what you're doing."

Did Kestrel know? She thought of when she sat to play Bite and Sting. When Kestrel turned the tiles, and flipped the blank sides onto their backs, and showed their faces and tallied their value, did she know? Sometimes the game went too quickly for Kestrel to understand exactly what she was doing. All she knew was that in the final play she would win.

Kestrel looked at Deliah. She wasn't certain of winning anymore, or even of what she could possibly hope to win. She didn't know what winning would mean.

Smoothly, she told Deliah, "Of course I do."

There was a hunt in the mountain forest behind the palace. The hounds bayed. A few courtiers brought slaves to load their crossbows for them, which would have appalled Kestrel's father, had he seen it. He'd chosen to stay behind.

Verex came, but refused to hunt. The emperor smiled widely. "There's my milk-blooded boy," he said.

"Walk with me, Verex," said Kestrel. "I've no interest in hunting either."

They took the trail ahead of the emperor. Kestrel's puppy bounded alongside her.

"What a sweet dog," Kestrel heard Maris say.

The emperor's cheerful voice floated clear. "Do you like her?"

Verex stiffened beside Kestrel.

"She's yours," the emperor told Maris.

Kestrel turned. "No. She's mine."

"What do you care if Maris has her?" There was that smile again. "You haven't even named her."

"Let her go," Verex whispered in Kestrel's ear. "Remember." He didn't say what she should remember, but Kestrel did anyway: Arin's stitched face.

The dog nudged her damp nose against Kestrel's trousered leg.

"Her name," Kestrel told the emperor, "is *Mine*."

He shrugged and looked careless. Maris, with a courtier's instinct, had caught the scent of danger and waited to see what would happen next. When nothing did, and nothing more was said, she moved to catch up with her friends.

Later that afternoon, the emperor shot a fox. "For my daughter." Blood marbled its reddish ruff. Its little black feet looked like dried paintbrushes. The emperor declared that its fur would be made into a stole for Kestrel.

When the court headed down to the castle and Verex was walking alongside Risha, the emperor fell in step with Kestrel.

He wasn't smiling anymore, but the smile was in his hardened voice, trapped there: an insect in amber. "Don't be more trouble than you're worth," he said.

"Give the dog away," Kestrel told Verex. She had held the prince back on the palace lawn, its grass soft and fine, the green brightly pale. The other courtiers had gone ahead. "Find her a home far from the court. Find the right person."

"*You* are the right person."

Kestrel's eyes stung. The puppy sat and happily chewed her paws.

Verex said, "This is my fault."

Kestrel said no. She said that she could no longer look at this dog, this warm and perfect gift, without seeing it hurt. It was different to give something up than to see it taken away. The difference, Kestrel said, was choice. A limited freedom, but better than none. Or so she had thought when Arin had given her two keys to his guarded house. She had thought the same when she'd offered him his country, nailed and bound and screwed tight with certain conditions. Better than nothing. She'd thought this before, and thought it again, but she didn't believe it anymore. Now she knew that to give something up *was* to have it taken away.

Kestrel said all this silently to herself. The words felt so loud inside her head that she almost forgot that she hadn't actually spoken them. But then she looked again at Verex and saw him waiting, worried, and remembered what he'd said last. She shook her head: *no.*

Quietly, Verex said, "My father needs for you to love him best. He needs for you to love what he loves. There's no room for anything else."

"I know."

"I'm not sure you do. Kestrel, your dressmaker is dead."

The news dropped hard. It sank and hit bottom. Kestrel saw Deliah, the woman's gray eyes lined with heavy lashes—Arin's eyes—as she lifted the ivory hem of the dress. The fabric went sheer, then solid as it settled. The skirt had swelled like a lung, then sighed.

Fear came over Kestrel in a nasty, shimmering breathlessness.

"She was seen meeting with the Herrani minister of agriculture," Verex said. "Later, the captain of the guard came for her. She killed herself with her own shears."

Kestrel remembered Thrynne's bloody fingers in the guttering prison light.

"The meeting with the minister wasn't why the captain was sent," Verex said. "That was an excuse. The real reason happened the day your governor left. The reason was the stitches on his face. Neat seams. Kestrel, don't you remember how perfect they were? My father saw. That dressmaker's loyalty to Arin was clear on his face."

The puppy was licking Kestrel's palm. Warm wet skin, cooling. Breath gently huffed into Kestrel's hand. The sky was a feather blanket of clouds, save for one blue hole in the fabric. A blue cloud in a white sky.

The hole grew wider, bluer. It pulled itself open. It silently stretched, like Kestrel's guilt, like the moment when she'd seen Arin's sewn face, like her father's gaze, drawn to the moth on the painting's frame. Kestrel saw satin blue, the color of Jess's dress. Powdered-sugar clouds, Kestrel thought. In her memory, Ronan handed her a cake. She tasted it. It ate into her tongue like poison.

Verex said, "You need to watch yourself. If you play against my father, you'll lose. This kind of game isn't about intelligence, Kestrel. It's about experience. And you're conflicted, and so . . . *hurt* that . . ." He shook his head. "Please, just don't do anything reckless."

"For how long?"

"You know."

Kestrel rested her wet palm on the big puppy's black skull. *Mine*, she thought. Then she lifted her hand away and told Verex to take the dog by the collar.

How long? Until the emperor was dead.

"Kestrel . . . one day, we could change things."

She looked up from the dog and at Verex, at his long, thin frame, the hunched shoulders, the shock of pale hair, the large, liquid eyes.

She wondered what would happen if she took his free hand. She wondered if he would imagine that Risha, not she, held his hand, and if this was how Kestrel's marriage to him would always be. She saw herself and Verex holding each other. She felt, almost, the kindness of it . . . and she felt, surely, its cruelty. Its claim on them. Its crime as they each pretended the other was someone else.

"I will never keep you from Risha," she said.

"I wouldn't do this to her," he said. "If—"

There was no need to finish. They both knew what the emperor was capable of doing to the princess if Verex defied him.

"We could remake the world," Verex said. "Would it be so bad, to rule the empire together?"

It had been a question Kestrel hadn't allowed herself to ask. Now she did. The question kept asking itself, an echo with no answer.

"We can do this," Verex said, "if we wait. If we're careful. Kestrel, can you be careful?"

In her mind, Kestrel played the tiles.

The emperor.

The water engineer.

The physician.

A favor.

Herran.

Valoria.

She noted the new engravings. She arranged them in different orders. She sought a pattern and came up empty. She mixed the tiles again. But the emperor made it hard to think. She flipped his tile so she wouldn't have to look at him.

Its other side, however, wasn't blank. It showed her father's face.

What game was this?

What did Kestrel think she was doing?

Hadn't she lost enough? Hadn't she done enough? She remembered Verex's advice.

The riddle of the engineer and physician wasn't hers to solve. She needed to stop.

Yes, stop playing, Kestrel, she told herself. Clear the bets, clear the table. Walk away from the game.

Now.

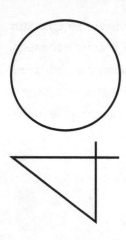

FIRST, ARIN MADE THE MOLDS. ONE, THE SIZE
and shape of a child's marble. The other, long and thin and
cylindrical. He made two of each kind from fired clay and
set the twinned halves aside. He heated lead in the forge's
fire until the metal oozed red.

Arin had been a blacksmith, but blacksmiths rarely
work with molds. His clay molds cracked. Hot lead spilled.
There was nothing to do but let everything cool into a mis-
begotten heap and shove it to the side.

It was maddening. And surprising, how Arin realized
that he needed those hours in the forge, how work he was
once forced to do was now *his*. He loved that feeling of
making something. He smoothed fresh clay, curving it,
hollowing it out with a measured tool. He watched new
molds bake in the forge's fire.

When they broke again, he almost didn't mind. He
would make more. One day, they would be right.

Arin had told the queen and her brother not to enter the forge. Roshar did anyway, his arm still heavily bandaged, the little tiger padding behind him.

"I think"—Roshar surveyed the disarray—"that you should have taken that dagger and been happy with it."

Arin handed him a list. "Supplies."

"My, how the lowly have risen. I'm not your messenger boy." He read the list. "What do you want *that* for? What are you making?"

"Your queen's *something more*."

Roshar laughed. "She asked you for 'something more'? I doubt that this"—he flourished the list at Arin's latest disaster—"was what she had in mind."

The tiger nipped Arin's ankle. He gently nudged its face away. "Roshar, why are you here?"

"I've named the cub. I named him after you."

"Roshar."

"When Arin grows up, you'll be sentenced to death by tiger in the Dacran arena. Arin will eat you alive."

Arin looked at Roshar's feral grin, and at the soft, mazed face of the tiger. The fire caught its eyes.

Roshar said, "I came to tell you that we burned the plains yesterday."

Arin glanced up. The green paint that lined Roshar's eyes made them look narrower, bright. Roshar's smile changed. It dug in deep. "Casualties?" Arin asked.

"Many."

"Good."

"Not quite good enough for you, I'm afraid. You gave sound advice, I admit, but that won't buy your alliance. I don't see how *this* will either." Roshar looked contemptuously at the items littering the forge's worktable.

Arin was tempted to explain his idea. "Do you remember the weapons in Risha's dollhouse?"

Roshar's expression closed. "Do you remember that seal on your pretty dagger? That knife is a lady's weapon. Don't think we don't know whose." He shoved at a broken mold. Ceramic dust scraped across the table. Yet Roshar saved the real damage for what he said before leaving, the tiger at his heels. "Don't wonder, Arin, why we won't ally with you."

Another article of clothing arrived for Arin. A pair of trimmed gloves. Tensen's woven code told him that the Moth had uncovered a connection between the water engineer and the emperor's physician. Sarsine reported that conditions in Herran had worsened. Had Arin secured an eastern alliance? the knots asked. He should return home.

Tensen, despite Arin's insistence that Kestrel have no colored thread, managed to work her in anyway. Firstsummer had almost arrived, Tensen said. She was a glowing bride. *Be happy for her, Arin,* said a knotted line as bumpy as a badly healed scar.

But Tensen didn't know what Arin knew. Tensen didn't know how cynically Kestrel had sold herself to the person with the most power. He hadn't seen her face above the sticky tavern table when she admitted her role in the murder of so many people.

Arin threw the gloves in the forge's fire. They smelled like burning flesh.

Kestrel would never have his happiness.

Roshar came again some days later. "It looks like a big, metal reed." He poked at the cooled object resting on one half of the opened mold. "I think I know what you're doing, Arin. I think it won't work."

"I told you to stay away."

"And didn't I? Notice that this time I didn't bring the tiger with me. Arin makes you nervous. As you see, I am attentive to your every wish, spoken or otherwise."

"Then leave."

"How did you ever survive, little slave, with that mouth of yours? Did you pray to your god of luck?" Roshar studied him, his gaze lingering on the left half of Arin's face. The scar seemed to prickle under Roshar's scrutiny. "You are luckier than I."

Roshar was right, Arin shouldn't have survived, not with his great skill for saying what he shouldn't. Arin said, "Were you with Risha when she was taken?"

"No." But it sounded like "yes."

"Was that when you were enslaved?"

"I *will* kill you."

"Why do you come here, if it's not because I'll say what no one else will?"

"What I want," Roshar said, "is for you to accuse me. *That* is what no one else will do. Not my people, who think I'm the victim. And never, ever the queen."

"Accuse you of what? Escaping when your sister didn't? Surviving?" Gently, Arin said, "If that's your crime, it's mine, too."

"Did *you* sell your sister?"

Arin recoiled. "What?"

"When the Valorians came for your country, did you trade her for something better? That's what we did with Risha. Our little girl. So gifted, even that young, with a blade. No river reed dolls for her. No, her bedroom was a fencing salle. Her toy box was an armory. Our older sister saw it. She knew what to do.

"We're twins, the queen and I. Did you know that? No? Well, if you cut off her nose and ears you'll find that we look very much alike. But oh, the key difference of four minutes. She was born before me. She got the country. Not that I wanted it. I didn't know what I wanted. But this is what I was: expendable.

"Tell me, Arin, the solution to this tempting conundrum. If you had a child assassin with lovely, innocent eyes, a princess your enemy was sure to snatch up if given the chance, what would you do? Would an idea cook in the heat of your mind? Maybe your older sister is the cunning one. She'll tell you the way to topple the empire. You: middle child, only boy, what do *you* do? You explain things to your little sister. You ride with her into enemy territory. You pretend to be her servant. You make yourselves noticed. You are conspicuous. And when you're captured, you let her go." Roshar's expression grew embittered, sly. "And then you wait. You wait, your queen waits, to see if Risha will put a knife in the emperor's neck."

It made unexpected sense to Arin. It explained Risha's claim that she belonged in the palace. It explained her haunted look. But . . . "She was captured years ago. What is she waiting for?"

"Revenge, maybe, on a brother and sister who used her. After the first year, we thought that she was waiting for the right opportunity to kill the emperor. More years passed. Now . . . we think she's become Valorian. Maybe that's what happens after someone grows up and understands that she was betrayed by her own family."

"You shouldn't have told me this. Why did you tell me this?"

"Because I know that what I said about that dagger isn't true. I knew, that day when they cut my face in your country, that you would never sell yourself. I could see it. You would never sell what's dear to you. Look at you, Arin. You're made of so many splendid, stupid *limits*."

Arin saw, in his mind's eye, the burning gloves, their curling fingers. He smelled that acrid reek. He remembered the Moth's coded news. "I don't think Risha is the empire's friend."

In his memory, flames shriveled the knots' message: *Have you secured the eastern alliance?*

Roshar's eyes were starving for news of his sister. Arin's people were starving, having run through the hearthnut harvest more quickly than thought. And Arin was starving as he remembered how the gloves had burned. He was hungry. He was hungry for this: to put his trust where it belonged.

He drew Roshar's attention to the long metal barrel on the worktable. "Let me tell you what this will do."

It took time to complete the parts of the miniature cannon. There was a chamber at one closed end for a paper twist of black powder, which rested on an internal pan behind where one placed the little metal ball. Arin cut a short, stiff fuse. He inserted it into the black powder twist.

He knew how to work leather from his time in the Valorian general's stables. He wrestled with stiff stuff used for saddles, making a packed leather handle for the end where the barrel would be lifted, leveled, and loaded with explosive. When Arin slid the barrel's end into the slim, hard leather box, he thought, oddly, of his family gardener. Long before the Herran War, the gardener had bred trees in the orchard, inserting a slip of one tree into the thick stock of another.

Arin attached his strange stock to the fitted barrel. He set steel pins through punctured holes in the stock and then soldered them to the barrel. Last, he cut a long strip of leather and fashioned a strap. This weapon was meant to be carried.

Arin slung it over his shoulder like he would a Dacran crossbow. Then he summoned the queen and her brother.

They cleared the castle yard outside the forge. Just before Arin fitted the black powder twist and metal ball into their chamber, he had a vision of the whole device exploding in his hands and taking his head with it. He'd used black powder before. He'd felt a cannon's burst. He'd heard it:

that single, booming heartbeat of the god of war. But it wasn't fear that he felt when he lit the fuse and set the stock against his shoulder. It was hunger.

The fuse burned.

The weapon cracked the air. It slammed into Arin's shoulder, punched the breath out of him. It seared his palm. He almost dropped it.

There was a brutalized silence. Shock had changed Roshar's and the queen's faces. A wisp of smoke trailed from the broad, blessedly big kitchen door. Arin's aim had been terrible. But that didn't matter. What mattered was the little lead ball, buried deep in the door. What mattered was the queen pacing the yard to stand tiptoe before the door. She touched the smoking hole.

Yes. He willed her to say it. As Arin found his breath again, his mind didn't think words like *alliance* or *trust* or even *something more.* Just *yes.* Later, he would consider the weapon fully. Later, he would shrink from what he'd done. But now there was only *no* or *yes,* and he'd had to choose. He'd had to find what would give him the word he wanted.

"That," Roshar said. *"That* against the empire."

"Think about how much black powder it takes to fire a cannon," Arin said. "The Valorians don't care. They have a lot of it. We don't, but we won't need much with this, and it can go anywhere. Let *them* drag their heavy cannon. Let *them* waste horses and soldiers maneuvering artillery into position. I know"—Arin shook his head—"the device isn't precise. Not yet. I can make it precise."

Roshar and the queen still stared at him.

"Come with me," Arin said. "I want to show you something else."

He led them into the forge, which was hot from the vat of molten metal Arin had prepared. Arin unslung the weapon. He strode toward the vat. There was a choking gasp from the queen as she realized what he was about to do. He dropped the weapon into the vat.

He turned back to the queen and her brother. "The Herrani will make more. I'll tell them how. We'll supply you with them. We would do that . . . for our allies."

"Did you have to *melt* it?" Roshar said.

"I need you to need me. You could have taken it, examined its mechanism, and found a way to reproduce it. Then you wouldn't need Herran."

"Arin, you idiot. What makes you think we won't torture the design out of you?"

"You won't."

"*I* might. I might enjoy it."

"You wouldn't." He looked at them. "Well? Can we fight together?"

It was the queen who said the word, but Roshar who made it real. He crossed the short space of the forge and placed one palm on Arin's cheek. It was the Herrani gesture of kinship. The queen smiled as Arin returned the gesture, and then the word came: beautiful, deadly, as small and hot as the hole in the kitchen door. In that moment, that word was all that Arin wanted.

"Yes."

Arin was coming from the baths. His face had been sprayed with black powder. It had been in his hair. Even in his teeth. He looked like he'd survived a fire. He'd cleaned himself, noting the massive bruise that darkened his scarred right shoulder and crept toward his chest. Then he returned to his room to pack.

The queen was waiting outside his door. She opened it for him to enter. Thinking that she needed to discuss something in private, perhaps a detail of the alliance, he was silent, too, as they walked in. When the queen had shut the door softly behind her, he said, "My people need to hear the news. I'd like to leave."

The queen came to him, then came closer. She reached to thread fingers through his damp hair. He froze. Whispering her cheek across his, she brought her warm lips to his ear. "Yes," she murmured. "But not yet."

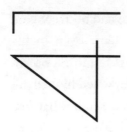

HE KISSED HER. HER MOUTH PARTED BENEATH his. Her hands were on him, and it was curious, it felt alien. He relaxed—shouldn't he relax? She seemed to think he should.

He remembered his hunger. Not for this. But she gave, and he took, and gave back, even while knowing what he really wanted instead. He didn't want to want it, and the thought of Kestrel, of that monstrous want—so stupid, so *wrong*—made him stop. He pulled away. He gritted his teeth once, hard, in a held breath, bright fury at himself.

"Arin?" said the queen.

He kissed her again, more deeply. This time, he lost himself in it a little. It filled him. It pulled him away from himself. That was good. He was tired with the way he had been. He forgot it all.

Except . . . he remembered other kisses, other times. It was impossible not to.

This was the truth: in his mind, Kestrel touched his scarred face. This was her mouth moving against his. This was the truth: what he imagined was a lie. The truth and the lie held him tight.

It made him think. The queen leaned into him, brushing his bruised shoulder, and he winced. He recalled his own soot-covered face after firing the weapon. What had Arin thought earlier? That he looked like he'd been in a fire.

Something in his mind began to burn. Arin saw again that pair of gloves in the flames. He remembered telling Roshar to burn the plains. *You're lucky the general didn't do that to begin with.*

Wait, wait. Why hadn't he?

Because Kestrel had offered him a different plan. The poisoned horses. *I can explain,* she'd said to Arin. He'd refused to listen. *I had no choice,* she'd said. *My father would have—*

Tentatively, with a dread that hissed into him along its quick fuse, Arin imagined the disaster that didn't happen and the one that did. He imagined fire and the plains-people burning . . . or dead horses and an exodus south.

The kiss went cold on his lips. Arin was numb with understanding. He broke away from the queen.

Arin imagined Kestrel. He saw her considering a choice: fire and annihilation, or poison and survival. He knew what he'd choose. He began to wonder if Kestrel had made the very same choice.

He grew pale. He felt the blood leave him. His warring heartbeat was loud in his ears.

The queen was staring. He'd pulled away from her; he remembered doing that as if it were a lifetime ago. Arin couldn't be sure if she'd touched him again after that. She wasn't touching him now. She eyed him warily. He saw himself as she must: hunched, seeming suddenly ill. Or as if he'd been assaulted. Cuffed across the head, or knocked back like when the explosion in the kitchen yard had kicked the breath out of him. "Arin," she said, "what's wrong?"

Arin's shoulder ached, his throat ached. *He* had been wrong, he had been kissing a lie. It would have sweetened, he would have kept doing it. He would have kept pretending the queen was Kestrel. But who *was* Kestrel? He'd been so sure, once. And then she'd appeared outside his besieged city walls with the emperor's treaty in her hand and an engagement mark on her brow, and his certainty became a wretched, crippled thing. He'd been a fool, he had told himself as he stood in the snow outside his city, back to the wall, cold to the bone. He'd been a fool of the worst kind: the one who can't see things for what they really are.

Arin raised a sudden flat hand, palm out, as if stopping someone. He remembered again how the siege had ended. But this time, he changed the way he saw it. This time, in his memory, he ignored that mark on Kestrel's brow. He saw only what she held in her hand: the treaty. It had saved his life and spared his country. In his memory, Kestrel offered him the folded, creamy paper. He took it, he opened it. In his mind, he now saw a meaning in that treaty, and the way she had given it to him, that he hadn't before. Sudden understanding made Arin's hand fall, and clench.

"I need to leave," Arin told the queen. "I need to leave right now."

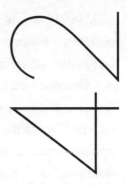

KESTREL LOOKED LIKE SHE'D BEEN DIPPED IN blood.

In the end, she hadn't actually given any orders for her wedding dress to be altered. The water engineer had already changed her bet, and although Kestrel wasn't sure if the emperor knew this, or what the consequences might be, she dreaded the malicious attention it would attract if she did anything more to upset the emperor's plans. He expected her to wear red, so the dress was red after all, in stiff, glossy crimson folds of rich samite. It was heavy. Structured in the bodice—it hurt when Kestrel breathed too deeply—with full skirts whose pintucked shadows created even deeper shades of red, almost black. The train was bustled now, but when Kestrel entered the great hall it would pour in a river behind her.

The new dressmaker's hands fluttered over Kestrel. "Is it too tight? Or . . . perhaps you'd like more embellishment? Crystals sewn onto the hem?"

"No." It was the last fitting before the wedding—barely more than a week away. What Kestrel really wanted was for the dress to be burned.

"Oh, but you haven't even seen it with the gold yet." The dressmaker gathered handfuls of golden sugarspun wire and began to weave it through Kestrel's braids and around her neck, trailing it in chilly patterns over her bare shoulders. The pain in Kestrel's lungs grew worse. Her eyes burned.

"Isn't that better? Isn't it?" the dressmaker's voice was high. "You are so beautiful!"

Kestrel suddenly heard the suppressed panic in the girl's voice. Kestrel saw her reflection. She wasn't beautiful. Her face was pinched and white, eyes shocked and wide. She looked ill. Kestrel pressed hands to damp eyes, pressed hard, and looked again. Kestrel didn't know what the dressmaker saw in her expression, but she realized that whatever it was, the girl read it as her own doom. She was a late-hour replacement for Deliah: a simple seamstress elevated to the role of imperial dressmaker. The girl was afraid. Why wouldn't she be afraid of Kestrel's dissatisfaction? The last imperial dressmaker was dead.

Kestrel turned from the mirror to face the brown-haired girl. Kestrel stepped down from the block, careful of the hem, and gently rested a hand on the girl's arm.

The new dressmaker quieted. "Do you like it?" she whispered.

"It's perfect," Kestrel said.

Her father was healed. He would leave the morning after the wedding to resume command of the eastern campaign. He would have left already if it weren't for the emperor's orders. Kestrel sometimes thought that the general would have stayed no matter what for her birthday recital and the wedding, but she tended to believe this only when not in his company. The moment he stood before her, his eyes increasingly restless, she knew that she'd been deluding herself.

He invited her for a walk. The wind was loud and brisk enough to make Kestrel's ears ache.

It seemed at first that Kestrel and her father wouldn't speak. Then he said, "I don't know what to give you for the wedding."

"It doesn't matter."

"I wish"—he squinted at a wheeling falcon high above the Spring Garden—"I wish I'd held back something of your mother's that I could give to you. I'd say that I'd been saving it for this." On the day she'd come of age, Kestrel had inherited all of her mother's possessions. He had wanted none of them.

A few months ago, Kestrel would have found another way—light, negligent, maybe witty—to repeat that it didn't matter. But now she felt keenly the damage of how they never really said what they meant to each other. Yes, they came close. They had understandings, such as the one that regularly brought the general to the secret space behind the music room's screen—if not into the music room itself—to hear Kestrel play. This was a kind of honesty, she supposed, but it wasn't *plain*, it wasn't true, and she couldn't help the hurt that came with the thought that she was just like him. She, too, couldn't say what she meant. She wanted to. She tried. The words struggled inside her.

Kestrel said, "Would you give me something if I asked for it?"

Carefully, he said, "That would depend."

"Stay. Don't go to the east."

"Kestrel . . ."

"Stay one more week, then," she pleaded. "Or a day. Stay one more day after the wedding."

He kept looking at the sky, but the hunting bird was gone.

"Please."

He finally turned to her. "Very well," he said. "One more day."

Events for the court continued. There was the spring tournament. There were masques, dances, feasts. More than once, Kestrel caught Tensen's gaze from across a room. She averted her eyes. She knew that he wanted to speak with her. He would press her for more information. He would urge her to take more risks, all for a very uncertain gain. But she'd made her decision. She would marry. She would rule. This was how she would change things. Her attempts at skullduggery seemed almost silly now: the games of a child who doesn't want to grow up. Worse—in her starkest moments, when Kestrel was most honest with herself, and honesty showed itself like a skeleton, bones clean and jutting, she knew that her efforts to be Tensen's spy had been a way to prove herself to Arin . . . even as she insisted that he never know.

It made no sense. Its senselessness was painful. How had Kestrel become someone who didn't make sense?

Two days before her birthday recital, which was two days before the wedding, Verex stopped the emperor on the palace grounds after a horse race where one of the imperial mounts had taken the prize. The prince had approached his father precisely at the moment when the emperor had his back to Kestrel. The emperor didn't see how close she was.

"Should we be concerned that the Herrani governor hasn't returned for the wedding?" Verex asked. His gaze flickered over his father's shoulder to light on Kestrel.

The emperor laughed.

"There's only one representative from that territory," Verex said. "It will look a little strange. Maybe the governor ought to be here." His eyes asked Kestrel's wish. She shook her head.

"Oh, the Herrani." The emperor chuckled again. "No one cares about the Herrani. Honestly, I had forgotten all about them."

When Arin arrived in the capital's harbor, he reined himself in. During the sea journey, he'd let himself pace the ship's deck, or curse faint winds. The waves didn't make him sick, not this time. He was too intent on the movements of his thoughts. Arin was incandescent, nervy, sleepless, and possibly mad.

Sometimes he managed to think of other things than Kestrel. He'd shudder at the memory of his cousin. He'd stopped in Herran to see Sarsine and resupply his ship. A Dacran fleet had sailed with him, as part of the alliance, and were stationed now in his city's harbor to protect it. Arin had been shocked by the change in Sarsine. She seemed so weak. Everyone did. He hated to leave her . . . yet he had, so possessed he was by the need to speak with Kestrel.

He needed to *know*. On the ship, his heart and brain galloped over what he knew and thought he knew, or hoped he knew, and then his thoughts would run right back over where they'd already been until they dug deep ruts inside him.

But when he dropped his boots to the capital's rocky wharf, he became nothing but careful.

He didn't wash the sea from him. He was too recognizable; the scar especially was a problem. His dirty hair hung just long enough to curtain his brow, but the scar cut clear from his left eye into his cheek. Arin kept his head down as he headed through the Narrows. He hoped he looked disreputable enough that no one would take him for the governor of an imperial territory.

He prowled the city. He didn't rest. The morning ripened into noon. Then it grew late.

Finally, Arin glimpsed a Herrani man about his size dressed in the blue livery of the imperial palace. The basket strapped to the servant's back weighed low on his shoulders—heavy, probably filled with foodstuffs for the imperial kitchens. Arin dogged him. He crossed skinny streets. His stride quickened, but he wouldn't let himself do anything so noticeable as to run.

It was at the edge of the canal, where the opened locks let the full spring waters gush loud, that Arin caught up with him. Arin hailed him, quietly. He called to him by the gods. He invoked their names in a way that made ignoring him a mortal sin. And then, for good measure, he spoke plainly. "Please," he said. "Help me."

In the palace kitchens, dressed in the servant's clothes, Arin asked for help again. Yet again, it was a risk. He could be reported. The moment his presence became known in the palace, what he wanted would quickly become impossible: namely, the opportunity to speak with Kestrel alone.

"The music room," suggested a maid. "Her recital's tomorrow. She's there practicing more often than not."

"What do you want with *her*?" A footman's mouth curled in contempt.

Arin almost gave a violent answer. He was anxious, he wasn't being smart, and for years now there'd been something hard and glittery—and stupid—in him that liked making enemies. He felt like making one right now. But he checked himself. Arin gave the footman a sweet smile. The kitchens became uncomfortably silent.

The cook decided matters. "It's none of our business." To Arin she said, "You want to get from here to there without being noticed, do you? Well, then. Someone had better fetch Lady Maris's maid."

The Herrani maid arrived soon, a cosmetics kit in

hand. She unscrewed a small pot with thick, tinted cream. She mixed it darker. As Arin sat at the scored and pitted worktable, the maid dabbed the cream on his scar.

Kestrel closed the music room door. The piano waited. Before that day in the slave market—before Arin—this had been enough for her: that row of keys like a straight border between one world and the next.

Kestrel's fingers trickled out a few high notes, then stopped. She glanced at the screen. She hadn't heard her father's watch chime. Then again, it wasn't the hour.

She set the sheet music on its rack. She shuffled the pages. She studied the first few lines of the sonata the emperor had chosen, and made herself slowly read the notes she had already memorized.

A breeze from an open window stroked Kestrel's shoulder. The air was soft, velvety, lushly scented with flowering trees. She remembered playing for Arin. It had just been the one time, though it felt like many more.

The breath of wind stirred the sheet music, then gusted the pages to the floor. Kestrel went to collect them. When she straightened, she glanced involuntarily at the door in a flash of unreasonable certainty that Arin was there.

But of course he wasn't. A needle of ice pierced her heart. What a foolish thing to have thought: him, *here*. Her breath caught at the pain of it.

Kestrel made herself sit again at the piano. She pushed that icy needle in deeper. It grew frosted crystals. Kestrel imagined the ice spreading until it lacquered her in a clear, cold shell. Kestrel lifted her hands from her lap and played the emperor's sonata.

The cook insisted that servants should accompany Arin. The maid's cream had softened the appearance of his scar, but it would fool no one who looked closely. "Walk the halls with a few of us," said the cook. A curious courtier could be distracted. The servants could flank Arin so that his features were obscured.

He refused.

"At least partway," urged a Herrani.

"No," Arin said "Think of what the emperor would do if he discovered that you were helping me walk through his palace unnoticed."

The Herrani gave Arin two keys and let him go alone.

When Arin mounted the steps up to the other world of the palace, the one with fresh air, he made sure to walk close alongside the walls, the left side of his face turned to them. A bucket of hot, soapy water swung from his hand. The steam curled damply over his wrist. He walked as quickly as he could.

Arin remembered little-used hallways, and had the advice of the servants, who knew which areas of the palace attracted the least attention at this hour. He followed their instructions. His pulse stuttered when he stumbled upon a couple of courtiers emerging, disheveled and giggling, from an alcove cloaked by a tapestry. But they were glad to ignore him.

The heavy keys in his pocket knocked hard against his thigh. He might not find Kestrel, or find her alone. It was astounding: the risk of what he was doing. Yet he picked up his pace. He dismissed that sinuous voice whispering inside him, calling him a fool.

But the treaty. Kestrel had offered it to him outside his city's gate. The treaty had saved him. Why had it taken Arin so long to wonder whether it had been *she* who had saved him?

Fool, the voice said again.

Arin reached the imperial wing. He took a key from his pocket and let himself in.

Somewhere in the midst of the sonata, Kestrel's hands paused. She hadn't been reading the sheet music, so when her memory failed her and she lost her place in the progression of phrases, she lost it completely. This was unlike her. The music throbbed away.

Her old self would have been annoyed, but the frozen needle in her heart gave the orders now, and it said that she should simply make a note of the mistake and move on. She found a pen and did just that, underscoring the forgotten passage. She set the pen on the rack that held the sheet music and prepared to play again.

Then it came: her father's silvery chime.

The corner of her mouth lifted.

All at once, she knew what she wanted to play for him. The general wouldn't recognize one half of a duet, and if he did, he couldn't guess whose voice was meant to sing with what she played. Kestrel thought again about how much she wanted to tell her father, and how little she could say.

But she could say this music. He would hear it, and even if he didn't understand what he heard, she would feel what it would be like to tell him.

Arin heard the music long before he reached the room. It came down the hall in an overwhelming tide. It called him like a question his throat ached to answer. He could feel the parts where he was meant to sing. The song tried to batter its way outside him.

He thought he might have dropped the bucket. He didn't know where it was. He was standing before the music room door. It seemed to have materialized in front of him. He set a palm to it. The door felt alive. The music pulsed in its grain.

Arin used the second key to open the door. The room was empty save for her. Kestrel saw him, and the music stopped.

FOR A HEARTBEAT, KESTREL THOUGHT THAT she'd imagined him. Then she realized that he was real. It shattered her. The icy shell around her shivered into a thousand stinging pieces.

He shut the door. He kept his palm flat against it, his fingers fanned wide. He looked at her.

Later, Kestrel understood what the shock had cost her. She'd been too slow. It wasn't until he met her eyes that she dropped deep into the knowledge that they were both in danger.

It took every ounce of will not to glance at the screen that hid her father. Her father, who would hear anything that they said, who could see Kestrel now. She saw herself as he must see her. She'd risen to her feet. She must be deathly pale. One hand gripped the music rack. She was staring toward the door, which was just out of her father's line of sight.

Kestrel raised her hand. *Stop,* she begged Arin. *Stay. Don't move.*

But the gesture set something in him on fire. His palm slid from the door. And she saw the determination in his face, the wild *suspicion*, the way it was already shaped into a question. With sudden horror, she realized what he was going to ask.

He strode toward her.

"No," she told him. "Get out."

It was too late. He was already at the piano. Her father could see.

"You will not shut me out," Arin said.

Kestrel sank back down onto the piano bench. Her stomach lurched: this was a disaster. She had imagined, again and again, Arin looking at her in this way, saying what he'd just said. Suspecting what he must suspect. She had even—tentatively, feeling like a trespasser—prayed to his gods for the chance to see him again. But not like this. Not with her father watching.

Her options dwindled.

She shuffled her sheet music, then stopped when she saw that her hands were unsteady. "Don't be so dramatic, Arin. I'm busy. Go away, won't you? You've interrupted my practice." She reached for her pen. *We're being observed,* she planned to scrawl on the sheet music. *I'll explain everything later.*

Arin grabbed the pen from her hand and threw it across the room. It clattered on the stone floor. "Stop it. Stop pretending that I don't matter."

She stared at the pen. She couldn't fetch it now. Her father was no fool; he might guess what she wanted to do with it. Even her attempt a moment ago had been a risk.

And then Arin asked his question. "What did you do for that treaty?" he demanded.

She wanted to drop her face into her hands. She wanted to laugh—or weep, she wasn't sure. Something was churning inside her that felt frighteningly like panic. She would have moved to leave if she didn't think that Arin might physically stop her—and *that*, if nothing else, would bring her father into the room.

She tried to speak coolly. "I don't know what you're talking about," she told Arin. "I'm sure I haven't done anything for any treaty. I've had a wedding to plan. I'll have plenty of time for politics when I'm empress."

"You know exactly which treaty I mean. You placed it in my hand. And I swear that it has the traces of you *all over it*."

"Arin—"

"It gave me my country's freedom. It saved my life." His face was pale, his gray eyes urgent. He towered over her as she remained sitting. The piano bench felt like a raft at sea. "What did you do to make the emperor sign it?" Arin's anxious voice rang loud. It didn't matter that he had spoken in Herrani. Her father knew Herrani. Kestrel knitted her hands. She thought of how her father had told the deserter to kill himself rather than live with his shame. Would he do that to her if she answered Arin truthfully? What would the general do to *him*?

"Arin, please. I did nothing for that treaty. I don't have time for your delusions."

"But you have time to meet with Tensen. Don't you?"

Innocently, she said, "Who?"

His mouth went hard.

Don't say it, Kestrel told him. *Please, please.* She didn't know if Tensen had somehow told Arin, or if Arin had guessed, but if he said the word *Moth* out loud . . . she remembered her father brushing the moth from Tensen's painting to the floor. The general's eyes had questioned the sight of a masker moth—infamous eater of fabrics, denizen of wardrobes—in such an odd place. It wouldn't take much for her father to guess what that moth was doing there, and why.

Especially if Arin asked her if *she* was Tensen's Moth.

Don't. She wanted to shake him. *Don't.*

Frustration rippled across Arin's face. She saw him war with himself.

Yes, Kestrel told him. *That's right. You can't tell the emperor's future daughter the code name of your spy, or admit the part Tensen plays for you at court. No, don't say it. What if you're wrong? You'd risk people's lives. Arin, you can't.*

With forced calm, Arin said, "If I've been deluded, it's because you have been *pretending.* You're pretending even *now.* You are not so cold. You tried to help the plainspeople. When we were together in the city tavern—"

Kestrel felt a sinking sickness.

"—I blamed you for the exodus. But poisoning the horses was better than setting fire to the plains. Isn't that why you chose it? Your father—"

"I love my father."

Arin drew slightly back. "I know."

"If I'd given him anything less than the best military advice I could, I would have put him in danger." She only now realized this, and was appalled anew at herself. "The east burned the plains we took."

"Yes." It seemed like Arin would say more, but he didn't.

"If my father had been there then . . . many Valorians died in the fire." She thought of Ronan. Her throat closed. She couldn't say his name. "If I did what you think I did, those deaths would be my fault."

"They deserved it," he said flatly. "All those soldiers cared about was feeding the empire's appetite. The empire eats *everything*. Everyone in Herran is weak. We've been taxed too much. There's been too little food. Now people are so weak they don't even want to eat what's left."

Kestrel glanced up. "That doesn't sound like starvation."

"You know nothing about starvation."

That silenced her.

Arin sighed. He rubbed hard at his brow, pushing along the line of the scar, which was poorly disguised by a cosmetic. "Everyone's thin, tired. Hollow-eyed. It's gotten worse. They sleep most of the day, Sarsine said. Even *she* does. If you could see her . . . she couldn't stop her hands from shaking."

Kestrel's mind snagged on his last word. *Shaking*. It made her think—inexplicably—about how she had dyed her villa's fountain pink when she was a little girl. She remembered telling the water engineer about it, not more than two months ago. She saw again the red dye spreading through the water and fading to pink. An experiment. Kestrel—had she been ten years old then?—had overheard the water engineer talking about a strange word, *dilution*, with her father at dinner. He thought well of the engineer, who had served with him in the war and designed Herran's aqueducts. The girl Kestrel decided she should understand how dilution worked.

But dilution had nothing to do with shaking. The grownup Kestrel frowned, and as she did, she remembered that *shaking* had been the imperial physician's word to describe the sign that someone had taken his medication for too long . . . long enough for it to become deadly.

Understanding seeped into her. It spread, red drops in still water, and she forgot that her father was listening and watching and judging behind the screen. She forgot even that Arin's shoulders were hunched in worry and doubt. She saw only the meaning of those six imagined Bite and Sting tiles she had mixed over and over in her mind: the emperor, the water engineer, the physician, a favor, Herran, and Valoria.

She knew how they all played out. The pattern stared her in the face.

The emperor had decided the Herrani were more trouble than they were worth. He decided to have them slowly poisoned through the water supply. A neat solution to a troublesome, rebellious people. He had eked as much out of them as he could. Once they were dead he'd claim the land again. He'd show the empire Herran's ultimate reward for rebellion.

It was more important than ever that she speak with Arin frankly . . . and that she not do so *here*. She looked at the door. She wasn't entirely sure her father wouldn't walk through it—maybe even with the palace guard.

But how could she get Arin to leave? How could she follow him, and not have it be blatantly obvious to her father why? He'd heard the rumors. He had seen her fight a duel on Arin's behalf in Herran. If all that wasn't enough, he must have surely heard the intimacy in Arin's voice. *You are not so cold. When we were together in the city tavern . . .*

Arin dropped his elbows to the piano's frame and leaned to press his face into his palms. "I shouldn't have left Sarsine. I shouldn't have come."

Kestrel wanted to touch him. He looked so miserable. Could her father see the longing in her face? It felt like a burning lamp. If she could, she would have touched three fingers to the back of Arin's hand: the Herrani gesture of thanks and regret. *I'm sorry,* she'd say. *Thank you,* she'd say, because somehow he still believed in her and had guessed what she'd tried so hard to hide. *I love you,* she'd say. She almost heard the words. She almost saw her hand reach out. She craved it.

Slowly, Kestrel said, "You wanted to talk about the treaty."

He lifted his head. His face reflected in the piano lid's varnish.

The decision fell on Kestrel like a white sheet. She would lie one last time, for her father. She would be composed. Convincing. Later she would set things right with Arin, and tell him everything.

She could do this. She must.

"You think that I somehow arranged it. Isn't that what you implied? That I swayed the emperor." Kestrel sank one finger down on a high key, but slowly, so that it made no sound. "Does the emperor *seem* easily influenced?"

"No."

"Yet *I* managed it?"

"Yes."

She played a merry trill.

"Please don't do that."

She stopped. "Arin, *why* would I persuade the emperor to offer that treaty? We do agree that it was I who told the empire of your rebellion, don't we? It's common knowledge. I sent war to your doorstep."

"Yes."

She said, "We were friends in Herran, weren't we, for a time?"

Arin's reply was hoarse. "Yes."

"Was what I did the act of a friend?"

"No," he whispered.

"Yet I did that, and then supposedly arranged this salvific treaty. It doesn't make much sense, Arin."

"It makes sense," he said, "if you changed your mind."

She raised one brow. "That's a dramatic change indeed."

He was silent.

Kestrel's fear, which she had briefly managed to squeeze shut, opened again. It spread.

She was afraid of failing in this lie. She was afraid of succeeding. And she was, she realized with a horrible clench of the heart, very afraid of her father.

Arin faced Kestrel fully: unblinking, eyes gray as a wind-torn sky, the scar livid against his drawn cheek. "It *was* a dramatic change," he said, "but you made it. I know you did."

Kestrel closed the lid over the keys. Something was coming that she couldn't control. The game was changing, and her best option now was to leave. She rose.

Arin stopped her. "I'm not *nothing* to you. I heard what you were playing."

She tried to laugh. "I don't even remember what I was playing." Arin's hand was on her arm. She stepped away from his touch. What must her father think? She glanced at the screen. She stared at the door. It didn't open.

"Why are you doing this?" Arin demanded. "Stop lying. I heard your music. And I *know.* You bargained with the emperor for the treaty."

She heard a faint, scratching sound. Had she imagined it? It was the sound of a sword drawn from its sheath in a hidden room. "I didn't."

Arin blocked her path.

"Let me go." Her voice sounded like it was falling apart.

"This is what I think: that there is no change more dramatic than you agreeing to marry when you have never—*never*—wanted to marry anyone."

"We've already discussed the many incentives to my marrying the prince."

"Have we discussed them all?" He dragged a hand through his dirty hair. "Kestrel, I feel like I'm going mad. That I'm seeing things—or *not* seeing things. Just tell me. Did you . . . are you . . . marrying the prince because of me? Was it . . . part of some kind of deal you made with the emperor?"

The silence wasn't just Kestrel's. It was her father's, too.

She sucked in a sharp breath. She could say this. She could do it, she promised herself, because she would make it better later. She would take it all back very, very soon.

Gently, Kestrel told him, "That sounds like a story."

Arin hung back, eyes uncertain, and despite his insistence that he knew what she had done, Kestrel sensed how new his belief was. How fragile. Yes, it could break. With just the right amount of pressure in the right place, it would crack like a mirror. Kestrel saw something in Arin that she'd never seen in him before, something unbearably young. She saw, for a moment, the boy Arin must have been. Right around the eyes. A softness. A yearning. There, in the lines of his sensitive mouth. There, to show her how to strike hardest.

"This isn't one of your Herrani tales with gods and villains and heroes and great sacrifices," she said. "I loved those stories when I was little. I'm sure you did, too. They're better than real life, where a person makes decisions in her best interests. Reality isn't very poetic, I know." She shrugged. "Neither is the sort of arrogance that encourages someone to think that so much revolves around him."

Arin looked away. He stared at the piano, its strung insides exposed under the propped-open lid.

She walked around him in a slow circle, sizing him up. "I wonder what you believe could compel me to go to such epic lengths for your sake. Is it your charm? Your breeding?"

His eyes cut to her. She paused, letting her gaze trace

his scar. He tensed. She made her mouth curl. "Not your looks, surely."

His jaw tightened.

Thorns pricked her throat, she ached with self-disgust. Yet she forced her smile to grow. "I don't mean to be cruel. But these ideas of yours are so *unbelievable*. And frankly, a little desperate. Like a fantasy. Hasn't it occurred to you that you're just seeing what you want to see?"

"No."

But she'd seen him waver. "You must realize that you've been telling yourself a story. Arin, we're too old for stories."

His voice came low. "Are we?"

"*I* am. Stop being a child. It's time you grew up."

"Yes." The word was slow. His tone was unexpectedly filled with something Kestrel recognized as wonder at the same moment that the recognition cramped her stomach. She knew that sound. It was the voice of someone for whom a cloud of confusion has been lifted. It was clarity, and the strength that returns with it.

"You're right," Arin said. When he faced her again she saw no shadow of that boy. It was as if she'd dreamed him. "I misunderstood," he said. "It won't happen again."

Formally, even clinically, Arin touched three fingers to the back of Kestrel's hand. Then he left, and closed the door behind him.

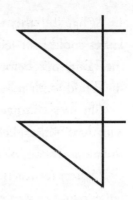

THE DOOR'S THUD ECHOED LOUD. A TOXIC fear ate at Kestrel. Even as doubt grew, and hinted that her strategy was the wrong one, or that no strategy could mend what she'd just done, Kestrel clung to the most important rule her father had taught her: *Deal with danger before it deals with you.*

"Father?" Kestrel called. Her voice rose higher. "Father?"

There was no answer. Had he been too shocked by what he had heard . . . suspicious? Was he refusing already to speak with her?

She rushed to the door and fumbled it open. The hallway was empty. Arin had vanished. An overturned bucket had spilled its foaming water. It was soaking Kestrel's shoes. She stood in the puddle for a moment, her feet wet and cold. Then she felt wildly along the corridor's carvings until she found the wooden button in the center of a blown flower. The panel slid aside, and light from the hallway illuminated the hidden room. It was empty.

What did this mean? Kestrel wondered whether her father could have left sometime after his watch had struck the hour, but before Arin had arrived. Had everything she'd said to Arin been for nothing?

She pressed fingertips to her temples. Her mind teemed with possibilities, her pulse soared, and she wasn't thinking so much as scrambling from one thought to the next.

Kestrel returned to the music room and picked up the fallen pen. She wrote Arin a letter. She wrote it on the sheet music, running words right over the notes. The ink flowed and smeared as Kestrel told Arin the truth, from the treaty to her engagement, from the Moth to her love, from the eastern horses to the poison that was killing his people. She wrote feelingly, fiercely, the nib of the pen sometimes puncturing the page.

The words came easily. In a bare minute, the letter was done.

It burned in her skirt pocket like a hot coal. Kestrel went to her father's suite—he wasn't there, his valet didn't know where he was—and then finally to her own, where two maids were so perfectly normal that their ordinariness was dizzying to Kestrel. She made an excuse and ducked into her dressing room. Alone, she tucked a masker moth into her sleeve. The buttoned fastening at the wrist kept the moth safely inside, and she wished fervently that she had done this earlier. If only she'd had a moth in the music room. She could have slipped it to Arin. A sign. She would have been subtle—a sleight of hand was all it would have taken, an absentminded rub of her wrists, and then the reveal.

Kestrel had a three-tiered plan of what to do when she found Arin. If she found him alone, and trusted their privacy, she would speak. Yet . . . would he listen? She remembered that clarity in his voice as he had finally and fully given up on her, the coolness of his touch . . . a lightness. That light, cool quality had been relief. She knew that. If she tried to speak with him again, he might very well just walk away.

Please, read this letter, she'd say, and place it in his hands. If all else failed, or they weren't alone: the moth.

There was a tap at the dressing room door.

Kestrel opened it to see one of the maids: a very young girl. Quiet, softly plain. "My lady," the maid said, "forgive me, but you seem upset."

"I'm fine." But Kestrel's voice was strained.

"Should I send for the prince?"

So this was the maid in Verex's employ. Kestrel realized that regardless of why the arrangement had begun, at some point Verex had asked the maid to watch over her, and to tell him if Kestrel needed help.

How like Verex. How like her friend.

It gave her courage. "No," she told the maid. "Truly, I'm fine. Everything will be fine."

At first, Kestrel felt better. She left the imperial wing behind her, clinging to her plan as if it were a guiding hand. But as she took a tightly wound marble staircase down, careful not to rush, careful to smile at a passing courtier and to ignore imperial guards stationed at the landings of each floor, that guiding hand grew cold. When she reached the wing that held suites for the lesser sort of guests, that hand felt like a fistful of bones. If she let go, they would scatter and roll.

Kestrel stole a glance behind her. No one seemed to be following her.

She turned down one last hall. The day's last light seeped in from a lone window. It cast the hallway into lurid orange.

Kestrel stood before the door. Could it really have been this easy? But then, the hidden room behind the screen had been empty. And the general was her *father*. He had taught her how to ride. He loved her. She knew it. Wasn't it a betrayal of him to fear that he had reported the conversation in the music room . . . if, indeed, he'd even witnessed it?

You have been betraying him all along, whispered a voice inside her. *You are betraying him now.*

Yet she knocked at Tensen's door. With a jittery gratitude, she heard someone stirring inside. Footsteps neared. The handle clicked. The door widened, and so did Tensen's eyes when he saw who stood before him.

She didn't wait for him to speak. She slipped inside.

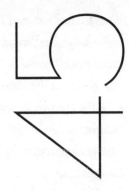

"YOU SHOULDN'T BE HERE," TENSEN SAID.

Kestrel ignored him. She threaded through the small suite, ignoring the very existence of privacy as Tensen trailed after her, protesting. She even entered his dressing room.

She rounded on Tensen. "Where's Arin?"

"I told you," Tensen said warily, "no one knows where he is, and I assure you that I haven't hidden him in the wardrobe."

"Well, he's closer than you'd think, and he hasn't been in Herran's city, or he would be dying." She explained what she knew about the poison flowing through Herran's aqueducts. The news made Tensen grow still. Stony. Telling the news had the opposite effect on her, because beneath her own words she heard the murmurs of everything Arin had said to her in the music room, and what she'd said back.

Tensen caught her wild hands. "Kestrel, be calm. Lower your voice."

Had she been shouting? Her breath felt shallow, as if she'd been running. "Where can I find him?"

"I need for you to calm down."

She pulled away. "The city's water supply is tainted. I have to tell him."

"It can't be you." His small green eyes were worried. "There are places in the palace you can't go without raising suspicion. Arin might even have left already. Your emperor's punishment for treason is death. Do you *want* to be caught?"

"It must be me," she insisted. "I have to explain . . . other things."

"Ah." Tensen covered his mouth and rubbed at his cheek. "He risked a great deal meeting with you alone. Would you have him risk that again?"

"No, but . . ." She felt desperate. The pieces of her were coming apart, jumbling out of order. She took the letter from her pocket. She could no longer believe that Arin might accept it. Not from her. Not after the things that she had said. "Find him. Give this to him. It explains."

He took the folded page gingerly. The black and white of the sonata's score looked up at them. "What does it explain?"

"Everything."

"Kestrel, what exactly do you hope giving him this will do?"

"Nothing. I don't know. I—"

"You're not yourself. You're not thinking clearly."

"I don't want to think clearly! I am *tired* of thinking clearly. Arin should know about me. He should have always known."

"It was better for him that he didn't. You believed that. I did, too."

"We were *wrong*."

"So after he learns the truth, you'll end your engagement."

"No."

"You'll run away with Arin to live in a dying country for a few short days before the hammer of another invasion falls."

"No."

"Why not?" Tensen said. "You love him."

Helplessly, she said, "I love my father, too."

Tensen looked down at the letter. He turned it over in his hands.

"If you don't give that to Arin," Kestrel said, "I will."

Tensen grimaced. Then he opened his jacket and placed the letter in an internal breast pocket. He refastened the jacket and patted his chest once, just above the heart. Kestrel heard the faint crackle of paper.

"You'll do it?" she said.

"I promise."

Kestrel's father was waiting in her suite. He must have sent the maids away. He was alone, sitting in a chair in the outermost receiving room. During daylight hours, the chair had a view of the barbican through which the general had entered months ago on his bloodied horse. He kept his gaze to the window well after Kestrel had entered. Night had fallen and the window was black. There was nothing for him to see.

She stopped wondering whether he had been in the

hidden room for some—all?—of her conversation with Arin. She knew. She saw it in his face. Her father had heard more than enough.

A crisis of words rose within her. She wanted to say so many things—to ask what he believed, to plead her innocence, to confess her guilt, to ask if he had reported Arin's presence to the imperial guard, and if yes, what would happen, and if no, please don't, Father, don't. She wanted to say, Love me anyway, even with what I've done, even with my mistakes, will you, would you, please?

And what she wanted most was to be small again, to be allowed to call him papa, to reach only his knee, because she remembered, in a flash like light from a curtain yanked open wide, how she used to run and topple against his legs when she was that young, and hug him, and she could swear that he would laugh.

Kestrel slowly crossed the room to him. She knelt beside his chair. She rested her brow against his knee and closed her eyes. Heart in mouth, she whispered, "Do you trust me?"

There was no answer. Then she felt his heavy hand on her hair. "Yes," he said.

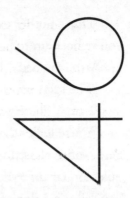

ARIN HID IN THE COAL ROOM NEAR THE furnaces that boiled water to be forced through palace pipes. He had asked a Herrani servant to find Tensen and bring him there, and thought that in the meanwhile he'd dirty himself beyond recognition, but after his first few minutes alone in the room, lit by a lamp set cautiously high on the wall on the far side of the coal pile, Arin realized that simply pacing and breathing was enough to deposit charcoal on him. He rubbed at his scar. His fingers came away grimy. Burnt-tasting dust coated his throat. He coughed, then choked, and somehow that choking turned into a black laugh.

The door unlocked and opened, and Tensen stepped inside. His face was furious. "The god of fools wants you for his own, Arin. What were you thinking, coming to the capital?"

Arin felt unreal, unstrung, bewilderingly light, like a workhorse stripped of his gear and let to wander. He drew breath to speak.

"Don't bother explaining," Tensen said. "I know what you've been up to."

Arin frowned. "How?"

"The servants told me. Arin, you *are* an idiot."

"I am." There was that dusty laugh again. "I really am."

"You're lucky that the whole palace doesn't know you're here—and blessedly lucky that the servants are keeping quiet. So far. *Everything* in the palace is too quiet. It's eerie. I don't like it, I don't like you here, and you are going to take my news and leave straight for Herran and never return." Tensen gripped his shoulder. "Swear it. Swear by the gods."

Arin did. It felt good to make that promise.

Tensen let go. "The treaty was a lie. Every minute we've spent here has been part of the emperor's charade, a distraction to make us believe that our independence was a serious thing, serious enough to demand attendance at court. The emperor wants Herran back. He wants it emptied of Herrani."

Arin listened as Tensen told him about the poison that had been seeping into Herran's water supply. Arin felt blood leach from his face. Coal dust caked his lungs. Air rattled in his chest. It was hard to breathe.

"You'll have to shut off the city's water," Tensen said. "Evacuate everyone to the countryside if you have to. Just go. It's nightfall. You might make it to the harbor with no one noticing."

"Come with me."

Tensen shook his head.

"If Sarsine's sick—if *everyone's* sick . . . Tensen, I need you."

"You need me here."

"It's too dangerous. You must be under scrutiny. Deliah can get word to us, your Moth could use the knotted code."

Tensen's face changed. "Deliah and the Moth can't help us anymore. They've done as much as they can."

"Then so have *you*."

"There might be one last thing to learn. What if I've missed something?" Tensen's expression softened. "Don't you remember when I asked whether you'd choose to help Herran, or yourself? You said you'd put our country first. Haven't I respected that choice? Can't you respect mine?" Tensen lifted a hand to Arin's face and ran a thumb across his cheek. The old man's thumb came away black. "My boy. You've been a little lost, haven't you?"

Arin wanted to protest that he hadn't been, then to admit that he had, then to prove that he wasn't anymore. "I didn't fail you."

"I never said you did."

"I secured the eastern alliance. I *made* something, Tensen, a new thing, something that might check the imperial army. The emperor isn't as secure as he thinks. He—"

"Better not tell me any more."

Arin went cold. Those had been the words of someone who feared torture. "Come with me."

"No. I need to know what happens next."

"This isn't a story!"

"Isn't it?" Tensen asked. "Isn't this the one about the boy who becomes a man and saves his people? I like that story. I acted the role once, decades ago, in a performance for

Herran's royal family. It ended happily." Tensen touched his chest, right above his heart. Arin thought he heard a faint, papery sound. There was a flash of indecisiveness on Tensen's face. Then it was gone. Tensen's hand fell, and Arin forgot what he'd heard with the minister's next words, and when he later remembered that look of indecisiveness, Arin hated himself, because he believed that the choice Tensen had been debating inside him had been about staying or leaving, and that if Arin had only found the right words, he could have persuaded Tensen to come with him.

"Go on, now. Go," Tensen said. "My grandson looked so much like you, Arin. Don't make me grieve him twice."

Tensen took the gold ring from his finger and offered it. "This time, keep it, will you?" He smiled.

Arin caught the man's hand. He kissed the dry palm. He took the ring. Then he said goodbye.

Kestrel's father had left her. He wouldn't stay for dinner, though Kestrel had said they could have it brought to her suite. He didn't claim he was tired, or that his freshly healed wound might trouble him, but his step was slow as he let himself out, and Kestrel thought for a moment that he would put a hand to where he'd been gutted.

After he'd gone, she felt shame in a solid rush. She realized that she had been *hoping* he was tired, hoping his wound was sore . . . it would explain why even though he'd said that he trusted her, he didn't want to stay.

Dinner came. Kestrel couldn't eat it.

She opened a window. The almost-summer air was soft and sweet. There was a high wind. It smelled like the mountains, which meant it was blowing out to sea.

Kestrel's maids came. They asked if she wanted to be changed for bed. She fidgeted with the wrist fastening that kept the moth inside her blue silk sleeve. She told the maids no. She wanted to send them away, then dreaded being alone. The maids stayed and gossiped quietly in their corners. It grew late. She sat, and worried. Had Tensen given Arin the letter? Was Arin still in the palace?

Later, Kestrel saw all of her mistakes, strung in such a crowded, ugly line that it was difficult to tell which one had come first.

But she knew the last. That was when she left her suite and went back to Tensen's rooms to find out whether he'd seen Arin and delivered her letter.

The halls were hushed. Even quieter than before. Though the sweat that trickled between her shoulder blades proved that it was almost summer, Kestrel had the sensation that it was snowing. Her ears rang with a white, mirroring silence. Anxiety pricked her skin in icy flakes. The stone heap of the palace held its cold breath.

Tensen's door was almost flush with its jamb, but it hadn't been closed completely. Kestrel thought for a moment that he'd been waiting for her, but a part of her knew better. That self had already guessed what the slightly open door might mean. Yet Kestrel refused to believe it . . . and so that other, wiser self turned away from her, disowned her, and refused to help any further someone who had wrought her own doom.

Kestrel lifted her hand to knock. Her knuckles stuttered against the wood.

The emperor opened the door. The captain of the guard reached around him and dragged Kestrel inside.

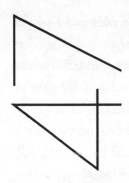

AT FIRST, KESTREL COULDN'T QUITE SEE. SHE
was straining against the captain's grasp, her breath coming in terrified gulps, and he and the emperor were tall. It
seemed that she saw nothing but the rich cloth of their
shoulders, their chests. Then she heard her father's voice:
"Please."

The captain let go.

Kestrel saw her father now. He stood in the far corner
of the room, on the other side of a dark spill of blood.
Tensen lay on the floor. His green eyes were child's mar-
bles. The body was already rigid. On the general's sleeve
was a short line of blood from where he must have wiped
his dagger before sheathing it.

Kestrel met her father's eyes. They were as cold as the
dead man's. She opened her frostbitten mouth, and she was
numb, too numb to speak, so she screamed.

The captain covered her mouth. Her father looked
away. She froze.

"We're trying to keep this as quiet as possible," the

emperor told her. "No one but us will know what you've done. It can't be public. I won't let your father be so dishonored." The emperor took Kestrel's dagger from its sheath. "This is mine. And *that*"—he held out the unfolded page of sheet music—"is yours."

Her letter. "No," she tried to say against the captain's salty palm, but he gripped her jaw, and the emperor lightly touched the captain's hand so that it turned Kestrel's face to meet him.

"No?" said the emperor. "Kestrel, if there were a trial, your letter is confession enough." His voice was filled with regret, but it wasn't for her. "I could kill you now. What a serpent you are. What a poor reward for a man like your father. He came to me."

Tears spilled down her cheeks. They trickled over the captain's knuckles.

"He came, and told me the truth, no matter what it cost him. He set no terms. No pleas for mercy or mitigation. He simply gave me the truth of your treason. Of all the lessons you could have learned as empress, the most important would have been this: loyalty is the best love."

Kestrel tried to look at her father, but the captain held her face firmly. She struggled. She tried to break free. The captain caged her in.

The emperor spoke again. "That kind of love tends to tarnish after the execution of one's child. So I can't repay Trajan's loyalty with your blood, or turn you over to my captain and his messy art of questioning. Something else you would have learned—had you chosen to learn from me—is that your father has my loyalty, too. I will protect him as he has protected me. This means that you're going north."

To the tundra. The work camp. She dragged in air.

"Did you think I had no clue?" said the emperor softly. "I've had the Herrani minister followed for some time now. He was seen meeting with a Valorian maid. I asked myself whether that maid could have been you. Whether it was really possible that you might betray your country so easily, especially when it had been practically *given* to you. But people are capable of anything."

Kestrel's words were strangled beneath the captain's hand. She wasn't even sure what she was trying to say.

"Maybe you think that I can't make you vanish," the emperor continued, "that the court will ask too many questions. This is the tale I'll tell. The prince and his bride were so consumed by love that they married in secret and slipped away to the southern isles. After some time—a month? two?—news will come that you've sickened. A rare disease that even my physician can't cure. As far as the empire is concerned, you'll be dead. You'll be mourned.

"You might forget, in the tundra's mines. I hear that people do, down in the dark. I hope that your father does. I hope that he forgets you, and your shame."

Kestrel bit the captain's hand. He didn't even flinch, but the blood in her mouth made her lose herself. She twisted. The sounds she made under the captain's hand were like an animal's.

"Let her go," said her father.

She ran to him. She skidded in the blood and fell against his chest, clinging, weeping. "Please don't do this," she sobbed, though he already had.

He didn't touch her. "I wanted to trust you," he whispered. "I tried. But I couldn't lie to myself hard enough."

She made fistfuls of his jacket. She pressed her face against his chest. Her shoulders jerked and heaved. "I didn't—"

"Mean to? How do you not mean treason?"

"Please," she begged. It seemed to be the only word she could say.

"I left your suite. I found the minister. I searched him. I read the letter. I killed him. And even then, I doubted. Even then, I couldn't believe it. I couldn't believe that this would be you."

"Papa, please." She choked on her tears. "I love you."

Slowly, carefully, he unhooked her hands from his jacket. The captain, sensing his moment, moved toward them.

The general's voice came low, so that his words were only for him and his daughter. "Kestrel," he said, "you have broken my heart."

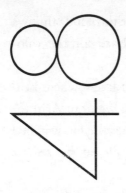

DAWN BURNED ON THE WATER.

Arin had been lucky. He'd slipped from the palace immediately after parting from Tensen. The elegant fortress had seemed absentminded, its energies turned inward, focused on something else.

Arin shrugged that thought away. Now, standing on the ship's deck, his face to the raw dawn, it seemed silly.

No one had noticed him. No one had cared. He'd made it to the harbor. The wind had been high and fair and seaward. His ship had cast off.

It was as he sailed from the bay that something finally changed. He'd seen, in the moonlight, Valorian doublemasters, the kind heavy with cannon, gun decks on two levels. They rode in his wake. It wasn't that Arin had gone unnoticed—just that he had been noticed too late. There had been a delay. Some slowness to realize. Arin had the image of Valorians scrambling to catch up—and catch him. But his ship plowed the waves. His captain had been a master sailor in the height of Herran's naval prowess. The wind favored them. It skipped them over the sea. It threw a scarf of dark cloud over the moon. By daybreak, the Valorian ships were gone.

It was a brief respite. The Valorians knew where he'd go. The empire was coming, and so was war, but Arin focused on listening to the wind gust the sails. He watched the sun lift dripping over the horizon. He let the sea air cram his lungs, and he felt free.

Arin unwrapped a small cloth bundle. Kestrel's dagger gleamed. Now that it didn't hurt him to look at it, he could see its beauty better. The sun set its ruby on fire and showed its pink heart. The chased gold became a liquid swirl. Arin weighed the weapon in his hand. Really, it weighed barely anything at all.

Yes, it was beautiful. But beauty seemed a feeble reason to keep something he didn't want.

Arin dropped the dagger in the sea.

He sailed home.

The wagon stopped. The horses needed to be watered.

The sun was up now. It came in through the wagon's small, barred window. It showed Kestrel her shackled wrists, limp in the lap of the same pretty blue gown she had been wearing last night. Though the wagon had stopped, Kestrel still felt jolted, sore. Her eyes were swollen. The sunlight hurt.

But something brought her to her feet. A voice in another language as familiar to her as her own. Someone outside had spoken in Herrani.

Kestrel went to the window. She couldn't see the guards. She couldn't see anything at first; the light was too bright. But then she saw the peaks of empty mountains. She heard the Herrani voice again: a man, talking to the horses. She heard the swing of an empty metal bucket. Footsteps in grainy dirt.

"Please," she called softly in his language. The footsteps stopped. Her shackles rattled as she fumbled to get a finger and thumb up her left sleeve. She pinched the moth she had hidden there and pulled it free. She put her hand through the bars. "Take this."

Slowly, the footsteps neared. She still couldn't see him, but imagined him standing just below her hand. Kestrel stretched. Her wrist strained, and her hand began to go numb. She offered the moth held in her fingertips.

Had he taken it? Had it fallen? It was gone.

"Give it to your governor," Kestrel whispered. "Tell Arin—"

There was a cry, a heavy thump. Valorian curses, boots scuffing dirt. "What did she give you?" said one of the Valorian guards.

"Nothing," said the Herrani.

The door to the wagon flung open. Kestrel shrank into a corner. The guard was a large shadow against the achingly white light. He advanced. "What did you give him?"

Outside, the rough sounds continued. Protests. An unceremonious search. But what, after all, would the guard outside see? A battered moth. Nothing precious. Nothing important. Just an ordinary thing, blending into everything else.

The guard grabbed her shoulders. Her shackled hands went up. She hid behind them.

All over, people were waking up to an ordinary day, as ordinary as a moth. Kestrel grieved for an ordinary day. She squeezed her eyes shut at the thought of how it would be, her perfect ordinary morning. A horse ride with Arin. A race.

I'm going to miss you when I wake up, she'd told him as she'd dreamed on the palace lawn.

Don't wake up.

On that perfect, ordinary morning, she would pour tea for her father. He would stay, and he would never leave to be anywhere else.

Someone was shaking her. Kestrel remembered that it was the guard.

She remembered that it was her eighteenth birthday. She laughed, chokingly, to imagine the emperor explaining her absence to everyone gathered for her recital. She thought she was laughing, but then that sound tore along its edges. It clawed at her throat. Her face was wet. Tears stung her lips.

Her birthday. *I remember the day you were born,* her father had said. *I could hold you with one hand.*

The guard hit Kestrel across the face. "I said, what did you give him?"

You had a warrior's heart, even then.

Kestrel spat blood. "Nothing," she told the guard. She thought of her father, she thought of Arin. She told her final lie. "I gave him nothing."

Author's Note

This book was exhausting to write and took a while for me to finish (having a baby in the middle of it might have had something to do with it). So first, an enormous thank you to those who read drafts of *The Winner's Crime* or portions of it: Ann Aguirre, Marianna Baer, Kristin Cashore, Donna Freitas, Daphne Grab, Mordicai Knode, Anne Heltzl, Sarah Mesle, Jill Santopolo, Eliot Schrefer, and Robin Wasserman. You always had the right words to keep me going and to make this a better book.

Such is also true for people who talked with me about knotty plot problems or thorny emotional questions, or worldbuilding ones. Thanks to everyone at Kindling Words, for excellent talks, advice, and comments that helped me piece together *The Winner's Crime* at a stage when I knew where I was going but not what I was doing. I especially thank Franny Billingsley, Judy Blundell, Sarah Beth Durst, Deborah Heiligman, Rebecca Stead, and Nancy Werlin. In Parisian cafés, Coe Booth and Aviva Cashmira Kakar helped me shape Tensen into the sneaky character he became. Also in Paris, at the Broken Arm café, Pamela Druckerman and I mulled over Arin, the bookkeeper, and the queen. Leigh Bardugo and I had an awesome conversation about guns, and Mordicai Knode contributed on separate occasions. He also told me about Quipu Code after reading an early scene about Favor-Keeping. Lunch with Sarah MacLean resulted in a plot point that I'm thrilled about but can't share (Book 3 spoiler, sorry!). Kristin Cashore brainstormed with me on so many points that it's hard to list them all. Robin Wasserman is probably the person you can thank (or blame) for this being a trilogy to begin with. Barry Lyga, aka my torture expert extraordinaire (he asked to be called that. Or something like that), suggested I go after Thrynne's fingers in the prison scene, and Kristin Raven, a doctor, gave very useful (and gory) information about how those fingers would look. She also confirmed my instinct that the general's abdominal wound could be "packed." Miriam Jacobson, a scholar and pianist, gave me (as she put it) *"le mot juste"* for a piece that Kestrel plays: an impromptu. Mordicai and Jenny Knode were consulted about ideas for the map. High praise to Keith Thompson for his artistry in representing this world. My husband, Thomas Philippon, is always my most crucial adviser when it comes to sorting out ideas, and he's especially great about anything to do with the military or horses.

My goal for this trilogy has been to read one ancient Greek or Roman text while writing each book. This time it was Herodotus's *The Histories*, which gave me some ideas about how to represent the East. I should also admit that I had the temerity to take a metaphor from Shakespeare and reshape it to suit my fancy for a particular line in the scene by the canal (hint: it's from *Much Ado about Nothing*).

Thank you to all the librarians, booksellers, and bloggers who have championed *The Winner's Curse*. It's been a real pleasure to get to know you in person and online. Your enthusiasm is so infectious—and appreciated.

Macmillan Children's Publishing Group! I'm one lucky woman. I'm very grateful to everyone who has supported me and this series. My amazing editor, Janine O'Malley. My intrepid publicist, Gina Gagliano. My designer of heart-stopping covers, Beth Clark. And a whole marvelous cohort of people: Nicole Banholzer, Simon Boughton, Anna Booth, Molly Brouillette, Angie Chen, Jennifer Edwards, Jean Feiwel, Jennifer Gonzalez, Liz Fithian, Katie Halata, Angus Killick, Kathryn Little, Karen Ninnis, Joy Peskin, Karla Reganold, Caitlin Sweeney, Claire B. Taylor, Mary Van Akin, Allison Verost, Mark Von Bargen, Ksenia Winnicki, and Jon Yaged.

Charlotte Sheedy, my agent, is a dream, and I thank her and Mackenzie Brady and Joan Rosen.

Sometimes people ask me what the secret is to writing books, and my very serious reply is "good child care." Thanks to my babysitters, parents, and in-laws: Monica Ciucurel, Anne Heltzl, Shaida Khan, Georgi MacCarthy, Sharon Singh, Marilyn and Robert Rutkoski, and Jean-Claude and Christiane Philippon.

My older son, Eliot (now five and a half), has an idea about why I sit in front of the computer instead of taking him to the Natural History Museum. My younger son, Téo (two years old), has only the sense of some great injustice and betrayal. Boys, I always miss you when I'm not with you, and I love you both best.

Read the first book in the sensational Winner's Trilogy

WINNING WHAT YOU WANT MAY COST YOU EVERYTHING YOU LOVE

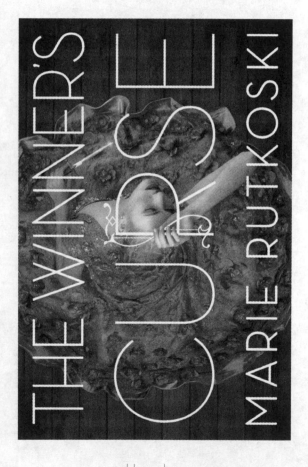

www.bloomsbury.com

 #TheWinnersCurse   #TheWinnersCrime